Praise for

ON THE ROOFTOP

"What happens when a mother's well-intentioned aspirations for her offspring conflict with her daughter's ever-changing vision of herself? In Margaret Wilkerson Sexton's showstopper of a third novel, *On the Rooftop*, this theme is explored with compassion, clear-eyed perception, and been-around-the-block delivery. And when placed within the context of racial segregation and prejudice in mid-century America, the results are soul-shaking. . . . A powerhouse novel."

—*San Francisco Chronicle*

"*On the Rooftop* explores a subject close to my heart: the shifting terrain between mothers and daughters, further complicated by grief. Margaret Wilkerson Sexton's powerful prose takes us to some familiar emotional places within an utterly original story. This searing, intimate portrait of family, ambition, and community from a bygone era feels deeply resonant for those of us still daring to dream today. Beautiful, moving, and truly unforgettable!"

—Deesha Philyaw, author of *The Secret Lives of Church Ladies*

"*On the Rooftop* beautifully captures the complicated emotions that arise when a parent realizes that what she wants for her kids doesn't necessarily align with what they need."

—*Time*

"A powerful drama set during a pivotal moment in US history."

—*Real Simple*

"I was not prepared for how this book would knock me over with its rich characterizations and intricate plot that handles major social issues such as racism and gentrification while telling an intimate story of a family in transition. . . . This novel is written tenderly with language that sings as much as the music it describes. When faced with enormous change, these finely drawn characters face the universal struggle of whether to accept what life has thrown at them or to resist change and lose everything they've worked so hard to achieve. I couldn't put it down."

—BuzzFeed

"An expansive, bighearted work of historical fiction about family, love, and what happens when children grow up to chase dreams their parents never imagined for them."

—*Good Housekeeping*

"Sprightly, emotionally savvy. . . . As much as this is a story about the lives of Vivian and her daughters, it's also a story about community—how groups serve as sources of support and liberation, too."

—*Alta Journal*

"*On the Rooftop* further cements Margaret Wilkerson Sexton as a deft chronicler of Blackness in America. A deeply felt, bighearted exploration of family, sisterhood, and gentrification, this is the kind of expansive, lush novel that envelops with charm while provoking with its fierce intelligence."

—Kaitlyn Greenidge, author of *Libertie*

"A masterful examination of family and community that celebrates the legacy of Black dreams and determination. . . . Sexton's work entertains and inspires at the same time, and with *On the Rooftop*, she urges us to find comfort in the triumphs of our past."

—*BookPage*

"Richly observed and beautifully written, *On the Rooftop* weaves the lives of its characters together into a story bursting with music and feeling. Margaret Wilkerson Sexton writes with power and nuance about matters of the spirit and the flesh. A moving, uplifting novel about art and ambition and faith and love."

—Charles Yu, author of *Interior Chinatown*

"In all of her work, Margaret Wilkerson Sexton invites us into the most intimate spaces of remarkable families during remarkable times. In this stellar novel, she takes us deeply into the dynamics of mothers and daughters, their individual—and collective—dreams and struggles. The harmonies of the Salvations are the literal soul music of this neighborhood in San Francisco during the turbulent fifties, and I will never look up at another rooftop again without imagining three sisters reaching for their stars."

—Luis Alberto Urrea, author of *The House of Broken Angels*

"Sexton does a wonderful job of capturing the complicated love that binds Vivian and her daughters. She also beautifully depicts the jealousies and rivalries that can tear once-close sisters apart. . . . A heartfelt tale of family and community."

—*Kirkus Reviews*

"Outstanding. . . . Sexton creates the place and era, with its sights, tastes, and sounds, and writes the feelings and thoughts the four women have versus their behavior with brilliant insight and perfect pitch."

—Historical Novel Society

ON THE ROOFTOP

ALSO BY MARGARET WILKERSON SEXTON

A Kind of Freedom

The Revisioners

ON THE ROOFTOP

A NOVEL

Margaret Wilkerson Sexton

ecco
An Imprint of HarperCollins*Publishers*

This is a work of fiction. Names, characters, places, and incidents are products of the author's imagination or are used fictitiously and are not to be construed as real. Any resemblance to actual events, locales, organizations, or persons, living or dead, is entirely coincidental.

HarperCollins books may be purchased for educational, business, or sales promotional use. For information, please email the Special Markets Department at SPsales@harpercollins.com.

Ecco® and HarperCollins® are trademarks of HarperCollins Publishers.

A hardcover edition of this book was published in 2022 by Ecco, an imprint of HarperCollins Publishers.

FIRST ECCO PAPERBACK EDITION PUBLISHED 2023

Designed by Angela Boutin

Library of Congress Cataloging-in-Publication Data has been applied for.

ISBN 978-0-06-313995-4 (pbk.)

23 24 25 26 27 LBC 5 4 3 2 1

To Thomas, for everything

By the rivers of Babylon, there we sat down, yea, we wept, when we remembered Zion. We hanged our harps upon the willows in the midst thereof. For there they that carried us away captive required of us a song; and they that wasted us required of us mirth, saying,
Sing us one of the songs of Zion.
How shall we sing the Lord's song in a strange land?

—PSALM 137: 1–4

PART ONE

VIVIAN

1953

Vivian didn't mourn St. Francisville, Louisiana. On the contrary, her memories kept watch against nostalgia. Still, she would never be used to the Fillmore's weather. She had anticipated mild and sunny. She had expected it would never rain, and it was true that it didn't dip below freezing, but she hadn't prepared for the summer chill, the fog and wind. She'd waltzed outside to work in a sleeveless dress her first June there, dipped her toe onto the sidewalk, then swung right back around for her front door.

She hadn't known a soul then who could have warned her.

That had been twenty-five years earlier. Now, she rounded the intersection of Fillmore and Post Street with her cotton car coat over her crisp white nursing uniform, past the looming theater, the Austin A40s lining the sidewalks, the streetcar perched at the stop sign awaiting Negro men with long coats and top hats. The bookstore let her know she was almost home, and she waved hello to Horace, who ran it; then next door to Miss Edna, who posted the winning numbers just before dark so the night ladies she ferreted out could anticipate their due; Mr. Gaines, the butcher, with the roaming eye; Miss Fox, with no teeth, who cleaned for them all in exchange for food. The beauticians at Gladys's were distracted, their gossip circling the parlor, but if they'd seen Vivian, they'd have called out her name, nearly inaudible beneath the dryers' hum.

It was the people she'd just passed who'd rebirthed her once her husband died. Vivian had begged Ellis to move her from Louisiana after a Klansman smashed her bedroom windows with shotguns and dragged her daddy to his death. Ellis had been her boyfriend then, but as soon as they crossed the state line, he'd married her, given her three children, then died, and she'd grieved, but her neighbors carried over stews and roast and potatoes and string beans. They bathed her children and greased the little girls' legs; more than that, they sat with her. When the pain was so deep she feared it would overcrowd her heart, they sat still beside her. If it hadn't been for them, she wouldn't have made it.

And there were the others, of course, two of whom she waved to at the intersection of Webster and Ellis, one whom she didn't recognize. In any case, they were all middle-aged white men who worked for the City, whose bellies stretched past their gray flannel suit pants. They'd drive west from downtown every two weeks with their clipboards in their hands, their hats over their eyes, and they'd peer through half-drawn curtains and ask children to number their bathrooms, then list the family members who used them. They pretended to be nice enough, even nodding now as Vivian passed, before they made note of the trash spilling out of the neighbor's garbage can. There had been talk years ago that if Mr. Gaines's meat had soured, if Miss Edna's girls ventured out too early, if her numbers weren't washed off her cloudy kitchen window, the men might move them all somehow, shut them out of their new homes, tear their haven down to make room for the unimaginable. But that talk had just been talk, ensconced in the City's incompetence. Anyway, Vivian never worried about it outright, for God had promised her her latter days would be plenty.

She was approaching the evidence of that same promise now. She could see her girls from where she stood, grazing her front steps in distinct positions of rest. Something about their lulls always heated Vivian up inside.

"I thought I told y'all to set out that garbage before I got home," she called from half a block away, and the sound of her voice sent them shuffling, two across the stoop, and one inside. They moved like they were synchronized, onstage somewhere, trying to convince an audience there was only one of them. Since she had them, it had been like that. Even when none of them made a sound, there was some guidance that lived inside their minds and joined them, and they'd wear the same color to school three mornings in a row, or style their hair in a French twist to the right, though they didn't share mirrors, or rooms for that matter; they didn't need to do so. They finished each other's jokes. Four years stood between the oldest (twenty-four) and the youngest (twenty), yet they all began menstruating the same day. It was why they were a perfect trio onstage too, why men and women shot their heads back, let their mouths hang; why the applause roared in like a freight train; why people didn't want to let them go. Vivian had never seen a show of theirs where they hadn't been begged for an encore, or where they hadn't ultimately acquiesced.

Vivian's neighbor Mary sat with them in her hard-back rocker, her feet on the base of it shifting back and forth. She lived next door, but visited so regularly she kept her designated chair on Vivian's stoop. Mary's son stood behind her, handsome, chocolate, with bushy hair, trimmed and neat. Vivian noticed he stood in touching distance to her oldest daughter, Ruth, too, but then again, Ruth had more old-world sense than a backwoods midwife—they were only friends. The boy's stability had saved Ruth after her father passed. He had been a gentle but strong child, and he had grown into that kind of man.

"At least we picked up inside." Chloe, her youngest, bounced back from the kitchen.

"Thank you, love. I can always count on you." Vivian kissed her baby's cheek. Chloe, being twenty, would still allow it. But it wasn't only that. The two of them breathed a different patch of air than everyone else. Ruth was her helper in action: combing the other girls' hair, ensuring they got off to school or work on time, but Chloe was Vivian's partner in spirit. She knew to smile when Vivian's boss had worn her down. She knew to praise her when she felt like she was flailing in every angle of her life. The thing was, Vivian hadn't been supposed to have her. She had been in a car accident when Esther was still taking milk, and the doctor had said she wouldn't give birth again. Ellis had been driving and Vivian swore he never got over that, the guilt. A year later, he'd died from a heart attack. Vivian had found out she was pregnant on the one-month anniversary of his passing. She'd handled the child as a miracle ever since.

"Go on in and finish setting up for dinner, though." She was talking to all the girls now.

"You took the fish out of the freezer?"

"Yes, Mama."

"And you washed the windows?"

"Yes, Mama."

"And you shined the floors?"

"Yes, Mama."

"And you scrubbed the baseboards?"

And something about that final "Yes, Mama"—the predictability of it and the solace, as the girls drifted inside, and Gerry walked upstairs—caused Vivian to smile. Something in her told her it would be okay to sit down for a spell.

"You reminding yourself of your own mama, huh, girl?" Mary was only seven years older than Vivian, but she could have been the woman's mother. Part of it was her look. Though she still set her hair and sat under the dryer every Friday so it would be crisp and curled for Sunday's service, the gray had overtaken it years before. Mary fought everything else: the postman when he was late, Miss Fox when she drank brown liquor, Lena's when the meat came to her white instead of dark. More than that, she spoke with authority on even the most benign subjects: whether you ought to brown beef before you roasted it, how long to hang the sheets from the line, whether a baby should take a bottle or the breast. She didn't ask questions she didn't think she knew the answer to already. She delivered her suggestions like expectations. "It might be time to prune those lilies" came out like "Girl, you better fix those flowers before I snap them off." So it had been astounding to watch her submit to the change at the top of her head.

Another thing about Mary was that she smoked cigarettes, and she held one now. She was careful to exhale in the other direction, but Vivian still felt dizzy from her seat beside her. She waved the air in front of her face before she answered.

"Hard not to these days." She smoothed her hands over her uniform, which had grown snugger in the last few years, especially in the middle.

"None of that. You's a fine woman, Vivian, you know that, though. I see you walking to the bus stop, walking back. Seem like every block there's a new gentleman trying to make your acquaintance." Mary had not only let her hair gray, but a shadow lined her upper lip. It, more than the gray, was likely the reason she hadn't had a man of her own since Vivian had met her. She had never mentioned Gerry's father, not once. Still, she seemed to be enlivened instead of threatened by Vivian's admirers. And Mary was right, they were many. Not that it mattered.

"Well, I ain't got time to stop in the street and I damn sure ain't got time for no whole man, Mary, you know that. Not with those girls. We're at the Champagne Supper Club every Friday. And that's just the beginning for us. I'm not even thinking about stopping there; even if I wanted to, I couldn't. Not with their talent. I mean, I'm talking the Dunbar Hotel in Los Angeles, the—"

"The Blah Blah in the Blah Blah, the Bleh Bleh in the Bleh Bleh." Mary made a point to blow the smoke in her face, hard.

"Hmph," Mary said now. "Don't look a gift horse in the mouth. You got some fine venues here in town. But I guess if it ain't Preacher Thomas's house, you ain't interested." That was a running joke between them, and the girls got in on it too sometimes. Vivian laughed—of course she did. And she supposed she wouldn't have been caught dead in the sanctuary of Shiloh Baptist without her lashes and her good brassiere. She supposed she caught him looking at her as he spoke to his congregation. Yes, she supposed in those moments she'd been looking at him too, but she'd been a friend of his wife's, a good friend, and it had been only three years since the woman took sick, and finally, mercifully, passed. And then there was that part she had just mentioned to Mary: she simply did not have the time.

"What? You see how ragged these kids run me already. We got rehearsal and shows, and I still got to go to work to earn a living. I don't know where anybody else would fit in."

"Hmph." Mary repeated herself, then paused. "There's one man who came by," she said after it seemed a whole hour had passed, "who you might want to pay some attention to." She was smiling.

Vivian turned to her for show. Like she'd said, she wasn't interested. "Oh yeah?" She paused. "Who?"

"A businessman. He had on a suit you wouldn't believe, and Stacy Adams shoes, and he didn't need to clean them with no Clorox. They was shining on they own, and girl, he wore a diamond stickpin and a long coat and I thought he was a man from a dream, I'm telling you I had to pinch myself. If I hadn't closed shop downstairs, I would have—"

"Mary!"

"Oh, excuse me, Vivian, I forgot you was sitting there." She fanned herself and crossed, then uncrossed her legs several times.

"You said he came by looking for me, Mary?"

"That's what I said alright."

"Well, what did he say?"

"Say?"

"Yeah, what did he say he wanted?"

"Oh, girl." She waved her hand at Vivian like only a fool would need to know what he had said. "Oh, girl, I didn't talk to him, just saw him through the window is all."

"You didn't?"

"No indeed, you expect me to go out there looking like who dunnit, and why? My rollers were in, my hair bonnet was on. I had only sat under the dryer for thirty minutes, and you know this style got to last me to Sunday school."

"Oh." Vivian sat back deflated in her chair.

"Yes, ma'am, Mr. Franklin Dyers. Name even sound like money don't it?"

Vivian whipped her head back around. "Mr. Franklin Dyers? Mr. Franklin Dyers? Mr. Franklin Dyers came here and you weren't going to tell me?"

"I just told you, girl, don't put all that on me. You wasn't asking the right questions, not outright."

"Oh, Mary, hush. How do you know it was him?"

"How do I know it was him? He left a card. Once my stories were through, I walked down and retrieved it." She pulled a small, opened envelope from her bra. Vivian reached for it without thinking and snapped the paper out of the flap, skimmed the words.

"He says he wants me to meet him at the Champagne Supper Club."

"Um-hmm."

"Tomorrow night at eight o'clock."

"That's what the man said."

"He says he has a proposition for me."

"I know that's right."

Vivian sat back in her chair. The pillow on its seat was thin and faded. The back was missing at least two rungs. Still, it was like the weight of her early years slid off her shoulders, and she felt unfazed for a minute, like someone whose life had been smooth and there was no reason to expect a bump up the road, like a new version of herself possibly. If Mr. Franklin was contacting her for the reason she imagined, and there could be no other plausible explanation, not really, it meant he wanted to manage the girls. He'd managed a boy from their youth group four summers ago, and that boy was a man now, and on the radio in regular rotation. He had only released a couple of singles so far, but his mother had bragged at last month's revival that he'd signed a deal with Columbia Records. And now the one who'd made it happen had set his eyes on her, on her girls rather. So far, she'd done well for them on her own: they performed at every club in the city, and just last month, they'd opened for the Caravans at the Oakland Auditorium, and met the manager of the Dunbar Hotel in Los Angeles. He had promised them an audition by the end of the year. Now she wouldn't have to hold out that long. Yes, He had graced them all with change this afternoon. Even Mary seemed to notice the shift.

"I'm happy for you, girl," she said. "If anybody deserve it, it's you."

"Thank you, Mary." Vivian said it cautiously, though. Mary didn't deliver praise. Vivian felt fatter on the inside because she knew this time it was seriously due, but she didn't quite feel comfortable accepting it either.

"I'm serious," Mary went on, but Vivian was already past all that.

"So you think he wants to take on the girls?" She asked it softly, slowly, like saying it might make it even more unlikely to be so.

"Of course, why else would he come by? Why else would he leave such a note?"

"Wow." Vivian stood and grasped the paper to her chest. She didn't spin around in a circle, but she considered it. She might have even snapped her fingers at her side and two-stepped.

"Should I bring the girls with me, then, when I go?"

"No, don't bring the girls. I read it two times myself and don't nowhere do it say bring the girls. Nah, do just what the man tell you. You don't want him thinking you hardheaded right off the bat."

"Alright, alright." Vivian nodded. "And what should I wear, Mary?"

"Now that's on you, girl. You the one who showed the block about those Chesterfield coats, pencil skirts, satin pumps. You better press that hair, slide on that red lip. You know you walk out here looking like cold hard cash."

"Right, right." Vivian settled into the news. It felt like she was slipping back into her ordinary self now, but the dimensions had been altered since she'd been gone. She had always operated as a crab, tough on the outside because the interior could bend, but now she could feel herself softening in her person. For instance, it was just a small thing, but instead of screaming, she turned for her front door and, from the entrance room, called out to the girls with a lilt:

"I thought I told y'all to pick up in there." She nearly sang it.

"We did pick up, Mama. We just didn't put it back again." That from Esther, the smart mouth, smart in general, but she could be melancholy too. The moods had started when she was in middle school. To this day, Vivian didn't know what had caused them.

"Alright now, clever girl, don't make me force you to pick those teeth up from the floor." Vivian stood in the kitchen with them now.

They laughed.

"Oh, Mama, can't we ever stop cleaning up? Cooking, cleaning, cooking, cleaning, is that any way for a girl to spend her life?" This from Ruth, the dreamer, only sometimes Vivian didn't know if the child's dreams matched her own.

"You forgot singing. Did you practice today?" she asked.

Silence.

But Vivian's calm sustained her and she almost smiled.

"Jesus, how are you going to surpass the Andrews Sisters if you don't practice like the Andrews Sisters? How far down the road you plan on getting without ambition? Huh?"

More silence.

"You hear me asking you a question, don't you?"

"Yes, Mama."

"'Yes, Mama. Yes, Mama.' Don't 'yes, Mama' me. Give me 'Please Tell Me Now' in three-part harmony."

The girls glanced at each other, then drew together. Vivian closed her eyes and listened.

"There you go," she said when they were done. "There you go. When you girls sing like that, it makes me forget all my worries. That's what you're going to do for other people too, just like Billie. You think Miss Holiday ever forgets to sing?"

"Sounds like from her songs if some man tells her what she wants to hear, she'll forget her own last name," Esther said.

The girls laughed, and Vivian found it hard not to.

"Alright, funny girl, maybe I got you in the wrong line of work, maybe you should be behind somebody's stage, writing jokes? In the meantime, finish cleaning up this house. You know Preacher Thomas is coming for dinner tonight."

The girls smiled between themselves like she couldn't see them.

"And Gerry," Ruth said.

"And Horace too, after he closes down the bookshop," Esther added.

"All the more reason, set the table with my mama's china. Put out the nice silver, Ruth. That fish ain't done. Lord, these potatoes, you could have smothered them a little more, but I suppose they'll do. And the green beans? From the can, but you added bacon, right? Alright, alright. Well, get yourselves ready then. Let me slide out of this uniform, put on something nice. My nose is shining, but I suppose I have a minute to powder it."

In the house Vivian rented on Webster, across the street from the New Home Market and the Crocker Bank, there was a hallway where, had the dinner guests not been just like family, they might have waited for one of the girls to escort them through the front parlor to the family parlor, then through the sliding doors to the dining room. As it was, they had all filed straight in to eat. The dining room wasn't as fancy as a predecessor might have kept it, but it was generations ahead of where Vivian had grown up, with its drawn-back velvet curtains, built-in china cabinet, a gold framed mirror opposite the table, and the silver Vivian's grandmother's mistress had left her laid out atop a bureau. They sat in armless chairs around the long oak table, a candelabra centerpiece between them, Vivian at the head across from Preacher Thomas, Gerry beside her, then Ruth beside Gerry, Esther beside her and Horace across from her, and Chloe next to him, then Mary so close to Vivian their knees touched. Their cloth napkins grazing their laps, their plates idle before them, they waited for Preacher to bless the table.

"Father Almighty, we ask you to preside over this meal, over the food itself that Vivian poured her heart into, her soul really," Preacher started. He was darker than Ellis had been, with straight hair that had thinned since she'd known him. Despite the thinning, virtually every woman at Shiloh had taken him pies with unspeakable hope baked into the filling. Vivian couldn't say she'd never been tempted to be one of them.

"We ask you to preside over the people seated before you anticipating their fill, but let them know that it's not just their physical hunger you're satisfying, Lord."

Esther and Horace side-eyed each other.

"Yes, Lord, let them know it's their thirst for you that they need to quench and that's not coming through this food, not through this drink either, Lord, no, it's not coming through their bodies, Lord. Not even the fittest among us are going to get satiated from that short thrill—" And he looked at the young men now. "And Lord—"

Esther cleared her throat.

"I beg you to fill them up with the water of your spirit, Lord, to infuse them with that holy fire, to let it burn through them, all the weakness, all the gluttony, all the sinfulness, all the pride, all the lust, all the earthly components of our indomitable nature, Lord Jesus, let it burn."

Esther and Horace were full-on laughing into their fists now, and Vivian shot a glance at Esther, who elbowed Preacher, and he looked up and threw his hands in the air, as if in acknowledgment that he had dragged.

"Oh, yes, Lord, and to not be attentive to this lovely woman's feast would be a different sort of sin, and so let's eat."

"Let's eat."

"Let's eat."

"I just hope Miss Viv didn't burn the catfish with all her holy fire," Horace said, and the people next to him snickered, and Preacher pretended not to hear, though Vivian thought she might have glimpsed a gentle smile.

There were a few minutes before every one of Vivian's meals where people didn't speak, their senses and faculties were so absorbed by the stimulation coming at them, and that happened again now. It made no difference that she hadn't cooked this meal. She'd shown all three of her daughters how to simulate the experience in the kitchen. It was Chloe's turn today, and she was best, but the truth was any one of them could run a house. Vivian had made sure of that, that while she rolled egged chicken in flour and waited for the oil to sizzle, her daughters were behind her knowing, just as she would, when it was time to drop the meat into the pan. When they were ten, they could blend a roux until their shoulders ached, could mash cinnamon and milk and banana for the moistest bread. Today they had baked a whole fish, and snuck kernels of corn into batter for muffins. There was red rice and gravy and green beans fried in bacon fat, and it was the final note of the prayer really to be swept up by it all. When someone spoke, it was like waking from a dream.

"This is something, Viv," Preacher said. "I'm mighty grateful, mighty grateful indeed. See, a man living on his own doesn't get to feast on home-cooked meals too often. This is a rightful treat."

She smiled. It didn't get old, the praise. And it didn't just move her; it felt like it connected her back to her mother, the past they shared that had been Vivian's life: hauling water and gathering eggs on the farm; accepting her first Communion in an old white dress the woman had restitched in lace; devouring fried fish on Lent Fridays, her napkin wet with grease; riding the streetcar tracks the summers her mother worked in the white woman's kitchen. On the way there, they sat, but by evening, it would be too crowded. The conductor would remove the COLORED sign, and they would have to surrender even the back. She had moved here to escape that part, and now Mr. Franklin had come. She would see him the following evening, in fact, and she reached for the appointment to coat herself. Things would be different now, not just for her, but for her girls too. They didn't show it, but she knew their yearning pressed so hard against their chests sometimes they ached. Especially Ruth.

"You got any news from home?" Preacher asked. He himself had come twenty years before from New Orleans with his wife, but she had woken one morning three years earlier with a lump in her throat that swelled until she couldn't talk or eat. It was only a few days after she stopped swallowing water that Vivian got the call, and she sat with Preacher that night. He didn't say a word then for eight hours straight, but his bottom lip never stopped shaking. Now he was smiling at her.

"None worth mentioning." Vivian shook her head. "Brother's working at Ford. Steady work," she added.

"That's good," Mary said.

"For now," she said back. "Anything resembling security down there bound to be a trap." And that was all she would say about that. She didn't like to talk about home, almost like it would call it back up, like she'd go to bed on the side of the country she could trust and wake up in enemy territory once again.

Anyway, the corn bread was divine, and she was about to tell Chloe as much when Horace cleared his throat. He was a big eater, and most of these meals he attended, he kept his head down like if he shifted his eyes away from his plate, someone might steal the contents. Today, though, he took a gulp from his glass of lemonade, wiped the remains from his mouth with the back of his hand, and then, as an afterthought, with his napkin, and began to speak.

"I got some news," he said. "My cousin live down there in Baton Rouge. He just got the City to pass an ordinance letting Negroes sit at the front of the bus if there's no whites there. It's something." He paused. "I'm on the lookout for similar progress out here." He took another gulp, neater this time.

"My daddy got lured here with empty promises and he was fool enough to believe them, we all were. They said, 'Work in our war.' They said, 'We'll protect you when it's over.' And yeah, I ate good for a few years, but almost ten years later, look at us: half of us opening doors for white people, shining their shoes, and the rest out on the street. They got us bottomed out in these slums"—he gestured toward the block outside—"and we just supposed to feel lucky. At least they didn't force us in those camps the way they did the poor Japanese." The Japanese—Vivian fought an urge to shake her head against the subject. She didn't like to talk about that either, not ever. One of the women who had been made to leave during the war had been her friend. Not like Mary or anything like that, but they had traded food: smothered okra for sukiyaki; red beans and rice for udon. Then one day she'd looked out the window and that woman was gone. It had been eight years now since the war ended, and when Vivian closed her eyes at night, she could still see the party streamers in the air, smell the victory. All of the rest of it, well, it was over now.

But Horace continued. "We might as well be back in Texas or Louisiana for that matter. Y'all might as well a stayed right where you were 'cause I'm afraid the improvement they promised you here is an illusion and it cost you a trip." He leaned forward in his chair and burped softly, then swallowed it back.

Nobody spoke for some time, and Vivian turned to her daughter sitting across from the man. Esther stared up at him like he was Jesus Christ Himself returned preaching the Sermon on the Mount. Vivian herself had to admit she'd been captivated all the while he was speaking, but now in the silence, for some reason, she felt afraid. He was an intelligent man, that much was clear, but all this energy and passion, wasted. She looked at Preacher. Preacher looked back at her.

"My mama used to say to my brother, 'Boy, you is an educated fool,'" she said finally and they all laughed. Even Horace seemed to smile a touch.

"I'm serious, though," she said as the uproar subsided. "You ever been in a house when it was firebombed?" she asked. "Ever seen the skeleton of it once it was all done? Maybe you ain't never seen a man beat beyond recognition, and don't get me started on the lynchings, so many at one time, my mama wept every time my daddy left the house. You see any of that in San Francisco?"

Horace seemed ashamed.

"I'm not trying to embarrass you, son," she said. "We need young people with heart, but don't say there hasn't been progress. It breaks my own heart to hear you say that 'cause I see the fruit of it every day."

"And thank God for the fruit," Preacher said. "And thank God for this beautiful meal," he added, "and the hands that prepared it." He glanced in the direction of the hands he was referencing when he said that, clasped in Vivian's lap, and for less than a minute he let his eyes linger at that level beneath her waist.

"And the hands that clean up after it too," she added, nodding at her girls, and he moved his eyes to hers, and they laughed.

SHE HAD MADE A JOKE ABOUT THE GIRLS, BUT THE TRUTH WAS THAT SHE cleaned behind them if she could. She didn't need to be as strict as her mother had been, pouring everything but milk into those white women's children. No, Vivian had it hard but not impossible. She worked twelve-hour shifts three days a week, one of two Negro women in all of the French Hospital, assisting Dr. Michaels and Dr. Phillips in pulling babies into this world. And there were the after-parties too. There would be one tonight in fact, where she'd serve jambalaya and finger sandwiches while the girls sang the neighbors' blues away. But those were more like homecomings than work. The rest of the time, she could oversee her daughters, their mood and their sound, their feel and their look, the eight-bar intros, the sequins and jewels she sewed atop the polyester fabric.

She let them sit now that the guests had gone. They enjoyed the remaining petit fours and warm tea, and even with her back to them as she scrubbed the pots and pans, she could tell when Chloe spoke that she was smiling that yard-length smile of hers. She could tell Esther was picking at her dessert, and Ruth, her firstborn baby, she could tell she was brooding over something, her brow furrowed, her hands clenched up in her lap. She had been that way for months now. When she was a child, she shared too much: "Mama, I'm nervous to sing.

Mama, no boy will ever love me." It had worn Vivian down, all the counseling she'd been made to do, all the stories, all the questions, all the "Look at me, Mama," from the morning she woke up to the time she beckoned the child to sleep. But if Vivian had had foresight, she would have warned herself, it was better when the children were talking. It was when they stopped that you had to worry, and that was where she was now. Ruth was hiding something. It was only a matter of time, though, as the Good Book said, before secrets would be made manifest. Everything hidden would become known.

"The corn bread was good, Chloe," she called out from the sink.

And the girls all groaned in agreement.

"Not a single square left," Esther said. "That's how you know."

"Did you see how many pieces Horace reached for?" Chloe asked.

"I wasn't looking," Esther said.

"You wasn't looking, yeah, alright, you wasn't looking, and I'm going to swim across the Pacific tonight, dip my hair under the water and all." This from Ruth. She was only kidding. She had a sweet disposition and it came out as such, but Esther was more sensitive than she let on, especially when it came to her older sister. She took everything Ruth said hard, then doubled down.

"Oh yeah?" Esther looked up fast. "I saw how many pieces of bread you ate, Ruth. Could you even fit in your swimsuit?"

Ruth's mouth trembled.

"The men at the club seem to like my new curves. I didn't see a single one checking for you."

"I wouldn't let those lowlifes touch me with a stick." Esther leaned forward.

"And they wouldn't let themselves either." Ruth pressed her back against her chair.

And it would go on like that if Vivian didn't step in. When those two were younger, they couldn't be separated; then their hugs turned to punches, then their punches turned to commentary, and that didn't seem to heal like the marks did. She didn't know what had provoked the rift, only that the slightest look by one of them would unleash all the resentment that had tangled and hardened.

"That's enough of that now," Vivian shouted, turning back.

"You both get more looks at the club than I do," Chloe said.

"Every one of you would be a fool to count on that," Vivian went on. She still gripped a wet spoon in her hand; she swung it as she spoke, and a drop of water flew to her wrist and curled down. "Every one of you. As much talent as God graced you with and you got the nerve to hang your hat on your looks, beautiful as you are, what's wrong with you? Now apologize to your sister, both of you."

They grumbled apologies, and Vivian made them repeat them, louder this time. She told herself she should be starting the greens for the after-party, at least washing the chicken, soaking the beans, but she didn't have the oomph for it, not right now. She was relieved when the girls started up again.

"Preacher sure seemed like he was in good spirits, huh, Mama?" Chloe asked.

"What was it he said, 'God bless the hands that made the meal,' huh?" Esther asked. "I bet he want to do a whole lot more than bless them." Esther and Ruth were both laughing now.

"If by bless them, he mean wrap them inside his own and never let go," Chloe said.

"If by bless them, he mean soothe the weight of his soul with them," Ruth said, and she and Esther slapped each other's palms.

"Nah, see, y'all getting along now when it's you against ol' Mama, huh?" Vivian dried her hands on the dish towel, walked over, and sat down in the empty chair between Chloe and Ruth. It was true what she had said, that they were all beautiful, if distinct. Chloe was black as her daddy, with Vivian's slight soft features; Ruth was Vivian's complexion, so white she might pass, if the very thought of it didn't sicken her, but she had Ellis's hair. Now it was the style to press and comb it, but when Ruth had been a baby, Vivian had plunged her hands deep into her daughter's curls and felt an ecstasy at every kink, almost like

God had found where she'd been lacking and through her daughter compensated her in full. Esther had come out as red as the dirt on Vivian's grandmother's land, Vivian's hair straight down her back. Sure, a certain kind of Negro man would always pick one of the older girls out in a crowd, on account of how he was made to detest his own skin. And sure, Chloe had had trouble for that reason, but as young as she was, Vivian could discern a sensuality inside her that was only a few moons from blooming.

"We not against you, Mama." Chloe leaned her head against Vivian's shoulder.

"Yeah, we love you, Mama," Ruth said, leaning in too.

Esther didn't repeat her sisters' reassurances, she never did. Still, she walked over and rubbed her mother's back.

Vivian started to hum "Underneath the Harlem Moon," and Ruth picked up the tune with her words. It was the first song the girls had learned, the only one they all still adored.

The other girls followed like taking in air.

Vivian had been a little girl herself when she heard a group of ladies from Mobile, fair-skinned too, singing this ditty. They'd come to entertain at a July birthday party her mother was working. Vivian was supposed to be setting out plates for petit fours, but her own birthday had been only two days before, and the fantastic nature of it still lingered, so she did too, next to the table, her mouth spread wide. One of the girls sat at the piano, the two others surrounding her in maid uniforms. The uniforms didn't lay on them the way they laid on her own mama. It almost looked like the women wore costumes. They were as lovely as the white ladies present. Their faces were as made up, their skin as smooth, their figures as tight. It was such a sad song, but they sang it like they were happy, their fingers snapping, their toes tapping the hard floor. If it weren't for their eyes, Vivian would have bought the act entirely.

The white woman Vivian's mother worked for danced in the center of the room. She wasn't old, but she was on her way and she hadn't realized it yet, with the low-cut blouse. She raised the hem of her skirt when she moved, stuck out her splotched thigh. The rest of the group cheered, some with mocking smirks. The sister at the piano watched while her fingers sprawled over the keys. It took a while for Vivian to mark what it was in her eyes. She only recognized it when the white woman's daughter, Vivian's own age herself, snapped at Vivian to get to work: "This ain't no nigger party." Vivian followed the girl back into the kitchen then, but she peered through the door each time it was opened. The ladies sang the whole night through, the woman and her daughter giddy off their show, and Vivian knew the feeling she had had trouble placing was rage.

She thought about those girls every night for years after, sang the song they'd sung, danced their dance. She had a feeling that she had been ordained to see them. She didn't have sisters. It was just her and her two brothers, Lowell and Egan. Still, she clung to the image of the singers, the unexpected surprise of the Negro women there looking just like her, the miracle of their talent lifting the room so high even the whites needed a part of it. All of it had restored Vivian so the white girl's taunts couldn't reach her, not all the way.

When she had one daughter, then another, then another, it occurred to her it might be fate, that that day over a decade earlier might have been the foundation for their destiny. Then she'd heard Ruth one morning in the sanctuary of Shiloh Missionary Baptist, with the press Vivian had combed in the night before glistening, belt out "Precious Lord" like a woman Vivian's own age, one who was tired, weak, worn. Vivian had yearned to sing as a child, and her mother had told her she could sing alright; she could sing as loud as she wanted while she sacked bags and bags of cotton. Vivian had clamped shut, but Ruth's melodies had picked up where she'd left off. The next morning, Vivian had led her two daughters onto the roof of their building, a smooth 1,500 square feet of concrete that they accessed through a fire escape set off from the kitchen. It was precarious walking up, especially in the winter morning's cold, but Vivian bundled the girls up in coats and scarves, and the children were brave and eager to learn. "See those houses to the north," she'd call out. "That's where you set your sights, you stick with this, you'll be there." She taught them about pitch and intonation until lunchtime called. Later, when Chloe was ready, there were three. The Salvations, as they called themselves, had spent two hours a day on that roof, rain or shine, every day since. As they aged, rehearsals dragged until sunset sometimes, and those nights, in the distance, the lights of the Nob Hill hotels sparkled.

Yes, Vivian had trained those girls as furiously as she'd twisted the cotton from the boll back home. But it would all be worth it one day. The Lord had promised her when Ellis died that He would repay her double for her trouble. There wasn't a day that went by that she didn't envision the reward, the baby blue Cadillac, the mink coats, the diamonds in her ears nearly the size of her fists. She wouldn't need to stand between a white woman's legs urging her to push out a child that would grow up just to tear her down. She wouldn't need to inform the new mothers she wasn't there to mind the babies, only to keep them alive. She'd buy the house Ellis had rented for her, just like Mary had bought her own years earlier, only she wouldn't need roomers to pay the note. The South would fog over into somebody else's memory. Of course, the material effects were just the top layer of her imagining, the fat at the top of milk that got skimmed for the real substance, because it wasn't that at all, was it? She already had an inclination the thrill didn't linger. It was the renewal of her faith she was anticipating, the final leg of a journey she had started out blindfolded over twenty years earlier, no plan in sight and $200 to her name taped inside her gingham dress. She had made something of it on her own. This last act would cement all she'd yearned for as hers, bind it to her so there'd be no turning back. The nursing degree, the white frocks and caps, the rubber shoes she tugged off each night were like signals to her that there was more coming. He had whispered that very message in her ear.

Now she stood for the dishes once more, still exalted from the card Mary had pulled from her bra.

"Hey, Mama." Ruth pushed back from the table, her chair legs abrupt against the hard wood. "I told my study group I'd meet them. We got the biology exam next week."

Vivian started to say no, then stopped herself. The girl was about to graduate from nursing school, and Vivian was proud of that, she was. Sure, sometimes it worried her too, how committed Ruth was to a backup plan. It was like the Good Book said, you couldn't serve two masters, but Ruth was a careful girl, always had been. Disciplined, methodical, *ambitious*, which had turned her into the star really. Of course, they all had talent. Esther's came through tireless effort, and even then, she'd stumble over lines, and Vivian had stopped letting her lead songs because she'd chime in off-key. Chloe's gift was pure, her range was wiiiide, delivered direct from God Himself, but she didn't have the power you couldn't describe in words, but that you couldn't mistake either. No, without Ruth, Vivian knew, deep in her heart, though she'd never utter it aloud, the life inside the dream would expire.

"Go ahead then, but be back soon," she said. "We got the after-party tonight."

"I know," Ruth said without looking back. And the door closed on the remaining two girls rounding out their final verse.

RUTH

Ruth and Gerry stood in an alley off the butcher shop, and she could still glimpse the unplucked birds and pig heads from the side window. She only had thirty minutes. It was Friday, and every Friday for the past five years, Mama had hosted an after-hours party in their basement. Ruth would need to boil beans in preparation, cut the chicken, not to mention curl her hair and squeeze her gut into a gown. It had been getting harder and harder to do that lately.

"I'm so sick of it," she complained even now. "The late nights, the nasty men, the liquor on their stank breath, the cigarette smoke on my dresses, my hair. The other day, I threw up after a show, Gerry, barely made it outside before it all streamed out, buckets of it. I can't sleep at night, I'm having nightmares about the performances—not like in the beginning, when I'd dream I'd open my mouth up and no sound would come out. It's the opposite. I'm seeing myself on stages hitting notes to perfection, and I wake up weeping. I don't know how much longer I can keep this going. I really don't."

Gerry stood against the butcher shop's brick. She leaned into him. They'd been kissing before they'd stopped for this conversation. She'd been wanting to have it more and more lately, and they'd ridden the same words down different tracks for weeks. Now he took her hand.

"I fell asleep in family nursing this morning," she started back.

"Shh." He put his finger to her mouth. "You know I'm going to take you out of there," he said. "You know I'm going to marry you."

"When?" She was tired, and the word came out with a desperate tinge. "I don't know how much longer I can wait."

"They about to promote me." He was a tall brown man with light brown eyes. He'd been skinny as a child, but he'd grown muscles now, muscles and a beard. He had a tic that made him nod when he spoke; he'd developed it when they were nine and a roomer had tried to step to his mother. He'd raised a baseball bat to the man's face, vowed he'd use it, and the man had fled, but the tic had lingered. That nod always reminded Ruth of the power of his word. He nodded again now. It was hard for her to touch him without wanting him fully.

"Myron aiming to open his package liquor store any minute. It's all he been talking about. Ain't nobody else to fill in for him. Nobody that know the business like I do. Ol' Barrett last week almost lost his finger to a handsaw. No way Mr. Gaines would put him in charge after that. No way in hell."

Gerry was confident, but he was fighting to be, and that worried Ruth, that there was an opponent on the other side of his conviction.

"It's not just that. I'm going to own my own butcher shop one day, just like Mr. Gaines. He started same way I did, apprenticing, then four years later, the shop on Post belonged to him. Then this one a few years after that. And cutting meat is like cutting hair, like burying bodies, there's going to always be a need for it, baby. It's not the bright lights"—he lowered his head—"but I promise you, you'll always be fed."

"I don't want all that," she said, lifting his face with her fingers. "Just enough light to see you by, that's all." And she kissed him again, harder that time.

"Just give me a few weeks," he repeated, and she nodded. She always backed down around this bend of the conversation because the truth was, if he proposed tomorrow, as ecstatic as she'd be, she couldn't begin to conceive of how she'd break it to her mother. It wasn't that she hadn't yet summoned the nerve; she didn't know if she had the capacity to. Even if all the courage in her body rose to its feet like an army inside her, she didn't think it would be enough. She had never been the type of person who just did things because she wanted to do them. There were people she knew like that, like Nubia, who yearned to be a star with everything in her, or even Katherine, who confessed she was born to bear children, but Ruth didn't know how to lead a vision from her mind into the world. All this time, her mother had been telling her to project her voice, to smooth out her steps, to mind her sisters, to boil the rice, to sort the bills, to run the house, and she had followed on her own mostly. But still, the drive of it had come from someone else, and along the way, her own will had been dulled, subsumed.

She was praying the proposal would give her some momentum. She was praying for certainty, a sign that might tell her when to move, what order the words should step out in to best capture her mother's agreement, a sign along the lines of the miracle at Cana in Galilee. Something she wouldn't be able to unsee or misremember later. But here she was outside the butcher shop counting the minutes until she'd hustle off to chase somebody else's dream.

Gerry sighed, shook his head, but he kissed her too.

He pulled her against him, then pulled back, focused on her middle. It was true that she had gained.

"Getting thick with it," he said. "I like it."

"It's all those bologna sandwiches." She nodded toward the meat inside.

"What I'ma do with you?" he asked, laughing.

"I don't know." She rubbed her hand up and down his hard chest. "But we only got ten minutes left to find out."

Ruth had known Gerry her whole life. When she was young, she would have sworn her father had sent him to her to protect her in his absence. She had been about to turn four when the man died, and she was twenty-four now, but she carried the memory of the day of his death with her everywhere she went with a freshness, a vigor, that belied its age.

The details were always the same no matter how many times she revisited them. Her parents had gone out for dinner, and Mary walked next door every ten minutes to be sure Ruth and Esther hadn't wandered from their beds and, once, to pour Esther a new bottle. After Esther gulped it down, Mary left again, and Ruth sang the toddler a lullaby she'd learned from their mother. She only had to finish the first verse before the child's heavy breathing resumed.

A-tisket, a-tasket
A green and yellow basket
I wrote a letter to my friend
And on the way I dropped it

Later, Ruth awoke to Mary hunched over on the edge of the bed whispering to herself, "Lord, help me, Jesus." Then Ruth was out again, and to this day, a small, buried part of herself wondered if perhaps that was the reason he had died. Maybe there was something she would have been able to do with her mind, with her spirit, should she have asked Mary what was wrong, should she have peered over her shoulder into the sitting room, where her father lay flat, her mother rushing to the window for the ambulance, rushing back.

When Ruth finally did get up, the details were hard to assemble into a story, her mother in a heap in the kitchen in front of the new icebox, Mary beside her rubbing her back, and Esther crying, wailing really, that interminable wail that wouldn't let up for months after. Every memory of that period seemed to have been infused with it. Even now, when she thought of her father, it wasn't the man with the soft hat, the mustache, or the bold cologne, the scratchy almost-beard struggling in; no, it was the sound of her sister's voice, Mary whispering, Mama in a heap. That last detail was the hardest to stomach. To this day, she'd do anything to keep that woman standing.

And she didn't hate singing as much as she hated performing, the frantic pace, the undying nights, the eyes on her, the expectations so heavy, and there was no satisfying them when they came to her so deep. Not that it mattered. She'd been in the youth choir since she was old enough to say, "No thank you," and Mama didn't expect anything out of it at first. It was more like holding your own bottle or buckling your own shoes. But then one day, her friend had to stay home sick, and it was Ruth whom the saints associated with her. They told her to get up on the pulpit and sing "Precious Lord" the same way Rosetta had sung it on the record, and so she shot her head back and she did just that, without any particular intention, or fear for that matter, only the way she cleared her plate when her pork chops and rice were finished, or ran the water for her bath. Though she stumbled over the line *Let me stand*, singing "*Let me sand*" instead, the church had erupted that day, and she was still so young she didn't know if their roar of applause was a blessing or a chastisement.

After that, she and Esther were on the roof every night, and for some time, Chloe was too young, but she'd watch. It was supposed to be a two-girl act, that was it, until one day, the baby girl who couldn't even use the bathroom reliably sang two octaves above middle C without strain. Her mother shook her head, smiled to herself, and looked up into the air like she did when she was conversing with Daddy, and she said, "Alright. Three? Alright. Three." Chloe joined, and they were the Salvations. Before Ruth could pronounce "intonation," she was sleeping with a humidifier to hydrate her larynx; gargling with salt water to prevent infections; jumping rope to ward off breathlessness. Even now, God forbid Mama caught them smoking, or drinking, or spreading too much mayonnaise on their deviled ham sandwiches, or shouting, or doing much of anything besides three-part harmonizing on the roof's concrete, watching the world beneath them press forward.

Gradually it had all become too much, and Ruth hungered for the girl who would hum along to the Soul Stirrers in the backseat of the car, for the Sunday morning sessions with her sisters, all "Just a Closer Walk with Thee." That would have been more than enough. Indeed, Mama had shepherded them from the roof to the basement to the high-level stages, but Ruth yearned to travel backwards. Most of the time she was crooning to jazz or gyrating to R&B onstage, she was reflecting on the simple things: breakfasts at Gerry's house on Father's Day because the holiday was less than meaningless to them both, drives with him to the Outer Sunset once she turned sixteen. Then there was the future beckoning: the click of the door weekday evenings, Gerry at the threshold, her children underfoot, the miracle of her husband making it home for supper yet again.

Back home, Ruth's mama sidled up beside her. She'd been acting funny since dinner and she kept it up now, held her hand over her heart, her eyes watering, bright red, and she walked up close to Ruth, and she cupped her face in her right hand.

"What's wrong with you, Mama?" Ruth asked now. "You coming down with something?"

And the older woman said, to Ruth's surprise, "No, no, your mama just got a little more hope in her cup than usual, that's all."

Then Vivian sat at the table beside her, and she didn't ask Ruth to get up either, though a hundred people were going to be in the basement in two hours looking for something to drive their hunger away.

"Who are you, and where is my mama?" Ruth asked.

And her mother laughed, in a loud, irreverent way that was not of her, though lately even Ruth had to admit she'd seemed looser, younger. Sometimes at night, she'd light a cigarette after rehearsal on the roof, and she'd talk about her early days with Ruth's father, how they'd walk to the general store for ice cream, how she knew she would marry him because when her mother was too sick to move, he'd lift her like she was a child, the way she knew he would one day lift his own children. Ruth would forget then she was talking to her mother, or any woman she knew for that matter. She felt the same sentiments, that she knew with Gerry by the way he took care of his own mama. Mary could be vengeful. She was known to start fights she couldn't finish, but each time Gerry would usher her away like she was incapable of harming a fly. Ruth started to say as much, but that was the thing with her mother—if Ruth inserted herself during these moments, Vivian would remember the usual order of things and pull back. She'd say, "Times have changed. The silliest thing you could do right now is chain yourself to a man." They wouldn't be like girlfriends any longer, and that wall between them would erect itself once again. For that reason, Ruth had learned to silently cherish the times her mother forgot herself, times like now.

"Who are you, and what have you done with my mama?" she repeated, just to hear the woman laugh again.

"Nothing's wrong, baby," she said, still in that same soft tone. "I got news is all. Good news this time. News that will change everything. News that we'd been waiting on, and I had just been about to doubt God, but no." And she shook her head and looked up to the ceiling like she did when she was grateful.

"What is it, Mama?" Ruth asked, though she knew. It was likely another audition, maybe the one at the Dunbar Hotel in Los Angeles, maybe somewhere farther away, maybe something worse. She almost shuddered. She loved her mother more than any other person in this world besides Gerry and her sisters, of course, but they were fundamentally opposed. Mama preferred Sarah Vaughan's fullness to Ella Fitzgerald's flexibility. She thought potato salad was what the devil prepared for his guests, and Ruth could devour bowls. She said idleness should have been rebuked in the Ten Commandments, and Ruth would just sit sometimes when her mother was at work and examine the thoughts in her mind, one by one, because when her mother was present, she swore the woman was privy even to them. Vivian was terrified of open-faced, raw emotion. Once she had glimpsed Ruth and Gerry beneath a door frame. They hadn't been doing or saying anything at all, but that had given it away, the way they'd been smiling like idiots over nothing, and the look in Vivian's eye, Ruth would never forget it.

Since Vivian seemed to have been lifted by her news, Ruth feared—no, she *knew*—that whatever it was, news like that would box her in, weigh her down, hold her back.

Her sisters scuffled in, Mary behind them carrying a fresh chicken from Mr. Gaines's. Mama stood to carry it to the counter, and Ruth took that opportunity to stand herself: "I better get to washing those greens." The girls followed her lead, headed upstairs to change. Vivian walked over and rubbed her arm. Ruth thought about telling her then about Gerry, preempting her news with her own, getting it over with, letting the what-ifs drift behind her.

"What is it, baby?" Vivian asked, rooting through the refrigerator now for the greens. "You always get nervous before a show," she hurried on. "The more nervous, in fact, the better you seem to do. You're going to soar up there. The thing is"—she whispered that part, probably so her sisters didn't hear; she didn't like to breed competition among them in that way—"you're a star, baby. And there's nothing you could do to change that, even if you wanted to."

"Yes, Mama," Ruth said. The collards were tough—Ruth could glean that from where she stood. Her mama passed her the bowl, and Ruth set it down in front of her, ripping the leaves from their hard stems piece by piece.

Gerry had spent more time than Ruth could measure setting up an after-hours spot in the basement, building a bar on the far end of the floor and drilling stools along its counter. Then a wooden stage with a red sequined curtain Mama had sewn and hung behind it, jutting out of the wall in the back. And every Friday night, he lined the frame of the room with chairs to free up the floor. Neighbors streamed in after places like Club Flamingo and the Gourmet Theater Restaurant closed, when they still needed a place to feel on each other or they needed bread to soak up their good times. Or they needed more of something else, anything else, a thing they could neither verbalize nor had ever located, and they were intent on finding it in the heat of Mama's done-up basement. Ruth understood, partly. She hadn't been able to claim that thing either, but she couldn't fathom searching for it there.

Anyway, she'd always been the one to start the food for the late nights, and they hadn't always provided dessert, but people more and more had requested something sweet, banana pudding or pecan pie. At first there hadn't been more than a trickle of folk, and the girls would rouse themselves from bed and perform in their regular house clothes, rollers in their hair, but as word spread, they began to treat it the same way they'd treat a formal show. The thing was the girls had built a following on their own, and now Ruth got the feeling people were there for them more than the corn bread, not to say her mother didn't put her foot in it, her foot and half a cup of sugar. Still, some of the audience didn't even eat; they just pulled their fold-up chairs to the tip of the stage, closed their eyes, and let their mouths hang, waiting on Ruth and her sisters to carry them elsewhere.

The noise downstairs started as a hum, but by the time Ruth had drizzled oil and vinegar over the tomato salad and poured milk in the biscuit batter, the hum had advanced to full-on song. That was her cue to head upstairs. Her mother and Mary would remove the greens from the fire once they were so tender Miss Fox with half her teeth gone would be able to swallow them whole. It used to be that Vivian would stand over the girls while they dressed, her voice straining with instructions: "Don't you want to paint your nails red to draw more attention to that microphone?" And the girls couldn't gossip and joke with each other the way they did ordinarily, not with their mother shouting: "Rest your voice now, that's your power."

Mama had to take up more responsibility downstairs, though, what with Mary and Miss Fox prone to starting fights with the other customers, and now, left to their own devices, the girls were free to bicker and complain. For instance:

"Is that Lil Viv?" Esther asked when Ruth opened the door. "I thought you had run off with Gerry, as late as you are coming in."

"Oh, stop," Chloe said.

"Yeah, before I tell Mama you want to sing an extra solo tonight," Ruth snapped back, shutting her bedroom door behind her.

Esther didn't say anything to that; Chloe only laughed.

There was an hour remaining before they'd head onstage, but Chloe was ready, perched on the edge of the bed, wagging her kitten heel pumps, tossing out compliments to Esther like she did, like she could build the girl's mood from scratch. And the thing was, though

Ruth seemed to bring out the worst aspects of her sister, sometimes, for Chloe, it worked.

"You might as well go ahead and get married in that dress, Esther," Chloe went on. "Just need to change the color."

Esther wasn't moved, not yet. "It's the same one you're wearing," she said. "Same one Ruth's wearing too."

"Yeah, but you not going to have to suck your stomach in neither, not like me. I made the mistake of stopping by Lena's on the way home. You know it's lemon butter pecan cake on Fridays, and I swear I can see it on me, like I didn't even digest it, like it just lodged itself in this roll"—and she squeezed the part of her stomach that folded over itself. Ruth tried not to laugh.

"Doesn't matter," Esther cut her off. "Ruth could walk up there in a garbage sack and she's all they'd see. Especially Mr. Gaines. Unless, of course, Miss Fox tries to fight him first," Esther went on. Mama let Miss Fox drink for free because she bussed tables, and she didn't have a dime to her name, but she would promise them she was going to make them rich.

"'I'ma get on the phone as soon as I leave here and see about my brother,'" Esther mimicked her now. "'He a promoter and he gon get you a deal and then you gon tell them all Miss Fox gave you that. Yeah, that came from your Miss Fox.'"

Ruth and Chloe bent over laughing. Esther was funny, but it wasn't just that—they were relieved. Her spells came and went, and it had seemed yesterday that one was brewing. Ruth had bullied her as a child, nothing extreme, simple name-calling, more so around certain days, Daddy-Daughter dances for instance. Then there'd been that one time when Esther had gotten unreasonably close to that grown man. He'd invite Esther to stay after shows at Flamingo, and standing behind the two, Ruth would have mistaken Mr. Sterling for Esther's daddy. Their bond had poked at a tender spot in Ruth she hadn't known was there, and she'd retaliated in her quiet way. Then she'd become kinder as her own heart healed, as Gerry mended it. Still, as much as Ruth tried, her sister didn't trust her. And most of her storms ended up spiraling in Ruth's direction. Sometimes, though, they'd shift before they touched ground.

"So, Ruth, how's Gerry?" Chloe asked in that singsong voice she developed whenever the topic was boys.

Ruth kept her face composed like she hadn't been worrying about the very same thing. "He's fine, why?"

"Is he coming tonight?"

She shook her head. "He's gotta work. He's up for a promotion you know."

"Ooh," Chloe said. "Maybe that's what he's been waiting on, before he pops the question."

"Please." Esther seemed to be relaxing. "Mama would answer that question for him with a pop upside his head. He's got too much sense for that."

"Maybe not," Chloe said. "Never know what somebody will do when they . . . in love. I wouldn't know, but don't they say it's like a brick hit you, you start seeing things that ain't ordinarily there. You lose control over your faculties. Shoot, I can't wait."

"You're only twenty, you better get comfortable with exactly that, waiting," Esther said.

"Ugh, might be another ten years waiting on you two." Chloe stood up and began powdering the spaces on either sides of her nose that tended to oil. She didn't need any of it was the thing. She had beautiful chocolate skin that even on the days leading up to her cycle didn't break out into the small bumps Esther kept on her forehead or the bigger mounds that dotted Ruth's jawline. But she didn't know it.

"Not too much," Ruth said in a soft voice, placing her hand on her sister's upper back. "Unless you expecting somebody tonight." She winked, glad for the change in subject.

"Not somebody, everybody," Chloe said. "And when they hear us, they'll be back the next week and the week after that and the week after that. Don't matter who else is open either."

Esther ignored Chloe, dashing her cheekbones with rouge. "Mama say how many songs we got to sing this time?" she asked. She was getting nervous, Ruth could tell, and if it grew in strength, it would reveal itself in some onstage mishap, hopefully one Ruth could distract the crowd from noticing.

"We gon go til the people through with us, that's what we gon do," she said like she was irritated. The truth, though, was that she was sustained by Esther's reticence. Her friends had stopped listening to her "made-up problems," as they called them; her mother thought she was spoiled, ungrateful. Even she did most times. Who wouldn't want to be transformed into a star? Esther was the only one who might have understood. She loved it like Chloe, but it ate at her too, that it didn't come to her straight, that she had to pour more effort in than the others, and she still wouldn't yield as much back. Ruth didn't know why she pressed on so hard with it, why she didn't let it go. They had never had an honest conversation about it, or anything for that matter, but the fact that it was inevitable that Esther would miss a note onstage settled Ruth's chagrin more than she could say. Esther would be upset if Ruth left, but in all likelihood it'd be best for her.

Ruth squeezed into her blue sequined gown, same exact one as the other girls' except hers stopped at her knees, and the other girls' reached their ankles. Esther eyed her up and down.

"Requiring more work than usual, huh, girl?" But she didn't seem judgmental, only interested, and her curiosity scared Ruth more. Ruth turned from her fast, snuffed her own concern out.

"What'd Mama say we singing?" she asked.

"You know I always like us to redo 'Sixty Minute Man,'" Chloe said, lighting up like she always did before a show, "and then 'I Didn't Know There Was a Reason.' That's the three of us. Then Mama wants you to take 'Walk Through That Door' solo, Ruth."

And as soothed as Ruth was by Esther's inadequacy, the idea that Ruth would yank this hope from Chloe worked the opposite magic. Whenever she was reminded of how much the singing meant to her baby sister, she would feel like a grown woman burning the Christmas list of a child who had imbued it with the previous year's supply of joy.

"Well, we better warm up then," Ruth said, letting out a deep, hard breath.

And she led them in their ritual: driving up and down the scale singing "Maaaa"; aligning posture; singing "Maaaa" with more vowels at the end; yawning, stretching their faces; thinking about their ribs and glutes and backs while singing "Maaaa" with all their might. And they never went onstage without running through "I Know Jesus Loves Me" a cappella, Ruth carrying the melody, Esther the upper part, and Chloe the lower, though the truth was Chloe's range was wider than either of theirs. Still, Mama said the men liked Ruth in the front.

It was nerves steady grinding after that, no matter how many times they performed, and they each had a different way of showing it. Ruth grew quiet now, eyeing the room for items she could organize, books off their shelves, sheets hanging beneath the mattress, but everything was in its place. Esther had it hardest, and she snapped at the girls about her lipstick. "The red color," she shouted, "I know you have it"—and then a minute later it turned up in her bra. And Chloe twirled in the mirror, flipped her hair, smoothed her gown, hummed the number they'd sing second, all the while beaming. Onstage she would take on a different persona altogether. Mama had told Ruth once she saw a seriousness, a power, in Chloe when she sang that she'd never ever viewed inside her otherwise.

They sprayed some more oil on their hair, hoisted up their pantyhose, glanced backwards in the mirror at their asses as they sashayed, and stepped out.

Downstairs was already hot and humid, though it was only eleven—the basement filled up fast in that way. Mama was running tables with Mary, and there were fifty people between her and her daughters at least, but she mouthed to Ruth, "You're going to be okay."

"I know," Ruth mouthed back like she didn't need it, though something settled inside her when her mother said it.

"You're going to be okay," Ruth said to her sisters, rubbing their backs, squeezing their hands. They always started with a prayer, and she led one now.

"Lord, carry us out of our own bodies so there's room for you to join us. More than that, move into us, Lord. Occupy our spirits, our hearts, and our minds. Be the words that we deliver, the sound that we emit, the flow we fall into, make us one with the audience so they tell us what they need and we hear it just as it's time to let it roll, Lord. Touch our feet, may they move like we're dancing on clouds. Still our minds so the rhythm is in our heart and we know it like we know our own name. Lord, energize the people before us, take the liquor off their breath—"

"Yes, Lord," Esther said.

"—and out of their brain so they can focus, so they can hear us, so they can appreciate the sound you and we are creating. Lord, let it be a testament to the gift you put inside us. Let us do right by you, Lord. Amen."

"Amen," the girls repeated.

They passed through the downstairs crowd to the front of the room where the floor had been scratched and Gerry's stage had been chipped, but after a few minutes nobody would pay attention to that. The band was ready, the drummer sliding his closed palm over his sticks one by one, the trumpeter cleaning his mouthpiece. The people beneath him were laughing, shouting, singing, dancing, though there was no music on, not yet. The girls would tame them, in time. Ruth was stepping up to do so when someone grabbed her arm, gripped it tight. She knew it was Gerry before she turned. He was supposed to be working tonight.

"I thought you couldn't make it."

"I took off." He nodded when he spoke. "Ruth"—and he paused here. "Mr. Gaines stopped me after work. I got the promotion. I got it, baby."

"That's wonderful," she said. Her foot had landed at the tip of the stage, but whatever powerful feeling his words lit up inside her didn't seem to belong in that venue. The feeling wasn't exactly joy: the decision wasn't on Gerry anymore, not Mr. Gaines either. She wasn't waiting on any outside force to save her. She stood arm's length from her sisters, and the gap between her and them might as well have been a mountain to scale.

"I don't want to put it off any longer. We need to tell her, your mama, she's going to have to know, Ruth. I love you, and—"

"I know," she cut him off. "I love you too. So much. But now I have to sing." She looked over to where her mama stood, Preacher beside her rubbing her back. She had said she needed to sing, but she didn't know if the words to the songs they had rehearsed would leave her mouth when she opened it. There might be an exclamation instead, a hymn of praise, a cry of alarm.

The music started, and she could hear Chloe in the back, crooning the chorus to "Sixty Minute Man." The girls all swung their arms, snapped their fingers. They rolled their hips forward in a slow swoon, and the crowd hollered, drunk as they were. She couldn't see them—it was too lit up onstage—but she could feel the energy, the free life, wild in the room yet directed straight at her too, and the thought of it all ending fueled her forward. It might be over soon.

And she leaned down for this part to offer the crowd the fingers that didn't grip the microphone, and the men who'd dragged their chairs to the stage leapt toward her, pitiful, though, on account of the booze, and she jerked her hand back just in time to make them laugh again.

Not that they needed the entertainment, not anymore. They were already coupled up, the song a stimulant in that direction. She could float away now if she wanted to, but there was "I Didn't Know There Was a Reason" to do, and the energy of her sisters occupied her through that, the fear of stepping on their feet, the mothering urge she could mostly manage, ensuring they maintained their notes above and below her.

They took a minute to receive the applause and to catch their breath. Ruth could glimpse Mama from the corner of her eye, chatting it up with Gerry, both of them staring straight at her, Mama calling out, "Alright now, girl." Ruth turned back to the song.

There didn't seem to be a reason to smile
I hadn't felt this funny feeling in quite a while
But then you came and shined your light on me
And I can't take another day without you, baby

Esther and Chloe sang the next two verses, and Ruth closed her eyes for them. In her mind, she was guiding her sisters through every note, holding their hands as they walked a narrow ledge, and it wasn't until Esther reached the final *But I must go on, But I will go on* without an error that Ruth exhaled, then called out to the audience to give it up for first Esther, then Chloe. Moments like these, she felt most intimately like her mother's child. The pride she felt watching them saunter off the stage, watching the people gaze at them, already hooked to them in that short time, well, she understood why her mother's eyes watered, why she followed them onto that roof every night. She and her sisters had been singing and dancing in harmony since they could talk, and somehow along the way, their insides had become connected too. She butted heads with Esther, sure, but she still knew when she was sick; she knew when her heart was broken. And now, when her two sisters had been glorified, she could feel their transcendence.

This was the part of the night Ruth feared—the part when she was left alone onstage. Her sisters, after all these years, were like padding to her. When she tripped over a microphone wire six months back at the Champagne Supper Club, it didn't sting as much when she stepped off the stage knowing they had had a bad night, that was all.

At least she wouldn't have to dance. That wasn't her forte, and it was all she could do to remember the words, much less know if she should step to the right *three* times before she dipped, or twice.

The crowd had erupted seeing her sisters off, and she waited for them to quiet down before she started, low at first.

I don't know exactly what I came here for
I don't know the reason anymore

She could sense her mama from where she stood, surrounded by patrons, overjoyed, and Ruth used to try to be too—to find pride in being the recipient of so many people's stares, to close her eyes and blend into the sound, to call up gratitude for her luck to be gifted such a talent—but she'd learned a few years back it was futile. She'd only feel more guilt at the end of it.

Just that what I'm getting isn't feeding me
Only that I stepped into a world that's not keeping me

She had finally found a way to match the joy she knew her mother felt watching them perform. But if she wanted to round out that joy, she would have to steal her mother's; she would have to talk to her; she would have to activate her own voice. She had promised herself she would do that very thing too many times now to count, but at the last minute, another audition would come through, another concert opening, another opportunity they simply could not forgo.

If this is what it is, then tell me
I've never been above settling

Because her mother would say, Ruth knew, that she wanted more for her than a life a finger-snap away from poverty. Her mother would say she wanted more for her than to be some man's wife, some children's mother, some milk to devour, some nerves to fray, some life force to suck dry. It represented danger to Vivian, anything that didn't showcase every form of ambition, but it was the opposite for Ruth. She would tell her mother if she listened. Her whole life she'd studied other people's families. The way a father would loop his jacket around his child when the outside air swooped in the sanctuary at church, and the way her friend Nubia's mother would set a plate before her man first before she tended to her own children. Those details fascinated her, and she'd unwind them and coil them back up, only to unwind them again many nights. If her mother were to talk to a girl in the church who wasn't her daughter, she would tell her that everyone had a compass inside them showing them which direction to go. Ruth had zeroed in on hers years earlier, but she had drowned it out with doo-wops and dance steps. The harder she went, she told herself, the more she could learn to love it, but the opposite had happened instead—the disgust had sharpened because she wasn't listening to it. And she sang that next part from her gut, with the weight of the urge to steer her own life.

The crowd was cheering now. She had hit the D on the head and let it linger, and there was wonder in that, sure. There was a peace there too, a stability. She had been on somebody's stage for as long as she knew. The crowd always overflowed with praise. She didn't know why she couldn't learn to be the type of woman to let that warm her. But she had learned she could not, and the certainty of that in the moment filled her up in a way that wouldn't seep out after the applause was done.

But if there's something different
Then let me walk through that door
Tonight

The song was almost over. She'd sing that last verse one more time, and she'd add some words to it, some oomph as Mama called it, and then . . . The truth was she was starting to feel funny again. It had been that way the last couple of nights, but the feeling was gaining strength now, as was her suspicion.

She set the microphone back on the stand and bowed. She usually stayed for as much applause as they'd give—she earned that and then some—but this time she walked straight down the steps, past the men whose eyes were strapped to her chest, only to get a sight of her backside; past her sisters, namely Chloe, who screeched and clapped; past Mama, Preacher Thomas beside her, who'd taken her hairnet off to say she was so proud. She could see Gerry too, walking toward her, but she didn't let him stop her from hurrying up the stairs. She wanted to talk to him, more than anything she did, but the noise, which she typically welcomed, the mix of odors, hot oil, Tabu the forbidden perfume, and sweat on top of hair grease, the sounds of palms slapping other palms, or butts, in greeting, the trumpeter leading the band in improv, all of it together was too frantic for the uneasiness rising inside her. She couldn't take the risk of throwing up in this setting.

She rushed up another flight of stairs and made it to her bathroom just in time. When she was done, she noticed that her sisters had come in behind her, Chloe stroking her hair and even Esther appearing contrite. The three girls glanced at each other, and an understanding passed between them, one Ruth had been bypassing the last few weeks, but in the familiarity of this setting, of this group, she felt safe staring it down and then absorbing it. Finally, when Ruth couldn't stand the smell of herself any longer, she told them to go, and she stood and washed up at the sink, smiling without meaning to all the while. There was something different, and she would walk through that door tonight.

ESTHER

All the while Ruth freshened up, Esther had to stop herself from smiling. She wasn't in the habit of celebrating her older sister, and the smile wouldn't have conveyed the meaning at its root. The thing was, Esther had been praying in her own vague and nondeferential way that Ruth would somehow be displaced from her star position, that Esther would be the one to displace her. And now her time had come. Chloe was good at this singing thing, better than good, but she didn't know it, and that hemmed her up in the way she'd let her voice drop when Ruth came in too heavy or the way she'd eat too much before a show, develop a leg cramp, and only half commit to the dance steps. That and Mama's blindness were why Ruth had always been set out front. And it was true that Esther had always had to work three times harder for the same level of skill, but she held her head up high when she arrived at rehearsal an hour before, tarried an hour later. And she maintained that spirit during the show. It was why onstage she could perform on par, why recently, at the Champagne Supper Club, she had outshined even Ruth singing "I Don't Want to Go On This Way." Half of stardom, she'd learned, was the belief that it was yours.

Of course, she'd learned a few minutes ago that there had been another reason she'd been trending upward, why Ruth had been slipping back, but that knowing only stoked her hope. Because it wasn't just the pregnancy—that state would yield a child, and Ruth would be the best mother, like she'd been to Esther before their feud, like she still was to Chloe. She wouldn't be able to split the effort between her home and the roof; she would make the right choice, she always did, and that would root up a path for Esther that simply had not been there before. Again, she had to stop herself from not only smiling but also tilting her head back and guffawing.

"How long have you known?" she asked. Ruth was back in her bedroom now, on the edge of her bed staring into space while Chloe rubbed her back. She had lingered in the bathroom for some minutes cleaning herself up, but Esther could still smell her, and she stepped backwards a few feet while she waited for her sister to confess.

"Really known? As long as you have." Ruth's eyes fastened on her stomach or the floor—Esther wasn't sure which. Esther wanted to extend her arm to her, maybe pull her in. It had been so long she wouldn't know where to start, how long to draw the act out, and she decided after a second of considering it wouldn't be close to worth the awkwardness. Instead she tried to will her sister to risk looking up into her eyes. It was the most tender Esther had felt about her in some time. Maybe Ruth could glimpse that if she looked her way. Esther understood why she might not; there had been only coldness there for years now.

"What are you going to do?" Esther asked. Her voice was softer here now, but no one seemed to notice it.

She was surprised at herself. In a matter of minutes, it was like history had changed, not the facts but her perception of them. For so long, when she saw or even thought of her sister, she could only find room for Ruth's taunts that had at first floated around her but then, in their adolescent years, circled closer, snuck inside her. The teasing had stopped years ago, but the discomfort had lingered, swelled even, encompassed most interactions involving Ruth, even ones where she wasn't to blame. For instance, her relationship with Mama: it wasn't Ruth's fault that she'd bent to the woman's will, that Mama didn't even have to say a word to Ruth and she'd know all the same to retrieve her slippers or her robe or whatever it was that would deliver her from her state of unease. Esther had found that state of unease to be permanent, but Ruth had worked a way around it. Then, of course, there was that man. Esther shook her head against the image of him.

Ruth shrugged, like they were talking about whether she'd finish off the leftovers from the after-party or send them home with Mary for her roomers.

"Well, you don't know a thing then, huh, girl? You don't know what you're going to do, you didn't know you got yourself knocked up, you're probably going to say you don't know how." Esther didn't mean to come out so strong. It was just that man's face, and humor had become a reflex for her, a guard. Her mama had tried to tame her mouth, even washed it out with soap when she was thirteen, but it didn't matter. Once Esther scrubbed the sharp taste off her tongue, she was back, switching Mama's gospel lyrics to sexually laced ones: *I need all of you inside me right this minute, Jesse* instead of *Jesus*; remarking on Miss Mary's smile behind her back, all "Be true to your teeth, or they'll be false to you." But this was not the time. She reminded herself of that.

"Of course I noticed," Ruth said. "Of course I did. Four months ago, it should have come and it didn't. But you know our cycles ain't never been so regular. And I been under so much pressure too, with the Dunbar audition approaching, Gerry's job stuff." She started to say something else and then she paused. "I'd assumed it had been stress," she went on. "I wanted to assume as much." She sort of smiled when she said that part, and Esther thought she might have noticed relief, not only that, but was it happiness? And that happiness seemed to invert itself and snake into Esther like it wasn't possible for her and her sister to match on the inside.

"Well, good for you," Esther said. "You got your ticket out. You know you never loved it, Ruth." There was more she had wanted to say only a minute earlier, so much more, maybe "Congratulations," maybe "You'd make a good mother, based on how you used to be with me, how you still are with Chloe," maybe "That's one lucky baby." But now handling it all a different way felt better, made it easier to walk out the door and slam it behind her.

Esther couldn't find downstairs fast enough. On her way, Mr. Gaines stopped her, trying to locate her chest with his eyes, but she had changed into her casual clothes now, a buttoned-up tailored shirt that nearly reached her neck.

"You sounded good," he said.

"You couldn't hear me over your own nasty thoughts," she yelled back over her shoulder. She would retrieve her coat, then be gone, but when she reached the basement, sure enough, Mama was busy trying to break up a fight between Miss Fox and Mary.

"She knew I wanted a square meal," Mary shouted. "Bringing me a slab of meat like I'm some heathen. I come in here every week and I order potatoes, greens, and steak, a square meal. You ain't never seen me in here not ordering no goddamn square meal."

"Nobody would argue with that. If anything, they might even say the meals were rectangular," Esther muttered to no one in particular, and a couple beside her snickered.

Mama was escorting Miss Fox from the basement, and she gestured at Esther to finish leading the woman upstairs. Esther reached down for her hand; her own coat would have to wait. Miss Fox was small, and it didn't require too much effort to guide her from one step to the other. Esther could smell the brown liquor straining through her pores.

"Oo, I could just strangle that bitch." Miss Fox turned to her when they reached outside. "Then your mama, that heifer, banned me for a month. Can't hardly stand none of y'all." She lit a cigarette and handed it to Esther. Esther hesitated—she had only done it once with

Horace at the bookstore—then looked around, took a long drag, and coughed the smoke out.

"Feel better, don't it?" Miss Fox asked.

Esther nodded, and the woman looked back at her like she was seeing her for the first time.

"Take another one, you might feel even better than that."

Esther reached for it once more and puffed before she heard the uproar. Mary had run out of the house and down the front steps, her arms swinging, Gerry behind her.

"You no-count geezer," she screamed, and Esther handed the cigarette back, started down the block. Last time she got caught up in one of Mary's grievances, her earring had been yanked out of her left lobe. She'd worn clip-ons onstage until a nurse friend of Mama's sewed her up again. From what she could gather, tonight would be that sort of night. Even now, she could hear Gerry, all:

"Mama, wait. Now stop all that now, Mama. You too old for all that."

Then Miss Fox:

"You lucky your son got you. If it weren't him, woulda been me."

Esther turned back for another peek. Ruth had ventured outside.

Gerry had set his mother at their front stoop and was standing beside his woman now, his hand grazing her stomach. He knew. Whether he'd known all along or Ruth had just told him, Esther would never know. It didn't matter anyway. He would be there; he would take care of it. Everything always worked out for Ruth. Esther faced the walk ahead with hot tears in her eyes. There was only one place for her to go.

FOR AS LONG AS SHE HAD WORKED AT HORACE'S DADDY'S BOOKSHOP, NObody called her by her given name. She was Professor Jones to Horace, and that had embarrassed her at first. In her family, her intelligence wasn't as much a gift as it was a distraction from rehearsal, and she had to learn to take the nickname as a compliment. Gradually, as customers increased and requested her, she'd meet their needs according to the piece of themselves they showed her—Ralph Ellison to men with anger dragging their heads to their chest, and Gwendolyn Brooks to girls she might have been friends with if she gave half a shit what they thought, if she had an ounce of energy to follow a crowd rushing nowhere. Instead, she began to find comfort, pride even, in deducing what needs a philosophy or a sentiment inside a book might meet, needs a person didn't even know showed up gaping. Just as customers returned weeks later lighter or fuller according to what their burden had been, the exchanges moved Esther. A person watching might have noticed midway through her frequent walks from Webster and Eddy to Post that in anticipation of hitting her spot, her everyday hardness seemed to melt off her body. She spoke to people more, not like Ruth and certainly not like Chloe, but she delivered hellos without rolling her eyes. Sometimes, she might even stop outside the shop and listen to Drunk Freddy reflect on the size of the roaches in his childhood home, large enough to choke a mule. She'd run the description through her mind after that, marveling at the precision. There was a notebook she hid under her mattress for lines like those, lines she might apply to something later, though what it might be she didn't know.

By the time she stepped inside the store, she was a different person altogether. She was no longer the girl who trained herself raw for impeccable footwork, the girl with a Billie Holiday arch to her voice, though she couldn't always control its stretch or bend. She was not the middle sister who sank so low sometimes she didn't know if she would ever be roused, the one people fought to be friends with before they realized that nearness to someone as prickly as Esther caused harm, that no matter how hard she tried, how tenderly they approached, proximity flagged danger to her every time. Here at the shop, she could feel joined without it threatening her. She was the one to categorize the stock according to its time period: slavery or Reconstruction or the Harlem Renaissance. She was the one to remind Horace to call his wife, let her know he'd be late; then, when they'd split up, she was the one to tell him life was long, and though that made him cry harder, at least she had been there. She was the one who read books straight through not once but twice because they became like family to her. And when business was slow, as it could be, she was the girl who wrote a newsletter every month, who snuck to print it in Horace's basement, who downplayed it when it came out because though her mother said, "That's great, dear," she wrapped her hollowed-out crawfish heads in it and plopped it in the trash before she sent Esther straight back to the roof. Esther had started the newsletter six months earlier mostly to commemorate the books she'd read, with summaries but also analysis. Her first issue had been about Gwendolyn Brooks's poem "Sadie and Maud," and she'd started with its synopsis, then critiqued the pressure applied to women to bear children. Esther had always identified with Maud, who went to college. She didn't want to go on like her, to die alone, but it was hard for her to imagine a different outcome sometimes.

Now she removed her key from her bra, opened up, turned on the light with a string that hung from the ceiling. When she oriented herself at the counter, she felt under the cash register for her current gem, *Their Eyes Were Watching God*. There was a sofa in the back room, and she carried the book there. The last thing she remembered before she fell asleep was Janie confessing to Nanny how badly she desired love. Come morning, Esther thought she caught the old woman's eyes in Horace's face.

"You knocked out in here again, huh, girl?" He reached behind her to open a window.

She sat up, stunned, though it had happened before, many times. As uncomfortable as the worn sofa was, she'd slept like a baby.

"One of those nights, huh?" he asked.

Even when she slept at home, she was the first one to arrive in the morning, and she'd turn on the lights and make coffee. When Horace joined her, they'd reflect on the *Sun-Reporter* while they downed two cups black. He tossed the paper against the counter now. The coffee would be late this morning.

"Now the City saying our neighborhood's slumming it," he went on. "Slum, huh? I read that article to my daddy, he said this was the nicest place he ever lived."

Esther stood for the bathroom. She kept a toothbrush there, and washcloths for her face.

"Goddamn shame." Esther could hear him as she splashed water on herself.

"You should write about it, Professor. In that newsletter of yours."

"That's not what it's for," she shouted over the sound of the running faucet.

"Well, that's what it should be for," Horace said.

"I don't get it, you want me elsewhere?" She had started to do something to her hair in the mirror, but she gave up, gathered it into a lumpy ponytail, and turned out the bathroom light. "You trying to fire me in language so shiny I don't realize til I get home that I don't have a check," she joked, because the idea was unfathomable, certainly now. Ruth would be gone, and as much relief as her absence had promised her, the relief didn't walk to her straight. Besides, lately Chloe was always off with Tony, and it wasn't possible to hold a conversation with Vivian that didn't involve performing, glorifying elements of it that had passed, or pining for more glory in the future, and those were the best-case scenarios. The alternative was listening to her critiques, the blocks to glory one of the girls had erected, and usually that girl was Esther. Here at the store, she worked and worked, but it was like the effort turned back on itself and graced her.

"Please, if you weren't getting paid to be here, you'd just sit up here all day anyway," Horace said. Esther had always thought it would be easier to have a brother, and if their relationship was any indication, she'd been right.

"Yeah, I'd have more space to lounge 'cause there wouldn't be any customers, though."

"Yeah right, they only started going to you when I had my baby last year."

"And once they started, they couldn't stop, it was like one of your mama's hot cross buns, boy, and I ate them until I was sick, but I was never full."

"Well, you got me sick and full listening to this mess," he said. She stood at the register now, and he reviewed the newest shipment: *The Street*.

"It's protest literature," she said.

"It's women's issues," Horace said.

"It's protest," she said back, "if quiet."

"I know it is," he said, and he had been about to cast it as the alternative, but she didn't say anything more.

"Baby not sleeping, huh?" she asked.

He shook his head. "And Vanessa on my ass about it 'cause it messes up his schedule the whole next day. Like I'm poking the child's foot in the middle of the night waking him up." They had split earlier that fall. They did well raising Malcolm apart, as long as he was sleeping. Horace had him Monday through Wednesday and one weekend day; Vanessa minded him the rest. From the beginning, Esther had warned him it wouldn't work out between him and the child's mother—they were too different—but she'd liked Vanessa anyway, and she'd been heartbroken to see her go.

"You're both tired," she said.

"Yeah, but don't let me complain about it. I'm not the one home all day, blah blah blah." His temple gathered sweat easily, and he addressed the issue now with a towel he stored in his back pocket. When he was done, he examined the cloth, though there was nothing visible on it, then slipped it back behind him.

"It's not just the article," he said, changing the subject. He didn't like to talk about his ex much these days. "A friend of my father's came over for supper yesterday. His brother-in-law works at the Redevelopment Agency."

"Oh yeah? Is he that one Negro I see with them sometimes? Looking like a raisin in a sea of milk. Better yet, a field of cotton."

Horace shook his head, laughed. "Girl, you crazy, but yeah, him. He said something's going down. I guess they got some new blood in there, I guess things are shifting."

Esther shrugged. "What's that got to do with us?"

"I'm telling you what, things about to go down. Something changed, he didn't say what. I mean, anybody with eyes could see the neighborhood has been struggling, and the City likes to send people in here to record the problems they created. But I never knew why. Until now. All this time, they've been planning to fix it."

"Well, that's good if they're fixing it then, right?"

"You not listening. They want to start over. They want to rebuild from scratch."

"Where the hell are we supposed to go while they're rebuilding?"

"Now you cooking with gas, Professor. Now you cooking with gas. They plan to remove us and ours. It's not just while they're rebuilding either. My daddy's friend said there probably won't be a place for us when they're done."

"Oh, boy, now you being paranoid." She waved her hand against him, his interpretation, all of it. "I can't take you seriously when you talk like that."

He paused. "Maybe you right," he said. "I told you I didn't get no sleep last night. Didn't have an appetite this morning either. Had a bad feeling about something."

"Well, I know something's wrong if you couldn't eat."

She couldn't help but think about Ruth's news when he brought up the sleep again. The part Horace was complaining about, about the toll the baby took, that wouldn't be an issue for her and Gerry. Esther could already imagine them gazing into each other's eyes in the late-night hours, fueled by their creation in a way rest couldn't match. There was Vivian, and she'd raise hell at the beginning, but she'd get over it and then Ruth's life would be sweet again, sweeter than ever before, because she would finally have her freedom. Then again, this time, Esther would have hers too. No more feeling like worse than invisible—seen but not worth viewing—beside her sister; no more measuring herself against someone whose complaints even came out in perfect key. She started to tell Horace about her new nephew or niece—she just wanted it off her chest—but his eyes were glazed over.

"Go in the back and take a rest then," she said. "You know I got you."

"You sure?" he asked, but she didn't bother answering him; he was already moving backwards.

Business was slow, so she went back to reading. A customer chimed in half an hour later with fury seeping through his smile, and Esther recommended Chester Himes and Frances Ellen Watkins Harper. The man had heard of Himes but not Harper, and Esther flipped the book to her favorite poem: "The Soul." Then some urgent sensation she had never experienced before moved her to recite her favorite stanza to him:

Could we drag the sun from his golden car,
To lay in this balance with ev'ry star,
'Twould darken the day and obscure the night—
But the weight of the balance would still be light.

When she was done, she found the customer staring. She didn't know what had come over her either.

Horace had ventured back by then, smiling all the while, and for the rest of the day, he'd called her Frances or Frankie, speaking to her about shipments and color coding through poorly rhymed stanzas. She told him as much, but that only sent him on harder.

"We all can't be brilliant like you and Frances," he said. He made himself laugh at that, but she didn't. "Nah. I'm not even playing, though, not all the way. Seeing you with that customer was something else." And hearing that, Esther longed for the proper response, pride, but the feeling betrayed itself like an ingrown nail. As she locked up, she didn't turn to look at him when she said goodbye.

NOBODY KNEW THIS, NOBODY, BUT TEN YEARS AGO, WHEN THE GIRLS worked the Flamingo every week, there was a man who managed the acts named Mr. Sterling. He was in his twenties and brown with soft black hair he slicked back, and every girl wearing a training bra nursed a crush on him. Esther and her sisters were the only performers each Wednesday night, so each girl got to have her own dressing room. Mr. Sterling would stand outside Esther's, and she would see him right before a show. On the days Esther's mother worked the night shift, he'd stand there after too, wait for her to change, then walk all three of them home. Esther was twelve years old and she'd started to think of boys, one in particular who brought double-stuffed ham sandwiches to school each day. His father worked for Mr. Gaines, and she'd watch the boy at lunch gulping down a quarter of a sandwich in one bite, and yet he always left half the meat on the table in front of him no matter how many times Miss Peters told him to clean it up. He'd stand and wipe his hands against his trousers, wind his tongue around his lips, and Esther got a funny feeling watching his tongue move. She asked Ruth once when they were undressing from church, rolling down their pantyhose and setting them in the sink to soap, what it was, that tickle down there. It seemed like if she touched it a certain way for a certain time, she could rush it to a gratifying stop.

"I'll tell you when you're older," Ruth had said. This had been before Esther had changed toward her, and Ruth said it with a softness Esther felt like she could blanket around herself, inside her body too. She could reach for it standing in line with girls who whispered about her for having a flat chest, teasing her mercilessly because though Esther was never seen without a book, she was left-handed, and the teacher had held her back from first grade to correct the deficiency.

One night on the Flamingo stage, twelve-year-old Esther wore a black gown that was too old for her narrow frame, and she pinned her hair in a bun, and when she came in with "*Oh dear, I wonder where my basket can be, Oh gee, I wish that little girl I could see,*" a man in the front row reached for her leg. She'd jumped back. It had been the first time anyone had looked past Ruth for her. Mr. Sterling had been angry and forced the man out, banned him for weeks after. That night, he dismissed Ruth and Chloe and asked her to stay behind. He'd taken note of her dancing, he'd said, and he wanted to show her more moves he'd learned. Ruth hesitated, then said, "Hurry home after you finish that practice, you hear?" And Esther sensed something new, a fear of some sort she could only interpret as jealousy. It was no matter. Mr. Sterling ordered the bartender to never leave her Shirley Temple glass empty, and he served her his sister's homemade cookies that the club was famous for, ginger molasses. Esther wasn't a big eater, but she loved sweets, and she lost track of how many times he refreshed her plate.

From then on, every evening her mother wasn't there, he sent her sisters home and kept her. Sometimes the drink was lemonade; sometimes it was a Shirley Temple; sometimes the cookies were the same; sometimes they were lemon, or chocolate chip.

Ruth would study her movements during rehearsal. A few weeks after the "lessons" had started, she approached her, felt for the groove on the other side of her elbow, and said, "I don't see any new dances. The ones he's supposedly been showing you." She paused. "I don't want you staying with Mr. Sterling anymore." And Esther had raged back at her with a ferocity she didn't know was in her. That had been the first time there had been anything between them but love, and the last time Ruth spoke on the matter.

One night, instead of giving her the snacks, Mr. Sterling asked her if she wanted to see where he lived. She knew what she was supposed to say. Her mother had warned her not to go anywhere with a strange man. "I'm not sending anybody to get you," she'd say. "If they say they're going to kill you if you don't get in their van, say 'Let me die then.'" But this man was the manager of the Flamingo. He hadn't yet, but he would gift her new skills, the secrets to her mother's smiles. And he stared at her the way men stared at Ruth, the way their eyes trailed her backside. When Ruth was in the room, it was like nobody else existed for Gerry, like he could take or leave the very world itself. Esther looked into Mr. Sterling's face and said "Okay."

Anyway, his house was only a few blocks away and they walked down Fillmore Street in silence. He led her straight to the dining room, which was much fancier than Esther's, with paintings of fruit and birds plastered on every wall and two crystal chandeliers hanging from the ceiling. The table had been set and Esther sat across from him, watched him move his cloth napkin from the table to his lap. She did the same.

"How old are you?" he asked first. He had set out sliced ham and rolls of bread, and he lifted the meat from a platter and uncoiled the rind from the edge in a slow circle. Esther followed suit, though she didn't like ham.

"Fifteen," Esther lied.

Mr. Sterling smirked, but he didn't object.

"You got a lot of friends at school?" he asked.

She shook her head. If she had had the wherewithal, she would have made up a lie. There were girls whose names she scribbled in margins of her notebook, girls whose friendship might have made life palatable.

"A girl as pretty as you, as sweet, and you don't have a lot of friends?" he asked.

"We practice a lot," she said. "There isn't much time."

He nodded. "I kept to myself too. After my daddy left. Was embarrassed for the kids to know me. I pushed them away so they wouldn't reject me."

Esther thought about correcting him, telling him it wasn't about embarrassment. But she lost track of all that considering his skin. It was browner than hers, brown like her daddy's had been, and he was eating now, and so careful about it, each bite more like a kiss than an act of devouring.

They kept on talking, and when he asked her questions, he really listened while she answered, then he thought about the response, and sometimes he leaned toward her for more, and sometimes he seemed satisfied. When he fell silent, she racked her brain for another question or consideration to prompt him, but she came up blank. Surely her mother would understand she couldn't just leave him floating. If she stood, it would be because she or he had delivered a response with an edge to it, a natural ending. Finally, it was the meal that announced itself done.

"I better get you home," he said. "Your mama may start looking for me."

"She doesn't get home until the morning," Esther said, and that seemed to make him smile, though they both stood anyway.

"I'll see you next week?" he asked a block from her door. And she nodded, though she didn't believe it. She wasn't Ruth; still, every Friday he asked her back. They ate together, and then he'd walk her home, and Esther's chores, her crooning, and her stepping out on the roof were all entwined now with the desperation of her longing.

One night, a few months into their routine, he brought her to his house, but he sidestepped the dining room and led her upstairs. In his bedroom, he took her hand, but he was skittish with it, his head darting over his shoulder every other step, though he lived alone. Esther wasn't skittish at all, not about being seen. She felt so removed from anything she had done or had expected to do, it didn't feel like she was using her own body. Surely even if someone saw her, they wouldn't recognize her as herself.

He told her to sit on the edge of his bed and he disappeared into a closet. While she couldn't see him, she asked questions like normal, more about his mama, a subject he seemed to fall into the last time, then his sister, but he'd only give one-word answers that came out more like grunts. Finally, he walked out with only his underwear on. She wanted to cry seeing the way his private part poked out of the cloth, but she was too old for that now. He sat beside her and guided her to his lap, and she sat on him, wrapped her arms around his neck. He kissed her hard like he had meant to hurt her, only got the move wrong. He ran his hands up her chest. There was nothing there, she knew—the girls at school had told her as much—but he moaned anyway and he moved her hand to his lap, where his private part was bigger than Esther had known it could become. It was nearly black except where it was pink at the tip, and it was hard and upright now. Esther had known to expect that because of the girls at school, but she also felt more unprepared than she ever had in her life. He did her work for her, up and down and up and down, and she was relieved that she wouldn't have to initiate the act on her own, that she wouldn't have a chance to mess it up. It didn't take long before he released, then exhaled louder and longer than before. His hand was still on her chest, but it only draped there, limp. His eyes were closed, and she stared at his face. She had never seen anyone's so peaceful. She thought he might have fallen asleep, but after a few minutes, he sat up higher and looked around. He reached for a handkerchief beside the bed and wiped her hand, then her skirt, then himself.

"I'm sorry," he said, gesturing to the mess he'd made, and she said, "That's okay, I can get it out." Then he seemed even sorrier, and he got up without holding her hand now, and she followed him home. Ruth had been up that night—Esther had seen her bedroom curtain rustle. When Esther made it up the stairs, she waited in front of her older sister's door for some time before she knocked, not once but three times. The third time, she even called out Ruth's name, but she didn't answer. The next week at the Flamingo, Mama accompanied them. Esther started to sing, and her throat began to close in on itself, though everyone was watching, including Mr. Sterling. Ruth took over her part, and Esther ran off the stage. After, Mama burst into her dressing room, shouting.

"You think Dinah Washington leaves a packed crowd for any reason at all?"

Esther just cried into her hands. Ruth knocked on her dressing room door, three times just like Esther had with her, and just like before, Esther didn't respond. She had spent the night after Mr. Sterling sobbing into sleep, then waking only to return to sobbing again, and in the break between her cries, she had wanted her sister. Then shame of what she'd done merged with the disappointment of her sister's silence, and by the time she woke up, she couldn't tell one from the other. After that, it was just a matter of time before she told herself that the look Ruth had given her when Mr. Sterling's interest sprouted was not of fear but of knowing. When she didn't hear from Mr. Sterling after that night at his house, it was only a matter of time before she believed Ruth to be smug over his absence. She didn't know what wrong thing she'd done to turn him away, but she knew that sort of thing wouldn't have happened to Ruth. Even with Gerry by her side, the men clamored for her and had to be told to leave.

The next week, they weren't asked to return to the Flamingo. That was when Esther's moods started, when she started finding fault with everything Ruth said, did. Sometimes she even imagined the girl's thoughts and took issue with them. She had calmed some once she found the bookstore, but that evening, the way Horace looked at her, with awe if she read it right, her resentment had returned with majestic vengeance, an unexpected summer storm.

Now, at home, Esther kept up with her sisters on the roof. It was clearer—as Esther knew the source of Ruth's impairment—how she had changed, how long it took her to catch her breath, how her stomach jutted over her pants when she dipped backwards. Still, it was Esther Mama focused on. "That's not the note," she'd call out. Or her favorite: "Ambition, girl. Not contrition."

As invincible as Esther had made herself out to seem, she couldn't access that sturdiness when she was singing. She was more the type to need reassurance, and after every show, she hurried backstage to her mama. Vivian would always say something positive—"Those swoops sure did improve" or "I could see where you practiced that C note"—but she didn't beam the way she would at Ruth, or even Chloe, and sometimes Esther felt like she wasn't dancing on the roof as much as she was chasing something, even now, tracking her mother's eyes to see if she had reached her target.

The woman only sighed. "Maybe we should nix it this evening. Y'all don't seem like you have it in you tonight." Still, she didn't call Ruth's name. She never would. "You can run a few scales, then go on to bed."

"You sure Mama?" Esther asked. She wanted to linger, to coax something, anything, out of the woman, maybe a compliment—she'd killed the high steps—but most likely she would let her down. Her mama didn't see her yet, not all the way, but she would.

IT HAD BEEN TEN YEARS, AND ESTHER STILL SAW MR. STERLING AROUND. At first, she had waited for him to approach her, relieve her shame, but he never did. At last, she stopped hoping. It had been easier that way. It had been easy too to hate Ruth, not just to hate her but to show her she did. The girl was tireless on the roof and outside it, pretending to be second mother, but like their first one, she didn't understand the role. Once, only once, Esther had needed her, and she hadn't opened the door.

After the incident, Esther had started to write songs, silly ones at first, pining after a man she learned later had defiled her. And then angry ones pinned at that same man. Now she wrote to unwind after a long day, to fill her heart up when it seemed wrung out, to match the mood she'd steal from a particularly resonant book, a high she hadn't located elsewhere. She'd shown her best work to her mother, and Mama had said someday she'd select one for the group to perform. The time had to be right, though, and so far it hadn't been. No matter; Esther took out her pen now and started.

VIVIAN

Vivian freshened up before she left to meet Mr. Franklin, pressed baking soda under her arms, and slipped on a pair of pantyhose, reaching through the closet for the form-fitting sheath dress she'd worn to Flamingo the night Fatso Berry hosted the talent show. People from all over San Francisco had come in dressed to the nines, and after the cowboy movies, the girls had won first place singing the Mello-Moods' "Where Are You (Now That I Need You)."

That had meant fifty dollars and a paragraph in the *Sun-Reporter*. She and the girls had rotated that excitement between themselves for weeks.

Vivian had washed and set her hair the night before, and the curls still held, more or less, though they'd fallen some. This was her favorite look actually, the second day's. There was more bounce around her face, a halo. It seemed to draw attention from the circles under her eyes she'd started to brush with powder, the lines on either side of her mouth. Oh well. She dabbed blush on her cheeks, slipped into her cloth coat with the deep fur cuffs, and then drew on another coat of lipstick and dabbed at the oil on her nose. She peeked once more in the mirror; circles or not, she still had it. She passed the same people on the street she always passed on the way home, Horace, Miss Edna, Gladys, Mr. Gaines, and Miss Fox, and they all called out behind her:

"Good evening, Vivian. What you know good?"

She started to say, as she always did, "Can't complain, no use in it," but this time, a different answer rose to its feet and she allowed it to preside.

"We shall see."

Mr. Franklin had asked to meet her at the Champagne Supper Club where the girls sang every Thursday and where *the* Miss Eartha Kitt had performed just last month. Vivian hadn't repeated this to her daughters—she didn't like to breed competition among them—but something about the woman's self-assurance as she sang "C'est Si Bon" reminded Vivian of Ruth so vividly she got chills. There was a line in front of the club today, mostly men congregating beneath the awning in suits, wide-brimmed hats, and smooth leather wing tips. The sign on the marquee read SHOW DANCING, but Vivian knew some of the major acts just ambled in without notice. There was no telling who would be playing tonight. Vivian made her way through the crowd, felt the men's eyes burrowing into her backside, and aimed herself at the door. There stood the owner, Mr. Bailey, a stout man with a deep voice and a hard smile, and he led her inside to the bar.

"Our best champagne." He nodded at the bartender, a quiet red man, tender when he did speak, though.

Vivian reached for her purse as both men waved their hands.

"You sure?" she asked, knowing neither would budge.

"Mr. Franklin's on his way in." The bartender slid the glass over to her, its bubbles sizzling on the top.

"How'd you know I was waiting on him?" she started to ask but didn't finish. It was the way it was in the Fillmore, the way it had been in St. Francisville too, but the twenty-block stretch of land here was narrower and news traveled within it like lightning.

"Lucky you," the bartender said without answering the question.

"Most people come in here to meet Mr. Franklin leave smiling wider than when they walked in. Most people."

Vivian smiled, not all the way, though. She didn't allow herself that, but she tipped the man half a dollar on her way to a booth.

Mr. Bailey led her there by the elbow. She had arrived early she'd been so excited, and the place was packed already with men dressed not unlike the ones outside, and women in slender or wide-skirted evening gowns and velvet bathing cap hats. Mr. Bailey stopped at a small round table draped in a white cloth right beside the stage where the chorus girls did splits in lace bras and panties. Pork chops were the special, he said, and she nodded, though she knew she wouldn't eat much; she couldn't. He left, and a waitress walked by with a big bottle of champagne. She poured Vivian a glass, and Vivian wanted to lunge for it. Still, she waited until the girl was out of sight. Then she looked around some as she sipped. The club was swanky inside, not like some of the places they'd sung in early in their careers, the kinds of places you'd have to leave early before a fight between a pimp and one of his ladies broke out.

No, this was a place for working people who had just been paid, especially considering Miss Edna had called the numbers. Men were out with their wives or their girlfriends, and in some situations Vivian noticed it was both, but there was laughter and yelps and women leaning into the breast pocket of a man and just resting their heads. Yes, this was the place for the high-end streetwalkers who occupied their own table. Their men would be the ones who could afford to drive them someplace with a view, but the ladies still had to steel themselves up for what would unfold, and glasses lined their table like rows of soldiers.

This was where the amateur trumpeter and horn man, hungry by the side of the stage, tapped their feet, patted the palms of their hands against their sides. They would get on soon, and it was only time and circumstance separating them from the greats. You would see that sometimes when Monk or Satchmo showed up and their sound blended together so seamlessly with the no-names you couldn't discern them as individuals any longer.

This was the place for the whites who came for the music, for the dancing—not to take part but to witness—for the food, for the cocktails the bartender doubled on instinct, and they sat off to the side and absorbed the regulars' soul.

This was the place for the young women who couldn't take a sip without a man signaling to the waitress that it was time to buy another. One of those men even approached Vivian, all "Oh, you sitting by your lonesome?"

And Vivian nodded, "For now," and she let the space around what she didn't say linger until the man understood her meaning and walked away.

Because this was Vivian's place too, hers and the girls'. Every Thursday, they slept right after dinner, set the clock to wake them before midnight, and then they dressed in the dark, hustled over in the cold just as the chorus girls exited the stage. They'd yawn through the comedians and the Samson and Delilah act. Then it would be time for their show, and they'd come alive for it, like they'd slept for years in preparation, and after, they'd linger for the greats. Then, even Esther, who'd complained every foot of the block there, would tear up listening to Ben Webster on the saxophone.

They didn't sit at tables like this, though, so close she could smell the baby powder one of the girls must have sprinkled between her legs before the show. Not only that, those nights were for education, and Vivian took notes, on how Miss Kitt moved like she was sneaking and that made it harder to look away, or how she made eyes with the audience like she was letting them all in on a story for their ears only, or how her voice dropped like a man's while she presented so thoroughly like a woman. That dichotomy was mind-blowing even for Vivian; the men might as well have flown away. Still, those nights with the girls were frenzied times and she didn't have the presence of mind to wonder if she belonged. Now she had the space for discomfort. All this time she had been waiting for something major to shift in her life, and yet all of a sudden she found she could have done without it. Maybe it wasn't worth it, the fear of all the dangerous ways this dream could implode; maybe she was alright as she was. The girls did well in school. Ruth was already studying nursing like her mother had, and most Negro mothers would have been ecstatic. Maybe Vivian could learn to be that type.

A red comedian she recognized but whose name she couldn't remember replaced the chorus girls onstage and recited poems ending in some sort of double entendre. The audience erupted each time. Vivian was observing them, wondering why she couldn't catch the joke, when she saw Mr. Franklin walk in. Mr. Bailey nodded at him in her direction, and he walked toward her, stopping at several tables to kiss a pretty woman or shake hands with a suddenly more serious man, a man who suddenly had reason to slip his shoulders back. When Mr. Franklin finally arrived at the table, she stood like one of those men and embraced him. The comedian finished up:

"And I told that man not to *ass* me any more questions."

More applause and laughter, but Vivian was sealed in from it now. The man in front of her was tall and brown with a slight paunch and gold jewelry on every part of his body like he measured it and there couldn't be more than six inches on his person that wasn't shining. He wore dark glasses with large frames and a bright purple tie. She had heard enough about him, and the information cycled through her mind now: he played with his own jazz band years back; he moved to Los Angeles but still had family in the area; he visited every now and then to scout new talent; there were even rumors he had found Etta James. Vivian had seen his signature baby blue Cadillac in the neighborhood weeks earlier, gossiped about the color to Mary, in fact, who said, "Only a real fine man would choose such a soft shade of blue," but she hadn't brought herself close to thinking anything about him could involve her, her girls anyway.

She pulled back before he did, but his smell was still on her, the smell of extravagance, and it was a tad too much, sure, but that made sense to her when she thought of it. It was probably impossible to hold back at that level. It fit him, and she inhaled.

"Well, damn, Vivian, if I didn't know it was you, I would have thought you had sent one of your daughters in your stead," he said.

"Aww, shucks, Mr. Franklin, stop all that now." But she welcomed it. She had to admit, it was difficult growing older. She had an aunt in New Orleans who never married. Vivian's whole life, people referred to the woman as the most beautiful in all of the 7th Ward, and every summer weekend night, Vivian admired her, watching her dress for a date. Anything Vivian wanted from her at this time, she could ask. Her new alligator handbag, yes; a coat from Woolworth, yes; a box of beignets, yes. The woman would submit because she held so much hope at that hour—Vivian never understood why. She never understood either why she returned home with her makeup worn, why, as time passed, she'd pull Vivian aside and ask if her outfit made her look too old or too young, depending on the day. Vivian always delivered the answer that would feed her, in exactly the tone that was needed, but she didn't understand the pain at the root of it at all, not until now, staring down fifty as she was. She had a feeling when it was finally all over, when her cycle stopped once and for all, when she didn't even expect the second glances out the car windows, when the urges that she saw to some nights had subsided, it would be a great relief. But the anticipation of the loss caught her every time.

"I thought about it, about bringing the girls, but my neighbor, the one who found your card, she said just do what the man says, go alone."

"Yeah, best for now, I think. I'll meet the Salvations soon enough. Saw them perform last week at the Town Club. If I had closed my eyes, you couldn't have told me Ruth wasn't Bessie Smith standing up there. Whole lot better-looking than Bessie, I'll tell you that too."

Vivian tried not to blush. It was like he was talking about her after all, in a way—Ruth was hers, she had created her, and as grown as Ruth was, Vivian still considered her an appendage more than a separate entity, which was why Ruth's new brooding irked her soul. She had the talent all on her own to be a superstar. If Vivian had had only half, if it had been a different time, if she'd had a mama who could have afforded to pass more than a second outside the fields—well, that part was over now.

"Oh, yes, no question she can sing, almost like a man, I mean with that power, but she can bring it down too, soften it, that's what makes it so shocking when she increases the force again. People have compared her to Bessie before, but not just Bessie, Eartha, Mahalia, it's like the instrument is not diluted, you know, the instrument God gave her. Training her, I see, she sets her intention on the sound she wants to deliver and she aims it and she hits the target direct, right on the money, I mean you can't teach it. You either got it or you don't." She realized she had been talking too much, too fast, and she paused. The host was announcing the main act.

"The lady who's about to grace this stage needs no introduction. She has toured with the Count Basie Orchestra, performed at New York's Club Ebony and Carnegie Hall. If I listed her hits, I'd be here til six a.m. and you wouldn't get to lay eyes on this beauty herself. She—"

Some folks from the crowd interrupted, "Sit down, big man. Get off the stage."

"You said it yourself, we knocking on daylight, and you still talking."

"Alright, alright, alright," he went on, "I am honored as ever to welcome her, our own, the immeasurable, the indomitable, the incomparable Miss Lady Day."

Everyone rose to their feet, Vivian included. Mr. Franklin leaned over and whispered through the shouting, "I know her, know her real well. Tried to get her to record with a friend of mine, but she went with Decca. See how that turned out."

The applause had subsided, but Mr. Franklin was still going:

"Maybe for the best: drug problems and such. You can see it on her now."

Vivian didn't respond; she was too enamored. When you stared, you could see the phenomenon might have lost weight, sure, but Vivian wouldn't have noticed it on her. She didn't evaluate her like that, like she was an actual person. It was more like Vivian was in Paris at the Louvre, or in Egypt beholding the pyramids, and whatever the creator had intended was fine. She certainly wouldn't burden His creations with her own expectations. Mr. Franklin was still rattling off his connections when the woman started "I Cover the Waterfront."

Vivian leaned in to Mr. Franklin, lowered her voice.

"We've been talking about Ruth, but you should hear Esther. It's a coincidence really that we're here on this night because people actually compare her to Lady. She's not as powerful, no, not by a long shot, but she has a voice that can travel, sweet as a baby's chortle, and when it lifts, oh my God"—Vivian brought her hand to her own heart—"she can hit notes that could break a windowpane, you have to hear it to believe it. She performs her own version of 'I Was Doing Alright.' Starts it out the same, but the second verse she raises it up an octave, and that *But I'm doing better than ever now* comes out so smooth, so sharp. The funny thing is I started to name her Ella, but—" Mr. Franklin wasn't listening; his eyes were on the stage. Vivian's were too, but watching anybody sing up close, royalty or not, always brought up her children.

"Yes, I saw her," Mr. Franklin said finally like she'd just asked the question, his voice flat, his gaze elsewhere, and Vivian saw he was motioning for another drink for the two of them. She was nearly finished with her first, and she told herself to slow down. *Slow on down, girl.* She hadn't even gotten to Chloe, and she was the one who had come out a mix between the two other girls, the bridge between her sisters, the older girls' perfect sum. Esther was the life of the party when she felt like it, but she could sink too. Lord, could she sink into moods so dark, Vivian couldn't get her out of bed some days. Ruth was kind, steady, sober-minded—Vivian could count on her to take the meat out of the freezer in the morning; to lay out clothes for herself and the girls, freshly ironed, in the parlor at night. She had been making groceries and assembling meals since she was eleven. But Chloe brought the joy, the wonder. It was Chloe whom Vivian could always depend on for a sweet word, for an "It's okay, Mama, I know you didn't mean it" if she had lost her temper. Vivian sometimes heard her from her bay window on the stoop with Tony or her other friends, nurturing them like she was somebody's mama. It was funny to hear such deep love coming from her little-girl voice: "I wish you could see yourself the way we see you." Vivian marveled at it because Esther wouldn't have been asked, and Ruth would have quoted the Bible without context, but Chloe, from the day she was born, filled up a part of Vivian's spirit that had been empty. She couldn't dance like Esther, and her voice wasn't as mighty as Ruth's, but that was why there was a group to stand up beside her. And anyway, it was like she had learned to glide between her two sisters, to occupy them in parts and to merge them inside her own spirit, and Vivian had never seen anybody, Miss Sarah Vaughan included, with more vocal range. She could visit three octaves in the course of one sitting. When Mr. Franklin saw that, it would bring him to his knees. She started to say as much, to try to figure out how to condense the sentiment into words, but the drinks arrived and the man took one long sip and then looked up at her again.

"You probably know why I called you here."

Vivian shrugged and smiled. "Of course I surmised—"

"That girl up there, Ruth, singing last week, what song was it, 'Stormy Weather,' and I almost started crying like an infant on his mama's ninny. Brought me all the way back to that farm, let me tell you, the crowder peas we picked, the hens we chased."

Vivian smiled. She did have that power. It was the power of her daughter, sure, but it had been cultivated in her and passed down, and it was the power of song too, of course, the reason Vivian had fled to it and locked herself inside.

"I knew right then, I had to have her, not just her, all of them.

See, it's got to be a girl group, that's the wave of the future, and that's the trouble too. Sure, you can find one who can sing, even two, but three? Nearly impossible, and every month I scour the country, East Texas and Baton Rouge, Chicago, Detroit, back rooms and motels. You wouldn't believe the places I've dug through just to find somebody, anybody, black, white, yellow, red, who can make me forget myself, all my trouble, and all this time they were hiding in my own backyard. Congratulations, Mama, you created them. Wasn't for you, we wouldn't even be sitting here right now. And three is a good number, a biblical number, the three gifts, the angels. And that girl Ruth, well, there was Jesus, there was the Holy Ghost, and there was God. Without her, why, you'd lose the one at the sacred helm."

Billie kept on alongside the compliment, and Vivian had to close her eyes to take it all in, she had to.

"And I hear you're quite the manager too. That you trained them yourself, taught them everything they know, got them performing onstage at Jack's, Flamingo, even here." He clasped and unclasped his hands as he spoke. "Yes, my dear, you've done fine for them by yourself. But if you want to take it further, you're going to need some help. Anyone would. And I'm in a position to provide it."

Vivian had to take a drink on that note, a long one, and she was a different person when she set the glass back down on the table than she was when she'd picked it up.

"See, I'd like to take them around the country," he kept on. "Ultimately the world. It's one thing to be in the top places here, to have the people scream for you here, but the farther away you venture from home, the more people know your name, the more you get paid for gigs, you know that, darlin'? You getting paid yet, sister?"

Vivian paused before she spoke.

"Some," she said, her eyes aimed right at him, though it was hard to keep them level.

"Well, alright, well, alright, I'm just saying, I don't want to step on your toes, but you get to a point where you got to release your children to the world if you want them to be worldly, you know what I'm saying? There's no reason we know Dinah and Sarah and Billie up there, but we ain't never heard of Ruth, not until last week when she sang that ballad so smooth it rounded out my heart."

"Now if I was their manager," he went on, "first thing I'd do is arrange bigger gigs for them, all over the country. I'm not meaning this chitlin circuit. I'm meaning more the likes of where Sam Cooke performs. I've been in Los Angeles for going on ten years now, but I'm not just talking there either. I'm talking the Apollo Theater in Harlem; I'm talking the Howard Theatre in DC, the Regal in Chicago. And that's just the beginning. See, I got connections you could only dream of, young lady."

"I have a friend at Columbia Records," Vivian interrupted, and the use of the word "friend" was a stretch, but she felt compelled to even their hand, to show off her own ambition.

"That's what I mean, that's exactly what I mean. What's Columbia Records going to do for them? I'm not talking about no Columbia Records, I'm talking about Chess, I'm talking about Wexler, they know Negro DJs. They know the way to actually get these girls on the radio. But I'm getting ahead of myself, first thing we'd need to do is hook them up with a musician, maybe a jazz bass player, of course I know too many to count. He'd make a demo for the girls, I'd drop it off at Wexler's doorstep with my own two hands. The rest would be in Jesus's hands, that's how smooth the process would flow, that's how ordained it would start to feel. You understand what I'm telling you, girl?"

And Vivian turned back to the stage, where Billie had started to beg.

She could have stayed that way forever, but Mr. Franklin had finished another drink, and was impatient for the waitress's attention, impatient for hers too. She got the feeling he had asked her another question aside from the one he had stretched out toward her a few minutes earlier, and she hadn't heard it. She found his eyes with her own.

"What do you say?" he asked. There was wetness around his lips, and he wiped it with a paper napkin, then crumpled it up and set it next to the now empty glass.

For some reason Vivian couldn't have foreseen, she didn't know. A fear had sprung upon her. Looking at Billie, she'd had to mentally command her eyes to focus, she was so stuck on envisioning herself in the cities he had named. She didn't know where to start in either of them, only pooled together images she had glimpsed in magazines, stories she'd overheard. Each city melted into the other and became a large fantastic one, Chicago's World's Fair Sky Ride ferrying millions of riders to New York's pea green beacon of hope. Vivian had the feeling she had had upon laying eyes on California, before she realized the streets were not actually paved with gold, that the rats were even bigger than they were in Louisiana, faster too, that white people were just white people, that the ones in the West had watched the same minstrel shows as the ones in the South. All they had room for in their imaginations was what had made them chuckle. But now . . . The deep, inexpressible wants she had been denied over the years always congealed in the center of her chest. From the first slight, the moment she worked up the nerve to tell her mother she would sing and that woman laughed like Vivian had never heard her laugh before, like she was free, through the moment she knew her husband had slipped off into another world, she felt the pain anew each day upon rising. Years ago, she had accepted she would go to her grave with that knot. Yet here was the analgesic she'd been searching for, and all she had to do was say yes.

"The girls and I always dreamed about traveling to New York City," she nearly whispered, clutching her mama's pearls at her neck.

"I would imagine, but it's a tricky lifestyle, especially in the beginning, living out of suitcases, in hotel rooms when we can secure them. I know people in almost every city I travel to who can put us up, but even then it's only back rooms, and after a month of it, it feels like you might kill somebody for a home-cooked meal." He shot his head back and laughed, a low heavy jingling of grunts.

And she tried to laugh with him, she did, but no sound would come out because, yes, it was true, all her life she had envisioned the big city. All her time as a mother, she had envisioned the four of them taking it in together. But that vision wouldn't pan out. She had work and bills and work again. This next step she had prayed for had come upon her, but it would not include her.

Billie was finishing up now. Vivian had sat at the base of the record player listening to this very song. She knew every inflection, every accent, every dip or leap, but the tone was gloomier now the way Billie was rendering it. Her voice was deeper, earthier, laced throughout with pain. The whole of all that had gone wrong shot through every word.

"You don't seem as excited as I thought you'd be." He smiled some more, motioning to the waitress again, and before Vivian knew it, she was on her third drink. She took a sip and felt more lonesome on account of it.

"It's not that, Mr. Franklin, it's not that. This is everything I have dreamed. It's just that . . ." She paused. "It's just that the thought of sending them off to the other side of the globe without any kin, well, it's . . ." She paused again, lifted her head so her eyes were level with his. "It's unimaginable."

"That's 'cause you don't get it." He stopped smiling, but he wasn't angry either, only methodical and patient. He was just getting started.

"That's 'cause you don't get it. Not yet, anyway. It's not just bright lights, baby, it's not just limos and furs, it's not just applause so loud you can't hear yourself think either. That's only the surface of it, that's just what the people who haven't been there have the capacity to imagine, but it's deeper than that. You know what it feels like to have a dream materialize, Vivian?"

He sat back in his chair and pulled a cigar out of his breast pocket. He offered her one, but she shook her head, though in the haze of the third drink it did seem appealing.

"There's two different types of people in the world, Vivian," he said, "two types only: people who know how to call up a desire, and command it into stone, and people who don't. I can show your daughters how to be the first type. Can show you too. If you'll let me."

And Vivian didn't know if it was the drink or the air wafting over from his smoke, but it was like she froze then, like time stopped, and she could see two parallel versions of her eldest daughter's life splayed out in front of her. In one, Ruth was headed down a road dizzyingly similar to the one Vivian had walked to the general store in St. Francisville for milk and eggs on credit. Maybe the face of it would be different, maybe it had been paved since Vivian had traveled west, maybe Ruth would wear heels instead of her brothers' hand-me-downs, but the feel of it was the same, the fear and the despair and the exhaustion. And maybe the way she would cope might vary, but the reason for coping would be the same, the need to excuse herself from the relentless monotony, the babies streaming behind her and a husband latching onto her inside the four walls of a kitchen piled high with dishes, bills, and with worry. At least Vivian had had this hope, something lofty to lift her from the mundane, the dreary, but now this man was offering a hand and, yes, charging too much, too too much for it, but maybe it was worth the cost. She'd outlined the girls' futures to herself too many times to count, but the picture was always limited, faded. The other road blurred even now in her line of sight. This man in front of her had reached it before. He had walked it even and could lead her along it just as easily as he signaled for the drink, if she would only say yes.

She took another sip and studied the room once more. The alcohol had cleared her in a sense, and she could see now that even here at Champagne Supper Club, one of the Big Three in the city, the stage was dusty, the chorus girls' wigs were slanted, their recent baby pooches hanging over their panties. The johns were losing their patience with the night ladies who took their time. Last week, Vivian had written FINAL ACT AT CHAMPAGNE down on a sheet of paper and taped it to the icebox as their next big dream, but now, in the last hour, she had begun to want more for her daughters, a hell of a lot more, and if sending them off was the path there, she would have to let them go. Maybe it was the only opportunity they'd get.

She looked up. "Yes."

"What's that?" Mr. Franklin asked.

"Yes," she repeated, feeling like she was coming to.

"Is that so?"

She nodded. "You got it, it's a deal." She stuck out her hand—and she was glad she had taken the time to polish her nails that evening, cherry red, just like her lips—and he squeezed it tight.

He was the type of man who seemed to always get his way, but he appeared surprised now, pleased but surprised.

"You serious, aren't you?" he asked, standing. No doubt the other people in the club thought they were forming more than a business alignment.

Standing too, she could feel how much she'd had to drink. She had to hold on to the edge of the table before she joined him in an embrace. When she pulled back, he signaled again to the waitress, this time for a round for everybody in the place.

"I'm managing her daughters," he yelled out to all of them, and the chorus girls were still shaking their behinds. They'd taken off their gowns, kicked them flat on the front of the stage, and they leaned toward the audience and shimmied their chests, their overflowing coconut bras jiggling.

"He's managing my daughters," Vivian called out to whoever hadn't heard, and the chorus girls cheered on their way offstage, arm in arm now, snapping their legs up to the ceiling in unison.

In the audience, a group formed around Vivian. The news had brought everyone to life: the bored wives, the impatient johns, the ladies of the night who had shielded themselves alright, shielded themselves five drinks deep. By now, these ladies would have celebrated a murder, but luckily it was goodness tonight that called their names. Even the whites stood and clinked their glasses.

The band joined onstage and played "A-Tisket, A-Tasket," and Mr. Franklin took her hand, and they came together and circled while she kicked her legs in short quick jerks, and then he extended his arm to swing her out, and watched her switch her hips on her own, and then he brought her in again, only to lift her and spin her on his back while the crowd cheered.

A lady usher at the church who cooked for Lena's Barbecue Restaurant accepted the hand of Deacon Washington, and they came together so tight there was no room for Jesus, but everyone was too mirthful to care and the likelihood was it wouldn't get carried back to Shiloh the next day. And then a john took a lady of the night, and then a man took his own wife, and then a different man took a different man's wife, and the whites didn't know the moves, but they switched their hips to a distinct pulse of their own, and the chorus girls who had been onstage earlier jumped back on and sang.

And then the trumpeter switched the tempo, and they weren't playing anything any of them knew. Now it was the saxophonist meeting eyes with the pianist and the drummer nodding back at the clarinet, and it was Vivian too, and not just her, but all of them, the collective soul of the place—the news Vivian had shared, the johns' hopes, the wives' fears, all melding into one frequency—it was driving the sound, which was also in their bones, and without realizing it, they were all kicking their feet out at the same rhythm, snapping their bodies into their partners' and back out again onto the floor, swerving and hopping and floating really, and the joy of having formed something streamed through Vivian, lit her up, made her feel like she was shining, and she had had that feeling before, when she was married, quick and simple as it was, and when she'd borne each of the girls, of course, she had slipped above the ordinary world for a moment, and then the most recent time, she was at Jack's in the front row, watching her babies sweep a room up into their command and she'd gone silent for some time, staring, in awe. And here it was again now. She could sell this moment, she knew. People would pay everything for it, she would herself if she could learn to carry it beyond these walls, but for now, it was free even to the whites who ventured down to the Fillmore for the barbecue and the blues, and who today for the first time had lingered.

BY THE TIME VIVIAN LEFT THE CLUB, THE DAY WAS BEGINNING, BUT NObody knew it yet. She had access to this hour when she worked her night shifts too, and on the way home, she'd sing quietly to herself, but this time she was alone and she shouted it out: "*A-tisket, a-tasket.*" Anyway, she still felt like celebrating, drunk as she was, and she realized she hadn't been so apart from her own senses since she was her oldest daughter's age, nearly pregnant.

She began to skip down the sidewalks, bypassing the old, scattered newspapers and bottles of pop, the food beginning to stink, streaming out of the cans on the corner.

Then she was twirling down Post, Club Alabam on her right, empty now, imagining a line of chorus girls beside her taking her hand. They'd lift each other, and she hopped into the air herself and tapped the heels of her shoes together as she'd seen them do, and she laughed when she landed. Then she heard a scream from the side of a house to her left and she screamed too. She almost broke into a run when she heard someone say quietly, then louder, "It's just me. It's just me, Freddy."

"Oh." She relaxed when she saw the man, his face smeared with dirt and the scent of liquor like a halo around him, not that Vivian could talk. Freddy was the neighborhood drunk, a Negro from Baton Rouge who'd moved there to work in the shipyards. When the war ended, he stopped making rent, and Vivian knew his people back home. They would have loved to have him return if only he'd go. She'd ask him sometimes why he didn't, offered to pay for a train down South, and he'd say, "I'm not walking backwards."

He stumbled over, and Vivian caught him by the wrist.

"Celebration, huh?" he asked. Vivian filled him in. "Ahh, that's wonderful, hope for the youthful. I remember that, I do." His eyes watered, but he stopped them in their place, and he danced around Vivian, of course not as sprightly as he might have moved before life had chewed, then spit him out. Vivian joined his dancing beside him, not a dance she had done before, but it was easy to catch on, bouncing really from one foot to the other in a circle. They held each other's arms just as she'd held Mr. Franklin, and the smell of vodka didn't bother her as much as it had minutes before. Once, Vivian nearly tripped on a curb, and it was Freddy who lifted her before she fell into a pile of peanut shells, and the two looked into each other's eyes and laughed.

She stood, and they walked along, Freddy gulping swigs from his drink and Vivian already feeling the agony that would await her later in the day. They passed the corner of her street where police cars sat sometimes at this hour, picking up Negroes for vagrancy when there was nowhere else to go. Today, she recognized the officer inside. White but decent—he would offer her a ride sometimes after her night shifts, and he rolled down the window now to bid them good morning.

"Good day," he said. "You're out late. Coming in the wrong direction for it to be work."

"My daughters," she said, and she told him what had happened.

"Wow, congratulations. You deserve it. That's what I love about your people. You always find something to celebrate. Even in the darkest times."

"What's so dark?" Freddy slurred, his eyes on hers while he spoke.

"What? You haven't heard about the redevelopment? Oh well, I hate to tell you now then on such a special occasion." The officer looked elsewhere, away from them both.

"What redevelopment?"

"Well, it's just that the City's redevelopment agency released a report." He still wasn't looking at them. "Your neighborhood was labeled as blighted."

Oh, yes, of course, there was always that talk. What did it have to do with the price of beans? Not a damn thing, Vivian had learned. She almost said as much, but she knew the order of things, and besides, the officer kept on.

"Now the agency's hired a new man, Mr. Belmont, just moved here from DC. He's taking the matter a bit more seriously than his predecessor."

"Talk, talk, always gon be talk," Freddy said.

"Yes, but tuberculosis is on the rise and there's overcrowding and fire hazards and, and"—he paused—"other moral issues." He paused again here like he might not say the next part. "I've heard talk of starting all over. Beautifying the city."

Freddy took another long swig of his drink, and Vivian was grateful for the distraction.

"That's enough of that," she said, reaching for the bottle the man hadn't even bothered to wrap, and Freddy snapped his hand back so fast, Vivian almost fell forward.

"You two be careful now." The officer's tone had straightened, and Vivian smoothed her dress, looked up the street to her house, which was beckoning.

"I'm always careful, Officer," she said, looking away. To Freddy, she called, "I'll bring some supper by this evening, leave it out." She said it like a question, though she did it many times a week.

"Didn't want to upset you," the officer said. "Just want you to be prepared. You're not like the rest of your people, and I don't want you to be taken by surprise." He was talking to Vivian's back now.

"I'm always prepared too, Officer," she said, uninterested in the rest, because if there was one thing she knew, it was white people, their whims and their fancies, and she wouldn't dream of taking action based on them. It was God who told her she would be safe here, that she'd earned a reprieve; God who'd given her a second home, that first one inaccessible to her now. And look how He'd shown out tonight.

She had reached her stoop, and she looked upstairs where her girls would be sleeping, no doubt presuming they would wake up beside their textbooks, the same girls they'd been before their eyes shut. Without them knowing it, their world had been transformed. And it would only be a matter of time before they started pulling in dough. Mr. Franklin had assured her of that sometime in the night. She wouldn't need her job forever. She would be able to join them. Vivian felt giddy just considering the turn.

Later, she would walk back outside with a blanket and spare ham sandwiches, dry because mayonnaise made Freddy sick. For now, she could barely wait to get inside. She didn't know what she would do when she was in there. She was a private woman. That tendency had been bred in her, and she couldn't forsake it now if she tried. She wouldn't knock on Mary's door or call her, not yet. She wouldn't yelp the way she had with the liquor hot inside her, but she might undress slowly in front of the glass. She might pick up the phone, pretend she was the kind of woman who'd call Preacher at this hour; she might lay the phone back down. She might touch herself and think of something other than those lights, that applause, someone, maybe him, she didn't know. She rarely sang these days, and when she did, the tune was wound up with her mother's hurtful laughter, but that song from the night before, which already felt like a lifetime earlier, was still hanging over the forefront of her mind, and she might slip inside it, no, but she might, no. That would be taking it too far, but she would stare into her own light brown eyes, her body the most youthful it would ever be, and mouth out:

Will the one I love
Be coming back to me?

She might recite the words aloud like she were reading a scripture. She might feel a surge of affirmation inside.

CHLOE

Chloe opened the front door, which was never locked, half expectant. Most of the times she returned home from school, Ruth was at the library, Esther was at the bookstore, Mama was working, and she'd enjoyed the small moments to herself. She'd prepare a double ham sandwich, drink Coca-Cola without her mama's side-eye, but today was different. It had only been two days since Ruth's news, and Chloe had stayed behind long after Esther left the room, slamming the door behind her. Chloe had even congratulated Ruth, told her she'd make an excellent mother, that she'd been mothering them all anyway; then she'd rubbed Ruth's back while she cried. At first she thought her sister was bereft, dreading the emptiness that awaited her, but somewhere along the way, something about the shallowness of the sobs, the way in between she'd sigh, Chloe realized it was the opposite. Ruth was relieved. It was only Chloe who felt that the rigor was all worth it when she was out on that stage and the lights were on her, obscuring the crowds. Those times, she'd be singing to them, yes, but mostly she'd be singing to her maker, who had gifted her with the call. It was all she could do to respond with the breadth of her song. That was the best way she could think to say thank you.

All this while, those moments apart from the world were the closest Chloe had found to heaven, and Ruth had been pining for a way out. Well, she'd found it. Gerry and that baby had come to rescue her. But who was going to rescue Chloe? She had had to fight off the urge to ask her sister, even as she sobbed, if she was going to stay in the group, if her leaving meant there would be no group anymore after all.

Now she dragged herself upstairs and collapsed into bed. Friends and family alike knew her to be the lit candle, the one on a stick that Preacher boasted gave light to all around it, but it seemed like a great big bushel had barreled in and put her out.

HOURS LATER, THE PHONE STARTLED HER AWAKE. SHE KNEW IT WAS TONY before she answered, and he started in on her before she could speak.

"Girl, if you don't get out that robe and put on some lipstick . . ." She could imagine his finger wagging from her end of the line.

"How'd you know I was wearing a robe?" she asked.

He didn't even bother to answer that, just kept on: "It's the Champagne Supper Club tonight, baby. I heard Sam Cooke was there just last week. You wear something lucky, he might spot you in the crowd and send you somewhere, if you know what I'm talking about. And there ain't no chance you gon be seen from inside that house hugged up underneath Vivian, on that roof screaming your lungs out, not with no fluffy robe covered in gravy stains and cobwebs. I'm talking about one of those party dresses, red or yellow. Don't think I didn't notice that black you came out to Flamingo in last night. I don't know what's come over you. It's like you grieving somebody. Somebody died, Chloe?"

"It's 'cause I was on my cycle and had been eating so heavy," she started. "It hides the extra—"

"Well, don't bring the fork tonight. I'm talking about strappy heels, baby, and short white satin gloves, and a rhinestone necklace. I'm talking about fiiine."

"Boy, I ain't got no rhinestone necklace."

"Well, steal one, do you hear what I'm telling you? Sam Cooke was in the building last night. Or the other night before that. He might be there today. Girl, if you don't take him, I will."

"Alright, alright, alright, Tony, for God's sake, I'll meet you there at nine."

"Um-hmm. Don't 'alright' me. Matter fact, 'cause of that, you better make it eight thirty." And she heard the click of the handset meeting its base.

SHE TOOK HER TIME GETTING READY ALL THE SAME. TONY WAS RIGHT IN some ways. She reached for her new yellow number. She needed to pop tonight, for her spirit more than anything. There wasn't anybody she was looking for—men didn't take to her the way they did to Ruth and even Esther, and she knew why. It was her color, a vestige of her daddy, but she would have preferred the man himself. When she went out with Tony, though, she could ride the night past its normal edges. She found that days later, even, she could smile and laugh. She could linger in the room with Ruth and Gerry without wondering when her day would come.

Chloe could boast of more hair than her sisters combined and Mama had pressed it the Sunday before, but it still took some time to curl. She painted her nails a neutral color so as not to outshine the dress. It was cold for strappy heels, but she could manage if she borrowed Vivian's fur. Ruth and Esther complained that Mama wouldn't have dreamed of letting them go out at night by themselves when they were her age. They called Chloe the golden child, but she didn't think it was that. She always reminded them Mama felt safe with her out with Tony any time of night on account of his tendencies. She wouldn't be popping up married or pregnant. Not only that, the older woman was getting tired. She was still as beautiful as she'd been marching Chloe into the first-grade schoolhouse. But if Ruth complained about rehearsal dragging, she ended it without quoting the Good Book, without referencing ambition; just last week, the woman had slept in her uniform, unheard of, and sometimes Chloe would walk into her room unannounced and catch her seated on the edge of her bed, staring hard at something, only nothing would be there.

Tony hadn't been the only one with the idea. The line to get into the Champagne Supper Club swerved and dipped around the block. Chloe didn't mind. Her favorite part of going out was surveying the other people, their swing dresses, overcoats, pencil skirts, gingham pants, backseam stockings, pearls, and button earrings. It was always lively on Fillmore, but tonight it was like you could reach out and touch the excitement brewing, like inside this night in particular lay the secret to eternal joy.

Of course that joy started with the bar. Often, on nights like these, Ruth would be tailing her. Even when Chloe went out with her friends, it wasn't uncommon for her to see her sister out of the corner of her eye, just come in with a girlfriend of hers and winking at Chloe. Chloe would be happy to see her—she had never stopped being enthralled by her, and more than that, she'd feel like she was in the proximity of a base, like she could reach out and touch the edge of safety should some threat arise. Before, with Ruth there, she might have taken one sip of Tony's drink, tops, but Ruth had stopped venturing out months ago. Now Tony knew to place her order as soon as he walked in, along with his own gin and tonic, his favorite until nine, at which point brown liquor kept him on his feet. And by that hour, there was no telling what he might do, where he might do it, or with whom.

"To a night of surprises!" Tony raised his glass, and she met it with her own. "I'm so tired of knowing what's coming from one day to the next."

"You want to be surprised?" Chloe asked, sipping. "Not me. I want to see the same people we always see and dance to the same music we always dance to. I want to be rocked." She held her arms around herself now, swinging in place.

"You need to be rocked alright," Tony said. "But you gon have to drink up if there's any chance of that happening."

They turned to face the stage, their backs to the bar, guzzling. Red velvet drapes separated them from the main room where people sat on mahogany furniture or stood talking and laughing. The owner, Mr. Bailey, sat at the centermost table surveying the room, T-Bone Walker wailing in the background.

Mid-drink, a plump woman from the block stopped by to ask after Chloe's sisters. Then she turned to Tony.

"Boy, when you gon find somebody?"

"I don't know," Tony started, and Chloe could tell from the sparkle in his eye the rest wouldn't be good. "You tell me. Yo' mama been awful busy lately. You call her and tell her I'm waiting on her, hear?" And that was all it took for the woman's man to hustle over from the corner, and skinny, medium-brown, handsome Tony would have gotten his teeth socked out of his mouth if he hadn't offered to buy them all drinks. They were back at the bar doing just that when Tony pointed at the door, in a strange man's direction. Chloe followed where Tony's finger led, and it was true what the gesture had implied—the man was beautiful by any standard. Tall and lean but not too much so, with brown hair and a slight mustache, and he was dressed to kill in a plaid button-down shirt and slacks that narrowed in the leg. He was white, so of course Tony had locked in on him immediately—most white men didn't step into that club alone unless they were interested in other men. Yes, Chloe had seen this part play out before. The first time she'd been sickened by it, not because they were two men, but because of the line around that particular man's ring finger where he hadn't tanned; because he wouldn't call or see Tony again and Tony was okay with that; because when she went to sleep at night, she dreamed of a man who would give her a life, and he dreamed of one night at the most. It didn't seem fair, and Mama would have said it was a sin, one worth loving, though. Preacher would have agreed. But mornings after, Chloe was the one who sat on the edge of Tony's bed and listened to him weep. One time the man had been in town on business and given him a whole week. Tony had let his imagination soar. Chloe didn't think he would ever get over that one. It was love that he was feeling. There was no other explanation for it.

"You see him?" Tony asked. "Two o'clock."

"How could I not? He's the only snowflake in here."

"Yeah, but it's still early." And he was right. More would come. Mostly they lived in Pacific Heights and Nob Hill. They walked in with their wives, and they sat in the back. They ordered martinis and they cheered for the band, but they kept to themselves otherwise. This one, though, like all the other ones who came for Tony, was alone.

"As many clubs they got in San Francisco, as fancy as they be, he got to peek inside the Fillmore."

This was regular too, Tony dumping on the boys before they approached him. It was how he would manage his nerves, how he would stand in their face and wink, bat his eyes, fling his wrist, and when it was time to go, say something smart like "It's time for me to get off my feet."

And her part was to agree with him. "Dumpster diving," she might repeat on her fourth drink and sliding into her fifth. Or she had been known to keep it positive: "Those downtown men ain't got a thing on you, Tony," she might say. Or "They're coming back 'cause you're the real deal. Ain't nothing sweeter."

They might dish out variations of that conversation for an hour some nights, louder and louder each serving, but this new man was shuffling over already, his head down, his hands in his pockets, when most of Tony's men came in hot.

T-Bone had taken a break, and one of the waitresses stood up there now singing "All I Have to Do Is Dream." She closed her eyes; her long fingers drummed against her waist. She was light-skinned with straight hair that reached her back, but that was all there was to it. If Chloe had been one more drink deep, if she was smart-mouthed like her middle sister instead of sweet as pie, as the neighborhood knew her to be, she might have succumbed to her sudden need to snatch the microphone from the amateur's skinny hand.

The song ended, and the audience roared. Tony was one of them, his head back whistling, demanding an encore, rolling his eyes all the while, and the girl had gone backstage, but she'd be back for T-Bone's next break. Chloe knew the deal. The white man had reached them, but he wasn't clapping as hard as everyone else, almost like he had been privy to Chloe's disdain. She studied him a beat too long, and he caught her. His eyes stayed with hers then, and that was strange, but it happened from time to time. Even in Negro corners, these men still needed to put on a show.

She turned away once more, toward Tony, but he was in his groove now, in whatever slot he snapped into when he was a few inches from a future lover. It was the happiest, the most confident she'd ever see him, but its lifespan was short, and at this point it was best for Chloe to grab another drink and stick to the sidelines. She reached the bar a second after a girl from Ruth's high school class. When the girl had paid, the bartender started toward Chloe; then his eyes shifted to her right. She turned. The man had walked up beside her. Chloe could see the bartender determining who to serve first. The man jumped in—

"She was here," he said.

Chloe was too taken aback to respond, and the bartender chimed in for her. "I already know you're a rum and Coca-Cola kind of girl."

"Another round for Tony too," she said once she had regained her bearings.

"My treat." The man shifted closer to her. She looked away. When the drinks came, she grabbed hers and reached for Tony's, but it was too late; the man had beat her to it. He had ordered a gin and tonic for himself too, and without saying a word, he followed her. Chloe glanced back several times to make sure they hadn't been separated, and each time she found him biting his bottom lip. There was a dab of sweat on his upper. He was nervous about something. Maybe it was his first time with a man. Chloe knew enough from Tony to know it wouldn't be his last.

When they reached Tony, she thanked him in a flat tone.

"Do you mind if I join you?" he asked.

"Who you trying to boss around? We all free in here," Tony said.

And the man became red in the face and he took a sip of his drink before he said, "I know that, I'm so sorry, I wasn't trying to imply anything at all."

"He's just kidding," Chloe said because Tony would have let him stumble over himself all night. "He does that," she added, "to everyone."

The man glanced back at her with a disproportional amount of gratitude. Without meaning to, she held his gaze for a second, then, again, looked away.

Tony laughed his high-pitched raucous laugh, bending and patting his knee. "Let's go sit down," he said after a while, and they chose one of the only tables available, on the outskirts of the center of the room, farthest from the band, where T-Bone was steady moaning.

"A West Side baby, huh? Yessir, Mr. T-Bone, yessir," Tony called out.

And the whole while he was yelling, his eyes were steady fixed on the new man, moving from his eyes down to his waist.

And the man, if Chloe caught it, was doing the same, only to her. But he must have been shy, or in denial up until the final moment—Tony had told her about those kinds.

"What's your name?" she asked.

"James," he said.

"I'm Chloe. This here's Tony. Nice to meet you."

There was silence then, and Chloe kept on to cover it.

"Where you from?" If she was honest, she was also trying to soften him. Tony was like a brother to her, and she hated that she knew how the night would go, from the loose, linked hands on the walk home to the silent, brooding days that would follow, but he depended on the rhythm of it, even its pain.

"I'm from Washington, DC," the man said, smiling now, relieved almost. "Is it so obvious I don't belong?"

"No, not obvious at all, I expected you to say Pacific Heights or something like that."

"That's where we're living. My father and I. My mother's moving up shortly. She just wanted to get my sisters through the end of the school year."

"Yes, Lord, so it's just you and your daddy," Tony said, and he placed so much weight on the word "daddy," lingered over it so long, the man's face turned even redder than it had been before.

If Chloe could have blushed, she would have too, for the discomfort of it all, the oddness. It usually didn't go like this; the men were more deliberate, more focused. She'd never said more than two words to any of them, in fact. It was like the man here was at war with himself. He wanted Tony, that much was clear by his presence, but he needed to resist it to the end.

A group of girls approached them then, Regina and Betty, and Claris right behind them. Chloe was somewhat close with these girls, but it wasn't like with Tony. They got dressed to go out together some nights. They carried Lena's pie to each other's mothers when they visited, but they wouldn't know how she longed for her sisters. She wouldn't invite them in to feel the ache, and she wouldn't offer to let them fix it either.

She squealed to see them now, though, and it wasn't an act as much as she was delighted for a reprieve from the awkwardness.

She stood, and each of them pulled her in with a sweet embrace, all "Where you been girl?"

"We been looking all over for you tonight. We couldn't hardly stand it."

"Did you see old Debhora on that stage? Look good enough, but can't hardly hum as well as the junior choir."

And they all laughed, but Chloe didn't, in her typical way, and she said, "Aww, she wasn't as bad as all that."

"Oh, Chloe, you always see the good in everybody," Betty said. Then she lowered her voice, peering out the corner of her eye.

"Speaking of, who is that?"

"You know, one of Tony's friends," she said, flinging her wrist.

"That's what I thought too, but he keeps looking over here." They giggled, and Chloe looked back. Sure enough, it did seem like he was eyeing her.

She and the girls talked more about who would win talent hour at Flamingo, and then the girls snickered at some of the audience around them. Once again, Chloe was the one to lay her shine on the ladies who needed it, like the girl whose mama had just died and poor thing didn't have a penny to her name. It was no wonder her clothes didn't fit proper, that her stomach oozed over her skirt, but Chloe understood it. Her own dresses had had to be taken out a few weeks earlier, and Mama hadn't said a word, only grimaced and sucked her teeth when the needle grazed her waist, and Chloe cried out. She could sense another session like that coming around the bend sooner rather than later.

Then her friends' eyes drifted back over to her table again, and Claris said, "Let's go see about old Tony." They crowded around him, and the only space for Chloe was beside the new man. For a minute they sat in silence. Then:

"I hope it's okay that I joined you," he said. "I didn't mean you any harm. It's just that I saw you when you walked in, the way you danced when that girl up there was singing. If you ask me, you could have switched places with her. You should have been the one on that stage, and she should have been at the base of it, you know what I mean?"

"I do," she said, her words coming out slower and slanted where they had been firm. She was nervous suddenly now that she saw the girls had been right. She didn't think it was about his color, more the way he had been watching her, and the way he'd admitted to it. It had been hard growing up beside women who looked like Josephine Baker. People liked Chloe's kindness, they liked her spirit, they liked her courage. They said things like "She's never met a baby who didn't cling to her, an animal neither," or "It's impossible to be in a bad mood when you around that Chloe." It was natural for her to be that way, for the most part, and where it wasn't, she had learned to play on what people liked. This man hadn't known any of that about her, though. He'd seen her sipping on her drink, laughing with Tony, shifting her hips, nothing more, and had been moved somehow. She knew her mother would say his interest was certainly none of her business. But there had been a way she'd been feeling before he walked up and a way she was feeling now, and she was too tired to turn back.

"She do sing on that stage most nights is the thing." This from Claris across the table.

She'd been ear hustling. The man looked from Chloe to her, then back again.

"It's true," Chloe said. "I'm a singer myself, dancer too, you're clever to pick up on it. I've sung on that same stage in fact." The girls had meant to insult his ignorance, but she shifted it. Something in her wanted to shift it for him.

"I'm not surprised at all to hear that. Not at all," he said.

"You sure seem surprised, red in the ears like that." Regina.

And again, Chloe felt the nerve to bolster the message before it reached him. She understood why the girls spoke that way. There were only so many times in a Negro woman's life she'd hold the authority to talk to a white man like he worked for her. Some people might not get one chance at that at all, and the girls had leapt upon this one, seeming to know even at its height it was already waning. Chloe didn't differ from the girls much in that respect. But he was gazing at her still, and his steep interest in her brought her loneliness forward and sat beside it, reached for its hand.

Then the bickering started, as it tended to: "You called yourself borrowing my dress, but you ain't never returned it," Claris said to Regina.

"Maybe I was doing you a favor, look better in it anyhow," Regina said back. Claris was silenced by that, but Regina kept on. "I mean even tonight you stumbling. You must have felt like Lena Horne when you was choosing your lipstick color, huh? I think a darker hue might do you better."

And the man cut in. "If I may," he started, "I've met Lena Horne up close, and if you don't mind me saying, that lip color looks beautiful on you. I mean, in that shade, you could really give her a run for her money."

The comedian came back on, Redd Foxx this time, and Tony loved him, but he was too dirty for Chloe. She finished off her last drink and whispered goodbye into Tony's ear.

"This one might not be worth the time I've spent," he whispered back, still none the wiser, and she shrugged and patted him on the shoulder. She glanced back before she stepped into the night air, and the man was still watching.

THE TRUTH WAS, CHLOE WAS LUCKY. HER MOTHER AND SISTERS HAD ALways encouraged her optimism since she was the baby of the family. And in the Fillmore, Negroes occupied a world among themselves. The butcher was a Negro; the seamstress was a Negro; the baker was a Negro, as was the loan shark. Her mother had told her stories her whole life about down South: the men who rode horseback with white sheets over their heads, the broken windows, the snapped necks, the beatings, the bashed heads, the blood. It was why she had moved here, to be rid of all that. Once, Preacher had told her mother that those stories weren't suited for young minds, but they fell like lullabies in Chloe's ear. They were what she'd grown used to hearing before she slept, and even now she repeated them to herself, flipped through the images to feel safe at night when she was alone. The contrast of her real life—the warm bed, the soft sheets, the full refrigerator, Miss Mary next door and nobody coming to get her, nobody who would—that was the music to her dreams every time.

Still, she knew to look down when the whites passed. She knew to let them sit on the streetcar first. She knew to stay on this side of Geary. And she knew, even if one was staring her down like he had some interest, it was out of the question, a hard no, an absolute. She reminded herself of that as she skipped down the street. Negroes and whites visited the Champagne Supper Club or Bop City or Jack's or Flamingo every night, and sometimes after three drinks they'd even leave together, hurry to the Negro person's house because the alternative would have been unthinkable. An hour later, if you watched for them outside, you'd see the white leave with a bouncier step, an air of relaxation that was missing before. It was unclear what the Negro was left with—Chloe would never find out. Still, that night inside her house, tucked away on the second floor, sealed into the blanket Mary had knitted for her fifth birthday, she remembered what the man said about her replacing the act: "You should have been the one on that stage, and she should have been at the base of it." He didn't know she had one sister, not to mention two, and he had imagined her up there, the audience hooked into the trance she had set for them. She and Tony had made a reasonable assumption—most white men didn't step into that club alone unless they liked other men. But maybe he wasn't like most white men. His words ventured back to her again. This time, she imagined herself singing the song instead of that waitress. There was no question that she would have let her voice climb to the highest note, and she would have delivered.

VIVIAN

The weekend had slid by and Vivian still hadn't relayed the news. She had imagined rushing to tell the girls, but Sunday morning, it had been like she couldn't lift her legs. She'd told herself any minute she would rise, and she tried, but by the time she'd made it out of her nightclothes, the girls had gone. She'd have been lying if she said she wasn't relieved. She didn't have to accept they'd be leaving if they didn't even know it yet themselves.

Now, there was no question they were home. They'd been arguing since Vivian woke up. In the kitchen, Chloe sucked her teeth at the bacon, which Ruth hadn't fried extra crisp. And when Ruth hummed "This Little Light of Mine" while she stirred butter in her grits, Esther snapped at her.

"Does everybody in this house always got to be singing?"

And the sweet whir of sound went flat.

"You didn't have to say it all hard like that, Esther," Ruth said. She still seemed to be brooding like she'd been the last few months, but she set the table anyway, spooning an extra helping of grits onto Chloe's plate. The second mother. She'd had to be when their father died and Vivian worked at the drugstore during the day and attended nursing school at night, and Mary always watched out for them, but there was only so much tending she could do, raising a son herself. Vivian would worry at first because she'd notice Mary would send the girls to school with bits of cracker around their lips, sleep in their eyes. It wasn't long before Ruth started to wet a towel after breakfast and dab it onto their faces. And Vivian learned things from her oldest. Like when Esther crashed the car and had to wear a boot on her right leg for some time, Vivian had lost it off the bat. Ruth, cool as midnight, turned to her before they'd left for the hospital and said, "She learned her lesson, Mama, you don't have to pound her over the head with it."

Now she would be leaving soon, what Vivian had always pined for, and yet her mind wouldn't let her celebrate it. Maybe it wasn't her mind. Maybe it was her heart.

Vivian sat beside her oldest, her coffee mug in hand.

"You sulking today, huh, girls? What, you didn't sleep well?"

"I was going to ask you the same thing, Mama. We didn't even see you come in the night before last." This from Esther, and Vivian play swatted at her, though the way the words had come out, it was almost like the child had meant her harm.

"Did Preacher get a taste of holy water?"

"Oh, please, don't start with that again." She swatted her harder this time. "You know I haven't seen Preacher Thomas, not like that. He's still grieving."

"It's been three years, Mama," Esther said.

"Well, maybe I'm still grieving." She laughed, but the sadness couldn't escape the sound.

"It's been even longer for you," Chloe said.

"Eons longer," Esther said.

"Preacher Thomas is a good man, now that's all."

The girls snuck glances at each other, and Esther was the one to speak.

"Did you learn a little bit more about how good?" And then the giggles started, and soon Vivian joined in, relieved for the change in their mood, but Ruth was silent all this time, staring down at her plate, alternating between it and the door like she was waiting on someone. Vivian's news would lift the child's spirits, that she knew. Maybe that was reason enough to let it out. Once she did, though, the plan to move them would be set in motion, and there would be no way to call it back. As happy as it made her, speaking it aloud would announce another loss, and she was running out of strength for that.

"I have something serious to share with you girls." She set her mug down.

The mood in the room shifted again, like a cake in the oven when you peer in at the wrong moment, or a child screeches too loud, and everything you poured inside the pan falls flat.

The girls glanced at each other again.

"What is it, Mama?" Ruth asked finally, but she didn't seem excited, only sad, and Vivian pressed her hand against hers.

"Well, it's serious, but it's good too, so that's something. You remember, Mama went out the other night. No, no, not what you thinking," she hurried along. "I went out with Mr. Franklin."

"Mr. Franklin?" Esther asked.

"Mr. Franklin? The one at the Champagne Supper Club all the time?" Chloe asked.

"I thought he moved to Hollywood." Esther rolled her eyes, scrunched up her face.

"Ooh, what did he want, Mama?" Chloe led the pack here. Ruth was the first to gripe about the practices, the spins and dips in four-inch pumps, the late-night routines, back-of-the-bus trips to Las Vegas each year. Esther didn't gripe, just had trouble keeping up all the while. But Chloe understood—Vivian could tell by how she handled her shoes, shining them in the morning without being told, by the care she took pinning sequins to her skirts. She wasn't the star, didn't have that power in her, but once, she didn't know Vivian was looking and she'd cried because her hair wouldn't flip into a backwards curl.

"Shh, shh, girls, okay, listen." It was happy news, she reminded herself. People would do any manner of things for this level of joy. She would have been one of them if her heart weren't breaking. "Okay, so listen, you know how I always tell you life moves forward in stages? You won't always see the end from the beginning, and when something big is happening, you have to learn to take it slow, you have to learn to not judge the whole experience by whatever aspect of it you're standing in at the moment. When I moved out here, I had—"

"Yeah yeah yeah, Mama, you had two dollars to your name but a millionaire's share of ambition. What about it?" Esther asked.

Ruth stayed silent.

"Well, so you're right, Mr. Franklin saw us perform last week and I guess we made a big impression on him, girls, you made a big impression on him."

She had expected Chloe to start squealing and even for Esther to smile, but that didn't happen. Nor did Ruth say a word. If Vivian could read it right, the girl seemed afraid, but she was always good about peeking into her mother's thoughts and maybe she had sensed Vivian would be staying behind.

"He wants to manage you. He wants to introduce you to producers, get you a record deal. He wants to take you on the road. It would be without me," she went on. "But Mama's going to visit." She rubbed each of their hands as she spoke. They were still babies in her mind's eye sometimes, and those newborn gurgles came back to her now. They were probably as keen to wrap themselves in her arms. Chloe looked up at Ruth, second mother, with what Vivian assumed was sadness, but not all the way; there was something else she couldn't name in Chloe's eyes. If she didn't know better, she might have read it as anger. Ruth was steady silent. Esther seemed to be smirking.

"To Los Angeles?" Ruth asked. And it was Chloe's turn to take her sister's hand now.

"No, sweetie." Vivian could almost cry at this moment. "It won't be just Los Angeles, it will be all over the country." She stood and swept her free hand across the room to indicate the scale of everything she was describing. In her other hand, she clamped her mug tighter.

She could see tears gathering in Ruth's eyes. The other girls looked back at her again. Chloe was about to speak, and Vivian begged her with her eyes to be the voice here. Sometimes her youngest daughter could make sense of the thickest jumble of life, and as she started, Vivian could feel the tangles separating, like hair that has been plowed through for knots, and now it could be combed through straight.

The doorbell rang, followed directly by a "Yoo-hoo." Gerry walked straight through the front parlor. Of course Ruth stood and ran to him. They had grown up together was the thing, sleeping in the same bed until they were five, and once, they had awoken and shared the same account of a dream, Gerry in Mary's house, Ruth in Vivian's. Vivian and Mary had happened to compare notes that day; otherwise, she might not ever have known. Still, the way Ruth was clinging to him now was different. Vivian supposed she needed something, someone, familiar. Vivian understood. Even now, she wondered if Mary was free, if she could go sit on the edge of her sofa and lay out every word, or say nothing at all.

"Ruth, baby, tell Gerry the good news." She waited, but the girl didn't say a word, just looked between her mother and Gerry, then back again.

"Fine," Vivian went on, almost angry now at the ungratefulness. "Fine," she repeated. "I'll tell him. Mr. Franklin wants to manage them, Gerry. He knows the right people who can get them a demo made. He even has connections for a deal. They'll travel all over the country, not just California. To fulfill their dreams. Finally. To be stars. Isn't that wonderful?" she added because no one had said a word.

Gerry looked at Ruth like he'd been socked. Ruth nodded. Vivian thought she heard the boy whisper, "No, baby." Then, "Are you sure?" Ruth nodded again and gripped his hand and walked them both toward Vivian. Vivian looked from him to her several times trying to imagine a situation in which that gesture would make sense.

"I can't leave, Mama," she said.

"What do you mean, you can't leave?" she asked, missiles in her eyes, and not all of them were aimed at her or at this very moment, but they might as well have been.

"I mean, I can't leave." Her voice was stronger this time around. "I aim to marry Gerry."

Vivian was too shocked to respond. Gerry gripped her daughter's hand, tighter.

"I aim to make her my wife," he said.

And it was like the two worlds Vivian had been able to visit that night with Mr. Franklin at the club sprang back upon her with even more color and precision. In one, her daughter performed onstage at the highest arena, a venue Vivian couldn't have imagined on her own, but she felt Ellis in the center of her thoughts, guiding her to the soft billows of seats surging beyond Ruth, applause so loud you couldn't hear your own fear, and her name spelled out in bold on the marquee. There was no question her daddy had a hand in it. It was too magical to have been made by their work alone, as dutiful as Vivian had been, as faithful and diligent.

And then there was the alternative, and the closer Gerry moved toward Ruth, the more vivid the details within it sprang to life. She could see a baby, for instance, not just hear it, a daughter who favored Gerry in her coloring and even in her temperament. There was nothing wrong with the man; Vivian adored him. He was dependable and trustworthy and reliable and safe. But his vision woke and slept within these four miles, and there was nothing she wanted less for her daughter than to be the sole carrier of ambition. Ruth would think she was okay through the thrills of the big stomach and the first cries, and then even the next life she brought in might spark a flair, but over time the dullness of it all the vagueness the sameness the recurrence would eat her alive.

"There's no way." Vivian walked toward the man she had bathed with her daughter more times than she could count. "You know me, and you know Ruth, and you know there's no way in hell she's going out like that, not while I got something to say about it."

And Ruth stepped forward at that moment, holding his hand even tighter, and she placed her hand on her own stomach and she said, "I want him, Mama. I always have. Gerry's working full-time at the butcher's, promoted to manager even, and he's able to take care of me. Enough for rent, and I'd keep on at the hospital. I never wanted all that, the bright lights and the big stars, I just wanted a home and I just wanted love and you gave me that, Daddy did too before he died, but now I have someone who wants to extend it, and—"

"No, hell no," Vivian cut her off where she stood. "You talking to me like you lived in this world as long as I have and you got information on it you been storing up, but it's the opposite." She heard herself getting worked up, and she tried to drop her pitch, the way she might instruct the girls who had veered past their note. "But it's the opposite, baby," she went on. "I know everything about the situation you're in right now, and you think it's wide and deep enough to fill your life, but in a year, maybe two, tops, it'll constrict, and all you'll have left is your longing, your should-have-beens, your could-have-beens. They won't let up, I promise you they won't."

"Mama, it doesn't matter. I'm prepared—"

"Just listen, okay, instead of talking, just listen to me now because I'm hitting on something you'll only hear if you're quiet." And Vivian was filled with a grace all of a sudden that steadied her tone and slowed her speech.

"I know you, I know you better than you know yourself. I saw your eyes light up when you heard your first song, saw how proud you were at your first dance recital, and to see you now onstage, to hear that deep voice, that earthy, wise, that heavy voice come out of a girl not even twenty-five, I know there's a spirit in you and it takes over when you perform. I need you to pull on that part of yourself right now and listen to me from that spot. I need you to reach deep inside and find your ambition. Can you do that for me, baby?"

Vivian felt good about where she was headed, no, where she had landed. Her daughter was really seeing her. Even Gerry was attentive. Vivian was good at this sort of thing, always had been. People had accused her of planting her own dream inside her children, but it wasn't that as much as she had been so prescient about observing it in them and plucking it out, conveying how delicious it was, and they had decided to taste and see for themselves.

"Mama, I'm pregnant."

And that's where Vivian's comprehension stalled. She tried to smile, but she couldn't complete the act. That other world with the lights and the sparkles and the applause so fierce it made your head spin had dimmed, so powerfully it might as well have been a different person's vision in the first place.

Chloe stood behind Ruth, Esther beside her. Neither child looked surprised, and their reaction to Mr. Franklin's news began to make more sense. Ruth stood straight across from Vivian, holding Gerry's hand. Mary had ventured in, and she walked over and stood next to Vivian, rubbing her back, up and down, and up and down again.

"Be cool," she whispered. "Be cool now, girl."

And Vivian wanted to, she tried it, she did. For a minute, she thought she might achieve it even, but then that hope was gone. The mug she was holding wanted to fall to the floor, and she allowed it its descent. A splash of heat slapped the backs of her calves. Then she walked through the kitchen and up the outside stairs to the roof. She sat and watched over the city to the north, up a hill of houses in Pacific Heights, where the roofs didn't leak, where the trash was picked up on time. Her eyes didn't see it, though. No, she might as well have been in Louisiana, wandering the rows, twisting the cotton from the bolls, beginning the terrible trek back home.

She didn't know how long she had sat out there when she heard Mary behind her. Maybe she didn't hear her; maybe she felt her. Either way, the older woman scooted her chair closer to her, grabbed her hand, and set it in her own lap. Sometimes the two women would sit in those very chairs and listen to the girls with their eyes closed, swimming inside their own private visions, whatever desires and silent exaltations the songs carried them to, but that was over now. Mary pulled out a cigarette and handed her one. Mary had been smoking since Vivian first knew her—her voice came out like gravel and people routinely mistook her on the phone for a man—but Vivian hadn't partaken since Ellis died. Now, though, she inhaled and let it out, then inhaled again. She did feel calmer somehow. Her hand shook and Mary squeezed it.

"Looks like we 'bout to be grandmothers," she said.

Vivian waited for her to say something else, but there was only silence.

She would have gone on about the imprudence of it all, the unsteadiness, the plainness, the mediocrity, except Gerry was Mary's son, and what could she say?

"I know you wanted something different for Ruth," Mary went on, stomping the cigarette out on the heel of her shoe. "We all did. I love that girl like my own. But we go against it and it's just going to make them stronger, you know that. I don't want them going through this next part of life alone. It's hard enough. Gerry will provide for her. I know that like I know my own name. If he has to work five jobs, walk ten miles in each direction for each one, he will see to it she never wants for anything."

"I know that, Mary," Vivian said. "I know that."

"Well, sometimes we have to be grateful for that," Mary said.

The noise downstairs began picking up, the neighborhood coming to life off of Ruth's and Gerry's news, no doubt. They listened to the fervor building for some time before Mary stood.

"I better go out there," she said, and Vivian nodded in her direction. Of course she couldn't join her; it would have made her sick to try. She stayed put, listening to the loud whoops and shrieks, peering out sometimes at the dancing on the sidewalk. The music blared out the open windows and doors. "A-Tisket, A-Tasket."

She hated that song. She willed herself to stand, and after some minutes, she rose to her feet. When she reached her bedroom, she took her time undressing. More than anything, she wanted to be asleep, but she didn't have the energy to rush. Finally, she took to the bed, but there was only so far down she could dip before she'd get yanked back into the new reality she'd entered, the music outside, the congratulatory shouts, and disappointment like a piece of wool layered it all. She needed to drown it out, so she got up and rifled through her old records, Nat King Cole's "Straighten Up and Fly Right" and Louis Armstrong's "Do You Know What it Means to Miss New Orleans?" She could tell you where she was when she heard songs from each of them.

Then she went for the pictures she kept in shoeboxes. The girls at Easter, their patent leather shoes shining bright, and gaps where Ruth's top front teeth should be. She talked with a lisp for months after while they grew back. All the girls had two plaits, one on either side of a part down the middle. It was easier that way, and Vivian remembered how tired she felt that holiday, an exhaustion that she knew would never leave her, even once the children were grown. It was a function of stepping into the territory of mothering, and yet she couldn't have imagined how easy she had had it then, shipping them off to school on time. Sure, there were small tiffs getting dressed in the morning because Esther could be so tender-headed and Chloe never did take to math, but who cared, she could see now. The world would become more complicated. She wouldn't be able to tap their little legs when they didn't clean their rooms on time; she couldn't catch them in a lie by glancing back at their faces. No, they were their own women now, Ruth at least, and she held her own secret life inside her. It would have been one thing if Vivian had known she was being cut out, but the suddenness of it, of coming apart from the child who had grown inside her—she didn't think she would have had children in the first place, in fact, she swore she wouldn't have, if she had known the shock would insert itself so deep.

And down, down in the bottom, because she didn't want to burrow into them without planning, lay the pictures of Ellis at Ruth's christening, him in his fur felt hat and trench coat. She had thought they would have so much more time, and "disappointment" wasn't the word for that realization that came not just the day of his death but every day after as she sat up in bed realizing she was facing the world alone. She hadn't learned the correct word for that despair yet, but at least the singing had held it at bay, and now here it stood, front and center, threatening to take her out.

"Oh, Ellis," she said as if she were praying. Her mama had always said, "No man can be your rock," but he had been, and maybe that was where she'd gone wrong. She fingered the photograph, brown at the edges, where his face had already dulled. She supposed she didn't need him. She could predict what he would say if he were there, that the child had to live her own life. If he were there, he would remind her that her mother didn't want her to move out West, that his mother didn't either, and where would they have been if they had stayed in Louisiana? *Not much would be different now, though*, she'd say back. *Not so*, he'd respond. *We'd still be picking cotton on a sharecropper's farm, deciding at the end of the month if it was worth standing up for the extra two dollars I was owed, if it was worth going to sleep and waking up with the white sheets outside ready to burn me alive.*

Yeah, she would say back, *but the Klan just wears suits and ties out here, that's the only difference*. Isn't that what Horace was always mouthing off about? *No*. Ellis would be adamant on this one point, she knew. *Maybe our family hasn't reached its destination, but there is no question that here, we are closer.*

She must have fallen asleep preparing her next argument. Ellis's picture lay beside her pillowcase when she woke, his eyes floating up toward his hat, his hands resting on his double-breasted front.

It was Sunday, which meant she'd boil water for coffee, then read her Bible in the time it took the bubbles to form. She always chose the scripture based on how she was feeling, and this was a day for Psalms, 27 to be specific:

One thing have I desired of the Lord, that will I seek after; that I may dwell in the house of the Lord all the days of my life, to behold the beauty of the Lord, and to enquire in his temple.

And that was where she stopped. She liked her coffee black, two cups, and she left the remainder out for Esther. The other girls didn't like the taste. Normally at this hour, she'd be whistling along to Clara Ward, and she and the girls would play around, clutching serving spoons in their fists like microphones.

She'd be the one to cook those mornings, let the girls rest their feet, fried bacon and drop biscuits and liver and onions over grits. They always attended the second service so they could afford to take their time ironing their blouses, applying polish remover to stockings, serving as mirrors for one another, asking one if she could see her panty line through her dress or if her skirt was too tight. But today she set her hot rollers and dabbed on her blush alone. She sat out in the moss green Pontiac when it was time to leave and turned the music on loud, loud when the girls filed in. They arrived at church early and were able to park right next to the preacher, and Esther made a joke about sliding in beside him in other ways, and Vivian pretended she didn't hear it; she certainly didn't smile.

Everyone she passed, Sister Henry and Deacon Bryant and the girls from the junior choir and the young ushers and even the youth group, congratulated her, and she nodded and smiled at them to be polite, but she snuck inside the prayer and petition room shortly after arriving and only slunk out when Lena stood at the podium to list announcements.

The woman seemed to drag on and on this morning—fish fries and prayer retreats and sick and shut-in visitation and book drives, and Mr. Franklin was kind enough to donate $200 for a talent show prize and would be in church the third Sunday of next month to review the acts.

Vivian normally took notes throughout the sermon, she depended on it so. Once, years ago, when Preacher Thomas was a young man, his late wife still meditating on the pulpit in a chair just beyond him as he preached the word, he said with a stammer in his voice that there were seasons in life. All of life was filled with seasons, he said, and there was a season for sadness and you had to tend to that season just like you would tend to the season of joy. You had to nurture yourself, you had to let yourself cry out, you had to soothe yourself. But whatever you did, you couldn't rush it, you couldn't gripe about it, you had to extend it respect. Back then, she still cried for Ellis every night, but sure enough, when the war was over, it was like a light shined on her, and it wasn't just her; it was the neighborhood. The next five years were some of the most pleasant she'd ever seen. She still thought of him every day, of course, but not with the sadness that filled her up and took her out, no. She still thought of home too but with the same buffer. Sometimes she'd tell Mary stories about her mother's crawfish boils, how hot the summers could burn, how she and her brothers would chase each other and forget they were born poor and Negro.

Today she only heard halves of phrases, meaningless without their counterparts—loneliness was like a poison, for instance, and forgiveness let it out, and death was really new life—and maybe if she could have held on for the remainder, she might have been delivered from the heaviness inside her, but her pain would whisk her away each time.

At the end of the service, she stood, though normally on the first Sunday, she was the one to walk the offerings basket around before Communion, then stay later to tally up the amount and source. As she was sliding back into her coat, Preacher walked toward her and reached for her hand. He nodded toward his office, and she shook her head, but he squeezed her wrist, so gently, then beckoned toward the room again, and she turned in its direction.

He would have to see to the rest of the congregants first, and she paced the room while she waited, dragged her fingertips along the window, peering just a touch behind his desk, staring for not so long at the picture of his wife in the corner, an eight-by-ten of the woman before she'd taken sick. Truly there had been no one as beautiful. Vivian could hear the events ministry outside setting up for a picnic, laying out the baskets of fried chicken and the bowls of god-awful potato salad, the pitchers of lemonade. There was a second where she wondered what they'd be celebrating before it hit her again, and she had to sit down in one of the seats across from his.

Preacher's voice carried from the hallway now, consoling a mother whose child hadn't come back from the war many years earlier.

"I know it is," she could hear him saying. "I can't even imagine it and you're entitled to feel it, but what do we know about feelings?"

The mother said something in a voice so low Vivian couldn't make it out, though she was stretching her ear toward the door.

"They come and then they go," Preacher said. "They come and they go," he repeated. "Even the ugliest can't stay, they just can't, it's not in their nature. They're paths to lead us toward God. What do we know about God's nature?"

And whatever the mother said must have been correct because she heard Preacher: "That's right. Praise God, that's right." They agreed to meet up the following Wednesday, and then Vivian heard the doorknob twist and the door budge. There was a flutter deep in her gut, but she didn't turn her attention to it. She looked back, and seeing him, she started to weep. She had never been that kind of woman. She could count on one hand the number of times even Ellis had seen her cry, and two of those occasions had been during childbirth when squeezing his hand and biting her lip were not sufficient to ward off the unfathomable. But now, seeing this man come in, feeling the tenderness wafting off of him after his conversation with that poor, poor woman, knowing the same nurturing lay in wait for her, she let it all out, and he walked over to her and clasped her shoulder. He didn't say a word while she cried there, her hands in her face, because as much as she trusted him, she couldn't let him see her. When the cry sank a little deeper and her sobs grew more guttural, he would sigh or squeeze her shoulder, or he would groan in commiseration, but otherwise he stood over her in silence, every now and then gripping her tighter, somehow knowing when the pain threatened to carry her off somewhere with no hope for return.

"I know it's stupid," she said. "I ought to be rejoicing. My first daughter getting married. That lady won't see her son again on this side of glory. But I had just been so excited." She filled him in on Mr. Franklin.

"Shh," he said. "Pain is pain, you know that. Don't care how you classify it, still eat at you the same, no?"

"Still," she said, her voice steadier, her breathing less bunched, "you hear the people out there. God must find me mighty ungrateful. They all using it as a reason to praise Him further, and I'm over here collapsing. I ought to be happy." The crying intensified then, and he sat down in the chair beside her and observed her like he was watching a beautiful sunset or a river's gentle rocking, and that just made her cry more. Then she surprised herself and calmed again.

"You're right," she said, "about what you told that woman, that feelings come and go. I remember that after Ellis died. I thought I'd never get over it at first. That ache was horrid in the beginning, it was too massive, I didn't think I'd ever be able to shake it out."

"Me neither," he said, "with Mattie. It was the same, but now, it's not that I don't miss her—"

"No, not a day goes by I don't think of Ellis, wish he were here."

"But you learn to live without them. It becomes routine, measured. Yes, you find the places in your heart where you can clear enough space to let some light in. Those spaces keep clearing, keep growing. The light brightens."

"But all that effort? Every day, Preacher, every single day, I was on that roof with them. There wasn't a day that went by that I wasn't. I sewed the dresses. I bought the makeup, the most modern shades, I can't tell you how much I paid, it didn't matter, and the shoes, I became a cobbler myself, setting and resetting the heels. The nail polish, the wigs, the jewelry, I'm still paying off that piano, the song lyrics, the dance moves, I know the jitterbug better than any young girl in here."

He laughed at that.

"But I don't care about that, if I never see a dime of that investment, I promise you it wasn't about the money."

"I know it wasn't."

She paused then.

"I just don't know what I'm going to do with all my hope," she said. "What's going to fill it now it's gone? You don't understand: it turned my head; it occupied me; it welcomed me to the day; it sang me to sleep at night. It steadied me; it filled me up." She paused again before she repeated the last part. "I don't know what I'm going to do without it."

"I know," he said, and she caught his eye. She had expected him to lay out scripture. There were so many to choose from—he knew better than anyone—that would slide right into this moment, nudge itself into a perfect slot.

But he hadn't, and somehow the omission fed her more.

"You got more teachers signed up for Bible study?" she asked.

"Barely. You know Miss Fox was first in line, but"—and he lowered his voice—"people are complaining that she repeats herself, talks in circles."

"She is sixty, and then, of course, there's the bottle. Let me guess, is her favorite verse still 'Give strong drink unto him that is ready to perish, and wine unto those that be of heavy hearts'?"

"No, I think this time, it's 'Let him drink, and forget his poverty, and remember his misery no more.'"

They laughed together for more time than the joke warranted, and then, against her own wishes, she stood.

"I guess I better run back for Ruth." She studied her watch. "She's got work in an hour. I want to catch her before she leaves." She paused. "To apologize."

"Good for you." He seemed like he wanted to say something more, but she waited for a minute and nothing came, so she thanked him and turned her back. She felt replenished somehow. Nothing had changed since she'd spoken to Preacher. The sadness she'd described had every right to linger still, but his fingerprints were on it too, holding it back, showing it who was its master.

When she got home, Ruth was in the front parlor changing into her oxfords. Neither woman said a word. They just fell into each other's arms before Vivian even closed the door behind her.

"I'm sorry, Mama," the girl said.

"No, it's me who's sorry, baby. It's a life you're carrying now. We're going to celebrate that just like it's Mr. Franklin, more even." It was hard for her to get the words out, but she managed; she finished. The girl pulled away.

"I'll be late if I don't leave now," she said as she tied her shoes. "Oh, but what are you going to tell him?" she asked.

"Tell who?" Vivian slid out of her trench coat.

"Mr. Franklin."

And the coat nearly fell off the hanger.

"I'll figure that out, baby," Vivian said like the question was inconsequential, the answer too. "You get on to work."

When Ruth was gone, Vivian hurried into the kitchen and picked up the phone. Preacher answered on the second ring, and she started talking like she was only continuing a conversation between them that had never stopped.

"You said Mr. Franklin is going to be here next month? For the talent show?"

"Yeah, why?"

"Well, I told you, we had made it a deal, and now I don't know what to tell him." The excitement dashed across her chest again then was gone fast.

"I don't understand. Can't he just take the others?"

"It needed to be a girl group." She felt herself slipping backwards, but she reined it in. "He won't take the two. He needed three," she repeated. "And he had set his sights on Ruth." She paused. "Of course, he's not the only manager in the Fillmore, not in San Francisco either." That hadn't occurred to her before, but the idea was here all of a sudden and so was that hope. She recognized it, though it was a stub of an emotion now; she, more than anyone, knew how to grow a feeling. "But I don't want him blacklisting me in the industry, well, not me, but the other two girls I mean," she went on.

Preacher Thomas didn't say anything else for a while. Vivian could imagine him folding and unfolding his hands.

"Mr. Franklin is an interesting man," he said. "Can quote the Bible backwards and forwards. Goes to church every Sunday. Not always here, but he's always in somebody's front pew. Tithes regularly, and generous to a fault. What I'm saying, Vivian, is I've never met a man of such means who's as obedient."

"Well, great, sounds like one of His most noble servants is an enemy of mine." She twirled the cord between her fingers as she spoke.

"No, I wasn't saying that, was saying he'll listen is all. I'll get him right in service if you'll let me. No matter what happens, I'll make sure he doesn't hold a grudge."

"I couldn't ask you to do that."

"You're not asking me," he said, and the pause that followed—well, it was heavy, and if she had doubted her daughters before this moment, she wouldn't again.

"Let me talk to him first," she said. "I should be the one to tell him. It's my own word that I'm breaking."

"Alright then, when it's my turn, you just say the word."

"I appreciate you, Preacher," she said, and she was twirling the cord much slower now.

"I appreciate you too, V," he said. "You don't know how much."

RUTH

Esther had only ever made snide remarks to Ruth since the year she entered seventh grade, but now she didn't even do that. There was just a silence that pierced the atmosphere whenever Esther walked into a room Ruth was in already or Ruth tore into a space that had previously felt safe for her sister. Ruth had grown used to that, but even Chloe, whom Ruth would sometimes tell Gerry she felt she had raised, would only half smile when she told a joke instead of belly laugh. When Ruth told her she wanted her to be the child's godmother, Chloe said she would, but she didn't spend much time with the exchange. She was off to another part of the kitchen where Mama hunched over the sink scrubbing plates.

The rest of the block helped her put it out of her mind—Mr. Gaines, with his extra helpings of ham hocks and pork roast, and Lena, who already wondered how many layers of buttercream cake she'd want for her shower. Lena had bought a new instrument that allowed her to etch roses into the frosting, she said. It was pricey, but for Ruth, her favorite girl, she'd make an exception. Ruth's girlfriends would beg her every lunch hour to tell the story of how she stood up to her mama, their mouths spread into an O, especially at the part where

Ruth recounted pushing her shoulders back and declaring with all the heat in her body that she was going to be married. Miss Gladys pulled her in, sat her down in the finest beauty parlor chair, spun her around to the mirror, and practiced different styles for hours. Ruth hadn't decided yet which one she favored.

Now she showed Gerry pictures of models with French twists. Vivian was off at work, and Mary didn't tolerate shacking up either, but the old woman slept hard. She permitted herself one vanity and wouldn't leave her room once she removed her teeth. Once Ruth had had to ask her to give an unruly boarder his ten dollars back, and she knocked and knocked on Mary's door for ten minutes straight before finally opening it herself. Mary was still out cold, but her teeth in the glass of water beside her seemed downright buoyant.

"I don't know which one flatters my face best," Ruth said, and Gerry had been good about indulging her since they'd gotten engaged. They'd rehashed what color his suit would be, how their vows would read, and the rings! They hadn't selected them yet, but they'd pored over the details, the cut of the diamond, the metal of the band. Once he responded to her about her hair, she planned to remind him to schedule the appointment with the jeweler. But Gerry was elsewhere, she could tell, even as he nodded at her questions about lipstick and eyeshadow. He was looking at her, sure, but his mind had begun its roam. That had been happening lately.

"What is it?" she asked again now, and he shook his head.

"Nothing, baby."

"I know it's something," she said. "The wedding? It's a lot to put together. I'm the oldest girl and Mama will want it done up right, and we have to rush on account of . . ."

"That's not what it is, baby," he said. "Marrying you is the best thing that's ever happened to me, the best thing that will ever happen to me, that I know." He paused to kiss her. She had unbuttoned her pants, which, though they'd stretched, had grown too snug, and he pressed his lips against the base of the stomach, which had started to jut out.

"It's work," he went on.

"But you love it."

"I do, I guess I'm just amped up to prove myself. Mr. Gaines has always been like a father to me and I don't want to let him down. I don't want him to think he made a mistake promoting me."

She rubbed his back. "You're going to do fine, I know you are. You were like this when you first started, and look how you soared. You'll see, after a few weeks, it will be like second nature to you. You'll start feeling like you were born to be manager of that shop. I believe in you," she said.

He kissed her.

"Maybe," he said. "For now, it's enough to come home to you, to my baby inside you." He lifted her shirt, and it was a relief to make love and know there wouldn't be a consequence. She felt herself relax beneath him, and she moaned louder than she normally did and pressed his backside harder until all the space inside her had been filled.

When they were done, he went to sleep off the bat. He was like his mama in that way. Though he had all his teeth, he would be out until the morning. She tried to join him, she did, but as exhausted as she felt during the day—so much so the other nurses had volunteered to stand in for the tail end of her shifts so she could rest her feet—come dusk, her energy would lift. One of her coworkers had warned her it would happen, that the body prepared itself for waking up to feed and change the baby, that starting at the fifth month, Ruth would be famished for more sleep but unable to slip inside it. Sure enough, more often than not, she'd find herself propped up beside Gerry until long after midnight, sometimes just watching him breathe. At least, she found a peace in the sound, its predictability, and sometimes she'd envision herself walking down the aisle to that rhythm of shudders, and sometimes she'd go over that moment she'd relived with all her girlfriends, where she sure did push her shoulders back and her chest out before she insisted she had a right to own her life.

Now she didn't feel like either. She could hear her sister Chloe out on the stoop returning from somewhere, probably a club with Tony, and she felt a sudden pang of sadness that she wouldn't be in the kitchen waiting for her, inhaling the elements of her night like she'd started to do once the first-trimester nausea had set in. She hadn't allowed herself to believe she was pregnant then, but she knew standing up too long made her dizzy, and alcohol on the breath made her want to retch. She'd stopped going out and started looking forward to Chloe reviving the night for her as much as she'd enjoy dressing up and dancing and cackling with her girlfriends herself. Those nights already seemed like years ago, but in Chloe's hands, at least she could reach out and feel their skin, hear what derogatory name Tony had called the man he'd wind up sleeping with, how long it had taken for him to feel powerful enough to let him lead him home. Ruth glanced beside her at her clothes, which Gerry had only had time to half yank off.

She stood and tugged a robe around her and headed off to the shower down the hall. There were two bathrooms on this floor. Because Gerry used the one adjacent to his room, Mary forbade most roomers from entering it. Sure enough, Ruth knocked and found it was empty. When she was done, she slipped back out into Gerry's room, tugged on the clothes she'd been wearing just an hour before, and hurried outside to her own house while it was still hers. There would only be a few more months when she could walk in without feeling like a visitor.

She expected it to just be Chloe inside the kitchen, but she walked up to the doorway to Esther's voice. Ordinarily Esther was the opposite of Ruth and Chloe. She spent more time in her bed than outside it. She slept surrounded by books, and oftentimes it was Ruth who turned the lamp out and slid her glasses down her nose, placed them folded onto the bedside table. Esther didn't know that, though. Now Ruth heard her say she'd been awake for the past two hours.

"That's not like you," Chloe said.

"I know. I got stuff on my mind, I guess."

"Is it Ruth?"

"No," Esther said, too fast, though. Too fast. "I mean, yeah, sure, it started to feel realer when she told Mama. I started considering the options more. I went up to Mama after and told her that it was okay, that I had been working hard and was more comfortable taking the lead, and she shook her head. She said Mr. Franklin wanted a girl group, and we're not a girl group anymore. She seemed so hopeless."

"Mama wouldn't stop over one man," Chloe said, but again, it was too fast. "I mean, do you even know her?" she went on. And she pretended to laugh, but Ruth knew Chloe too well to believe it. "She wouldn't be Vivian without us singing and dancing; she wouldn't have a place in the world without the roof."

"Yeah," Esther said, "that's what I thought at first. And then I thought more about it. Have you noticed, since Ruth told her, she hasn't mentioned rehearsal? I guess it didn't cross my mind that Ruth leaving might mean the end."

Chloe didn't respond for a while, and then, in a low voice, Ruth heard:

"Well, maybe we could still get Mr. Franklin to take us on, just the two of us, Esther. It might go different for you without Mama breathing down your neck. I always thought part of the problem was that you clashed. I always wondered if it wasn't the anxiety of it causing you to slip up sometimes."

Esther must have pushed her chair back or scowled or only sighed because Chloe stopped right there.

"Mr. Franklin only wants girl groups," Esther repeated with an edge to it now. "Look at that last act he signed, four ladies. Fat as cows but can sing better than Jesus. And Ruth just didn't consider—"

"It's just that we had made so much headway in the last few months," Chloe cut her off. "The Champagne Supper Club, opening for the Caravans. The Dunbar audition is still an option. It wasn't all

Ruth. We were there too. You were there too. That has to have counted for something. You have to believe that. You have to love it all enough to trust that belief."

Ruth waited for Esther's response, her hand clutching the front door like she might walk in, though that was no longer a possibility. Finally it came in a near whisper.

"I do," Esther said. "I do love it enough. Maybe that's the problem."

There was silence for a while after that, and Ruth realized Esther had walked upstairs. Just as sure as Ruth knew Chloe was still at the kitchen table, she could peek inside her little sister's fantasy too, the glow of the stage she'd be dreaming of, the audience she'd imagine at her feet. It was all too much, and Ruth turned her back and tiptoed next door so she wouldn't be heard.

When she tucked inside Gerry's room, she took off all her clothes, even her panties, and lay down beside him. It had been hot at night lately, 80 when they'd grown used to 60, and she didn't wake up with a film of sweat over her when she lay down naked. In bed, she didn't watch him sleep like normal, and she didn't reenact her bold display to her mother. Suddenly, it didn't feel so bold. It wasn't that she regretted the baby or being with Gerry, that was what she wanted, but she hadn't wanted it to cost so much. She hadn't wanted to be acquainted with the price.

She closed her eyes, and there Chloe's view was again, the lights, the audience, but Ruth was there this time, and though she tried to squeeze her eyes shut against herself in the center of the stage—and how it shined—it was like her pumps were stuck to the stained wood floor. There it all was, the steps, the sound, the beauty. There was no wonder the people screamed, and their applause, she let it ride over her; she let it glide inside; she let it fill her up and push her higher. The feeling she'd had just an hour ago beneath Gerry didn't have anything on this—plus, it had been over so fast. But this, that rush she could access anytime she sang for a crowd, there were only so many moments you'd get like that in a lifetime, and now hers had been spent. She had always been like a mirror to her sisters' hearts. When they were in pain, she was too, and walking back home from her mother's front stoop, she had assumed the sorrow she felt was on their behalf. Now she wasn't so sure.

ESTHER

"Stupid heifer-ass slut." Esther slammed the books into the used and discounted bin. "Fucking ho-ass tramp. Bitch-ass, frontin'-ass cow." And another pile was established with a dull thud. It had been a week since Ruth had changed all their lives, and Esther had expected her older sister to be pummeled with shame. Most women who got pregnant before they were married didn't tell a soul. You only knew by their mothers' tired eyes and downward glances at the church supper, the fabric stretched taut across their daughters' middles. Once, Lena's sister, Miss Beverly, faked a pregnancy to cover for her daughter, and that baby was ten years old now, and none the wiser. Then too, Mama had always whispered about an old woman fifteen miles from her in Louisiana who, for a fee, could send a baby back where it came from, wherever that was. It wasn't that Esther thought any of these approaches were sound. She was undecided on the existence of God and sin, at least in the way Preacher Thomas waxed on about it. Mama had even told them over dinner a few days before that she'd decided they needed to move forward. She had been trying to convince Mr. Franklin to take Esther and Chloe on, arguing that a duo constituted a group. So there was hope. Esther had expected to be relieved by that hope, but no. What if she couldn't hold a candle to Ruth after all? And that was the part that made her want her sister scorned.

Esther couldn't see the door from where she stood, and she hadn't stopped muttering when Horace walked in with his baby on his hip.

"Everything okay?" She nodded at Malcolm once she heard them enter. Horace cherished his breaks, and he only brought the boy in when he had no choice.

"I should be asking you the same thing. Who you in here cursing about? Somebody stole your bicycle?"

"Boy, nobody. Is everything okay with Malcolm?"

"Yeah, Vanessa had a doctor's appointment, that's all."

"Oh." Esther didn't like the little people, but for some reason she could tolerate this one and he seemed to know it. Every time he saw her, he stretched out his arms and babbled, drool slicking his chin.

"I got Lena's." Horace handed Malcolm to her, and she had no choice but to accept him while his daddy sat at the other end of the counter and emptied an overflowing paper bag. "Fried chicken for you, grits and the pepper sauce too."

"I ate my mama's breakfast."

"I figured. But maybe for lunch. You don't eat enough."

"You already know you gon eat my order and probably go back and get another."

"You might be right. You might be right." He had made the sign of the cross before he started, and now he dipped his fork in the container, closed his eyes, and moaned. "You had the gumbo there yet?"

That was what he was eating now. Esther ate like a bird—everyone in the family said it. She often said she wished she could take a pill instead of going to the trouble of preparing a meal, but she did remember Chloe raving about the food, and of course the girl had been gaining weight to match. When they were younger, people would tease them, saying Chloe should pass some of her excess weight over to Esther, who needed it. Ruth was perfect in the middle. Of course, Esther would always say something smart back, like "And your mama need to transfer some of her mustache to your daddy's bald head." Whoever overheard her would erupt. But the laughter seemed to only double her own pain.

"Now you know I don't eat everybody's gumbo," Esther said.

"Well, yeah, but that's what I'm telling you, you need to be eating this one. Lena was spooning tomato paste into hers and I stopped that. She wasn't using oysters either. People are coming asking for two bowls off the bat now. Her revenue went up 15 percent since I started learning her."

"We get it, we get it, you can cook."

"I don't know how you can smell this and not want a bite." He stood and held his spoon out to her, and she laughed and backed away, set the baby down on a rug in the center of the floor.

"Boy, you crazy. Leave me alone with all that." He chased her to the back room, the spoon so close to her face she could smell the oil in the roux when the bell on the front door chimed. Esther didn't pay it much mind; she more than assumed it would be Mr. Gaines or Lena, who ventured in during breaks to shoot the shit. She kept running, letting Horace approach closer each round. Then she caught the men out of the corner of her eye, and her mood drained on the spot.

There were three of them, all white, staring back at her, two she recognized and one she didn't; she supposed he was the new man she'd heard about from Horace. "Nice shop you got here," the new one said, and the baby started to cry. Horace and Esther both hurried to lift him and collided. Esther lingered next to her friend for a second longer than necessary for the comfort. White men didn't come into this store. They just didn't.

"Can I help you?" Horace stood up taller on the spot, and she could feel the men, white as they were—suited up and slack-bellied as they were, tweeded up and wing-tip-shoed as they were—become intimidated, and they backed up.

"I'm Mr. Belmont. How do you do? I'm looking to speak with the owner of the store," the new man said.

"That's me." Horace's words shot forward like they wanted to knock the man down. "My father passed it to me when he got too sick to run it."

"Family business, the cornerstone of the American dream." Mr. Belmont smiled.

"Something like that," Horace said, not smiling.

Mr. Belmont fixed his face too. "Is there somewhere private we could go to discuss matters, man-to-man?" he asked.

And Horace seemed embarrassed, though he was a big man and Esther had never seen him flinch, even now. She knew him well enough to know he was warring with how powerful to hold himself out to be.

"I don't have a problem with that." He passed the baby to Esther, and it seemed he was pleading with her with his eyes not to say anything too flip. She hesitated before she took Malcolm—she'd run through the other options in her mind and, out of protectiveness of Horace, she dialed them all back. She watched the men retreat to the back; then she carried the baby to the children's section, where she sat him against a bookshelf and read an alphabet book in high-pitched voices she'd sworn she'd never use. Her hands shook every time she flipped a page. Of course he squealed for her to read the book again each time she finished. She was on her third rendition when the white men walked out. She stood abruptly. She could see Horace was angry, red in his eyes and tight-lipped, but he opened the front door for the men anyway.

"Don't think too long," they said, and they winked at Esther and the baby and were on their way.

Esther started screaming before the door shut.

"Men's talk?" she said. "Men's talk? And I can't believe you accepted that. You, of all people, know how much I give to this store. I know our supplies backwards and forwards. I'm the one who opens in the morning. Most nights, I'm the one who closes too. I'm the one you call when you need a rush from the distributors. I'm the one the customers depend on to get them the right cure at the right time."

"I know all that, girl." He walked over and held her arms to her side where they'd been swinging before. The baby switched his head from one to another like they were characters on a big screen.

"But those were white men in there," Horace said. "White men. I wasn't thinking is all. I just wasn't thinking." He had lifted his hands from her now and was pacing. "I'm sorry, Esther," he said. "I know I couldn't do this without you. You know I know that."

"Thank you," she said. She had lowered her voice some, and the baby seemed bored by the calm, started to fuss. "I'm sorry too. I shouldn't have blown up. I just hated that I couldn't be in there with you. I was scared for you, Horace. What did they say?"

"They said they want to buy the store. They want to offer me money for my daddy's building, the only thing my family got left and the only way I feed that boy there." He nodded to Malcolm on the rug. His food at the counter where he'd been sitting had firmed and cooled. He broke off a piece of corn bread. "That new guy, Mr. Belmont or whatever, he offered a price." He pulled a white sheet of paper out of his pocket and passed it over to Esther. She gasped and covered her mouth. "They aim to buy up this whole block," he said.

"But I can't believe that," she said. "All these years, and nothing. Why today?" She had gone back to the books midway through their talk, and she focused on them now; organizing them in alphabetical order established a stability inside her.

"I wonder if there was a misunderstanding," she said. "I mean I just can't believe—"

"Believe it," Horace cut her off. The baby had crawled to his daddy's chair, tugged on his shoes, and reached up for him now. Horace lifted him, offered him corn bread, but the baby was busy grasping for his daddy's ear, trying to stuff the lobe in his mouth.

"That's more money than I ever seen at one time, Esther, but I'm not a fool. I'd take it and be through with it in a year, maybe two.

Then what? It took my daddy his whole life to save for this lot. I'm not throwing it away for a chunk of change."

"Everybody will feel that way." Esther felt shielded by her words.

"I don't know," Horace said. "A lot of people starting to fall on rough times. The shipyard jobs dried up. They not hiring us otherwise." The baby had grabbed a hardcover, plopped it between his lips, drool darkening the pages.

"You could talk to the neighbors," she said. "People listen to you. You could organize them, convince them what they're holding is worth more than what they'd get. We know that to be true. I mean if it weren't, white people wouldn't be offering it."

"That's for sure. White people ain't never struck a fair deal, and ain't no reason to expect them to start now."

"Amen"—they said it at the same time.

"I could help you," Esther said.

Horace raised his eyebrow, seeming as surprised as she felt.

"I mean, just because I already send out the newsletter. I could include an article in the next one."

"I thought it wasn't for that type of thing," Horace said.

"You want the help or not?" she asked.

He didn't answer her for some time, and they both just observed Malcolm. They'd have to air the book out to dry. Not a thing else had changed in his world.

"Alright," Horace said. "We ain't got nothing to lose, I guess."

"Alright," Esther said, and it came out more as a question, so she repeated it, tried to deepen her voice this time. "Alright." She paused. "It's just that the store means so much to me," she went on. "I don't want to even imagine who I'd be without it."

OVER THE NEXT WEEK, THEY WORKED ON THE NEWSLETTER ARTICLE together, a call to their neighbors to consider their legacy over short-term reward. Esther found that Horace had more animation than even she'd known, more spirit and more fire, but she had to pull his thoughts out of him one by one. Once she laid them down beside each other, she had to position them in the order that would maintain each one's shine. It reminded her of her mother orchestrating a sound, lining her and her sisters up so they'd blend, but this was different. She and Horace were equal here: she made them so by rooting for the stuff inside them both that was the same, the same frustration, the same hope, the same fear, and she distilled that on the page. When she was done, they looked at each other like they had been somewhere. Esther finished the September newsletter with Horace's story on the front, "Negro Ownership Is Negro Power," and within days, the neighbors began swarming in during their lunch breaks for copies.

The next week, they made their rounds. Of course, everyone they spoke to seemed to have already built a rapport with Horace: Lena, whose pies filled their bellies for every wedding, funeral, and baptism, and even Freddy, whom her mother spoke to sometimes but who otherwise wandered the Fillmore streets in silence. Horace greeted him like he was any other person, where even Esther's mother maintained an air of courtesy that read like superiority around him.

Not only that, Horace encouraged everyone to keep their property according to who he knew them to be, slanting his message so it was aimed at each person accordingly. To Mr. Gaines, he said, "I'm so tired of these people trying to reach in our pots, take all the meat out for themselves before it could provide any flavor," and the man turned his head up, considered Horace's words, and nodded.

When they visited Miss Gladys, whose hair stuck up in every direction, though she took such care with everyone else's, she pushed back, "But that new man, Mr. Belmont, is a gentleman. Always bringing the candy for the babies, always with a smile." Then, "We could sure use the money. If the price is right, shit, I might consider." She glanced around the salon, which was crowded like always, with women in various stages of improvement.

"It's not just about you, though," Horace started. "That's where you go wrong, when you start thinking about it that way, what might work for you, what might satisfy yours. And yeah, you know, maybe you're right, maybe that lil check they write you will tide you over til retirement and you been wanting to get off your feet anyway."

"I mean, he said it," Gladys said. She stood over a lady in a full roller set, and the two laughed together.

"Yeah, maybe so," Horace went on. "And maybe you could even find another spot of land elsewhere, if you did want to continue on, and maybe it'd be smack-dab in the middle of a sea of Negro heads, Negro customers. Maybe."

"From your mouth to God's ears."

"But it's like a stack of dominoes. How many ladies you got in that salon washing hair, drying hair, cutting hair, adding hair? Three, four?"

Gladys smiled a cautious smile. "Six some weeks," she said with pride.

"And what's gon happen to them when you sell? They gon be out of work. How they gon pay their rent? And it's not just you, when you sell, everybody else gon say, 'Well, she getting hers, we might as well get ours,' and then the whole block's out from under us." Gladys seemed embarrassed.

He turned to the woman beside her sitting under the dryer. She raised the hood to hear him better. "Then what you think they gon replace everything with?" he went on. "They been scoping out this neighborhood for years now, trying to steal something of value out of it. You think they gon replace it with another beauty salon like yours? Nah. It's gon be dolled up, sugarcoated, fanciest of the fancy businesses for them, businesses we can't afford, restaurants with food on the menu we can't even pronounce or banks where they won't let us borrow. Or maybe it will be a shopping center or a parking lot, and what you think gon happen then? You think they gon let those shiny white patrons come in here with the likes of us? Nah. They gon raise the prices on all this, on our storefronts, on our homes, and how many of us you think gon be able to afford it? How many?" he repeated.

Most of the customers were listening now, and a few passersby had lingered by the doorway.

"Pretty soon, it's not gon be the Fillmore no more; we won't recognize half the people we pass on the street; pretty soon, we won't be able to walk half a block for pecan pie or fried oysters; pretty soon, we'll have to start locking our doors, and that's the people who are able to stay. Pretty soon, you'll walk around these streets and you won't see yourself reflected back in it."

He turned away from Gladys toward the others, who had silenced their morning gossip and complaints to hear him. His voice rose.

"See, we can't just be thinking about ourselves. That's the way they do it, but Negroes have survived only off the strength of each other. And if we gon keep surviving, we gon have to keep nurturing that mentality. I'm not just thinking about me, I'm thinking more about your mama, your grandmama, your daddy, your sister and brother. And we don't have no choice but to be generous like that in our intentions 'cause nobody else is coming for us. If we don't build each other, we're going to be at the bottom of the barrel for the rest of our lives. That's what they want, Lord knows that's what they want, but we can't stand around and let them get their way. We can't let them take our basic rights from us. We've got to demand what we deserve."

He went on longer than the original comment warranted, and people listening absorbed him; they didn't want to let him go. It wasn't only them.

Horace caught Esther's gaze then, her total and absolute surrender to his words, and she was embarrassed, but not as much as she would have thought she'd be. She didn't have time to pretend, so she let her face be, and it seemed like Horace held tears in his eyes as he smiled.

"YOU WERE AMAZING," ESTHER SAID WHEN THEY WERE BACK INSIDE THE bookstore that evening. It was hard for her to look at him. There seemed to be light falling off of his person. "Where did you even get all that from?"

"It wasn't me," he said. "It was your newsletter. I never would have put all those ideas together. I wouldn't have been able to if you hadn't laid them out so easily."

"You're being modest," she said.

"I mean it. When I started, I didn't know what I was going to say, but it poured out of me as soon as I opened my mouth. I just saw myself talking to you, and when the words stopped flowing, I knew it was time to be silent."

Every night after that, she would go home and tug her notepad out of her mattress and craft lyrics. Later, she'd sit on the edge of Chloe's bed and hum the melody the way she envisioned it, and after a few runs, Chloe would sing over them. Chloe seemed to cherish them all, but one was her favorite, Esther's too:

You may see me as a distance runner
A fast-paced juggler on the road to a blunder
Oh no
Oh no
The world is changing fast

Then Esther would join her in harmony:

People are different now
No matter where you turn
The world is changing fast
No matter where you turn

"I feel this deep in my spirit," Chloe said when they finished. "Where did it come from?"

"I don't know," Esther said back. "I don't know."

Horace kept on canvassing the block, sharing the newsletter, urging people to ignore Mr. Belmont. Inevitably, his urging would evolve into a speech. At first there were just a few others in attendance, then crowds developed, and after a couple of weeks, people started to look for him. Esther would open up the bookstore in the morning and they'd be waiting outside the door. He'd apologize to her, but she'd shake her head. She didn't mind not being seen in lieu of him. Standing onstage next to Ruth her whole life had lowered her, but this was different. She was glad to see Horace getting recognition. She'd been the lone recipient of his brilliance for too long. Now he'd practice with her while they worked, outlining ideas, and she'd fish through her purse for her pen and clean his thoughts up, set them upright. That kind of thing had come so easily to her all this time, she hadn't known it could somehow be useful. And they were succeeding.

Gladys had been convinced that first day; Lena was on board. Mr. Gaines had all but agreed, and though he fussed and whined about it, Esther assured Horace it was just how he was. He would do the right thing. The only person they worried about was Mr. Bailey. He was known for forsaking any and everything for a dime, and the Champagne Supper Club was prime real estate. Horace had sat outside the club three days in one week, then traipsed back to the bookstore each time after with a worn-down expression on his face.

This last time, Esther had been angry at Mr. Bailey on his behalf.

"That ol' evil-eyed greedy piece of—"

"Not in front of the baby," Horace said.

"I'm just saying. You too nice to these people. You ought to let me go in and tell him what I think."

"That's exactly what we don't want," he said. "You saying something he won't be able to forget."

"Everything I say is unforgettable," she fired back. "This time I'll try to make it sweet too, though."

"No." He was serious, Esther could tell. "This is my daddy's shop. Let me handle it."

And she was hurt to hear that, of course she was, but she shrugged and said, "Fine, fend for yourself."

She didn't talk to him for the rest of the day. When he asked her questions about stock, she'd direct the answers to the baby in a singsong voice. She made a big to-do of shelving, though she knew he liked his quiet while he read the paper and drank his second cup of coffee. Finally, when it was time to close up, he stopped her at the door and gripped her wrist.

"Alright," he said. "You can come. But promise me you'll be on your best behavior."

"I won't say a word," she said.

SHE DRESSED UP FOR THE OCCASION, NOT ANYTHING LIKE WHAT SHE'D wear to a show but a basic shawl and a pair of slacks. She caught a reflection of herself in the club's window, and if she didn't know better, she might have thought she was her mother. She and Horace waited outside for an hour, and the whole while, people strode in and out of the club, mostly cooks and a bartender who had offered her a ride home one night. Everyone recognized her and nodded in her direction, asked about her mama and sisters, and with Horace there, she smiled and chatted with them like it was the most natural thing in the world, human connection. She was in the middle of a conversation when Mr. Bailey pulled up.

Horace stood and waited for him to step out of his dark blue Roadmaster Skylark. When he finally approached, Horace held out his hand, but Mr. Bailey looked past him to her.

"I'm Esther," she said in a soft voice. She reached out for him with a limp hand; seeing him there had whipped her back ten years at least.

"I know who you are," he said. "Come in off the street. I never do business outside."

The office off to the side of the entrance was pristine. Before they sat down, Mr. Bailey called for the nice bartender to bring him a whiskey straight. He didn't ask if they wanted anything. Once his drink arrived, he took a long sip, then set the glass back down on the chestnut desk. He wiped his mouth with the back of his hand, and then he looked up at Horace and Esther.

"I got a busy day ahead of me. How can I help you?"

Horace told him what he'd heard about the offers being made all over the block. He said he knew the club had been targeted too. He handed him the newsletter.

Mr. Bailey shook his head.

"It don't matter. I've already decided." He shrugged. "The price isn't near what I've built, but then again, business is slow. Especially since that girl got knocked up." He nodded in Esther's direction. "Didn't realize how popular you were, huh? I can't fill half my seats without you there. Too bad what happened with your sister."

"She's been blessed."

"Is that what they're calling it these days? Anyway, business is business. She got hers, I got mine. I figger these white people think they can come in and do it better, I might as well go on and let them."

He held up his hands. "I tried." He gestured for the bartender again and pushed back from the table. Esther felt like they should leave, but Horace kept on with the same points he'd been dishing out to the neighbors. There were Mr. Bailey's workers to consider for one, and then the Negro people in general. But it was futile; the man was unfazed. In the middle of Horace's sentence, the bartender interrupted with a pile of pancakes and bacon Esther had smelled frying. Mr. Bailey gestured to him—"You can see them out, Edward"—and first Esther, then Horace stood.

They were silent on the walk home. Esther took jabs at Mr. Bailey, the scant patches of hair he tried to disperse over his scalp, the gold rings barely visible on his fat fingers, but it only upset Horace more.

"I guess that's it then," he said.

"How can you say that after all we've done? How can that be it?" Esther said back.

The truth was, she didn't know if Mr. Bailey would change his mind, and she didn't know what would happen if he didn't, if that would trigger the rest of the block to concede too. All she knew was she had found something independent of her that demanded her attention. It was like a plant she'd need to water, a baby she'd need to feed, and she felt urgent in a way she hadn't in as long as she could remember. She couldn't give it up. She wouldn't.

AT HOME, CHLOE SAT AT THE KITCHEN TABLE, SPOONING LARGE HEAPS OF gumbo into her mouth.

"Lena's?" Esther asked, sitting too.

Chloe nodded, wiping her mouth with the cloth napkin on her lap.

"I understand Horace made it," Chloe said, in a singsong voice Esther had been trying to avoid.

"Is that right?" Esther looked down to hide her smile.

"You been seeing a lot of him lately, huh?" She plopped a slice of smoked sausage in her mouth. Esther didn't love gumbo, but the way

Chloe was eating and her knowledge of who the source was pressed on her stomach. She stood for her own bowl and spoon.

"It's not him," she said. "It's the cause, it's the movement. They're trying to run us out of here, starting with our businesses, and if they go, it's just a matter of time before we're all out on our feet." She spooned half of Chloe's remaining food into a new bowl.

"You sound just like him," Chloe said, "the little bits I've heard from the bookstore stoop. Seems like it's working too. Seems like everybody is in agreement."

Esther shook her head. "Everybody but Mr. Bailey." She was eating now like she hadn't in days. She spoke between bites. "We just left him. He's still mad about Ruth. He says his business went downhill since we've gone. He said he's lost half his customers. He said, 'You didn't know how important you were, huh, girl?' Something like that." She was figuring something out as she spoke.

Chloe finished and got up to wash the bowl, dry it, and place it back in the cupboard.

Esther could hear her mother turn her key in the lock.

"Other people have said the same," Chloe said, sitting again. "It's not only that for me." She paused. "It's just been so lonely without it." She rushed through the words almost like she wanted to get them out before her mother could hear them. There was a look in her eyes Esther recognized but couldn't name. It was odd. As much as Esther had devoted herself to the routines, the practices, the steps, the songs, as much hope as she'd had around taking the lead, she didn't miss it as much as she'd thought she would.

"It's been over a month," Chloe went on, and Esther found she was surprised to hear how the time had flown.

Her mother stood in the kitchen now.

"Everything okay?" she asked. And the girls nodded.

She joined them at the table and the conversation stopped in its tracks. Esther ought to have been used to this new silence. It had been over a month now with Ruth pregnant, over a month without rehearsals, over a month of wordless suppers, the relief at the end so enticing she'd rush through meals, though she normally labored over each bite. Sitting among them now felt as daunting as the first time. She made the mistake of locking eyes with her sister.

"Don't worry, Mr. Franklin can't run from me forever," Vivian joked. "We'll come up with something." But Esther could sense her heavy sadness. She had thought her mother would have bum-rushed them by now with another plan, one involving the two of them or others—she didn't know. But the woman seemed resigned. Every day she accepted Ruth's pregnancy more. Esther was starting to think Vivian might let the whole dream go, as unthinkable as that seemed.

And Chloe, who normally propped their moods up on instinct, looked away. Esther did too. Vivian's joke seemed to cut through the sadness, only to turn back and double its texture. Esther took the new slice of pain as an invitation to leave. Upstairs, though, she couldn't stop thinking of her sister. That had been hopelessness in Chloe's eyes. It had seemed foreign to her in that context, though Esther had been intimate with the feeling for many years now. She fell asleep with her clothes on and woke up with the feeling of cotton in her mouth that even when she brushed she couldn't escape.

"And this would further it," she heard herself say to Mr. Bailey the next morning. She and Horace had agreed to go back for one more attempt to dissuade him from selling. They'd only been seated three minutes when she spoke. She could see Horace in her periphery staring her down, his lips pressed together, probably waiting for her to revert to cursing, but she didn't think that was a possibility anymore.

"We could come in again, sing every week. Ruth wouldn't be there, so maybe it wouldn't work, but we could try it for a month, see how it goes, see if business picks up."

Before she'd left the house that morning, she and Chloe had embraced for a long time. If she looked back, it was the way the girl had clung to her that confirmed her decision.

Now Mr. Bailey sucked crawfish heads while he read the news. He set the paper down and licked his fingers before he cut Esther off. He offered her a tail, and she shook her head.

"You think you can put on just as good of a show without your sister, girl?" he asked.

"I know it," she said back. She didn't recognize the certainty. If you had asked her an hour earlier, she would have said with as much conviction that she knew the opposite.

He sat there in silence again, sucking the juice from the red capsule, pulling his handkerchief from his pocket, and wiping it from his chin before it dribbled down his neck anyway. She could see Horace without shifting her head. He had never turned away from her. She couldn't read his expression, some juncture of fear and respect.

"You sure now, girl?" Mr. Bailey repeated. "You talked to your mama about this?"

She nodded, though it wasn't true. She wouldn't have had to. If there was one thing she knew, it was that Vivian would have approved of chasing a dream.

"Alright, I'll tell the white folks to hold off. We'll see how it goes. And mind me, don't embarrass me, girl. The Champagne Supper Club was the first of its kind, the best of its kind. The magic you find here you can't re-create anywhere. Why I was so resistant to selling it in the first place."

Esther was already on her feet. She reached out her hand, then thought better of it and clasped his elbow instead.

"You won't regret it," she said. "You won't regret it."

"I already regret it," he said back, but he was smiling too, and soon, she was out the door, and Horace was on her heels. They reenacted the conversation together for some time. After, he said he just wanted to unwind. Vanessa had the baby. Would she go to a movie with him? She wanted to, of course she did, but more importantly, she didn't have time to come up with an excuse. They saw the new Audrey Hepburn flick, *Roman Holiday*. Esther loved movies and usually she arrived early, engrossed even by the previews about Communist spy rings or biowarfare. Then she lingered in the theater after the credits ran, after the Negro men with brooms turned on the lights to sweep out the popcorn and ticket stubs, because it was so hard, harder to explain, to step back into her own small life. But this time, she stood up as soon as the theme music started. She had tried not to look at Horace when the couple onscreen kissed, but she'd shot glances at him otherwise, marveled at the way he couldn't keep still, like his mind was roaming, and his hands couldn't tell who to pledge allegiance to, his creased and veined brown hands. They'd lie flat in parts, and then he'd hold one and smooth it out, then shift to the other. By the end, his foot was tapping and his leg was shaking, and Esther, on instinct, the way she might have with Chloe or even Ruth, placed her hand atop his knee to calm him. He stopped in an instant and she jerked back.

When they had left the lobby of the theater, she rushed into conversation: what she would do to see the Spanish Steps, the Mouth of Truth, and the Colosseum.

"Same," he said. "And the pyramids and Table Mountain and Victoria Falls. When I was a boy, I used to dream about the sites we'd read about in school: Yosemite and Joshua Tree and Alcatraz and Golden Gate Park. I lived right here, but I hadn't even seen the beauty of the place. My daddy was always working. Even in the best months, you know we not making out like bandits. That was always an issue for Vanessa."

He glanced at her fast like he wanted to catch something, like her reaction in that exact second might be monumental, might have the power to change the course of his assessment of himself, of his life. She didn't know what to say that would meet the magnitude of his stare so she just gazed back.

"It's good work," she said. "Noble work. The best kind doesn't reward you in the ways you would expect."

And she swore she saw him exhale.

At her door, she was about to make some kind of joke to discharge the heavy silence between them, but before she could start, he leaned in to kiss her.

She laughed. She could see the hurt spread across his face.

"I'm sorry," she said.

"No, it's me, I'm sorry. I was just, I think I got carried away with the news today."

"Of course, of course you did," she said. "It's no problem. "I'll see you in the morning then." She was already halfway up the stairs.

"See you," he said. She couldn't make it inside fast enough, though once she was in there, she wanted to be anywhere else. She hadn't thought about Mr. Sterling in months, but he was back now, laughing in her ear. She couldn't even remember his face anymore, just the color of his skin, so similar to Horace's, and his eyes when he came to, full of regret.

VIVIAN

The Sunday Mr. Franklin was scheduled to attend Shiloh Baptist, Vivian washed and rolled her hair, sat under the dryer reading the word, then dressed in her purple three-quarter-length-sleeve knit swing dress. She set her black circle hat atop her long curls, and she rooted through her cosmetic bag for a pink shade of lipstick that accented the blush on her cheekbones. She let the girls sleep in and played her gospel numbers low. She hummed instead of singing; she fried shrimp to go with the grits, and she sat on the roof with her coffee for some time before she called for everyone to get ready. She didn't rush them. She pulled the car up to the front of the house and waited, humming all the while. Late as they were, they got the best parking spot again, the one right next to Preacher Thomas. And as if to welcome them, when they walked in halfway through the second number, the heaviest woman in the choir, Sister Nancy, fell to her knees, calling out for the Lord to hold her place back home.

Soon one morning
I'm gonna lay down my cross

Vivian wasn't healed, far from it, but talking to Preacher weeks earlier had peeled back a layer of her anguish, enough so that, though it still sat firm inside her, she could maneuver around it. She could smile at the patients at work, access the soft tone she reserved for the ones she favored. She hadn't spoken to her children much, but she could cook beside them; she could listen to them laugh among themselves. And when those moments too became unbearable, she revisited Preacher's words.

Because of that, when he got up on that podium, she felt like the two of them were joined. As he paced back and forth, she felt her own heart picking up speed. And as he shouted "Can I hear an amen?" she didn't need to respond, not verbally. It was her own mind and heart that had caused him to say that phrase in the first place, and so answering it would have been redundant.

And then he asked, "How many of y'all follow Christ?"

And they all raised their hands, including Mr. Franklin from the first pew. And Preacher went on and asked again, "No, I'm serious, how many of y'all actually follow Christ our Lord Jesus? Not in the church with your hats perched just so and your lipstick lined up and your dress sashaying in that good Northern California breeze. I'm not talking about how you rallied yourselves to get here and present like you do. I'm not even talking about the prayers you mouth back to me or the saints up there on the stage knocking their heads back, all 'Lalalalala,' and Lord, you know I love the singing. I love the heft of it, the surprises inside every verse, the sacredness of it, the sensuality of it, yeah, I said it, there's something sensual about praising God. It feels almost like—yeah, you know what I'm talking about." And he winked at Vivian, and though she hadn't known that feeling, not from another person in so long, she could feel it now as sure as another body was inside her.

"I'm not talking about all that," he said. "I wish I was. Don't I wish I was. Wouldn't it be easier? Wouldn't it be easier if we could just buy our way to Him, if we could just impress Him with our short skirts and our manly arms? If He was moved by our learning? If we could memorize our way to Him? If I could recite my favorite verses and that would win His favor, I'd be fine. There are a few I keep tucked in my heart for my lowest moments, and we all have those moments, and they lift me during those times, but they can't take me all the way. As powerful as they are, they just can't get me to Him.

"Not even my personal favorite: 'One thing have I desired of the Lord, that will I seek after; that I may dwell in the house of the Lord all the days of my life, to behold the beauty of the Lord, and to enquire in his temple.' I used to recite it every morning, but no. No matter how many times I repeated it, I'd be met with silence. Silence. And as believers, we're going to always run up against that silence when we think we can bribe God. When we think we can say, 'I'll give you this, and you give me peace,' or 'I'll give you that, and you'll give me salvation.' It doesn't work like that. I'm afraid it doesn't work like that. There's something more, and I'm not saying I found it."

There was a gasp from within the congregation.

"I'm not. I'm trying to find it same way you are. It's a constant quest and I need help from you today to get there, but I've had moments along the way where I've been reminded, with a conviction I can't put into words, that I'm close. And I want us to put our heads together and study one of these moments today. I have to admit, I'm almost embarrassed to reference it in front of the godly folk in front of me this evening, people who may have forgotten about youthful indiscretions. But when I'm going through something, church, I like to look back at other experiences when I've questioned Him to remind myself that doubt, weakness, and confusion are only designed to carry me forward, to Him."

The church let out a loud, harmonious moan as they were wont to do anytime Preacher spoke, and he let them go as long as they needed to, smiling all the while.

"Tell it, Preacher," one of them shouted and the others followed suit.

"Nah, I think it's safe, though, I think I'm among friends, am I right, church? Alright, I'll go on then. This story is about a woman I wanted when I was a young man. My sister's best friend. Fellas, let's shout out 'Amen' right here on the spot on behalf of our sisters' friends. I'll tell you a little bit about this one in particular: She kept up one of those Coke-bottle shapes, was a nice nutmeg shade of brown, long hair past her bra strap, and don't get me started on that strap. What? I'm a preacher, I'm not blind, church. And I would have done anything to be with that woman, anything, and I'm talking about just being with her, just talking to her, just hearing about her life. It was like my calling was tied up with how close we could be, how much I could know about her."

"But there was just one problem. She was engaged to be married to somebody else. Yeah, just one little small problem. I was young then, so I didn't know any better, and I fought it. I sent her chocolates, I brought her my mama's fresh hot cross buns, crawfish wrapped in newspaper, I even bought her a ring. Like I told y'all, I didn't know any better. I would invite her places pretending I needed a friend, like I didn't want to make her my wife. And I thought my plan was going well until I saw my sister in our living room being fitted for her bridesmaid dress."

The church groaned on behalf of his younger self.

"I know, I know, but you know what, I told myself my woman just didn't have the nerve to tell her beau yet, that she would. I got a wedding invitation in the mail, all sparkly and white, and I told myself she was trying to save face. Then the actual day arrived, and I dressed up in the only suit I owned. Mama had to take the hem out the pants for them to cover my socks, but I looked good. I had a fresh haircut, laid the kinks down into waves with pomade, had grown in a new mustache. I was young then, church, twenty-five pounds lighter, and you couldn't tell me I wasn't Nat King Cole in my daddy's church. See, my daddy presided over all the Negro weddings in the parish, and I walked inside that small brick building, through the crowds of people

I'd known all my life, and I snuck toward the back where the ladies had dressed, and I said I had a message to take to my sister. I folded up a note I'd written and handed it to her, told her to give it to the bride straightaway. How many of y'all already know what the note said?"

The church hollered here, all "Read it, Preacher."

"You know what, you know what, I won't read it. I don't need to embarrass myself in front of y'all again. It doesn't matter what it said. I watched my sister walk down that aisle with her beau at the time, the man she'd eventually marry, and then I watched the other bridesmaids. Then the flower girls walked down in their tiny white gowns, and I just knew she wasn't going to meet her father at the top of that aisle. I just knew she wasn't. I actually stared down her groom with a hint of smugness, but sure enough, she was the prettiest bride I'd ever seen, and I bawled into my handkerchief like a baby, my mama beside me rubbing my back. I don't think she ever realized why I was crying and I never made her any the wiser."

The church was offended now, moaning in vicarious shame.

"Oh, Preacher, you didn't deserve that, Preacher."

"For a year I cried every night over that woman. I never been closer to God than that year. I read the Bible and I cried. I read the Bible and I cried and I prayed. I didn't understand why God kept me from that lady until the day I met my wife.

"Mrs. First Lady Mattie Jefferson Way. Mm-hmm. Yes, Lord. I'm going to say it again for the people in the back. Mrs. First Lady Mattie Jefferson Way. I knew I was going to marry her the first time I laid eyes on her. We were in my hometown, New Orleans, and there was a French market there every Sunday. I went looking for a pound of beef for my mama—she wanted to make stew for Sunday dinner. Well, this girl was standing next to her mama at one of the stands, calling out, 'Fresh seafood for supper.' I looked at her, and she looked at me. One thing led to another, and next thing I knew, Mama and I enjoyed a fish fry that evening. And it was like that ever since. She called up something in me that made me want to do for her, anything she needed, and part of it was she didn't take advantage of that, she gave it back to me tenfold, and so when she died—" He stopped here to steady himself, and from deep inside Vivian's own grief—the grief she was to this day afraid to poke at the wrong time because though it was often dormant, it ran deep—she could tell he had run up against a tender spot.

"It was like there was an envelope of my heart she opened up when I met her, an envelope I didn't even know was there, and when she died, that envelope closed, but it wasn't a tight seal, and anybody in this room who's lost somebody"—and he looked at Vivian when he said that—"anybody in this room who's lost somebody knows what I mean when I say I don't know if it's going to ever shut, not all the way, and that's where I am now, church, just like she died yesterday, and I know what it means. I know what it means because I've been there before. It means I've got to get close. Church, I've got to get close. Because what did He say when Paul asked Him, when he besought the Lord thrice, that the thorn he spoke of might depart from him? What did God say? God said unto him—what did He say, church? Tell it." And the congregation recited the verse with him.

"'My grace is sufficient for thee: for my strength is made perfect in weakness.'"

"'My strength is made perfect in weakness,'" Preacher repeated. "My strength is made perfect when we're close. And this is just like the last time. For years I didn't know why my sister's friend hadn't become my wife, but I had to trust in those years that God knew, that God had a plan that was greater than any I could envision. And that's what I'm doing right now, in the midst of this grief, in the midst of this despair, I'm leaning on Him. And just like last time, I'm close. I'm close, I'm close, I'm close. Look at your neighbor and touch him and tell him I'm close. I'm so close I can feel that He and I are one. I'm close when I've surrendered to him even in the deepest pain. It's one thing to get on your knees and pray that He'll relieve you, it's one thing to beg it of Him, even to praise Him once it's done, but sometimes it's not in His plan to salvage you. You ever notice that, church? That sometimes it's not in His plan to set you free just yet, sometimes there's something you need to see on your own to free yourself, and He's waiting for you to hit on it. And that surrender, that faith in His plan, in His comfort over my own, that's when I'm a follower, that's when I am indeed in Christ and He is in me. When I say to him, 'Lord, you have your way, I don't need to be joyful right now. I don't need to be in understanding right now. You take the wheel, Lord, and I'll wait on you to tell me when it's time to act.'"

The congregation was out of their seats now, winding their way through the cramped aisles, the ushers tapping on boxes of Kleenex, wiping their own eyes where they leaked or holding women up who were threatening to fall out, fanning men whose eyes popped, mangled words streaming out of their mouths. And Vivian didn't remember standing, only that she found herself upright, running up and down with the other saints, speaking in a language she had never been taught. But if someone had asked her what she intended to say, she would have been able to provide a perfect translation: that she had found in the depth of her sorrow some justification for it, some recompense, that He was with her.

"And the Lord doesn't just knowest my downsitting and mine uprising, He doesn't just understandest my thought afar off, but everybody else's too, and if I"—and Preacher looked at Mr. Franklin deeply when he said this—"if I were to take another servant of the Lord off His course, or begrudge her for obedience, though it impeded my own worldly plans, well, 'Let us not therefore judge one another anymore: but judge this rather, that no man put a stumbling block or an occasion to fall in his brother's way.'"

And that was when the choir started, directing them all to sit, and the song came out a low rumbling at first:

Let us break bread together on our knees;
Let us break bread together on our knees.

"But how many of y'all have tried to do it your own way, tried and tried to do it your own way, and it just never materialized?" Preacher slowed his speaking down now, raised his voice a notch to be as clear over the choir. "What does a follower do when her dreams don't materialize the way they were supposed to? When things change? When God's path looks different than yours?"

Vivian clutched her own Bible to her chest.

The choir rose higher now.

Let us drink wine together on our knees;
Let us drink wine together on our knees.

"What about when you finally found a job that would make you want to get up in the morning and they went with the white man, didn't even let you through the front door? What about when you poured all your heart and soul into that new restaurant and you got the best barbecue in the Fillmore and you just know the line's going to stretch down the block just as good as it stretches for Jack's or as good as it stretched for New Orleans Swing Club back when it opened, and then you show up and nobody's there? What about when you made a business deal and something came up, somebody came up and stole it right from your lap? What about then, church? What do you do then? What does a follower do, church?" And this time, he was standing right in front of Mr. Franklin and he rested a hand on the man's shoulder before he walked back to the altar, still going:

"You have to surrender. That's when you have to say, 'Lord, I might not get it the way I want it, but I know there's something out there for me, and it may look different than my little mind might have imagined it, but it doesn't mean I won't have glory. It may not be the exact kind, but it doesn't mean my life won't hold favor.'"

And seeing where this message had always been intended to land filled Vivian with a grace she hadn't known outside her daughters' gigs. She couldn't look away. Preacher didn't look back, but she knew he could feel her just like she could feel him this whole time.

"And that's the real test. Because it hurts. Everybody in here has gone through something that hurt like hell getting through because we put our everything into making it happen. It was our Eden, it was our baby, it was our ark, it was our burning bush, it was our deliverance, and we did everything we could and we just couldn't yield fruit. But what if we just said, 'Okay'? If we just said, 'Okay, God, I'm going to give this over to you. It hurts me, but I'm not going to fight it anymore, I'm going to give it to you anyway.' That's what it means to abide in Him, church, that's when you know your soul belongs to Him."

And the choir took it away.

Let us praise God together on our knees;
Let us praise God together on our knees.
When I fall on my knees
with my face to the rising sun,
O Lord, have mercy on me.

And when the ushers reached her aisle with their baskets, Vivian dug into her purse to reach for ten dollars she didn't have, and after closing announcements, she stood and shook everyone's hand hard and long. She let the other congregants greet Preacher before her and listened to them praise him, watched him lower his head with humility. Depending on the person, sometimes he smiled, and sometimes he closed his eyes, rested his hand on their backs, and offered a prayer. When it was her turn, they stood there in silence.

"That was some mighty good preaching there," she said finally. "Haven't heard it like that since I was back on the farm."

He laughed. "I'm glad it suited you."

"Yeah, there were some points I wanted to explore with you,

though, some that flew over my head. Maybe you can come by and we can talk them through." She had been looking at the ground, and now she lifted her head so her eyes fixed on his.

He seemed like he was stopping himself from laughing, his eyes dancing, and she remembered that boy in his daddy's church who wanted a woman so bad he believed he could stop her from meeting that aisle.

"That'd be some nice," he said back, still smiling with his eyes.

"Well, alright then, let's plan on it."

On the way to her car, she passed Mr. Franklin in front of his Cadillac, all decked out in his gray-striped suit. He had been dodging her since she told him about Ruth, but seeing him now, she wasn't desperate, nor was she afraid. She nodded at him.

"Good day, Mr. Franklin," she said.

"Good day, Miss Vivian," he said back. "I'll see your girls at the club on Friday then?" he asked.

And she was about to tell him he was mistaken when Esther walked by, squeezed her arm, winked, and kissed her on the cheek.

"We'll see you then, Mr. Franklin," the girl called out over her shoulder, seeming like a new woman. A new woman indeed.

CHLOE

Chloe wasn't fully asleep when the phone rang, but she was close, and it took a few rings for her to lift the receiver.

"You remember that white boy from the Supper Club?"

"Good morning, Tony." Her voice came out like a growl. She hadn't even brushed her teeth. It had been weeks since she'd gone out with him and they'd encountered the white man. All this time Tony hadn't said a word about him. She didn't know what had sparked one now.

"And I've been wondering why he didn't step to me. Then I ran into Betty last night, and she told me he's been coming to the club asking about *you*."

"Oh, Tony, you know you can't believe everything ol' Betty says. People see what they want to. He didn't ask me for my number. He let me leave separate. How interested could he have been?"

Tony was silent for a while like he was considering her angle, like he wanted to believe it, to accept it and roll it up into a bundle that might warm him, but after a minute, he broke in again.

"No, ma'am, I heard it direct from Betty. Chloe and white boys, I never would have thought it. I'm through with them anyway. On my way home, I got a whistle from that red bartender. Joann's brother, matter of fact. I always thought he took to men, but this confirmed it. He asked me for my number and everything. Didn't even make me work for it. We're going out this weekend. I'm glad that lil white boy was into you the whole while. I mean, at first I was embarrassed, of course, and to hear it from Betty, of all people, but the more I thought about it, the more I thought about that handsome red thang, I started thanking my lucky stars. I thought, damn, 'The Lord is my strength and my song; he has given me victory.' That's how they say it at Shiloh, huh? That's how my mama used to say it." He got quiet then, and she knew to change the subject.

"I'll be at your house Friday for the supper."

"You better."

"And I'm singing later that night. At the Champagne Supper Club."

"I know, and ol' Red Ed gon be working too. I wouldn't miss it. You better put on a show."

She paused. "You really think Betty was right, Tony?" she asked. She regretted it as soon as it was out.

"Of course she was right. Betty ain't got but two licks of sense; ain't enough moving around upstairs for her to be inventive. Anyway, once I thought about it, it was obvious to me too. Not like it matter. Vivian would tear up your hide if she found out you were fondling anything but a microphone. And then for him to be white? Please, girl. Better luck getting a camel through the eye of a needle. Is that what they say? Yeah, that's what they say. I got to go. See you, bye."

REHEARSAL HAD STARTED EARLIER THAT WEEK, AND AS GRUELING AS IT was packing routines made for three into the shape of a duo, it had been glorious to find her way back to the sound, to lose time on that roof while she spun and dipped and swooped, and she'd walked down to the kitchen and declined the 7Up cake her mama pulled out of the oven. It seemed extraneous to indulge again when she had so thoroughly been filled.

That weekend, Chloe convinced her mama to end rehearsal early so she could make groceries: ham, chicken to fry, cornmeal, yams, pasta, milk, and cheese. She didn't have to read a list anymore, nor did she consult her mother's old cookbooks, her pristine handwriting in the margins. The first night, two years ago, in Tony's aunt's hot kitchen, they'd eaten, then played bid whist, then eaten again. Tony had said it was the best food he'd tasted since his mama left. His mama had kicked him out once she found his dirty magazines, and he'd moved in with his aunt, who died of a stroke two weeks later. His aunt hadn't paid off the note, not by a long shot, but it was hers, and she had left it for Tony. It had been Chloe's idea to start the suppers. She'd fix them, and Tony would stand outside every Friday at five hustling them to anybody who passed with an empty belly. The money went to the mortgage, as did collections from Tony's various men.

Now Tony hurried down his front stairs, his arms outstretched for the bags. "You got the drumsticks?"

"Of course I got the drumsticks."

"I'm just saying. 'Cause last time you ain't get the drumsticks. And that white meat just sat there all cold and neglected. Like a pair of perfect C cups in my bedroom."

WHEN CHLOE WAS DONE COOKING, SHE DRESSED FOR THE NIGHT. SHE could hear Tony from downstairs hawking the meals.

"Beans and rice so good you gon swear you back in Louisiana sitting in somebody's bayou. Make you think you Creole, Black Millie. Yeah, even you. And that cobbler, make you slap your mama. Well, not your mama, Lexington, she'll knock your teeth out. But somebody else's. Shit, mine, if you could find her."

Chloe always did herself up, and today in Tony's bathroom was no exception. Mama had trained her on that front, but this time she surpassed even Vivian's instruction. There was the gown and the eye shadow and the powder and the eyeliner and mascara, and it was true she had put on weight, but it hit her in the right places. She hadn't lost the hourglass shape that dripped from her bloodline, but her hips had spread out, her breasts too. She stared at herself until she could no longer hear Tony's voice; then she made her way back downstairs.

"Hot mama!" Tony walked back in with the now empty cardboard box and set it on the counter.

Chloe just nodded, reached into her purse to re-dab her lipstick.

"What you going to sing?"

She told him and he nodded.

"One of my favorites."

"I remember."

"And where's Esther?"

"Meeting me there; she had to work."

"Had to work ol' Horace. Nah, I'm just playing. I know she wouldn't be late for that. Well, I guess I got to be the one to tell you to make sure you punch that high note at the end, that's the one that's gon send the crowd straight to the top."

"All your advice, you might as well come out there just like Esther. Or Ruth."

"No, lil mama, don't get no ideas now, I was just telling you to make sure you hit the top note hard."

"I always hit the top note hard."

"Well, then hit it hardest tonight. I'ma go get dressed. Between you and me, we'll give that lil red thang something he ain't never seen before."

OUTSIDE THE CLUB, THE WHITE MEN WHO SCOURED THE NEIGHBORHOOD in their suits, silk ties, and saddle shoes stood like they were waiting for somebody. Esther and Horace had been up in arms about them. To Chloe, they were harmless just like always, though it was true a new man was with them today. They all held their hands in their pockets, sweat visible on their red brows, their eyes on their shoes, then around them again. Esther had said Mr. Bailey promised not to sell, so she didn't know why they were still lurking.

"Don't pay them no mind." Tony pushed past them. "They just beggars"—and he said it loud enough for them to hear as he and Chloe stepped inside and felt the door flutter at their backs.

ESTHER WAS WAITING BY THE BAR, THOUGH SHE DIDN'T DRINK, AND CHLOE had the nerve to be disappointed. She would never admit it aloud, but the few times she had performed alone had been her favorites. She wasn't sucked dry wondering if Esther was going to remember the bridge. And there had always been a faint resentment hovering over her spirit whenever she heard Ruth hit a note she could have surpassed if she ever had the opportunity to prove it. Still, she had come to depend on her sisters, and she hugged Esther tighter than normal. Like always, the place was packed. She didn't drink before she sang, but Tony bought two rum and Coca-Colas anyway. "This one's for you," he mouthed from the bar, and she nodded, her attention elsewhere. The girl scheduled just ahead of her had started rounding out her show. She was a beautiful woman, like Ruth, and men who didn't know the difference between a soprano and an alto had pulled their chairs up to the lip of the stage, hanging off of her every line, her every move, like it was all they could do not to jump over and rip her out of her gown. And just like always, once the bridge hit and the chorus trailed off and the two-stepping off the stage began, Chloe could feel the flurries in the pit of her belly mounting. Ruth would say, *Eat something*, and her mama would say, *Girl, if you don't calm down right this minute, they gon boo us out of here*. But they were both gone now.

"You're going to be okay." Esther gripped her hand, and Chloe had the feeling Esther was the one who was most nervous.

"I know," Chloe said in a near whisper.

She told herself to pull it together. Tony was back beside her. He had already sucked his drink down and was sipping on hers. "They filled it up too high," he said. He seemed to sense her nerves. "That girl up there ain't got nothing on you, Chlo. You neither, Esther."

"She got the attention of all the men in here," Chloe shot back.

"Not for long, baby. Not for long."

The girl was nearly off the stage now on the final leg of James Brown.

The women in the audience rolled their eyes, staring into the bottoms of their drinks, and not many clapped. But the men raced over to the stairs just to be there when Miss Thang would descend in half an hour. Chloe and Esther would be mid-show by then, and half their audience would be occupied following her over to the bar.

The announcer was talking up the girls now.

"They have opened for the Caravans, won Talent of the Year at the Flamingo, and of course they'll be gracing our stage every week here at the Champagne Supper Club. You may remember them as the Salvations, but they are all grown up now. Let me be the first to say we are so glad they are. Please give it up for Miss Esther and Miss Chloe Jones."

They were halfway on the stage by the time he finished. Chloe was glad they had chosen "Teardrops from My Eyes." She would lead it, naturally, and she could sing the song in her sleep. Sure, she was used to Ruth's rendition, but she had soared beyond her mother's strict standards since her older sister left, practiced twice a day instead of once. Mama had been right about the jump ropes, right about running the chords, right about all of it really, the ardor she demanded, because when it came down to it, when Chloe was on top of the stage, all the self-doubt, all the worry vanished, and there was nothing taking up space in her body but the thrill. She felt like she was floating above herself, out of space and time, watching with amusement, admiration too, at the body she'd been given—who had taught it how to move like that? And that voice—even in her darkest hours, she knew she had been dreamed up by some sort of creator; she must have been to have arrived in this world with such a gift.

The truth was she was looking around too. There was Mr. Franklin to consider, scarcely visible in the back, and maybe she was being naive, but she still held out hope he'd consider them as a duo. And of course, though she hadn't mentioned it to Tony, she was half hopeful the white man would return. She hadn't seen him since the first time, but she remembered everything about him, his gray wool trousers and loafers, the fedora he wore until he'd walked over and taken it off. She remembered that his hair was a light brown color, not quite blond but close; that he'd shaved that morning, but an aggressive patch resisted, especially above his chin. And then there was the way he looked at her, like he had discovered something precious and still couldn't believe no man had come before him to claim it. Times like these, a microphone in her hand, she came close to feeling that way about herself.

The crowd floated with her now, more than usual even. And she felt the reason for it. She had found her way inside this song, to the chord that enveloped it and also the one that had prompted it in the first place, like she was with Mr. Rudy Toombs when he wrote it, sitting at his feet. Miss Brown was there too, swishing her hips and snapping her fingers, and they were all one in this wave of God they had found to ride. She wanted to soar with it higher and higher, but the tune was softening now.

And that's when she saw him, standing right in the spot he was last time. She was belting out a word here or there, and Esther must have been too, but it was like Chloe couldn't even hear her, just her own groans and moans, exhalations. Normally she felt odd delivering sounds and tones so primal, but they fit today, seeing how close she had come to the light. Any second, the crowd would be clapping. Most performers craved this part, but for her it was an announcement that she wasn't in charge anymore, that she had surrendered the miracle to the beholders, and some of them would accept it for what it was and some of them would not. She didn't know which category the man would fall in, but it mattered to her and she was only halfway ashamed.

The crowd lost it, even less confined than she'd seen them for Miss

Thang earlier. They begged for an encore, and she would have done one, would have done more than one, but Esther was already offstage, and anyway there was the man whom she would have to see to. Of course nothing would happen, but the crowd's applause right now made her think that this club had accessed magic somehow, that the constraints of the world didn't affect it, and if they spoke for a few minutes and a power flowed between them that kept her standing the rest of this week the way it had the last time, then so be it. It wouldn't leave this place. What business did Chloe have with a white man, as well as Vivian had taught her?

She took her time taking off her stockings. If she knew Esther, she would be out the door and back to the bookstore in ten minutes flat, and Chloe wouldn't want to beat her downstairs, not with the plans she was already half forming. She didn't always bring a second dress, but she had hoped to linger, and it turned out she had been right. And even that was a touch of magic that had bled onto the night because most of the things she had wanted—a boy in middle school she had named all of her kids behind, her sisters to stay with her until they were old enough to move far off together—those things hadn't come to be, not one of them.

She walked down the stairs like each one was its own destination. She was afraid of what she'd see on the other side. When she did make it down, he was there. Though there were more whites there tonight, there was no mistaking him, in a different plaid shirt and browner slacks, but otherwise looking just as he had before. Only this time she was looking back. He nodded toward the bar, then turned toward it, and she followed.

He placed an order for both of them, a rum and Coke for her and a gin and tonic for himself, just like last time. He handed her her drink. Another comedian had come onstage, and the white boy would start a sentence or she would, and then the crowd's laughter would cloak their words, and they'd have to ask each other to repeat themselves. After a while, they stopped trying to talk, but she would glance at him while he watched the stage, then turn away when he glanced back. At one point she caught his eye and stayed with it, and an interesting sensation filled her, a connection despite the odds against it. She recognized it, like in that story Preacher told, when the crowd from different countries heard the apostles speak and understood them, each in his own language.

"You were amazing," he said when the comedian finally finished up his act.

"Thank you," she said, embarrassed.

"I'm serious. It was like watching somebody with superhuman powers, the way you swept up that room. I went to jazz clubs every night back home. Crystal Caverns and the Howard Theatre and the Lincoln Theatre too. I've seen all the greats up close and I'm telling you, you're right there with them. Of course you know this already." He blushed. "I'm sorry, I'm going on and on about something that's obvious to you. Forgive me, I'm just in awe."

She smiled, took a sip. "It's okay. I appreciate it; it's the kind of thing you can never hear too much." She laughed.

"How long have you been performing?"

"Since I could talk," she said without thinking, the liquor quickening her pace. "I can't even imagine my life without it. Of course, my mama wouldn't let me even if I wanted to." She laughed again. "It started out as her dream, see. My mama is more lioness than woman. She's not of this world, not really. I never met somebody with so much energy, with so much ambition, too much for her small body, and she has to pour it into all of us. It's just me and Esther now. My sister Ruth gave it up." Her speaking slowed here. "I wanted to convince her to stay. She hated it, I knew she did, and I'm not usually a selfish person, but I couldn't imagine getting out of bed in the morning without this. I just knew if she left it, it would be taken from me too. But Esther talked to the owner and convinced him to let us try this duo out. I just hope she continues with it, she's fallen in love with writing these speeches, and if she left . . ." She trailed off, realized she'd been rambling. "We were lucky," she finished. She looked up with that last declaration like he had asked her a question.

"Why can't it just be you anyway?" he asked. "Today, you were unbelievable out there." He asked the question so casually, it frightened her. Of course that had crossed her mind many times, but he complimented her like it was a fact, irrefutable. She was flattered. Still, it felt like she'd be taking something away from Esther, from her mother, if she agreed.

"Nah." She shook her head, sipped again. "You can't get anywhere singing by yourself these days. Mama's clear on that. So is Mr. Franklin, why he needs a girl group, why we lost our chance." She pointed Mr. Franklin out at the bar. She told the story of him and Ruth, the sermon and all, and the white boy laughed so hard his shoulders shook. Chloe didn't drink for a while, beholding that. It was Esther who normally induced that level of glee when she spoke, or Tony, but here she was, altering this strange man's mood.

"The deal is most likely off," she said, "but we'll see," she added.

"So is it your favorite thing to do in the whole world?" he asked.

"What's that?"

"Performing."

"Oh." And she looked down and smiled a private smile before she answered. Nobody had asked her that before. She hadn't known it mattered.

"Maybe." She looked up. "Maybe not as much as my mama. She wakes up inhaling music, and for the rest of the day that's what sustains her. It's the glory for her. But me, I've dug out a part of it that's mine. Even my mama can't touch that part. She's never been on a stage, she's never battled the nerves just before, she's never sung to people whose minds were so far off the club might as well have been empty. She's never heard the applause, not that it changes anything for me, not anymore. The feeling I get up there is the same either way. I disappear inside that song and sometimes I don't want to come back." She paused. "Except today, once I saw you."

"You saw me from up there?"

"At the end."

"Were you glad? To see me?"

"More than glad," she said, and she didn't take a sip that time either. "Much more than glad. What about you?" she asked, loving the banter, but already fearing its ending. "What do you do?"

He shook his head. "Nothing like this. I've been apprenticing for a lawyer downtown," he said. "A friend of my father's. He's the one who got my old man this big job for the City, why we moved. I've got sisters just like you, two of 'em, but they'll be teachers, then mothers. It's on me to carry the name."

"So what do you do for the lawyer?" she asked.

"Not much so far." He looked away like he was embarrassed of something. Maybe humble. "Go to meetings with him," he went on. "Try to look like I'm paying attention. Afterwards, I give him a lot of compliments, like 'The way you talked to that council member, that was something.'"

Chloe laughed.

"And is it your favorite thing to do in the world?" she asked, winking.

He paused, laughed. "Absolutely not. Not even a little bit. But it doesn't matter. I know that. My father's made a good living. I'll be able to provide for my family like he has."

And that prediction hung there between them, taking different shapes according to the size of their hope and then wilting.

"He's a domineering man. Not just to me but to my mother. The things he's done to her. I put a stop to it when I got old enough, but he still carries the seed for it." As he spoke now, he looked Chloe dead in her eye. "Why jazz speaks to me so much, I guess. I feel its pain, but somehow it doesn't add to my own. Nights I couldn't stomach being in the same house as my old man, I lived in those clubs."

He had bought another round of drinks, and he took his down quicker, talking about how his father had promised him he would love the move, that the new city would be sophisticated, that he would be swept up by all the promise, but that hadn't happened yet. He was mostly alone.

"I feel alone too most times," she said. She was picking at her fingernails while she talked, careful not to uproot the polish. She hadn't told anyone this except Tony, and he had waved it away with a joke. This man's face didn't shift an inch.

"I didn't used to," she went on. "But my oldest sister is getting married, and my middle one is caught up by this cause; even my mama has a man she's been getting closer to. He grew up like an uncle to us, but things are deepening between them, I can feel it, though she doesn't realize it yet. I'm happy for her, I guess. She's been by herself since before I was born, but I just feel so forlorn in that house, replaceable. Like everyone moved on and found something that fills them up so fat they don't have space to remember me."

"I know," he said, and he placed his hand over hers. "I know."

If Tony hadn't come over then with the girls, she might have let him touch her all night long. As it was, she came to, dabbed at her eyes where they had watered some. The man stood up to guard her from the group while she wiped.

"You remember James," she said to everyone.

"James, huh?" This from Betty. He held his hand out to her, and then, when she didn't take it, to the others, but they all just sized him up.

"Um-hmm . . ." They looked from one to another. "Um-hmm," they repeated.

"Seem like y'all had a good talk and now it's time to come dance, Chlo," Tony said.

"Okay," she said, but she shot James a look as they dragged her, and he followed them to the dance floor. At first, he just stood there, sucking on his drink and nodding. Occasionally, he'd tap his feet or pat the side of his pocket with his free hand. Then he set his drink down on the nearest table and started hunching his shoulders up and relaxing them again and shuffling his feet from one side to the other. The girls, all of them, had mastered dances like the jive and the bunny hop, and after a while, he would mimic them or try to, and they would collapse into fits of laughter. It was true, he had no rhythm, but there was a sweetness to it, how embarrassed he was. He'd look over at Chloe as if for reassurance, and then he'd look back at the girls and mimic another impossible move.

Of course Chloe hadn't forgotten he was white, magic or not inside that club, but his difference here was a reminder of it, a tangible one, and she noted it to herself for real this time. It was endearing, to see his discomfort, more so because in the street, she'd be the one who was afraid. Still, even reflecting on that distinction brought her back to what was waiting outside for them. She moved closer to Tony.

"You having fun?" he whispered in her ear.

She nodded and made herself smile.

"Just as long as that's all it is," he said. She could sense his worry. "Fun."

And she waved him off like she didn't need to be told such a thing, while his caution added to her own and gathered weight.

James bought them drinks the rest of the night. When they finished dancing, they sat at the table regaling him with stories of their world, nodding at the woman across the room, for instance, who was sitting with a white man as though she herself were white, but her sister had gone to school with Betty's brother. The man next to the stage had sex with men, Tony could verify, but he'd cry after, and it wasn't worth the scene. And the man the owner was talking to right now was Mr. Franklin, and every one of them was tied to an event he had secretly funded, Betty's mother's cousin's repast, and Tony just needed to be spotted two winters ago after his mother left him and his aunt died, and he hadn't been able to make it to a real job since.

James listened like they were teachers, and he might need to put the information to good use. He would ask follow-up questions, like how long it had been since the passing woman drifted over, and it would make Chloe think in a way she hadn't, inhabiting the world so thoroughly she hadn't questioned it before. As the night wore on and her friends became drunker and quieter, the mood thickened. She could feel it in the weight of the waitress's feet, heavy as the dead shuffling between the tables. The prostitutes' makeup was fading: their eyeliner had smeared; their lipstick was straight-up gone, their faces washed out. Tony stood behind the bar making eyes with the bartender, and from Chloe's vantage point, it seemed like the bartender really was making eyes back.

James offered to walk her home and she said okay, but she was already home in her mind. There was nowhere this could go, and it was best, she had always thought, to preempt grief. She hadn't known it but had grown up to fear it. Her mother had let it tower over her for so many years. Despite how much they all laughed and sang and danced and sang and ate, there was always this specter hovering over their affairs, hovering over their hearts too, and she wondered sometimes if her mother had loved too hard and they were all being punished. Yes, better to preempt grief and whatever emotion might lend itself to it.

Mr. Franklin stood at the exit talking with the owner, and he touched her arm as she passed.

"Well done," he said. "Well, well done."

Chloe thanked him and turned to Mr. Bailey, but his face was hard and stern.

"I told you," James said once they were outside.

"Oh, hush," Chloe said. Then, "I'm only at Webster and Eddy. You know where that is?"

He shook his head.

"It's not so far."

"I'll walk you, then take the streetcar back to town," he said.

And she shrugged like she didn't need it.

They didn't talk as much as they had, though the truth was now she was feeling an urgency to say something that might bind him to her, and many options flooded her mind at once. She saw the block the way he might be seeing it: crazy Freddy, who was thankfully sleeping; the smell of urine that would soon be replaced by the scent of honey buns in the oven, cinnamon glazing their tops, though it wasn't that time yet. She wasn't ashamed; these were her people. This was her home. If he was going to get to know her, he would have to know that, but of course he wasn't going to get to know her. She bit her lip against the thought and could taste the blood.

"This is it," she said, stopping at the stick-style flat, the largest one on the block, only now she could see the cracks in the paint. The roof was peeling. It would be obvious to him that it leaked something awful in rainy seasons; that the house was dotted with buckets spread apart like landmines in the place, and halfway through the day one of the sisters would need to come home to be sure they hadn't overflowed. Still, she felt herself brace up with pride.

"It's beautiful." He sized it up, and he seemed genuine about his assessment. "I had such a good time with you. The best time I've had since I moved here. Now I feel like I have something to look forward to." He leaned into her and she let him. He pressed his lips to hers and she let him do that too. No one would be watching. Even if they were, it was too dark to see. Just because it happened this once wouldn't mean it would happen again.

One kiss was followed by another, then another. And finally, Chloe stepped back. Maybe this was all he was after. Maybe he expected to be brought upstairs like one of Tony's men, but he seemed shy.

"I'm sorry," he said. "I don't want to pressure you."

"It's okay. I had a good time too, but I'm a lady, and this was one night." She intended to follow that up by saying it was one night and not the world they lived in, but it was so obvious, she didn't need to spell it out.

"Of course you are, of course you are." He was even more shy now, stumbling and red in the face. "I didn't mean to imply otherwise—"

"It's okay," she cut him off. "It's just that I better be going. It's so late."

"Yes, your mother must be worried." She didn't bother to tell him Vivian would be working the night shift. She would probably never see this man again. Why did he need all of the details?

She walked up the steps. She told herself not to look back, but she couldn't help it, and when she did, he was still standing there. He was still standing there as she fumbled for the key and opened the door, and even as she shut it behind her and leaned against it, just before she peeked beneath the curtain Mama had hung years ago to keep the light out, he was still standing there. She walked up the steps to her room, quietly in case her mother had decided to stay home, but no, the door was open and the bed was empty, a quilt she'd knitted when Chloe was in her stomach strewn across it. Chloe's own bed was unmade. Her mother was always on her about that. She passed it, the clothes littering the floor, the drawers half open, to look outside the window for him. But he was gone now, and she felt a wave of sadness already pulsing through her, sadness at the loss, even as she knew she would see him again.

VIVIAN

Mr. Franklin was so moved by Preacher's sermon, he reserved the back of the Champagne Supper Club for Ruth's wedding reception and even offered to spot all the drinks. He'd taken Vivian aside too and whispered that he'd seen the girls perform without Ruth and was impressed, that he'd consider signing the two if they proved themselves. "You know, with a gig at a club or hotel," he'd said, "someplace fancy that draws a crowd."

Vivian had nodded, but she wasn't putting stock in him any longer. Mr. Franklin wasn't God. No, God had sent him, but He'd send someone else too, someone with flexibility, someone who knew real ambition when he saw it. If she gave up before that happened, she'd be no better than the men who used to work the shipyards and who only played numbers now. Vivian would see them sometimes creeping into Miss Edna's house. She would never let the girls go out that way.

On the other hand, Vivian was so relieved by Mr. Bailey welcoming Esther and Chloe back, she could pour herself into the wedding details. What texture of fabric would go best with Ruth's skin tone? Would they have to invite Mr. Gaines's wife *and* his girlfriend? Vivian hoped Miss Fox wouldn't show up with all her goddamn kids. Just in case, she gave up on cooking herself and enlisted Lena to prepare the shrimp, deviled eggs, fondue and fresh bread, meatballs, chicken wings, beef Wellington, macaroni and cheese, and green beans sautéed in bacon fat. Lena would bake the cake too, of course, five tiers of fruit and cream. Vivian had offered to sew Ruth's dress, but Ruth had insisted she buy it from a new, fashionable shop in Union Square, white tulle that gathered at the waist, then flowed outward to her ankles. The war was over, she kept exclaiming, Gerry had been promoted, they had enough.

Sometimes at night, Vivian's disappointment would cycle back on her without mercy. But then she'd overhear the girls on the roof. Esther and Chloe had already started practicing a duet for Ruth's wedding. Chloe would sing the first verse; then Esther would take the second. There were four days of preparation remaining, and they were right at the point they were supposed to be. They could perform it right now if necessary, sure, and no layperson would be any the wiser, but these final hours were for polish. These hours made the steps seamless, the harmony tight and clear, the words like lullabies your mama used to sing, and Vivian could tell by the shuffle of their feet, the rhythm reflected on the ceiling now, that they were almost there.

THE DAY OF RUTH AND GERRY'S WEDDING, IT RAINED HEAVY-HEAVY AND hard-hard. The day before, there hadn't been a cloud in the sky, and the discrepancy spooked Vivian as she dressed and tugged the hot curlers from her hair. She and Mary hadn't picked the same dress—Mary's hung loose; Vivian's held her hips, which her children had gifted her, and clutched her stomach from behind, another unsolicited gift. She stared at herself for some time in the mirror. No, she wasn't the young girl whom Ellis had married, but he would recognize her if he came back today; she was certain of that. She thought he would be pleased with what she'd made of herself.

Preacher Thomas had arranged for the families of the bride and groom to be picked up in a stretch limo, and she, Mary, and the younger girls, as stunning as Vivian had seen them in their bright yellow knee-length swing dresses, piled in and waved at the regular cast of characters at Lena's, Horace at the bookstore, Miss Edna at her gambling house, Miss Gladys smoking a cigarette outside the shop, Mr. Gaines whistling. They would all be at the wedding too—no one in the community would miss it—but Vivian would arrive early to help set up, to help Ruth, who hadn't dressed yet and whose hands were shaking now in her lap.

"Everything's going to be just fine," Vivian said, rubbing the child's back.

"I know, Mama," she said, but she fixed one hand over the other to keep it still.

At the church, they followed Preacher Thomas to a back room off the sanctuary where Ruth would dress. There was so much to do: Ruth's makeup, which Esther had promised to apply; her scent, which Chloe had compiled from three different perfumes; and of course they would all be needed to pull the gown over her, to adjust the bodice and lay out the train at her back, but Vivian didn't have the energy for it all of a sudden. She sat on a chair and motioned for Ruth to sit beside her.

"Come closer," Vivian said, and her daughter scooted over. "Closer still," she repeated, and Ruth sat practically in her lap, the bump of her stomach settling on her thighs.

The other girls laid out Ruth's toiletries in the bathroom. It occurred to Vivian that she didn't know how many times it had been just her and her oldest daughter together. After she turned four, Ruth had become the mother, the assistant, the cook, the housekeeper—hell, the preacher, when Vivian had no one else to turn to with her woes—and now she was leaving, and Vivian didn't know if Ruth knew all she had been to her. Maybe Vivian hadn't known it before this moment herself.

Ruth's hair had been washed and dried already, and Vivian tried to rub the back of the girl's neck without interfering with the rollers on top.

"I can't believe you're the little girl who made me a mother," Vivian said, surprising herself even.

"Oh, Mama, don't start. If you cry, I'm going to cry, and if I start now, I guess I'll never stop."

"Nothing to cry about. Just telling you how I feel. I thought you were a boy, you know," she went on. "Your daddy did too. He thought he wanted one, but once you came out, I saw he'd been wrong. Dead wrong. Wasn't nothing you could do to upset him, nothing he wouldn't alter to see you smile. When he'd get dressed in the morning, you'd hold onto his legs and say, 'Daddy, you're not going anywhere.' It's amazing, I can still hear it. When you first came out and they held you against my chest, it was like magic; something was healed in me in that moment, something I didn't even know had been wounded. You fixed me, Ruth. I wasn't all bad. I didn't drink or fool around or do drugs or nothing like that, but I doubted myself. I didn't trust my own ambition. I never would have done all this for us"—and she motioned toward the girls in the bathroom, but she didn't spend too much time on them because she meant for this to be about her firstborn. "And now my baby is leaving."

"I'm not going nowhere, Mama, just up the street." And it was true that Vivian would be able to throw a rock and hit her daughter's new window. Still, it wasn't the same. It never would be again, and she'd be a fool to think otherwise.

"I just don't understand where the time goes," she said now, and she felt herself drifting to a place so far back she might not be able to retrace her steps and recover. "Never mind, Ruth, the main thing I wanted to tell you, well . . ." And she felt herself stumble here because she wasn't used to this part, any of it really, but she started out again, the same way she'd taught her children to stand right back up during practice when they tripped so they'd develop the muscle memory for correction onstage. "I want to apologize to you, baby. For trying to say I knew best, about your life. My mama did that to me, and I swore I wouldn't do the same to my own children, but here now . . ." She stopped herself again. And they both looked at the dress hanging in the closet. "You did the right thing, baby, I can see that now. I'm so happy for you, so so happy, and so proud."

"Oh, Mama, I am too." They embraced, and Vivian forbade herself from crying; she didn't have time to redo her eyes. Then she passed Ruth her mother's brooch. The older woman had pressed it into Vivian's hand at the train station the last time she'd seen her, told her to gift it to her oldest daughter the day she married. Doing so now, Vivian felt the impossible sadness of leaving home all over again. Her memory was already fading. At first, Vivian allowed her mother's spirit to guide her in that new city so thoroughly she could have convinced herself she'd taken her with her, but lately she thought of her sayings only once every now and then. Her mother's recipes had become her own. Vivian had had to tailor them because crawfish was indecently expensive in the city, because her second daughter couldn't abide as much dairy in the oyster soup. But she'd drift to her dresser drawer as if guided by a quiet otherworldly power every time she needed sustenance for her insides, and sure enough, she'd lift that brooch, its emeralds shining, and a word would spring to her mind, the word she needed, a word she didn't even think she'd memorized, but there it was. There her mother was, she was sure of it, and now, where would the woman be once the last item she'd touched Vivian with was gone?

There was no time to answer that question because the girls swept in and carried Ruth off. After a moment, Vivian rose and followed her, stood in the bathroom doorway.

"Be still," Chloe said, bobby pins in her mouth, towering over Ruth, who sat; firming what Gladys had twisted and gelled hours before.

"Be careful with her," Esther said. Vivian couldn't remember hearing her be so tender toward her sister. She was dabbing powder all over Ruth's face now, blowing it in parts where it had congealed. She leaned in closer to line her eyes, then to brush mascara onto her lashes. When she was done, she lifted a handheld mirror from the counter and set it in Ruth's lap.

"What do you think?" she asked.

There was so much yearning in that question. Vivian didn't know if Ruth could hear it as well as she could.

"It's perfect." Ruth handed the mirror back. Tears were forming.

"Now, don't ruin all my hard work, girl," Esther said. Then, when Ruth calmed, she whispered so low Vivian could barely hear her, "You're beautiful."

And Vivian held onto the edge of the counter so she wouldn't collapse.

GERRY WALKED DOWN THE AISLE FIRST, WITH MARY ON ONE ARM AND Vivian on another. Then Esther and Chloe followed with Gerry's two friends from grade school, boys with soft voices Vivian had seen sprout into men. Then the little flower girls from next door, Ava and Maya, drizzled orchid petals down a white cloth runner, and Vivian had to remind herself every now and then that the festivity was all for her daughter. She had to remind herself to feel it out while it happened; to smooth the front of the program with Ruth's full name, the one she and Ellis had given her, listed for the final time; to admire the poinsettias the ushers had taped to the sides of the pews; to absorb the warmth of the crowd gasping at the sight of her baby walking in, her shoulder-length veil covering her face. Through the veil, Vivian could still see Ruth's eyes glistening, scampering the way they had when she was a child, when she had searched for her mother in a crowded room, but now she was searching for Gerry. That other part was over now.

Then it was time for her girls to stand on the tip of the altar and sing as they had so many times before, but it was different too. Chloe was crying before she could even get the words out. Esther's face was like stone, but Vivian knew that meant she was feeling more than any of them.

Preacher Thomas stood up front and he winked at Vivian and she winked back. He had asked earlier if he could sit at her table at the reception, beside her, and she had said yes, of course, though now the thought frightened her. It would be the first time they would be seated as a couple in public, although people had been talking for years. Of course, she and Preacher had flirted after that powerful Sunday message. She had said she would visit him and he had said it would be just fine. It was true that it had thrilled her to step back into that side of life after so long, like dipping her toes into warm, lapping water. But after a day or two of spending most of her waking hours reliving the conversation between them, rejoicing at the way her heart felt knowing his was open to hers if she needed it, she'd started to pull back. There was just so much pain when you ventured out too far, too much pain when you started to love, and cementing the feeling, forget about it. It had taken her too long to come back from it the last time.

"We come together today to celebrate Gerry and Ruth," Preacher started. "To celebrate their love, their bond, their commitment to each other, and we know how strong it would have had to be to overpower a woman as mighty as Vivian."

And everyone laughed, Vivian included.

"No, but we celebrate even that, the might of their family's love for them, the power of that bond, and today, when we join them, we're not just joining these two, we're joining Mary, and we're joining Vivian and Esther and Chloe, and we're announcing them all formally as a united force."

Ruth seemed afraid then, moving her hands at her side, but Gerry reached for her, and she seemed to calm. Vivian remembered that feeling, meeting Ellis someplace just as they had planned, a simple gesture. If there was a greater comfort in the world, she hadn't found it yet.

The couple drank wine from a chalice passed between them, and then Mary's brother got up and read from Corinthians, stumbling over every other word, and it was more endearing that way.

The girls sang again, then Preacher Thomas talked about how he had known the children since they were in diapers scrambling around with each other, and now, of course, there was a different sort of scrambling that would be done, and everyone laughed. There was a broom laid down at their feet, and when Preacher pronounced them man and wife, Gerry lifted Ruth's veil, kissed her, and they jumped over it so tenderly Vivian held her heart.

NOW THE RECEPTION WOULDN'T BE AS TENDER. MR. FRANKLIN HAD MADE sure the bar in the back room of the Champagne Supper Club was stocked, and Lena had laid out platters of appetizers to tide the guests over until the main event. The men drank whiskey and the women drank vodka with a splash of grenadine, and they danced the boogie-woogie, their skirts shifting up, and every time one platter of food was emptied, another one was delivered in its wake. Even Esther and Horace cut up on the floor, and Vivian sucked her teeth at Mary, but she allowed it, the merriment of the day pressing into her better judgment. Friends of Gerry gave toasts that were more like roasts, and Chloe stood up and talked about how Ruth had been like a mother to them.

"Her disappointment hit me harder than Mama's. Maybe because I always wanted to impress her, always wanted her to be proud of me. But her praise, I'll always carry it with me. It was simple things, my bread pudding, my rendition of 'A-Tisket, A-Tasket.' I don't know what I'm going to do without her." She wept into her hand, and Esther rose from her seat and walked her off.

Vivian stood in place of her husband and talked about how proud he would have been on a day like today, how he'd had faith in Ruth since the beginning, and how his faith had materialized, only in a different way than she'd imagined. Then everyone went back to the dancing again, more raucous on account of the break from it. Vivian mostly skimmed the edges, accepting congratulations, and occasionally she'd get caught up in a dance. It was only midway through that she found herself in the same vicinity as Preacher Thomas. He grabbed her hand and sat her down next to him and sighed.

"You didn't eat," he said.

"I tried to join your table," she started.

"I know how it is at these things. I made you a plate." He pushed one toward her, fist-sized servings of macaroni and beef and green beans. Meanwhile, Ruth and Gerry cut the cake, but Vivian's feet hurt so bad, she was so worn-out period, she didn't have the oomph to stand.

"People are complimenting you, Preacher," she said, trying not to shovel the food into her mouth. "Everybody I talk to says Preacher sure did preach that wedding today."

He smiled. "That's nice to know. I wanted it to be special for them. Wanted it to be special for you. You all deserve it." He sat back in his chair and crossed one leg over the other, watching Ruth smash the icing into Gerry's mouth.

"Young love, huh?"

"Yes, and it's so young."

"Well, they'll make their way."

"Yes, they will."

"What about you?" he asked.

"Oh, my love is so old I don't even remember how to spell it."

He laughed. "That's not what I mean."

"What you mean then?" She paused, a new vigor coursing through her. Maybe it was the food. "You gotta say what you mean, Preacher."

"Will you dance with me?" he asked.

And she set her fork down and wiped her mouth at the corners.

She didn't answer, but she stood and reached for his hand.

He led her to the floor. It wasn't as crowded as it had been. The music had slowed, and people were tending to their last drinks, homing in on their third plates, devouring cake. Jimmy Forrest's "Night Train" played. Preacher held her close, and she felt her body sigh in his, his shudder back. She hadn't known what a relief it would be. She thought of things she might say, but nothing came to her mind, and she'd look up at him, then down, and they'd laugh, and once, he stepped on her foot and she laughed again. He hummed the melody to the song in her ear, a nice baritone—she had known that from the many services she'd attended—but when had she started to feel so comfortable? She didn't know. Her children were in touching distance; so were her friends. She was losing Ruth, but the other girls would step up. Look how well they had done today.

When the song ended, the MC announced there would be just one more. In the meantime, Vivian and what felt like an army began clearing through the mess. They piled the leftover food into plastic containers; they swept, then mopped the floor; they washed the tables and counters down. There wasn't much cake, so many had worked their way into the line a second time, but what was remaining Vivian boxed and covered. Ruth and Gerry would eat this on their first anniversary, and they'd be able to count on innumerable years to come.

Even with all the hands, it was hours before they stepped outside. The rain still pressed forward, and they huddled at the doorway as they adjusted their jackets, aimed their umbrellas at the night sky. Ruth and Gerry held hands; Horace and Esther did too, but Vivian was past caring about that, Preacher's arm looped around her waist.

Any minute she and her party would step outside into the wet cold, but as it was, it was like they were immobile, like the energy that had coursed through them had been left inside on the dance floor and anything supplemental wouldn't be available until the morning. It was the sign of a good party. She would be sure to write a note to Mr. Franklin, Lena and Preacher too, take them sweet potato pies, her mama's recipe, one of the only ones that still came to her intact. And then, to her surprise, they all filed out, ready to brave the storm, and she was too, she supposed, her bed positioned foremost in her mind's eye. Maybe Preacher would tarry a bit in her parlor before making his way home. Maybe not. It had been so long. As she turned to close the door, she imagined his hand at the base of her spine, and the tingle that image lent her was how she missed it, why it took her longer than it should have to zero in on the white page, the typed words therein. There was a notice on the door. Even when she saw it, there was a gap between her sight and her understanding, a gap she would have extended further if she could. She gripped Preacher's hand. The gasps came out in waves: first Esther and Horace, then Chloe, then Gerry, next Ruth, who wore her after-dinner dress but still glowed like a bride.

A silence fell over the group that was unnatural in the neighborhood, in the context. Fifty of them had been screeching, had been singing, had been dancing, and then, like a curtain falling over a show, it had stopped.

"But we just walked in," somebody said, her voice rising and cracking.

"Someone must have taped it there while we were inside," another one answered.

"He said he wasn't going to sell"—this from Esther. As pleased as Vivian had been to sample her daughter's joy at the reception, it was like the child's heart had been turned over, and the other side presented as extremely, only with an opposite meaning.

"He said he wasn't," Esther yelled, facing Horace now.

Chloe held her hands to her face and cried as she had just hours earlier when she toasted her sister.

Vivian could still see Horace, Lena, Gladys waving back, on her way in this evening. So much had changed, and the most remarkable twist hadn't been her daughter marrying.

"Well, things are different now," Preacher said, and that's when the scene clarified, hardened. It was true what he said; there was no mistaking it.

Horace ripped the sheet of paper from the front door, balled it up, and clenched it with his fist.

He had been so lighthearted inside. Now he banged his empty palm against the window. No one else said a word. Vivian stared at the houses beyond this block, upright and whole, trying to tell herself she was imagining what she'd just read. The festivity, the alcohol, something was making her see those words—"redevelopment," "thirty days," "demolition"—when this was the land of the thriving. This was the land she had traveled to to make a way when there was no way to be had down in Louisiana. This was the refuge still as it withered. But she couldn't keep her eyes on the distance. She was forced to look away when Preacher gripped her hand to lead her home.

PART TWO

RUTH

Ruth had had the baby four weeks before, a healthy girl, a little red thing with a head full of slick black hair and a pudgy nose like her paw. Ruth had lost the weight, and her thighs had contracted, as had the hard, then soft mound of her belly. The child drank formula some, and Ruth's supply had decreased; even her breasts had started to deflate. And Denise was a good baby, she was: she only woke once in the night, so Ruth could rise almost every morning to bathe herself, dress, and even curl her own hair. She was lucky, everyone said so, and she'd repeat those words to herself in the mirror every time she needed to remember as much.

But what Ruth didn't know, what she had begun to consider ceaselessly with no target to aim the question at, was when she would locate herself again, that part of her she sat with alone sometimes; the part that would fantasize about the life she now held with Gerry instead of taking notes in Statistics; the part that would loathe the toil of rehearsal and performance; the part that would laugh with her head stretched back and her mouth slack with her friends at the Champagne Supper Club after a show, a martini in her hand, all the while keeping an eye on her baby sister and Tony in the corner.

There was the waking and the feeding and the shushing and the rocking and the laundering and the folding, and when Gerry came home, there were his needs, distinct of course, but accompanied by the same note of obligation. There was a fist in her chest that compressed tighter over the course of the day, and Ruth was waiting for it to reduce its pressure. She thought any minute it would have to let up (how could any human thing keep up such strain for so long?), but it hadn't happened yet, and the most peace she could secure was in the nighttime, the house finally dormant. She didn't even sleep then; she wouldn't waste such precious hours. She'd sit and breathe in and out, in and out again, with a new lightness, the weightlessness of not being needed.

SINCE RUTH'S MOTHER WORKED AT THE HOSPITAL AND ON THE ROOF MOST days, it was Mary who came over in the mornings to relieve her. She would clean up the breakfast table and wash the pot of grits and pan of eggs and bacon. Then she'd sweep the baby out of Ruth's arms and say, "Girl, don't you got something better to do?" Ruth would retreat into her bedroom and sometimes shower and sometimes nap and sometimes stare at a wall with her thoughts that didn't feel like hers, someone else's maybe, someone she knew only distantly, a face but not a name, and this person was sad and lonely and unfulfilled. Ruth didn't understand it. "You have everything you ever wanted," she'd want to shout out at the ingrate, but she didn't raise her voice, and anyway, the other woman didn't seem to know she was there. Today Ruth made up her bed and applied some makeup. That made her feel like herself. She hurried with the eyeliner, and the line above her eyelashes swerved upward on her right eye, but she didn't fix it; she didn't like to leave the baby with Mary too long. Of course she trusted her. It was just that when she didn't recognize herself when she was nursing or heating a bottle, at least it made sense—those were foreign acts. But sitting alone painting her fingernails, she had done that countless times before, and to be removed from herself in the midst of such familiarity alarmed her.

"Back already?" Mary asked only an hour after she'd relieved her.

"I couldn't sleep."

"Hmph, well, she didn't have that problem." She nodded at the baby on a cotton gingham blanket on the floor. "She's been out for half an hour now. You know what I told you. When she sleeps—"

"I sleep," Ruth cut her off. "I know, I know."

"You not acting like you know." She paused. "You not acting like yourself either. You need to get up out of this house. When's the last time you left it? Too many weeks to count." She went on without letting Ruth answer. "That's a goddamn shame. When I had Gerry, I would walk him up and down Webster. He took all his naps in his stroller. At noon, I'd wheel him into Lena's, she'd serve my gumbo piping hot. When he got big enough, he and I would share it. Those were the days." Her eyes glazed over, and if Ruth noted correctly, they watered.

Then, without wiping them or turning her head, Mary kept on as if one tender moment reached out its hand for another. "I saw Lena the other day, at the bus stop. She's lost weight. Said she don't cook as much without the restaurant. She's still not skinny or nothin like that, but it don't look right on her, like her cheeks are caving in; I can see her collarbone too clear. It's a shame what happened."

And it had been. Mr. Bailey had pulled out, then Lena, then Gladys, then Mr. Gaines. Now Gerry was commuting to Vallejo to work in Mr. Gaines's brother-in-law's butchery. He brought home more meat from there, beef, pork, and sometimes lamb. Ruth had a freezer full of anything she'd need, but Gerry hated the long hours on the road, and he missed his mentor. He'd perk up at the door for the baby's sake, but when Denise went down, it was like he didn't have enough else for Ruth anymore. Anyway, Esther's friend Horace was tackling the City now. Mama said he was wasting his breath, arguing with devils. Best to let them run themselves in circles, then collapse. But Horace led protests on Webster and Turk every morning, and so far, though the businesses had closed, at least none of the buildings had been touched.

“She must be relieved, though, as much ripping and running as she was doing,” Ruth said. “She must be relieved to be able to sit down.”

And then Mary turned to look at the baby, who was stirring.

“Some people don’t know how to sit down,” she said. She looked at Ruth right in her eyes. “Lena’s one of them.

“It’s a shame,” she said again, this time in a baby voice as she lifted her only grandchild. Ruth had never heard her speak that way. People were already starting to ask when Ruth would have another. It was something, the power behind creation. Truthfully, it had been the most appalling part of Ruth’s transition to motherhood, witnessing how this person she’d borne could tear down brick walls in people’s hearts.

IT DIDN’T START ALL AT ONCE. THERE WAS A SLOW, STEADY RISING, A COMing forth. For instance, after Mary left for her afternoon stories, Ruth dug through unpacked boxes for her records. The Salvations had sung Faye Adams once at the Champagne Supper Club, and Ruth stood and reenacted the steps for her daughter now. She didn’t know who she was singing about, but the loss between the words, in the center of the melody, felt intimate, like she’d known it for some time. She was at the B section, a wooden spoon tight in her fist, bending her knees and beckoning to the baby like she was the source of all the pain that might ebb, if only she’d take her hand, when Gerry walked through the door.

He usually hurried straight for the baby these days, but this time, his eyes zeroed in on Ruth first, and he laughed. He walked over to hug her, but she was embarrassed and she slunk away to her room. She had been planning not entirely consciously to squeeze into one of her old sequined numbers, and she was relieved he had come home ten minutes early today, that she was spared the extra humiliation of that scene. She expected him to follow her into the room, but he didn't. She could hear him from her bed with the child he'd practically spit out. He was using the same terms of endearment with the baby that he'd used with Ruth, "darling" and "sweetheart" and "honey pie," and each time he said it now, she had to fight the urge to call out to him, "Yes, my love? Here I am."

THE NEXT DAY, SHE LOOKED THROUGH THE PICTURES. THERE WERE PHOTO albums of the Salvations her mother collected, and Ruth had snuck one out the day after her wedding. Her mother and Preacher had been in the kitchen speaking in hushed tones about the end of the night. The orange tape, the sign. Preacher had predicted the rest of the block might follow suit, but Mama had protested. The last thing she would have noticed was the photos. Now Ruth flipped through the pages. She and Esther and Chloe at the Champagne Supper Club the first night they'd performed there. Mama behind them looking like if she smiled any harder, her cheeks might burst. Then the three at Bop City. That night, they'd taken home the prize for amateur hour. The crowd had started out booing because Esther had missed the intro, but Ruth had taken over, poured her vicarious embarrassment into the chords, and those people had given her an encore; they'd refused to let her go. Matter of fact, she had never been abandoned on a stage. Maybe that was what she missed. It was her decision when to turn around, when to give them more. At the end of the day, she'd always felt wanted, and she hadn't known to appreciate that.

Gerry stood at the doorway now.

"I think she's wet." He held the baby forward.

Ruth reached for her, kissed Denise on the top of her head, smelled her, really took her in. There was nothing like it; there wasn't. If she wasn't careful, she'd look back at this moment too and it would be gone.

She'd already started Gerry's dinner. There were five more minutes in the oven for the chicken, and the string beans were ready; so were the potatoes. Gerry liked his food hot, so she'd covered the vegetables in foil. She'd run them through the oven for a few minutes once the chicken was out just to be sure they hadn't cooled.

Once they'd depleted the baby topics—that Denise was trying to hold her head up, that she slept better on her back these days, that before they knew it she'd be ready for solid foods—and the sound of the fork scraping the plate became too awful to bear, Ruth stood. Gerry turned on the television and sat in front of *I Love Lucy*, and she cleared the table and washed the dishes, then set them to dry. The baby was fussy by then, so she bathed her, fed her from the bottle this time so she would sleep through the night. She could hear Gerry's laughter from the living room, and every time it sent a strain of rage through her that she let herself feel all the way through and around. She thought if she were thorough, the feeling might run its course, but it seemed to return each night on a loop.

In bed, Gerry tried something, but she said no. "That's alright, baby," he said. "I know you're tired. I don't know how you do it. I don't know what I'd do without you."

If it had been the old him and the old her, she would have clarified: she wasn't tired, she was exhausted, but it wasn't an exhaustion that would submit to sleep, she'd learned that now. And it wasn't that she didn't want him; it was that she felt like he didn't want her anymore. The ways he'd used to show it, the sweet words, the caresses, had been a straight shot to her heart, and him grazing her lips with his in the morning didn't cut it.

When she heard him start to snore, she walked over to her closet, to the dress she'd selected a few hours earlier in her mind's eye, the one with the slit up the front and the cinch at the waist. It looked better on her now than it ever had. Even with her breasts deflated, the baby had granted her a new plumpness, her hair had come in fuller, her skin had cleared. Esther and Chloe had started performing at

Bop City since Champagne Supper Club had closed. She didn't plan to walk there, but twenty minutes after she slid on lipstick and powdered her face, she found herself in front of the marquee. She hadn't even been sure it was the girls' night to perform but sure enough, their names had been spelled out in full. Ruth was still used to seeing THE SALVATIONS, and there was some jealousy wrapped tight inside her momentary confusion. She would have to accept that things were different now.

When she walked in, the lights onstage were already set low, and Ruth could imagine her sisters holding hands behind the curtain. The room was packed, and before she reached the bar, a gentleman offered to buy her a drink. She nodded and waited for the bartender to hand it to her. Then she pushed her way through the crowd, not so close to the stage that Chloe or Esther could see her, but close enough that she could breathe them in, just as the girls burst out into song.

My loving ain't no river
That ebbs and flows with time
My love is the ocean, baby
It rises with the tides

Ruth knew the song, had sung it in her mother's basement in fact, and it was impossible for her not to join in now, low, under her breath. Before she knew it, she was rocking in place. She bumped into a man in front of her who was about to make a scene before he turned back, nodded in recognition, then asked her if she needed anything. She shook her head.

"I'm good," she said, still sucking on her martini. "I'm good."

And it was true then, for the first time in a long time. She sniffed her old self out in the way she smiled now, not at anything in particular, but from a warmth that had lived inside her for as long as she could remember and which she couldn't help but dole out. And the way she stood with her shoulders back, the way she swung her hips.

Before, she'd associated this song, the performance of it, with disgust, with resentment, with longing for a different life, and now all those same emotions were there but they were aimed in the opposite direction. She wanted to be on that stage just now, dipping as Esther would, belting out the bridge like Chloe, receiving the crowd's dreams—and, displaced as those dreams were, she knew that for a brief time onstage she could make them seem real.

She kept her head down as the lights rode up, as she trudged through the audience who was applauding for her, well, no, for her sisters now. She was almost at the door when she felt someone grip her arm. She turned back—Mr. Franklin. She hadn't seen him since her wedding. Here now, all she could summon was her mother's disappointment that afternoon she'd told her daughters they were on the brink of stardom.

"What you doing here, girl?" he asked. She could smell the whiskey on his breath, his cologne. She inhaled the mixture and calmed, like she had ascended to his level somehow. "Don't you got a baby to mind?"

"I'm on my way back for her. Just taking a break is all."

"Un-huh." He looked at her like he didn't believe her. That was fine.

She stayed there with him for longer than she should have—Esther would be leaving any minute, and she was the last person Ruth would want to notice her here, clinging to the past. She was waiting for him to say something that would make sense of her presence there, though, her absence to herself all this time, but he had turned for the stage, the next act.

He looked back, even more quizzically, then that expression transformed into a smile.

"Your sisters are doing better than I expected, better than I could have foreseen."

"Oh," Ruth said like she was happy to hear it because her soft betrayal pained her beyond recognition.

"It's a shame what happened between us, but some gems are

forged through fire, am I right? It's that little one," he went on. Ruth could see Esther out of the corner of her eye now, keeping to the side of the club so as not to be seen, the same way Ruth had done. She turned her back in her direction.

"Chloe? She's always been a star," Ruth said.

"Yes, I can see that." He took a sip from his crystal glass. "Yes. I bet Mr. Bailey is regretting closing shop now. Bop City has never been so popular. It's just a matter of time before these girls move elsewhere, to higher ground."

Esther was past her now, and Ruth turned again to avoid a final glance. She had made it.

"I'll tell her you said that," Ruth said.

"Sure. I'll tell her myself too. As soon as she finishes with that crowd." He laughed, taking another sip. The brown liquor burned Ruth's throat by extension.

Ruth looked behind her to where Mr. Franklin had gestured, and Chloe hadn't stopped in the dressing room at all apparently. She was already on the floor, surrounded by men and women both, like they could waft who she had been for them and transport the essence wherever they needed to carry it. Ruth remembered that. Mr. Franklin moved over to the group with the same intentness as the others.

"I'll see you later." He stared straight ahead. "Take care of that baby, now."

"Will do," Ruth said, though it was the last thing she felt like doing now. She walked toward the exit as Esther had, then looked back for Chloe one more time. The crowd was still there, though slightly dispersed. Mr. Franklin had made his way through it and was shaking her hand. Ruth had never been a jealous person. She wouldn't start now. She closed the door of the club behind her. The men outside studied her back, she knew that without turning, and she let their attention guide her all the way home.

She tried to open the door slowly so she wouldn't wake Gerry or the baby. She held her shoes, tiptoed inside on stockinged feet, felt for the light. When she turned it on, Mary was seated on the sofa in front of her.

"Un-huh, you think you slick, huh?"

"Mary, what are you doing here?"

"Forgot my pocketbook, came in and saw you weren't in bed. I was worried, to tell you the truth. Didn't want to wake Gerry, he got work in the morning, figured I'd sit back and wait. And here you are. Where you been, superstar? I hope you didn't forget you had a man and baby at home."

Ruth stopped tiptoeing and walked over to her on the sofa.

"How could I forget?"

"Exactly," Mary said. "Exactly. I know it's hard." Ruth looked at her fast. She was surprised was all. Mary didn't abide feelings or comfort or anything of the sort.

"With Gerry, I didn't even have time to nurse him, I had to return to work so fast, and I knew it would be cruel to treat a child to a bond I couldn't maintain. I got out of the house every day, though. It's easier for you in some ways, and in some ways it's not." She placed her hand over Ruth's. "We all do what we can to get through. I started renting out to roomers. Brought money in, and more importantly it kept me alive." She paused for a long time. "I don't see any reason Gerry needs to know about this."

"Thank you, Mary."

"Hush. Yes, Lord, we all got to have something in our back pocket."

Ruth kissed her on the cheek, then stood. "I better call it a night. The baby will be up whether I'm rested or not."

"You got that right." She stood too. "Oh, Ruth?" she called back.

"Yes, Mary?"

"You're not the only one with secrets, you know. Catch this. When I got home this afternoon, a little white man called himself Mr. Belmont was standing at my door, yes, he was, said he wanted to change my life. I told him, the last time a white man wanted to change my life, my daddy was carted off to jail for a crime he didn't commit. Oh, yes, he was."

Mary laughed too loud and Ruth could hear the baby gurgle.

She lowered her voice. "The man said, 'None of that, Miss Jenkins, none of that. How would you feel about making more money than you've ever dreamed of?' I said, 'I'd feel goddamn amazing about it,' and he said, 'Miss Jenkins, the City wants to buy your house.'"

"What, Miss Mary?" Ruth covered her mouth with her hand.

"You heard me. Offered me a pretty penny for it too. A pretty penny."

"But you can't be thinking about it. This is your home."

Mary shrugged. "I'm not sure. Now don't go and tell your mama," she went on. "No need for her to worry herself crazy for no reason."

Ruth started to push back, tell her Mama deserved to know just in case, and then she remembered that she'd been caught. Mary opened the door now.

"Where were you anyway?" she asked before she stepped out.

"Bop City. My sisters had a show."

"Just like I said." Mary smirked now. "We all got our ways."

She turned her back, and Ruth stayed on the sofa for an hour, breathing in and out, in and out. She thought back to the song her sisters had sung, hummed it under her breath.

Tell me how you feel
Something to let me know you're true
'Cause I've been hurt before

Mr. Franklin by the exit. Chloe surrounded. There was no question Ruth would go back. For the first time in a long time, she slept through the night.

ESTHER

Esther had expected to be the new lead when Ruth left, but it was Chloe who had taken on their older sister's role. She was running the house too, halfway managing the group, and when Mama was working, Chloe would be the one to call out, "I can't hear you from the back. You trip and you get right back up. You fall down like that in practice, you're going to fall down at the show and not know how to right yourself again." Practices dragged even longer. Mama invented more routines she wanted to edge in, different ones that would fare better with two people, and it was harder on Esther—without a third person for the audience to observe, her mistakes were clear to everyone watching, and she made more of them. Before, she had gotten by on hard work alone, but that didn't seem to be enough lately.

At the bookstore, Horace ate his meals standing so he'd have time to write his speeches. There was so much disappointment inside him at Mr. Bailey and the others folding, but it seemed he had learned how to channel it, how to let it spill out onto his words. He met with Mr. Belmont to propose that some new buildings benefit the community as recreational centers, or low-income housing. The man had nodded and smiled but had resisted committing in writing. At least, Esther often reminded Horace, demolition hadn't started yet; maybe the City was considering all he'd said. But Horace wasn't satisfied, and he'd taken to organizing protests. They'd started small, twenty-five people mostly from the blocks themselves, but then they'd advanced to one hundred, then two hundred, and Esther saw people at his demonstrations she'd never met before. She couldn't go to every one—she was a singer again, after all—but he'd walk her home from the bookstore at night, and if Vivian was still at work, they'd sit outside on the stoop. It wasn't like Gerry used to do with Ruth, where Esther would approach and they'd pull away from each other in scattered haste, Gerry rearranging his pants, Ruth patting her hair down and reapplying her lipstick. Horace must have been confused that one night at the movies, but she hadn't mentioned the scene again, and it had blown over. No, with Horace, it was their minds that were joined. They shared their woes from the day or their wins, and when Esther had ideas, like that he needed to appeal to the elderly more—they were the ones with the most allegiance to this neighborhood—or that she could fashion newsletters out of his speeches and distribute them to the crowd at his protests, he'd pluck a pencil from behind his ear and jot it all down.

She'd walk up to her room and write songs based on the feelings their talks would stir up inside her, and they weren't only love songs anymore, inverted or otherwise; they were songs about the whole movement, songs about freedom.

Now at Bop City, thirty minutes before the show, Mama hovered over them behind the stage, doling out last-minute recommendations.

"Esther, when you cross over on that last verse and switch places with Chloe, make sure you slide your foot over delicate like, lately you been looking more like you galloping. And Chloe, don't stress your voice out too much on that first high note 'cause you got a few coming after."

Chloe took Esther's hand and squeezed it.

"You're going to be okay," she said the way Ruth used to.

And as much as Ruth had irritated her, that affirmation just before a show had always been a comfort. Even in her sister's absence, it was again.

Then Esther heard the club manager announcing their accomplishments one by one, that they were down to two members, but just as mighty, just as sweet, and when he started welcoming them to the stage, their mother stood between them and gripped their hands and said something Esther had never heard her say before.

"Forget everything I told you. Just have fun."

But it was too late for all that now.

Onstage, Chloe took the lead, and for a minute, while she sang "Oh What a Dream," Esther just beheld her like she might have if she were a member of the audience. When she observed her this way, she could see why she'd made her way to the front. It did seem like the voice of God was beckoning to the crowd from her heart.

Esther almost missed her own part she was so in tune to her sister, and when she started off that way, so rushed, it carried over into the rest of the show. She sang two of her notes off-key, then made the mistake of glancing back behind the curtain at her mother, whose face drew in so tight it appeared like she might not be breathing. Esther was always good at footwork, she had studied the greats, Katherine Dunham and Lena Horne, and that was a gift tonight, but then they got to the bridge. They had sung this song so many times with Ruth, so many times at Shiloh Missionary Baptist Church, at Mama's afterparties, at Flamingo for amateur night, so many times that she could hear Ruth coming in with an A-sharp any minute. The expectation wasn't even as active as a memory, more like an instinct, so deeply embedded that it was only when Chloe belted the part out that Esther remembered Ruth was gone. It was her part now, only she had missed it and come in late. Chloe had taken over for her, but now their voices were scrambling all over each other, and when it was time to leave the stage, the crowd didn't applaud like they normally did. They didn't boo them either—it wasn't Flamingo—but Mama didn't say a word the entire walk home, and Esther would have preferred the crowd's retorts to what she knew occupied the woman's thoughts.

At work the next day, Esther relayed the same.

"It was terrible, Horace." A month ago, she wouldn't have shared the humiliation with anybody. It was enough to know that there were real people there who would retain the sight of her failure for the rest of their lives. But he had been so vulnerable about his own cause, his own disappointment around it once half the block backed out, and she felt comfortable now saying things hadn't gone the way she'd hoped they would. They just hadn't.

"It couldn't have been that bad, Professor."

"No, I'm serious. You know my mama talks a mile a minute. You never have to worry about what she's thinking. She didn't say a word the whole walk home."

He paused, seeming to think. "Well, it's hard. Ruth's gone. You got to adjust to that. Your mama should understand as much."

"Chloe didn't need time to adjust."

"I'm not talking about Chloe, I'm talking about you. It's a lot, going from three to two. It's going to take some time for you to get comfortable out there, I'm sure. I wouldn't expect any different. Definitely don't let it kill your shine, girl."

"You don't think?"

"Absolutely not. You've put so much into this. When's your next show?"

"Friday."

"What time?"

"Seven o'clock."

"Um-hmm, seven, that's a lucky number, my daddy always said that."

"The shows always start at seven, boy."

He walked over to her and touched her shoulder. Before she could register it, his hand was gone.

"You gon be alright, Professor," he said. She didn't believe him, but his hand there, what he'd said in general, did soothe her in some way she couldn't source, and she still replayed the night's mishaps, but only when the plot in her new book stalled.

OF COURSE, ON FRIDAY, HER NERVES WERE BACK AS YET AGAIN THEY SANG "Oh What a Dream." Onstage, Esther told herself not to look into the audience, to hold her gaze level at the exit sign in the back of the room. But before she knew it, Chloe was filling in for her missed part. Esther let her eyes drift to the crowd in front of her. The faces blurred into one. She might not have singled Horace's out if she hadn't also heard his voice.

"Alright now, Esther."

She looked down at him, and the connection, identical to when their eyes met at his speeches, steadied her, reminded her of the escape she found among the words he uttered. She flew away again now. She stood upright. She puckered her lips. There was something about him beholding her from afar that enabled her awareness of herself. He was twelve feet from her; she wasn't threatened by his presence. Rather it was there like a shield outside herself, and nothing could come close to her that didn't live in agreement with his assessment. She felt an understanding of her own femininity, an appreciation of it, gliding up her body, and when she sang that same verse Chloe had, she let that understanding infuse itself into the lyrics.

She let those lyrics ring out, but the truth was, she was elsewhere. She was running through speeches with him. She was giving birth to new words, relatives of his own. She was singing those words to a crowd this size, maybe larger. The thrill of that dream, half unfurled already, took her to a place she hadn't seen onstage or anywhere else before.

And it was like the audience could hear the words in her mind, in her heart, like they were responding to that more than the show, which she had put on too many times to spark awe. They were on their feet now. She didn't dare stare too hard or too long, she didn't want any one face to crystallize, but she imagined Horace gazing up at her like she was gold.

She had never hit notes with as much precision as she did that last "Oh What a Dream." She looked to the side where her mother always hugged the curtains nights she didn't have to work, and there were tears in the woman's eyes. She clapped like if she poured all her spirit into it, the effort was going to land her next to Jesus.

Esther danced offstage, Chloe behind her, and Horace met her there. She fell into his arms for a moment before Vivian cleared her throat. She wasn't clapping anymore. Esther pulled back, walked closer to her mother.

"That was a good show, girls," she said like that was all it had been, not a deliverance. "We better be going now." Esther followed her off, glancing back at Horace behind her, who was still grinning. She realized when she stepped outside she'd forgotten her coat, and she hurried back into the club. The crowd had multiplied since they'd left. She didn't know which big name would be there tonight. The coat wasn't at the table where she'd been sitting before they took the stage, so she danced over to the bartender, and he said he'd moved it to the front office to be safe. She thanked him and declined his drink. She could hear voices from the office as she approached, deep ones. Big fancy men usually drank in this room and she didn't want to disturb them. She'd be quick. She had heard the shell of the talk from a distance, but there was the content of it too now that she'd come closer. One voice she couldn't help but recognize. "Those girls weren't half bad tonight, huh?" It was Mr. Bailey speaking.

"No, not bad at all," Mr. Franklin said back. Esther was nervous standing there, her name on the tips of these men's tongues, but she had done well tonight, and she had the nerve to be excited too.

"Nothing like what it was with that other one, but life goes on, like Preacher says, does it not?"

"It sure does."

"Funny thing is, I had it wrong. I wasn't looking at it the right way. My mama always said that. She'd send me to fetch something for her, a sewing needle, or her good linen, and I wouldn't always catch it at first. She'd say, 'Boy, you got to look with your eyes open.'"

"Mine would say, 'If it had been a snake, it would have bit you,'" Mr. Bailey said.

The old men laughed like those were the funniest expressions they'd ever heard. Ordinarily Esther would have walked in then with a wisecrack that would have really made them chuckle, but she needed to hear the rest.

"I think on account of how Ruth looks, you know what I mean."

"Well, I'm a married man."

"Yeah, married, but not blind."

"No, not blind, but those hips will smite you."

The old men laughed again.

"But it's Chloe that's the star, you know that now, don't you?"

"Yeah, that had crossed my mind tonight. Not to mention the other night."

"Yeah, it's unfortunate, the mama is going for a girl group and so am I. And that other one, well, she was cut from a different cloth, that's all. Any group with her in it is going nowhere fast. I'd just take the little one, but you gotta give the people what they want, you know what I mean?"

"Yeah, but man, those trends come and go. You gotta follow the talent."

"You right about that, remember that young man I signed in '51, thought he was going to be Nat King Cole, turned out he was more like his country cousin."

"Pat King Cole."

"Nat King Ol'."

The old men laughed again and Esther might have, the last joke held some merit, but she was too sick with what she'd heard to stick around; if she did, she feared she'd be affirming what they said, affirming their right to say it and their capacity to discern it. She was relieved her mother and sister hadn't waited. She arrived at home shivering on account of never having retrieved her coat. Vivian and Chloe waited at the kitchen table, but she bypassed them without saying a word. She locked the door of her bedroom, and she lay down on the cold wood floor beneath the base of the record player and listened to the song she'd just sung until she fell asleep. It had been a dream alright. The last decade of her life. What a dream.

AT THE STORE THE NEXT DAY, HORACE WAS WAITING.

"I never saw anything like that," he said while she fumbled through her purse for her key. "You were amazing. It wasn't even the song itself, just your presence there." He held her wrist for a moment as she turned the doorknob. "You stirred up so much in me last night. I went home and called my cousin in Baton Rouge. You know that ordinance that passed, nobody ever followed it, but then he led a weeklong boycott. Now he's working on a protest. They're expecting five thousand people. Can you believe that?"

They were in the store now.

"It was like seeing all that magic in you was contagious. I woke up thinking about a demonstration out here. I heard a rumor the City's going to start demolition on the Champagne Supper Club next week. Next Friday. But they can't start if we're standing there every day. We tried to get them to compromise. We said, alright, y'all going to tear down some buildings, but just keep a portion of it for our community, for our needs, but nothing came of it; they're not hearing us. Now it's time to escalate. And it won't just be us. We could invite preachers to speak too, maybe the president of our NAACP. We'd need to choose a spot that could handle a crowd. We'll need signs and megaphones. I can see it like it's in front of me right this instant."

He sat beside her behind the counter, rubbing his leg. "I can see people there I ain't never seen before in my life. You were so bold last night, girl, and it traveled over to me. I believe I can do it now. And next Friday is the first Friday of the month. Payday. People will be ready for action."

She tried to exude the excitement she would have had before she'd eavesdropped. Mama always said, "Some things ain't for you to know," and Esther understood her now.

"That's wonderful," she said, but even that came out flat. She tried to compensate. "I want to be there too." She felt better saying that, still dismal but not as sharp.

"Of course."

"I want to help you, with your speech, with whatever you need," she added.

"That's wonderful, but you been so busy with rehearsal, and I don't want to take away—"

She cut him off. Her offering wasn't an act as much as she'd thought it had been.

"No," she said. "Let me help you. I need it."

THE NEXT DAY, MAMA WALKED IN EARLY FROM WORK WAVING A PIECE OF paper in the air.

"They're going to take us," she screamed. "The Dunbar Hotel still wants us to audition, even without Ruth, even with the baby. God has blessed us, God has blessed us, my children." She pulled Esther and Chloe to her hard. Esther jumped around with her and squealed; she wasn't completely faking.

"When is it, Mama?" she asked.

"Friday, in Los Angeles." Next weekend. The same time as the demonstration.

"And I didn't mention it because I didn't want to get your hopes up," Mama went on, lowering her voice for the next part, "but Mr.

Franklin said if you two get a big gig, a fancy gig with a big crowd, he'd consider signing the two of you."

Chloe squealed. Esther didn't cling to her mother as tightly at that, but she didn't drop the embrace either. She didn't have the heart to tell her there was no way Mr. Franklin was going to sign her. "Unfortunate" was the word he'd used, and he was right, the diction was precise, the whole thing had turned out to be so unfortunate.

"I HAD HOPED WE WOULDN'T HAVE TO GET TO THIS POINT. I HAD HOPED we could settle this among our own, but it was our own people who sold the neighborhood to them," Horace said. They were in the bookstore, preparing for Friday's demonstration. "I'm worried there aren't enough of us fighting them off. And just based on sheer numbers alone, they're going to win. A few of us can protest with all the force in the world, but if the rest just give our places up, not giving a hell what they're replaced with, then what's all our work for? Nothing."

"That's 'cause they're not free," Esther said. It slipped out before she'd even known she was going to say it. "We're always talking about whites giving us freedom, and yeah, that would be nice, but we have to free ourselves first. We have to see ourselves from a place of power. So many of us aren't even used to having the capacity to say no. It's not in us. The strength was just never developed. We don't even think we have the right."

Horace copied what she said in furious motions, like there was something supernatural flowing through him and his fingers could clasp the bulk if they just kept going. When she was done talking, he set the pencil down and looked between her and his notes.

"I wish I could be there," she said. She'd told him about the audition. "It's just that Chloe has so much riding on this. I don't want to let her down." As she spoke, she realized she didn't know what would let her sister down more, staying or going.

"I know," he said back. "But you'll be with me in spirit."

When she got home, she carried her notepad to the roof. There was a tune that had come to her that morning.

ESTHER COULDN'T SLEEP WEDNESDAY NIGHT. YES, THE AUDITION WAS ON a Friday, but Mama wanted to leave Thursday evening so they'd have time to familiarize themselves with the new environment.

When Esther woke Thursday, she dressed and brushed her hair. She tiptoed down the stairs and through the living room, then the front parlor so as not to wake her sister before the appointed time. She sat down and wrote a quick note, folding it into Chloe's satchel, already there waiting. She didn't know yet if the girl would need to read it.

She stopped at the bookstore and just sat beside Horace for some time.

He had been whistling: "A-Tisket, A-Tasket."

"Penny for your thoughts?" he asked.

And when she only shrugged, he said, "It's nice to see you in a better mood, Professor."

"You too," she said.

HE DIDN'T SEEM TO REMEMBER THAT SHE WAS LEAVING LATER THAT DAY, and she didn't mention it either. As the hours passed, she tracked them according to what she should have been doing. At one, she might go home and prepare a light lunch on account of the long ride ahead of her. At three, she might pack, then freshen up, place the remaining toiletries in her suitcase. At five, Chloe would be on her way home from school. Esther would remove the note from her sister's bag in anticipation—there being no need for it as long as she was where she was supposed to be. At six, they would catch a ride with Mary to the train station. Mama would meet them there. But when five thirty came, Esther was still inside the shop.

At closing, Horace asked if she wanted to go to Ocean Beach, and without thinking, she said "Sure." She had been there so many times, but it looked like a new place that afternoon. She sat on the large rock where they would usually throw pebbles, and she didn't just see the water; she let its rhythm move inside her.

She felt the smoothness she'd accessed that last night on Bop City's stage, and she knew she would sit where she was until she was sure Chloe had read the note, sure the train had departed. The note had said something had come up at the store and she would meet her in Los Angeles on Friday. There was still time for that second part to be true. She was guilt-ridden thinking of the state the girl would find their mother in, the state she'd find herself in, but maybe that would be for the best in the long run. Anyway, like she'd written, she'd be there. Just not today.

Horace didn't ask any questions at first. He was too focused on fretting over who would be coming to the demonstration, what he planned to discuss. Then he glanced up at her.

"So I wanted to give you your time," he said. "But what happened? Why ain't you where you supposed to be?"

She took a deep breath. "There was a delay," she said. "Tomorrow."

He reached for her hand, and she let him.

"Thank you," he said. "I know you didn't stay for me, but thank you. I needed you here tonight."

He kept on cycling through his fears; then he'd turn back around and cycle through them again from the other direction. He had never spoken in front of a group that large. What if he got stage fright?

"You never do."

"What if people don't show up like they say they will?"

"They always come."

"What if I say the wrong thing and I miss the message?"

"It also resides in your heart."

"What if this all fails? What if they all rise up against me for playing with their hope?"

"At least you tried," she said. "You'll always sleep at night knowing that, that you saw something that needed fixing and you tried to make it right. You owe it to yourself to do that, but that's all you can do."

"You're too much," he whispered. "You're too much."

And then she heard herself say, "What if I sang?"

"Do what?"

"At the demonstration. What if I sang? I've been working on something." She pulled her notepad from her satchel, stood on a rock, and let him hear everything that had come to her the night before. When she was done, he lifted her and swung her around. She was so giddy, she rested her head against his shoulder.

She could see the relief in his eyes. But he said, "It was amazing. You're amazing. But what about the show? What about your sister? Your mother? You've been practicing and practicing. I don't want to see you throw that away for me."

"It's not for you," she said. "It's for the people. My family chief among them. And it's for *me*." She said it again because she so enjoyed the weight of the words. "For once," she added, "I want to be there at the turning point. I want to see this through."

She had never told him about the conversation she overheard, and she did so now.

"There's so much riding on Chloe's performance, yes, and that's why I shouldn't be there."

He pressed her into him, and again, she let him.

"There's not an ounce of truth in what they said," he said. "I hope you know that. You're going to see that for yourself tomorrow. Are you ready?"

She nodded. "I think so," she said. And then, "Yeah, more ready than I've been."

THAT NEXT MORNING, ESTHER FINISHED GETTING READY IN HALF THE time it would have taken her just a day earlier. The phone rang, her mother no doubt, but the ring might as well have been the theme song to her new life. When Horace knocked at the door, she felt like she was spinning.

"Ain't you supposed to be elsewhere chasing your mama's dreams?" Mary called from her kitchen window, and without a tinge of fear, Esther shot back, "I got my own dreams, Miss Mary." She clutched Horace's arm and pressed forward.

Horace was right about the turnout. He and his brothers had built a stage in front of the Champagne Supper Club. They'd blocked off the street, and there were at least three hundred people standing an hour before start time, some holding signs and some empty-handed, some dressed for nighttime and some in work pants and boots. The first to speak were preachers, Reverend Wilson and Pastor Brown, and she found their talks were so different from what she'd grown up on in church. They roused their people up with logic here now, the simple and long-gone deduction that their neighborhood was every bit as valuable as the white ones; they had built the community and deserved a chance to enjoy that hard-earned plenty. And instead of the passion being directed toward praise, it was lit up and inflamed, angry.

When the time for Esther to sing had come, she watched Horace approach the podium. The crowd in the street had thickened, and Esther's nerves kicked in noticing that, but they flattened when she looked up at Horace. There was a sense inside her rising that she had nothing to do with what was about to happen. A version of her, sure, stood in her clothes, at the hem of the stage, and was even now stepping on, but she was elsewhere, sort of like that moment when Mr. Sterling put her hand on himself, and she wouldn't have made it through if her eyes had landed on her body then, if her spirit had stayed inside it.

Horace introduced her, and the crowd clapped and cheered her on. If she had been herself, who she had been, she might have recognized Gladys and Horace and Mary in the front, the high school girls some rows behind them, but as it was, she stared ahead at a void. A part of her wanted to search the stage for her sisters, wanted to prepare to scamper across the floor with them, all the while singing along to foolishness. Back then, she had always been most nervous before she opened her mouth, before the hosts even called out her name. But now, she didn't have to tell her feet to twirl; she didn't have to count out beats in her mind. This song she was about to reveal had come through her. There was no way she could forget it.

She opened her mouth and watched the lyrics take flight.

The world can't change without me
No, the world can't change without me
When I reach into my soul
And dig out what it knows
That's the first step to being free

On the first few lines, she had heard her voice stagger, but she didn't critique herself for it like she might have if she were singing something that had come out bolder, more natural, from Faye Adams's lips. The words themselves, the meaning behind them, seemed to preclude an attack. She only kept on, and as she progressed through the song, her voice made it its own.

I've scaled mountains, I've journeyed rivers
I've crossed bridges that broke me to my knees
I've endured burdens, I've been bonded my whole life
But I'm claiming today
I'm free

And there was something about making that declaration to a group that made the words more accessible to her spirit, like teaching Chloe how to fox-trot one day had chiseled her own quarter-turns.

There's no white man to tell me no
There's no law to make it so

There's no government to grant me liberty
There's no leader, there is no power
That trumps the one that comes straight out of me

And she felt the glory of that belief, realized down in her soul.

When it was over, the applause overtook her, and she submitted. The people rushed the stage, wanting to be near her, but Horace swept her along to the front of the crowd, and they walked back through the Fillmore, the others behind them now.

"HOW DID ALL THAT FEEL, COMING OUT OF YOU?" HE ASKED LATER THAT night. Whatever all that was had affected her in other ways. He was in her house with her right now, for instance, in her bedroom, and she had removed her shirt.

"It was just like you said." She traced her fingers along his side. "I started singing and it all came pouring out. It was the safest I've felt, being removed in that way."

He nodded, smiling. "I told you right? Didn't I tell you? Everybody was saying it. They want to know where I've been hiding you. I mean, you should have seen the people. As many as there were there, young people and babies, and nobody made a sound. And the women. Think about what it meant to them to see you."

They kissed some more and then agreed they needed to slow down. She walked him to the stoop, and he told her he loved her as he stepped into his truck. He drove away before she could respond, but if he hadn't, she would have said it back.

She was about to walk into the house when she saw Ruth approaching.

"Mama sent me over here to see about you, girl." She sat down on the stoop, and Esther, surprised as she was, collected herself after a moment and sat too.

She was still buzzing from earlier, but it had started to wear off even before Horace left. Her mother would be back tomorrow, and it wouldn't matter how many people had been at the protest, how high she had lifted them, how high she had been lifted. And now this.

"She looking every which way," she went on. "I told her I seen you this morning, that you safe. I figure you betta be the one to tell her why you stayed."

Esther turned. Ruth had lost the baby weight, but she seemed older somehow, tired in the eyes, even more tired in the spirit. "You were there?"

"Of course I was there." Ruth rubbed her eyes like she had been privy to Esther's thoughts. "Mama's been through a lot. I can see it clearer since I had Denise. She think she got us doo-wopping for money, but it's safety she's after. She figure you on that roof, you not in somebody's bed, in no jail cell. They locking women up too, you know."

"I know." Esther lowered her head.

"I'm not saying that to scare you. I'm just telling you, if she act up when she get back, and you know she gon cut up something awful, that's why."

She paused, and neither of them spoke, but there was information streaming between them like always. Ruth had been her best friend before she could say more than a dozen words—they had had to feel each other's meanings out, and that trail that stretched from one woman to the other was worn down now, but it was still there.

"Y'all butt heads, but I believe that's 'cause you the one remind her most of Daddy."

Esther hadn't expected her to mention him, and the day had been so transformative, invoking him touched the soft spot inside her she had learned to block.

"If something happened to you, to you most of all, Esther, I believe she'd die. I do believe that." She reached for Esther's hand. "Either way, I'm proud of you," she said. "The way you showed yourself, your full self, to those people, girl. I always knew you had that spirit in you. That spirit of fire. You get it from Mama, that's the funny thing. She gon see that for herself one day."

Esther paused before she asked the question. "And if she doesn't?"

Ruth didn't say anything for a while, and that trail between them seemed to have coiled back in her direction, out of Esther's reach. Esther looked back toward the house, focused her gaze on the knob at the center of the door. She could stand up, prop herself there on the other side of her sister, preempt whatever it was Ruth was about to say, whatever it was that might sour the sweetness budding between them now. She was about to do so when her sister spoke.

"A woman like you, you'll make her see."

VIVIAN

It had been a week since Esther had skipped the audition, and though Vivian had known she wouldn't come before they'd even boarded the train—she didn't care what the goddamn note said—she still thought about it every day. The betrayal. The gall.

Vivian had trucked it to Los Angeles with her baby daughter, imagining the whole while the train rolled past sand dunes and strawberry fields what she would say when she got the chance. It was always about Esther, wasn't it? For once, couldn't she think about what it would do to Chloe to fall flat on her face? And yet Chloe, as shocking as it had been to behold, had shined. They had hailed a taxi to the Dunbar Hotel and rode in an elevator with *the* Miss Lena Horne all the way to the third floor. At the last minute, Vivian had to change the routine since there was only one, and Billie Holiday worked best, what with the mood she was under. Chloe hadn't sung by her lonesome before, but at rehearsal, she delivered the song so hard Vivian feared the next day her voice would be gone. And at the actual audition, Chloe had been more nervous than Vivian had ever seen her. But the adrenaline seemed to be like a formula for her daughter; she performed according to the intensity of it—that day, Chloe didn't just hit notes, she bent them, and when it was time for the bridge, she climbed so high, Vivian couldn't locate her anymore. Vivian couldn't help but rise to her feet. She knew standing there that the moment had been fated, yet she still felt gutted somehow.

This evening, Vivian's anger had dulled just a touch, enough for her to wait in the kitchen for Esther to come home from work. She planned to tell her in a tone devoid of all heat that there was one path to living in this house rent-free, and it was obedience. It wasn't about the show, she'd say. It was about trust, dependability, family. What was more important than that? Certainly not this Horace character. She wasn't a fool; she'd seen them giving each other goo-goo eyes, heard he was prophesying all over the neighborhood. And for what? Yeah, the Champagne Supper Club was still standing for now, but it was only a matter of time. One day she and everybody else would walk past it expecting life, and it would be reduced to rubble. She had to prepare herself for that. Esther and Horace would need to too. Yes, best to design your own life, erect walls around it, effect change inside those walls. Vivian had learned that the hard way, and every time a white woman at work moved her files, every time she had to stand—fresh off a twelve-hour shift—the whole bumpy, windy ride home, she remembered the bloodshot eyes of the men swinging from those trees. There had been progress; sometimes it was enough just to sit with that. She was lifted from the memory by the sound of footsteps.

It was Esther, no doubt. Vivian had prepared a speech more or less, but she was taken aback by what she heard from the stoop: Esther whistling a tune Vivian couldn't place, whistling like a child, like she'd been cleansed of something. She had never known why the girl had started to fade sometime in middle school, and Mary had sworn it was just a phase, but she had never come back, not fully. Except now, she was here reminding Vivian of the child who used to squeal for homemade whipping cream, and it had nothing to do with Vivian, nothing to do with the roof.

Vivian stood to start talking—the speech was on the edge of her tongue—but the girl barreled into the kitchen, still whistling, intercepting her, and for a minute, they faced each other in silence close enough to hug, but that would have been unthinkable in this context.

"Mama, I know you're mad," Esther started, "but Chloe told me she did great, that she'd never performed better in her life."

"Chloe's responsible," Vivian heard herself say, sitting. She had had to take several breaths to even out her words, to keep them sturdy. "She had a job to do and she did it, though the circumstances had changed, that's all. That's going to be more necessary than ever, at the stage she's brought us to now. But if you can't commit to it, just say the word, and I'll make my arrangements." She was back on track now. This part she had meant to be only a threat. She had become desperate, as painful as it was to admit. There was too much riding on this. If Esther didn't understand that now, she would in some years, her own children at her feet looking up at her for security, and yet she was a Negro woman: there were only so many avenues that could provide it.

"I can't," Esther said before Vivian had even gotten the last word out. "I can't. I have news."

And something in her expression gave Vivian pause, a sense of déjà vu. She suddenly wished she'd made herself a drink. She rarely indulged, of course, but now this conversation was bound to be something about a protest, or whatever all else they had planned, and Vivian wouldn't be able to bear it without something better than good coating her stomach.

"Mama, I have news," she repeated.

"Yes, I gathered that."

"I found it."

"You found what?"

"That thing, that thing, that feeling you have on the roof, that feeling Chloe seems to have there too. I found it for myself, Mama. At the demonstration the other day, you should have seen me, all that power that had been waiting to spring forth, Mama, people are still talking about that afternoon. All this time I didn't realize how much I needed to feel good at something."

Esther moved her hand from her side to wipe her eyes. "It swelled the part of my heart that I had let recede. It—I don't want to just sing old covers at clubs anymore, Mama, now that I know this, now that I have this—" She paused. "I want to sing for our people, Mama, for their liberation. I don't want to, I need to. I love it, Mama. I love it," she repeated softer this time.

Vivian stood again, walked across the kitchen, and poured the rum for herself. She had barely eaten, but it was no matter. That fool had ruined her appetite. She wiped her hands on her apron and turned to walk toward the parlor. She would head upstairs. Something was twisted up inside her stomach. Best if she lay down for a spell.

"Mama," Esther called to her, reaching for her, but she was too far away. Vivian was too far ahead. "Mama," she called out to her back. "Can't you see? It's better this way. I did it for Chloe, I did it for both of you. Can't you see that?"

But Vivian didn't see anything but red, and this time it wasn't the future; it was the past. It was the men at her door, the dogs barking and racing, the glass breaking, the shots ringing out from both sides, the fire erupting and her mama scooping her up and carrying her out in the nick of time because there was an explosion and she would have lost her limbs. She heard her mother tell someone later, "There are things worse than death," and Vivian had nearly been one of them. She had heard her mother beg her father months earlier: "I plead of you to stop that dangerous preaching." But he hadn't, and Vivian had had to flee halfway across the world.

She was up the stairs when she heard herself say, "Get out," without even turning. "You betrayed me, you broke my heart." She was on the landing now, leaning down, full-on shouting. "You would have made a fool of me, you would have made a fool of your sister, you didn't care. All her hard work for nothing."

"But it turned out alright, Mama."

"Only by the grace of God, only because we stay ready, only because I trained you all to be the best no matter the circumstances. You stay if you want to be loyal, but otherwise, you have got to get out."

And Vivian was surprised to hear Esther for once actually obey her. She'd expected her to tarry in the kitchen for a few minutes, then retire upstairs to her room, but Vivian heard the front door open, then click back into place. It was Vivian who reached her room and retired without brushing her teeth or covering her hair.

She tried to sleep, Lord knew she did, but it wouldn't come. After she heard Chloe's bedroom door close, she ventured upstairs to the roof. She had finished her first drink and then another, and she could run through all their shows now in her head if she wanted to; something in her wanted to, needed to, now. Ruth's baby had been born months earlier, and she loved being a grandmother; she did. Denise had turned her inside out, but she missed the early days, the trio, the disparate scraps of routines that would blend into sound and dance and looks so intact, it was as if they had been crafted by someone outside herself. More than anything, she wanted to act it out here, now, relive it, convince the part of her mind that might submit that she was safe again, but she had a feeling when the song was over, she'd find herself more hollowed out than when it began. She turned back to the house to get dressed instead. She curled her hair and dabbed on lipstick, slid into a pencil skirt, smoothed it down in the middle where it lay flat; she knew where she was going. Even walking, she knew, but she didn't acknowledge it to herself until he opened the door. If she told herself, if she prepared for the moment in any way, she might be let down. She couldn't bear the thought of more disappointment.

"Hey," Preacher Thomas said like it was the most natural thing in the world for her to show up to his place past dark. "Come in."

He had just finished dinner and was poking at a sweet potato pie one of the congregants had brought him that morning.

"Which one?" she asked.

"Miss Thompson," he said and Vivian scrunched up her nose.

"You can't be picky when you're an old widower," he said. "Most of the days I eat, it's through their kindness."

"I should send you some plates. I didn't think about it," she said back. "We've been so busy with . . ." And her voice trailed off.

"How's it going?"

She shook her head. "Not well," she said. She sat and told him about Esther.

"Oh, I'm sorry, Viv. I know that must be so hard. It didn't ever really seem like it was her thing, though, did it?"

She paused. "No, I guess not, but I thought she would improve. Esther's the type who needs validation, she needs proof. I thought when we got to the top of the mountain, she would meet its height."

Preacher shook his head. "Not if it wasn't for her," he said. "Wouldn't be enough proof in the world."

"But this movement? That can't be it for her either. Traipsing all around the city. I already did that for her. I came this far. And she's trying to go backwards.

"And because of love," she went on. "Can you believe it? She didn't know what a protest song was a few months ago. Now she loves it, now she's got to have it, now she's so riled up she's willing to forsake everything she poured her life into."

"Love is a powerful thing," the preacher said. "When it's real. I understand that. What wouldn't you do to maintain it?" And he looked up at her the same time she looked at him and their eyes locked.

He didn't say anything, but he didn't need to. She could feel what he was telling her with everything in her. She had been feeling it all this time, she saw now. "I better go." She stood.

"Stop, V, you always do this. When we get close, you pull back, and then we get close again and you pull back. I can't keep going through the cycle. It's too hard on me. I've been through so much loss as it is. If you can't meet me here with this, then tell me. I'll always love you,

I'll always be your friend, but I can't keep hurting myself." Then he paused. She reached for the doorknob.

"Before you go, I just have one question," he said.

"Anything," she said back, because it was true. What wouldn't she tell him if he needed to know?

"Do you love me?" he asked.

"Do I what?" Her head swung slowly back.

"I said, do you love me?"

"Boy, stop playing with me. We too old for all that now. What does that even mean?"

"Do you love me?" he repeated the question this time like he was reading a script and was surprised at the line written across it.

"Preacher." She placed her hand on her heart. "How can you ask me that?"

"How can I not?"

"You know how much I have on my plate. The girls, work, your wife not cold in her grave. My husband—"

"Do you love me?"

She turned back for the door, stared at the cold, hard wood. It was an easy question the way it was presented. For most people, it would have required no thought. Even her. She could say yes or no. Many questions provoked complex responses, but this one could be addressed in one syllable and filed away. In a way that made it harder.

He sighed. "You got to think about it all this time, I already know." And he stood too then and headed toward his parlor stairs.

But she stopped him. "Wait."

She still didn't know what to say. She knew the answer, of course, but to say it, that was different. It was the sort of difference that would swallow them up, all they'd been, and she didn't know how their new form would be rendered. He was the person she called when she needed prayer, the person she thought of when enough space cleared in her mind. Right before she drifted off or at the very tip of the morning, when she was already regretting coming to, he was there. Once, when she needed tuition for the girls, he had spotted her. On Ellis's birthday just two weeks earlier, the grief she'd warded off for decades had coursed back hot and tough, and he'd sat on the line with her for hours listening to her weep. She had come here again now when everything she'd banked on had been swept out from under her and she couldn't reclaim her footing. She had known in the part of herself that led the way, though she hadn't admitted where she was going yet, that he would be able to soothe her. And he had, but now he wanted this. Did she love him?

"Do you?"

She'd brought him food; she'd watched him grieve; she'd seen his first smile months after he'd buried the woman he'd thought would never leave, and she'd rubbed his back when a month later the smile receded once more. Her girls bought him Christmas presents, cooked his favorite fish; he taught them to ride a bicycle; he didn't miss a major show. He had folded Vivian into his life and she, him. They had never said the word "love." They hadn't had to. Of course it had been there.

He was walking up the stairs finally now, and she flew from the door to head him off, reached for his arm.

"Of course I love you," she whispered. It wouldn't come out stronger. She hadn't said it to a man in so much time.

His eyes shined. "You don't want to hurt my feelings."

She shook her head. "It's not that. It's never been about that. I love you. I continue to love you. I always have."

She fell into his arms, and he tightened them around her.

"You love me," he said.

"I love you," she said. And then he led her upstairs and she didn't go back home that night.

WHEN SHE WOKE, THERE WAS A MOMENT WHEN SHE DIDN'T REMEMBER Esther in her kitchen, the proclamations streaming from her mouth.

Just a minute, though, and then it returned. The shock of it, the nerve. Esther had just told her how it was going to be. No one outside that hospital had directed information at her in that way in more than a decade. But then the girl had said she'd done it for Chloe, for her too. And Preacher had said she never would have come around if her heart wasn't in it. And look how well Chloe had done. Maybe Esther not showing had been some sort of gift.

Vivian turned to her side. Preacher snored. She hadn't known that about him yesterday, but now it was something she would never forget. She stood to get dressed and he reached for her hand and groaned.

"Not yet."

"I got to," she whispered. "You do too. Any minute the saints will be here with their breakfast platter."

"That's not the kind of meal I was envisioning."

"Ooh, Preacher." She leaned toward him and kissed him hard. It took everything in her not to fall on her back. "The girls'll be worried. They'll start looking for me." She stood, rediscovering her underthings in the sunlight.

"Nah, they grown," Preacher said back.

"Still live at home, though, two of 'em at least." She remembered then she'd kicked Esther out and kept talking to ward off the shame. "And I've got to think about the example I'm setting."

He didn't say anything to that, just watched her stuff herself into her bra and then her pantyhose and skirt. She tried to slow down, to stretch it out—it had been so long since somebody was watching. Downstairs, he kissed her before she opened the front door. The guilt she'd thought would greet her with the sun was there, but she found she was tall beside it.

Still, there was the regular cast of characters to consider, and Preacher lived in the direction opposite the hospital. She couldn't just blame it on a late shift.

She walked down the sidewalk with her head up, and nobody said anything outright, only, "Oh, okay, Miss Vivian," and "I see you, lady. It was just a matter of time."

Luckily Mary hadn't set her stool out on the front porch when Vivian reached home, and the girls weren't up yet either. She eased the door into its slot, tiptoed through the parlor and up the stairs. She showered Preacher's cologne out of her hair, off her breasts and elsewhere. She would have cried if she were in the habit of it, but she didn't understand why. She was reminded of those moments at the clubs on the heels of a show, watching the audience go crazy for the girls, but it wasn't exactly that; it was more personal. If Preacher's heart was like a tree, she had reached its innermost ring. Ellis and Mattie, she thought, would say they had mourned long enough.

When she got downstairs, Esther was leaning against the counter in her robe like she had been waiting for her. They were the only two in the house who drank coffee. Esther had prepared a pot, and Vivian didn't say a word until she poured her cup. She was poised to speak when she sat, but the girl beat her to it.

"Mama, I'm sorry," she started.

"Shh," Vivian said. But she didn't say more, not yet. She took a sip, then another. She didn't know what would come out of her mouth, only that she was still thinking about the night before, how it had felt when she had reached his bedroom, lay down on his bed, and closed her eyes. By that time, the need had become so strong, it had gained control of her body. She had still been considering his wife then, Ellis, and the church besides—but none of it was steady enough to matter. She had taken off her shirt anyway, peeled back her legs, surrendered to the thrill of having a need matched. She set her coffee down.

"I thought about it some," Vivian said. And it was true, she had thought about it some, but more than thinking about it, she had not thought about it. She had occupied herself with Preacher's hands, the lines on the palms that she had always viewed from the corner of her eye but which she now had the opportunity to study and feel in private. She had been able to absorb the tenor of his voice at home, which was different than it was on the pulpit, on the phone, surrounded by her children, but it was the same too. The same spirit that occupied him there seemed to course through him in his bedroom. And when that voice grew softer and fainter, then higher and higher still, it was that same power, but she had accessed it now. It had streamed through her and filled her. Even remembering it seemed to enlarge her. Her daughter, for instance, stared at her from across the room like she had transformed into Dinah Washington, and maybe she had. Vivian shifted in her seat some, crossed, then uncrossed her legs.

"I thought about it some," she repeated. "And Esther, you're right. If you love it, you love it. Who am I to stand in your way?"

If she had been Dinah Washington a minute ago, she was Sam Cooke now. The girl's mouth hung open.

"Mama, are you being serious?"

"Of course. You know I wouldn't joke about something like that."

"Mama." The girl walked closer now. She felt safer, that much was clear, but she stopped at the other end of the table. "So you're not mad?"

"Mad? No. I never was that. I was disappointed. I still am. I have my hopes. I have my dreams. If I had had the talent you were blessed with, well, it's too late for me, but I hoped for you all. But if you don't love it, it will never feel that way to you, I guess, no matter how hard you try, and you say there's something you really want to pursue. How many times do you come across that in life? Some people don't even get one shot. Miraculous really to have two." She paused. She wanted to tell her to be careful, but she didn't know how to get the warning across without highlighting the need for the care. She couldn't bear it if something happened to Esther. Instead of speaking, she held out her arms.

The girl seemed to have lost herself there, rushing over to hug her. Chloe had come downstairs sometime in the middle of their conversation, and Esther clued her in in that quiet sisterly way Vivian had always envied. Today, she admired it knowing she would never be a part, and they all danced around in a circle, reenacting the moves they would have shown off on somebody's stage. They were in the middle of the small celebration when the phone rang. Vivian excused herself and hustled over, caught the receiver on the final ring. Oh. It was the Dunbar Hotel. They had come to a decision. They wanted Chloe to come back for a final audition, this time for the head manager; this time, he would meet them at the San Francisco location. And this time, they intended for Chloe to sing alone.

CHLOE

Ruth had started back at work weeks ago, and Chloe minded the baby. Today Denise was colicky and fussed if she was out of her arms for even five minutes, so Chloe slept with the girl on top of her on the couch, though normally she used that time to fix supper. Today she rushed through the tasks, browning chicken on the stove, then baking it, and she knew she overboiled the rice, but at least it was tender, and at least the string beans were salty and divine. The baby plopped them in her mouth with both fists, and Chloe was the one to wipe her cheeks with the napkin.

When Ruth got home, sometimes she would sit at the table for nearly an hour in silence, just staring off into space. The baby still wasn't sleeping all the way through the night, and Ruth was working twelve-hour shifts. After smiling in people's faces all day, maintaining her voice along an upward slope, asking about patients' wives and their husbands, telling the dementia patients the weather then telling them again, she was worn down, simply worn down. She needed to retreat into herself before she could utter another word. Chloe normally let her determine when that time had come, but she was antsy today—not in a bad way, only like her spirit knew a surprise was awaiting her, and it was overtaxed trying to determine what it might be.

"Ruth?" she asked, shifting the child in her arms to another hip. The woman didn't come to. "Ruth?" she repeated. "How long have you known Gerry?" she asked once her sister glanced in her direction.

"Since before I was forming memories, you know that." She smiled.

"Yeah, I just remember you two chasing the ice cream truck together, and you'd always split the dessert."

"Ice cream sandwich."

"Ice cream sandwich. It would have melted and y'all would still be dividing it in half, the vanilla dripping down your fingers."

Ruth came to life again at that, and Chloe could imagine how she might show up for her patients, dog-tired, but there was always a light inside her, and it was like she couldn't help but let people tug it to the forefront.

Chloe paused before the next question.

"When did you realize you liked him like that?"

"Like what?" Ruth raised her eyebrows.

"You know what I mean, girl." Chloe turned toward the stove, then back again.

Ruth smirked, rubbed her eyes, and held out her arms for her baby.

"I don't know."

"I know you started hanging out secret a few years ago."

"You noticed it a few years ago. I had started thinking about him as more than a friend before I even got my period. I remember thinking something was wrong with me because it hadn't come. I remember worrying that if he knew about whatever deficiency it was, he wouldn't want me. Funny now to reminisce on it. I was only twelve years old."

Chloe laughed, but she felt sad all of a sudden, like the experience Ruth was describing was out of bounds for her.

"Have you seen Mama?" she asked to change the subject.

"Um-hmm, at work, though, only place I see her now that she all hugged up with Preacher."

"Don't I know it," Chloe said.

"I'm glad she's happy, though," Ruth said. "She's been alone for so long. You'll understand what that's like when you're older."

"I understand now," Chloe started to say, and then Gerry walked in and Ruth stood to greet him, kissed his cheek. It was hard to watch that, harder now that she wanted it for herself.

Gerry greeted Chloe next just like always, but before he could ask about her day, the baby started crying for him. Only when he had kissed her about thirty times did he turn back.

"How did everything go today?"

"Good, we walked to Hamilton Square. There was a family of geese, and she stared at them for nearly an hour."

"She loves animals," he said. "Maybe she'll be a veterinarian, yes, maybe you'll be a veterinarian." He turned back to the baby and sang the words at her, and it was endearing, it was, but it also made Chloe sick.

"And how's everything else?" Gerry went on. "You got any new gigs coming up?"

She told him about the audition, that Esther hadn't been there, that even without her, she'd gotten a second one.

"Congratulations." He sounded genuinely pleased. She knew they both had been worried about her when the Champagne Supper Club closed, and she'd thought her dreams had shut down with it. She had been worried about herself too. She hadn't known if it was the loss of her sister to that aisle or the loss of the club or both, but she didn't sing for days after. She didn't eat either. And she'd never had a bad word to say against anyone, anyone, but whenever she saw the white men from the City around the neighborhood, she cursed them in her mind, even once she'd started flourishing despite them.

"I know Vivian's happy," he went on. "Sometimes I catch this one"—he nodded at Ruth— "singing in her sleep, dancing in the mirror too while she's getting ready for work. I think she misses it."

"Boy, I always did that," Ruth said.

"Not like now."

"Anyway. Even if I wanted to miss it, how could I? Mama won't let me forget I left her. You should hear her at the hospital, all 'Chloe is a star, don't get me wrong, but girl groups are the wave of the future, and I just hope we didn't miss our window on account of . . .' Then she'll just let her voice trail off, let me fill in the rest. It's a nightmare."

"Tell me about it," Chloe said. "Now she's on the hunt for other girls, since Esther's gone too. 'It was fine with two,' she'll say. 'But we gotta pull out the big guns now. Three is a spiritual number. Don't get cocky just 'cause you got that one lil gig.'"

"I can hear it," Ruth said laughing. "You'd be alright by yourself, though. Better than alright. It hit me last time I saw you sing, the spotlight should have always been on you."

"You haven't seen me in so long," Chloe said, and Ruth started to refute her, then stopped herself and looked away.

Normally, Chloe started packing as soon as Gerry walked in; she didn't want to be in the way. Ruth had assured her that wasn't possible, that this was her home, but she didn't believe it. This time, though, she sat. She watched the two of them. Ruth had been exhausted, but she stood to fix him a plate. While she was arranging his, she asked if Chloe wanted some too, and Chloe nodded and said she'd get it herself. Ruth looked back at her and smiled. It was a tired smile, but it was kind too.

They all sat around the table watching the baby stuff balls of rice in her mouth, listening to Gerry describe his day. A customer had come in asking for a pound of ground beef. Gerry had given him a little over. Mr. Gaines had encouraged that type of generosity, but his brother-in-law laid into him so hard. Ruth didn't even respond, like she'd heard it all before.

"This is good, Chloe, real good," she said. She had taken a bite from Gerry's plate.

"Not as good as your spaghetti, though," Chloe said. She had woken up craving it for some reason. Mama used to make it every Tuesday, but these days, she was out with Preacher most nights.

"That's funny you say that," Ruth said. "This morning I woke up wanting that very dish, if you can believe that. Smoked sausage and all. I've watched Mama make it so many times I could run through the recipe in my sleep, you know that? I'll make it for you this weekend, drop off a platter. Would that be okay?"

And Chloe felt like she might weep.

THE CALLBACK FROM THE DUNBAR HOTEL HAD BEEN UNEXPECTED REally. The promoter had wanted a duo, but when Esther hadn't made it, a calm had descended over Chloe. She'd remembered how James had encouraged her, and she'd released Billie's words with all the longing and desire pent up inside her. When it was over, she felt a certain relief, a liberation from the white man who'd overtaken her very being since he kissed her on her sidewalk months earlier.

She hadn't seen him since, and that had been by her own doing. Tony had asked her to accompany him to the Blue Mirror first, then Club Flamingo, where she just knew in her spirit James would be, but each and every time, she declined. He'd stopped asking soon after because he'd been making it with the bartender, and the dual losses had been a hard pill to swallow, but Chloe filled her mind with her rehearsals, the new routines Mama had been studying, and they fit the width of her attention mostly if she focused. If she lay down at the base of the record player with her eyes closed and imagined the person she became onstage, that person who breathed cosmic air and ate moon crumbs, she didn't need anybody else.

IT WAS THE DAY OF TONY'S SUPPER, AND SHE'D WANTED TO CANCEL, BUT he needed the money. She was halfway down his block, the food in tow, when she saw the white men a few yards from his house, Mr. Belmont at the front. There was no missing the gray flannel business suits or the impudence, standing on Tony's across-the-street neighbor's stoop as if they owned it, their heads high to the sky, shoulders pulled back.

Tony opened the door, nodding at the men. "Now they coming after our houses, offered a pretty penny too. Of course I told them no, hell no, and they went on. I heard it's the other end of Webster they're focused on anyway." Chloe's side. He held a Coca-Cola in one hand and a bologna-and-cheese sandwich in the other. He wore a robe that reached his calves, and his hair, which he was meticulous about grooming, hadn't been cut in weeks.

"That mighty dollar," he went on. "How's your lil white man anyway?"

"Come on, Tony," she said, following him inside. "You know I ain't got a white man."

"Um-hmm, but you could. The way Drunk Freddy said you was locking lips with him outside your house, seem like you even considered it."

She turned back toward him fast. "I told you to stop bringing that up."

She opened the refrigerator and pulled out a Coke for herself. She gulped it down, then lifted the groceries from the shopping bag. The television was on, and she could hear Ozzie and Harriet from the kitchen.

"Speaking of guilty pleasures, I want you to meet somebody," Tony said.

"Let me guess, the bartender?" She rolled her eyes as she chopped the garlic for the chicken.

"Well, we don't call him that anymore. His name is Ed. He seems"—he paused—"nice. It's been hard to adjust to that. I'm afraid he's going to yank it all back. But then, it's so sweet. Chloe, you know

I have terrible judgment in men." And it was his soft side now, which he rarely surrendered to, and she couldn't help but feel compassion.

"It's not so bad," she said.

"Stop. And he reminds me of my daddy so. My uncles too, if I'm being honest. I need you, girl, to tell me if he's good for me or not. He's probably not, of course he's not. But just in case, I was thinking I could have you two over next week."

"Oh, that's wonderful, Tony." She tried to make her voice smile when she said it. He deserved as much. "That you have somebody you're serious about. I've never you seen you so"—she paused—"serene."

"Yeah, that's one word for it."

"I'd be happy to meet him," she said, though it wasn't true. "You know I'd do anything for you. But your hair—" She reached out to touch the tips, which had roughened. Tony typically brushed them down with hair grease and covered them at night for waves.

"He like it like that." He shrugged. "And nowadays it don't bother me none."

CHLOE HAD TURNED IT AROUND, BUT THE TRUTH WAS SHE COULDN'T ENdure another upset. Everyone had left her in the last year, and now Tony. If she was honest with herself, she'd admit part of the reason she'd always felt secure with him as her closest friend was because he'd seemed like he'd be perpetually single. That had stabilized her more than she could say, and now even their bond would fade. Still, she felt guilty about her response. How many times had he suffered? How many times had he cried into her arms, asking her why God had made him the way he was? How many times had she assured him he would find someone, had she prayed for as much? And now it had happened, and she owed it to him to praise God on his behalf.

Later that week, she called him and offered to cook for him and his new friend.

"I'll just pick up something quick from Lena's," he said. "Tonight is for you too, girl. Let your hair down once in a while."

She fought back once or twice, but ultimately, she acquiesced. She wore a pink full-circle skirt and a white sheer blouse. She normally pinned her great heft of jet-black hair up in a bun, but today she let the loose curls hang. There was a show the next day, and on her way over she ran through the words to the song she'd chosen.

Ed was already there by the time she reached Tony's—she could hear their banter from the stoop.

"You only got them little bitty crabs? Lawd, and ain't there more in that bag? They look so lonely on that platter. I think I'ma jump in there and ask if they'll be my friend."

"Boy, stop, I got as much as they had."

"Well, I hope you not gon be stingy with me like they was with you."

"Hello, hello," Chloe called out from the front parlor before she heard something she couldn't unhear.

Tony rushed over and kissed her on both cheeks, then handed her a rum and Coke.

"Eddie made it." He winked at Chloe and blew the man a kiss. Chloe smiled and called out hello again, but she felt that same feeling she'd known when Ruth announced her pregnancy, when Esther started preaching with Horace, when Mama stopped staying home, only now the feelings had been stacked on one another, and with this addition, she felt like they might overtake her.

It was the same through dinner: the head leans on the shoulder, the brushing of hands. Tony wrapped his arm around Ed's waist, and once, before leaving to refresh their drinks, he kissed him on the cheek. Ed wasn't as affectionate, but he didn't resist the advances either, and he seemed to be a different man altogether from the one she'd known to pour the strongest drinks at the Champagne Supper Club all these years. With Tony, here, he was gentler in a way, firmer in a way too. She'd seen him laugh with his shoulders shaking and his head back; she'd seen him touch Tony's knee when one of his jokes went too far. She'd seen him.

"Any more gigs?" he asked when Tony had gone in the kitchen.

She repeated what she'd told Gerry, that she'd been called back for a second audition, and he raised his eyebrows. "They'd be lucky to have you," he said. "Everybody at Bop City asks about you when you're not there."

"Oh, go on," she said. "You're just trying to get on my good side. On account of Tony."

He shook his head, laughing, though. "I'm serious," he said. "Since that day you sang 'Teardrops,' they been looking for you."

"Not the only one either," Tony said, walking back. His voice had changed, taken on a singsong quality. She'd known him so long she knew that inflection wasn't one he'd invoke in this group. It was more formal, the tone he'd use when he was out shopping, for instance, or when he was talking to her but wanting someone adjacent to hear what he was saying.

She turned back and saw James beside him.

She stood up fast. She didn't know why. She didn't intend to walk anywhere, but the shock of seeing him in a place she considered a second home sent her upright, the way she might stand if they were inside a club or on the sidewalk. It just didn't make sense to be comfortable if he was in the room.

He seemed to think so too. He shuffled his feet; he looked down at the rug, then up again at the ceiling but never landed on her face. If he did, she could have settled herself, she knew she could have, and then—

"I hope it's okay that I'm here. Tony invited me. I ran into him at the Blue Mirror the other night and I asked about you."

"Girl, he was there looking for you," Tony cut in. "I saw him before he saw me, and every few minutes he would scan the room, like a little rat scampering out a hole for cheese."

"Not a rat." This from Ed.

"He's right," James said. "I have been trying to find you."

"She didn't want to be found. I had to take it into my own hands." Tony was talking to Ed now, and as was typical, he couldn't control the sound of his whisper. Chloe wanted to kill him. If she thought about it more, she'd see it wasn't him she was angry at. Since James had walked in, she'd felt that pull toward him, heavy and full, pleasant too, and so much of it was outside her control. She could feel shame as well. It was her mother's mostly, but it was the world's. Maybe Esther could have turned her face from it. Perhaps Ruth too, if it involved her child. But Chloe hadn't trained herself to stand apart from the group in a real way.

Now she and James were so close they could touch; she didn't know if he had moved or she had. There was a lone hair sprouting on his neck beneath his beard. She wanted to pluck it. If he were her man, she would have. At the second audition, she'd planned to sing "Angel Eyes," at Mama's suggestion. Chloe didn't know yet what kind of song hers and James's would be.

"Is there somewhere we can talk privately?" he asked.

"Up the stairs, first room on the right," Tony said. "Shit, I need my privacy too."

Chloe started up, and he followed her to Tony's aunt's old room. She sat on the edge of the bed and rubbed the patchwork quilt the woman had knitted before she died. She had heard Tony say there wasn't much else she left behind. James sat across from her.

"I've been looking for you." He repeated what he'd said in the living room.

Chloe tilted her head down. She was nervous to see him really.

"I know," she said. "I needed some time. It was too much."

"What was?"

"Being with you."

She looked up, and he paused before saying,"I haven't been able to stop thinking about you."

She almost didn't say it. "I haven't either."

"Then what's the problem?"

"The fact that you have to ask tells me everything I already knew." She picked up a throw pillow and set it back down again. "We're from two different worlds."

"Of course we are. Nobody said we weren't." He paused. "But are we going to be like everybody else and let something so meaningless stop us?"

"It's not meaningless, it's real, James. Realer to me and my family than it is to you maybe. It's already hard enough." But as she said it, she knew she'd had it easy compared to her mother, who'd had it so easy compared to her own. The introduction of hope. Maybe he was right.

They were silent for some time. Chloe had never been one to argue. She didn't think she was afraid to, only that habit had dimmed the impulse. By the time she was old enough to talk back, Ruth had already become second mother. Nobody could compete with Esther's sharp tongue; even Mama would sigh sometimes instead of responding. Later, with Chloe's friends, it was easier to go along with the movies they picked, the restaurants they frequented. And now she'd said what she thought. He had wanted to hear her confirm his feelings, he had wanted her to agree that their love might be powerful enough to alter the world, or, if not alter it, then hold it at bay, but she hadn't agreed, and she felt a strength she hadn't known was possible. It almost didn't matter that, talking, she didn't think she sounded like herself. If you had recorded the words, replayed them back for her and her sisters, they all would have identified them easily as their mother's.

He seemed resigned. "So Tony heard about us kissing then?"

She smiled—she couldn't help it.

"Who told him?"

"Probably Drunk Freddy. But it could have been anyone in this neighborhood. There's no such thing as a secret in the Fillmore."

"Who's Drunk Freddy?"

"Oh, he's just a man who fell on hard times. Drinks to get through them. I don't blame him. Nobody does, and everybody helps him out, Mama on Mondays, Miss Mary on Tuesdays. He'll never starve."

"That's amazing," he said, "the way you take care of each other."

She shrugged. "It's always been that way. My mama came up from the South with my daddy, but he passed. Then she met Mary, and she was the one who took care of us when my mama was in nursing school. It's not like that where you stay?" she asked.

He shook his head. "Well, maybe?" he corrected himself. "Maybe, and I just don't know about it. There was one family we were close to across the street. The daughter was a year behind me in school. She still writes me letters sometimes."

"Um-hmm," Chloe said, sounding like a woman and liking the new shift. "What kind of letters?"

"Nothing like that," he said, blushing. "She's like a sister to me really," he added. "I didn't think you would care. After everything you said."

"You didn't hear me then. You weren't listening clearly. I don't want to care, I don't think it's a good idea for me to care, but"—she lowered her voice—"of course I care."

He smiled then, and she smiled back, and he pushed up closer to her on the bed. When he leaned in, she didn't pull back, and he kept his hands at his side except for when he reached out to caress her neck. They kissed for some time before they started talking again. He was liking work okay. Things were more peaceful at home on account of his father's heinous job heating up, keeping him elsewhere. Even still, James was scheming, saving up for his own place.

"Heinous?" Chloe asked. "What could be so bad?"

"I couldn't bear you lowering your opinion of me."

"Nothing would," she said. "My own mother runs us like dogs. I understand."

He didn't answer her. It was late, and when he lay down beside her, she joined him on her back. She ran her fingers over the side of his arm, where the hair was lighter than on his head, a soft yellow glistening.

He turned so they were facing each other.

"Maybe we could all go out one night," he said. "The four of us." He gestured to the room downstairs where they'd left Tony and Ed.

By this time, Chloe was half asleep, and she knew what he was asking, but she wasn't alert enough to dissect it. She yielded to the smoothness spreading across her mind's eye. She agreed.

They were holding each other, lying down still fully clothed, and all they'd done was kiss, but she felt satisfied.

She woke up to the sun streaming in through Tony's aunt's lace curtains. She jumped out of bed and hurried into her shoes, ran across the hallway to the bathroom to slap water on her face.

"What's wrong?" James asked when she rushed back.

"My mama, that's what's wrong. If she's not with her boyfriend, she'll have my hide."

"Just tell her you were with me," he said, and he grinned saying it, but it only highlighted the sadness between them.

On the front stoop, they kissed out in the open. The sun was up, but no one was out, not yet. Fifteen minutes later, and there would have been an audience.

"Remember what I said, about the four of us, next weekend?" he said, and she paused before she nodded. "Until next time," he said, and he looked at her like his whole life was riding on her answer to that one question.

"Until next time," she repeated. She had sounded out the exact opposite response in her mind, she had started to say it, but it didn't sound like her.

HE CALLED HER THE NEXT NIGHT AND SUGGESTED THEY GO OUT IN OAKland that weekend. He said he'd been thinking about her, and she said she'd been thinking about him. She screamed when he hung up the phone, then called Tony right after with the news.

"Alright now, heifer, so you moving forward with this thang, huh?"

"I didn't say that, Tony."

"You didn't have to say it. I can hear it in your voice, all pressed, 'Are you sure you're free, Tony? You can't be late.' Bitch, I'll get there when I get there."

"Look, Tony, I just think it would be nice for us all to get to know each other better, that's all."

"Um-hmm. Seem like you got to know him a lil better last night in my auntie's guest room. I saw that bed all disheveled."

"It wasn't like that, Tony," she said, and he started to say something smart back, but she heard Vivian and Preacher downstairs and she excused herself for rehearsal.

IF SHE HAD UNDERDRESSED FOR TONY'S HOUSE, SHE DID THE OPPOSITE the following weekend. They had agreed to meet on Tony's street, and the three men were all waiting on the stoop when she approached. Tony and Ed whistled, and she laughed and tried to play it cool, but her eyes were on James. When she reached him, he held out his hand and she took it. He leaned into her.

"I've never seen anyone so beautiful in my life," he said.

And as much as her life had prepared her to disregard the compliment, standing there before him just then, she believed it.

They walked in a line to the bus stop, like they weren't together at all, or like she was with Tony or Ed, and James was their boss, or like she and Tony and Ed were siblings and they were showing a strange man how to get to Powell Street.

There was no one on the bus, so they spread out all over, and then Tony started singing "Tell Me Why," and he and Ed danced up and down the aisles and Chloe leaned into James's shirt. She had an urge to apologize for their animation, but she stopped herself. James didn't say a word, just glanced from Tony and Ed back to her again, smiling.

In Oakland, their nerves strengthened. Each couple walked hand in hand, and people stared, mostly Negro, but it was a holiday weekend, and there were some whites too. Chloe wasn't certain which couple garnered the most attention. She had feared this exact thing, but there was something about having Tony and Ed there that steeled her up inside, and she stared straight back at the onlookers. After a few blocks, she stopped noticing, and she'd look at James mostly and he'd look back at her, and she understood why Mama was never home anymore.

At the restaurant, they sat at a proper table, and a waitress came by with menus and glasses of water and asked what they'd like to eat. She'd done this before, of course, with Tony, with her girlfriends, with her mama and her sisters. But this was different. This was her out with a man, and she had money in her pocketbook from her earnings, and Tony had made extra last Friday from her suppers on account of the catfish. Sure, she was nervous at first. If James's color stood out to her when it was just them, it announced itself with a megaphone in the restaurant. He was the only white person there, and as on the street, people weren't shy about their curiosity. Then her rum and Coke hit, and Tony's mouth started—now it was the woman at the table next to them who "knew good and well she was too skinny for a sheath dress." By the time the food came—steak and asparagus and mashed potatoes—she ate like she was at her mama's table. James offered her a bite of his meat, and she accepted it just like she would have with Tony or one of her sisters. When Ben Webster came out and played "Pennies from Heaven," she lay her head against James's shoulder and closed her eyes, and she didn't care who saw. She really didn't.

The music picked up speed after that, and Tony and Ed stepped out onto the dance floor.

"Stay here," Tony called to James. "Whatever you do, don't repeat what happened last time." And they all laughed. Anyway, Chloe would rather talk to him. They ordered another round of drinks and watched Tony and Ed—they couldn't dance with each other outright, so each one grabbed a lady and swung her around his back.

"I think that's my new favorite song, 'Pennies from Heaven,'"

James said. "I never told you this, but I grew up wanting to play the sax. I have every Ben Webster record ever made. I took lessons and I used to perform at clubs, not like you, not even close, but at night I'd imagine myself with the greats. I wanted to live in Harlem in a brownstone apartment and venture out to clubs each night. I told my father that a few years ago, and he laughed and laughed, said I had always been attention-seeking, that it was the stage I wanted and not the skill. That wasn't true, though, because I'm mostly content to just listen to music now. Maybe that's enough."

"I'm sorry," she said back. She was rubbing his arm with her fingers now. "I think that's my new favorite song too." And she kissed him so fast, anyone not looking at that exact instant wouldn't have known it had happened at all.

After a while, Tony and Ed returned. They sat and ordered more drinks, and every now and then, they would get up, and then they'd come back and assess the women they'd danced with, some who were light on their feet and others who moved, according to Tony, like his grandmother with gout.

Chloe would laugh; then she'd look back at James and marvel at the miracle that the nights she had grown so used to with Tony, the ones that had filled her up to capacity, hadn't been capped after all. There was more that could fit inside them. She used to stare at a picture of her father and pretend he was on a trip down South to see his brother, but he'd be back in time for Christmas. She'd even imagine the mornings, the cinnamon rolls and bacon and eggs, the gifts, but that had never been the core of it. Of course, the day never met the dream, her father dead and gone, but this was the feeling she'd generated in herself when she was hopeful. She could go back and tell that child it was coming, only not how she'd imagined.

Then the liquor haze started to firm and the gaiety it conferred hardened. Tony and Ed couldn't keep their hands off each other, and it was dangerous how careless they had become. Chloe was the one who ushered them out. They were alone on the bus again, thank God, but on the street back in San Francisco, it was more of the same, the hand-holding, and once, she even saw Tony touch Ed's butt. James stepped in between them.

"You've got to stop that now," Chloe heard him say. "It's no problem with me, you know it's not, but the people out here won't stand for it."

"Please, you think I'm worried about a bunch of drunk snowflakes. This my neighborhood," Tony said. Ed was normally more reasonable, but he had had more to drink than Tony, and he only laughed.

There was a group of whites approaching up ahead, two couples arm in arm. James turned and gestured to Chloe that he'd stand between Tony and Ed until they passed them, and Chloe nodded back. Tony was in full force, though, all: "What, you trying to get between me and my man? These white men greedy, Chloe, you better come see about him, 'cause ain't nobody getting between us, is they, baby?"

That seemed to rile Ed up, and he stepped around James so he was on the other side of Tony, and he was loud when he answered him: "Nobody, baby." They were about to kiss when the whites reached them, and Chloe heard the women shriek at Tony and Ed's closeness. The men approached soon after, gawking, and then, without warning, they pointed at the two Negro men whose arms were still linked and laughed. The women were reticent at first, but soon even they were chuckling with their hands over their mouths. Chloe didn't look at them, only at Tony. She had known him since he was a child, when he was teased mercilessly for the way he walked. Since they'd grown up, she hadn't seen any trace of that boy, not until tonight. She wanted to rush over to him, but she was frozen in her spot.

Finally, James shouted to the whites, "That's enough of that now."

"Whatever your thing is, buddy," the man in the front said, and the laughter followed them, it seemed, all the way to Tony's stoop. At their door, Tony and Ed walked upstairs without saying goodbye.

Chloe let them have their time before she and James passed through the door back into the bedroom they'd shared a week before.

This time, they locked the door and Chloe undressed. Several times over the course of the night, she had to place her hand over James's mouth to quiet him. She thought she wouldn't be able to set aside the ugliness she'd just witnessed, but it was the opposite—there was no space for it between them. All the while she felt him inside her, she was thinking of that Ben Webster song, snaking, rocking, moaning along, and finally giving way to its height.

VIVIAN

Vivian had started attending Wednesday night prayer revival at Shiloh now that she'd been spending more time with Preacher. At the beginning, the married ladies would smile with their eyebrows cocked, and the single ladies wouldn't even bother with that, but gradually people grew used to her in the front row, a half-baked first lady. She'd sit through the sermon, then talk with folk about their jobs, cut off with no fair warning; she'd cradle their fears that there would be more of the same to come. The shops on Post had mostly closed, and everyone knew somebody who'd been let go on account of it. Esther and Horace were still carrying on with the City, but absolutely nothing had come of it. Still, Vivian thanked God every morning that she worked at the hospital. The grace the world allotted for white people would cover her too for now.

The sermon today was about God's voice.

"How do we know when He's speaking to us, church?" Preacher asked, and Vivian still got chills when his eye caught hers, though there weren't just the chills anymore. There were the disputes. He wanted to be married, and she was happy as they were. As it was, if she didn't feel like spending five nights in a week at his place, she didn't;

when she stayed up late to usher Chloe through a performance, she didn't always worry about calling. It wasn't because she didn't want to. The more she'd known him, the hungrier she'd become to spend every minute beside him. But that was the problem; it all reminded her too much of Ellis, what they'd had, and any minute it could be snatched away. She told herself not to hoard love. There were verses she studied to echo the same, but there was a primal terror she felt when he came too near, and she didn't know any other way to ward it off except to distance.

"How does God speak to us?" Preacher repeated. "People are quick to say they heard a sign from God, but how do they know? Anybody?"

"I feel it in my spirit," Miss Fox called out, and Vivian wondered if it was the spirit of Jim Beam or Jack Daniel's she was referencing.

"Yes, Lord, and when we feel it in our spirit, that's the Holy Spirit that dwells in our heart communing with us, and it's always there; we just have somehow, someway, entered into an intimate enough relationship with Christ that we can finally hear the voice.

"But what else, what else? What more does He do? Aww, shucks, you telling on yourselves now, running out of ways He speaks. That tells me you not talking to Him, and if you not talking, I know you ain't listening. Come on now, church?"

"Life," Gladys called out. "I got the salon up and running because my friend thought to call me over for dinner one day. I walked by the empty storefront on the way home. If I had waited a week, it would have been sold."

"That's right, some people call it being in the right place at the right time, but we as Christians know that's not a matter of luck, that's God putting us where He wants us to be, church."

"Prayer," Mr. Gaines shouted out, and Vivian had been praying about his prime rib since she'd had it at the wedding, that it would go on sale, that it wouldn't stick to her hips, that she could fry it up with onions and not think about her daddy. But his shop had closed.

"That's right, church, and sometimes He answers that minute, and sometimes it can take years. Sometimes we're stuck in a lesson, and if He gives us the answer straightaway, we won't have earned it yet. Yes, my God is a comforting God, He's a healing God, He's a nurturer and a friend, but His love comes through correction, my friends. Am I right?"

Someone beside Vivian groaned.

"It's not to blame you, it's not to judge you, it's to love you, church. It's to love you with the love of God that passeth all understanding. To get you closer to Him. That's what it's all about. To be in Him and to have Him in you." He looked at her now, hard. "There's nothing sweeter."

AFTER, SHE SPENT TIME WITH THE CONGREGANTS AND CLEANED UP THE pews. She helped Preacher prepare the announcements for Sunday, from the same chair in his office she'd sat in before she'd known him, really known him. When they were done with business, he lifted his head.

"You coming over tonight?"

"Not tonight," she said. "I got to talk to Chloe."

"I thought you said Chloe was doing her own thing these days."

"That's why I got to talk to her. I got these girls lined up to audition with her and she can't make the time to run through one number." She could sense his hurt. "Tomorrow, okay, baby?"

"It's not about tonight." He had split his Bible open, his notebook too, preparing for Sunday's sermon, but he closed both. "I'm a pastor, I'm telling these people how to live right, and I'm over here shacking up. My daddy would be rolling in his grave." He paused. "It's not just that either. I love you, Vivian. I want to make a life with you, all the way, but you won't let me in. You start and stop. I thought it would get easier with us getting . . . closer, but if anything, it tears me up more. I've opened up my heart to you. I got past all the fear of losing somebody again, the guilt of being with anybody but Mattie. I plowed through all that for you because that's how important you are to me, but it can't just be me pouring out. I need for you to meet me halfway, to give me something."

"Don't you think I'm giving you all I got?" Vivian asked. "I'm sorry I'm not as fast on my feet as you are, Preacher. I'm sorry I can't face the hurt head-on, but you've seen how far I've come. You can't deny that. I've opened up as much as I can. If you rush me, I'm afraid I'll clam back up." That seemed to jolt him. "Just give me my time, okay? I'm moving, but I can't push myself harder than my feet are able to carry me."

"And I can't push myself harder than my partner's willing to go." He stood and walked over to her. She let him sit and then joined him in the chair on his lap this time.

He kissed her cheeks. "I didn't want to make you cry."

"I know that. I'm sorry too. I'm not going to stop trying."

"I need you to try harder."

"My intentions are pure."

"Yes, but faith without works is dead."

She stood and walked to the door, turned back.

"Love you," she said.

"I love you too," he said. There was a flash of something in his eyes that she caught before it faded, something she hadn't seen before. She had known about the hurt, but this new thing was fear. She had considered her own, but to see that she was inspiring it in him swept her out of herself for a moment.

SHE HAD SAID SHE WAS GOING HOME TO SEE CHLOE, BUT SHE WAS SURprised to actually see the girl at the table, dressed to go out, she didn't know where. It was like her daughter had become a different person in the last month, an entire woman, not a fraction of one grasping for parts from her mother, her sisters, and, further back, Ellis. Now Vivian found herself nervous to initiate conversation.

She washed her hands and sat down.

"You're home, huh?" Chloe sounded more like Esther than herself.

"This is my house isn't it? Unless you volunteering to pay the rent. Which I'd accept, gladly." She thought the girl would laugh. It seemed maybe a week ago she might have. But this time she just looked away. "You haven't been here much yourself lately."

"No, I haven't."

Vivian waited for her to say more, she hungered to hear it, but her daughter was silent. Wherever she had been, wherever she was already in the mindset of going, she wouldn't say. And then—

"I wanted to talk to you about something important, Mama," she started.

"Oh?" Vivian was happy at the prospect of getting more information, but she had learned to fear her children talking to her about something important. "Important" might as well have become a synonym for "life-altering," "tragic."

"Yeah." Her daughter was becoming nervous again, more like her old self. Vivian was ashamed to realize it settled her.

"What is it, baby?" she asked.

"Well, I know you wanted to start auditioning those girls next week."

"Not 'wanted.' Already got them lined up. Mary's niece for one, and then Gladys's best friend's daughter. They want to come by tomorrow and run through a few numbers. I thought I told you that. Six o'clock at the church, you'll be there, right?"

"Well . . ." She paused. "What if we didn't audition them?"

"And just took them? Well, I mean that's something to think about. I've heard them both sing in the choir. Just last Sunday, Mary's niece busted out with 'Take Me to the Water,' but I've learned with this type of thing not to let on just how desperate we are. I mean, you and I both know we don't have any other options, not anymore, but I've told them we got a line of girls who can't wait to bust through this front door." She laughed. It felt good to laugh with her daughter. "That tends to keep people on their toes, you know. Keep them on their best behavior. At least at the start."

"That's not what I meant, Mama," Chloe cut her off. "I mean, what if I was the singer? The only singer. What happened at Dunbar confirmed that it's at least a possibility."

"Oh," Vivian said. Well, it was just that; that was nothing compared to where she'd been. Chloe was confused was all. She didn't get the vision. Wasn't that what Preacher had warned them all about that evening? That God spoke, but not everybody listened. Not everybody had the capacity to, that was all. Even with a willing heart. The Dunbar was one stage; Vivian had learned not to pin her hopes on one *anything.*

"You didn't see it," she said now, smiling, shaking her head, feeling settled again, though, because it could have been worse. Oh, yes, she had seen it be worse. "It was three, not one," she went on. "Three ladies singing. And we lost Ruth, and I tried with you and Esther, but I think that's where I went wrong, see, trying to do it my way, when it was God who delivered the Trinity. You remember what I told you, don't you? About those ladies I glimpsed when I was just a little girl?"

"'Underneath the Harlem Moon,'" they said together.

"Right," Vivian said. "Right."

Vivian was about to stand, but the girl beat her to it. She was dressed to the nines, Vivian saw now.

"Where did you say you were headed?" she asked, her head curling back because Chloe was already behind her.

"Just out with Tony."

But Vivian knew that was a lie, not dressed like that. That was okay, that was okay, she had been too pushy with the others. Too rigid and controlling. As long as Chloe performed the way she'd been doing, the rest of her time was hers. It had to be for this to work, she saw now.

"You'll see," she called out to the girl's back.

"Alright, Mama." She was barely audible, almost out the door, and it had slammed when Vivian heard herself say, "Three ladies. Not my will but His will. Six o'clock tomorrow. You'll be there, won't you?"

SHE HAD TOLD THE GIRLS TO MEET AT THE CHURCH. CUTE GIRLS, THOUGH one wore a pencil skirt that might have fit before her second helping of biscuits, and the other didn't seem to have run a brush through her hair that morning. That was okay. She could work with that. What she wanted to find out was, could they saaang?

"Alright, Lucinda, Joyce, on the third count, I want you to belt it out, 'Precious Lord.'"

"Both of us at the same time?"

"Of course at the same time—what are you talking about, girls? Chloe will be here any minute and she'll join you, but we can't waste a minute, Preacher needs this room in an hour."

The girls looked at each other, then at her again.

"Come on now. One, two, three, *Precious Lord, take my hand . . .*"

And Vivian without warning flashed back to her time on the farm. The pigs would get so excited for the slop her father carried into the pen in a barrel, she could hear the squeals from her bedroom.

"Alright, alright now, girls, that's enough, come on now, I don't want to break the new stained glass windows. Maybe sing it one at a time. Maybe you had it right the first time. Joyce, from the top."

First Joyce went, then Lucinda, and Lucinda could carry a tune better than Joyce, but her diction was sloppy, and she stared at the ceiling when she sang like the audience lived in the church-house attic. It was a mess, but Vivian liked a challenge, and Chloe would join them, and the girl saw the good in everybody, or she used to at least. Vivian had a feeling it was the camaraderie she was missing, what turned her so sore lately. These girls had been in the same grade as her. They'd attended Sunday school together. They weren't friends, but they would be. Sometimes it was better for these types of arrangements not to exist between kin. The bloodline complicated matters. The last thing Vivian needed was any more complexity.

"Very good, girls," she called out. "Take a break, get some water. Lucinda, see if you can take my purse to the bathroom and slick that hair back. You got to look the part to fill it, didn't anybody ever tell you that? Chloe will be here any minute, and she can sing with you; sometimes you need a lead to reach the harmony. Yes, Lord," she mumbled that last part.

Chloe scrambled in once the girls had gone.

"You're late," Vivian started to say, but she held herself back. Nobody wanted to be made acquaintances with their own failings. She had learned that, and it had been a long time coming, but her daddy used to say, "So often wisdom never comes. We can't complain if it comes late."

"You missed the bus?" she asked instead.

Chloe shook her head.

"What's the matter? Cat got your tongue?"

"No, I'm just tired, Mama."

She looked tired too. Vivian leaned back and observed her. When she was a baby, Vivian could take her in with her instinct and know within seconds if she was hungry, or gassy, or sleepy, or wet. Vivian had to squint now, though, nearly close her eyes to get a sense for her own child. She was tired, it was true, but it was a tiredness of the spirit, not the body. Vivian would be a fool to push her in this state.

So when the girls returned, she didn't ask Chloe to stand beside them, and when Chloe barely greeted them, she didn't cut her eyes at her or urge her toward courtesy.

Instead, Vivian had them run scales; she answered their questions, informed them rehearsals lasted three hours every other day. They nodded, so expectant and hopeful, it was like their feelings activated the corresponding opposite. Vivian felt something she hadn't felt in a long time. She almost couldn't place it, but as she watched the girls walk down the aisle through the swinging front doors of the church, swishing their behinds (and she swore she glimpsed the white cotton of Lucinda's panties underneath that short, short slit of her skirt), and after Chloe had mumbled about a school project due the next day and hurried off, Vivian realized, sitting alone in that church, that she had doubt.

RUTH

Ruth wouldn't have been able to explain to a bystander how she found herself back at Bop City. She had been resisting the temptation to visit again since her first time. At first it hadn't been hard. With the shame at having been seen by Mary burning hot in her chest, she had doubled down on mothering, folding the laundered diapers before Mary's visits to make a point of her diligence, even going out of her way to do more for her husband, if you caught her drift. He'd appreciated it and started taking the baby out on days she worked late at the hospital. Tonight, after some special attention, he'd told her he'd bathe and feed Denise, put her to bed.

"Go visit one of your nursing school friends," he said. "You haven't seen them in a while. It'll lift your spirits."

And she paused before she accepted the offer, though she knew she'd say yes. What she didn't know—but what she would have if she'd given it any serious thought—was that she wouldn't call a friend. She intended to, of course. She even played the part with Gerry.

"I'll check on ol' Ynez, see if she can find a way to get from under Brennan, I guess"—and they laughed. "If Mama's not with Preacher,

I'll stop by her place for some pound cake on the way home. You want a slice?"

"I'm alright, but girl, you have all the pound cake in the world if it's going to keep you looking fine as you look tonight." And she'd giggled, genuinely so. In the last month, she'd gone back to work, she'd gone back to Gerry, she'd gone back to herself, mostly. It had all started when she'd visited Bop City that first time. She thought this final visit might cement her resurrection.

HER SISTERS WEREN'T PERFORMING TONIGHT, SO SHE WOULDN'T HAVE TO worry about running into them. It was that waitress instead, and the girl couldn't sing to save her life, but at least she wouldn't inspire any jealousy, any awe. Ruth recognized half the crowd, and they occupied an echelon below the folks who had frequented the Champagne Supper Club. She'd been so frantic to not be seen she must not have noticed that last time. Now it was the pimps who looked her up and down, the mothers looking for a new daddy who sized her up as foe. It was all a matter of the light cast upon it. She'd sit and have a drink just so she could sleep tonight, and she'd be out of there. She had a bustling life at home. It was sad, in a way, that she couldn't pine after the fantasy of this world any longer, that the illusion of its perfection had been burst, but there was relief too. She didn't need it anymore.

She was halfway through that drink when she zeroed in on one of Chloe's friends, Betty, a girl she'd known since she was drooling spittle onto her onesie. The group of women she stood with held their backs to Ruth. There was a white man in their midst. That was happening more and more now, their kind venturing out, and some said the neighborhood would soon be theirs to claim. As Ruth watched, the white man slipped his arm around the lady beside him, then squeezed her shoulder.

"Another drink?" The bartender jerked her attention away.

She shook her head. "Just the bill when you get a chance."

"You got it."

She stood at the same time the mixed couple turned toward the door. Ruth gripped the edge of the counter.

"My God." She didn't think anyone had heard her, but the bartender clasped her wrist.

"Be cool," he said. "Be cool." He must have known it was Chloe too.

She and the white man had made it to the door now. It wasn't like the last time Ruth was there when she'd been dodging her sisters, not wanting to be seen. She wanted Chloe to look at her, to know from her face that what she'd done was unfathomable, impossible to continue. She had the urge to call out to her, but it was like the scene blocked her out, the absurdity of it, the danger; she would intend to walk toward them and feel a force pulling her backwards.

"Be cool," the bartender kept saying.

"I'm alright," she said back. "Just catching my bearings." And if Ruth was blocked out from the scene before her, it was like Chloe was trapped inside it, blind to anything that might exist otherwise. Just now she squeezed through the door, the white man beside her, with the confidence of someone who had made herself invisible for the night.

SEVERAL TIMES ON HER ROUTE HOME, RUTH HAD TO CONFIRM FOR HERself she wasn't in a dream. She needed to tell someone, but Gerry would hold it against Chloe, might think she'd lost her mind, forbid her from watching the baby. Esther wouldn't keep it to herself; she wasn't good with holding back impulses, and she'd demand an answer. She might even tell Mama. On the other hand, maybe Mama deserved to know. She was surely the only one who could talk some sense into Chloe, but Chloe had been like a child to Ruth. The thought of unleashing her mother's rage onto someone she still envisioned sometimes with missing teeth and pigtails was blasphemous. She handled the secret all the way home like a hot stone she had to shift from one hand to the other so she wouldn't be burned.

At her own front door, she heard talking. Gerry should have been fast asleep by now. She opened the door, and Mary stood across from her pacing the floor, the baby in her arms. Gerry sat on the sofa like he'd been waiting.

"What's wrong?" Ruth rushed in. She snapped Denise from Mary's embrace, and the baby woke with a start, then rested her head on her mother's shoulder. She was burning up.

"What happened?" Ruth kissed the baby's flushed cheeks.

"I could ask you the same thing," Mary said.

"She woke up with a fever," Gerry said. "I gave her a bottle, I took her clothes off. She wouldn't cool down. I called you at Ynez's. She said you hadn't even been there. I had to call my mama. She came and drew her an ice bath. She's not as warm as she had been now. She's been resting."

"She's going to be okay," Mary said. She snatched the baby back and carried her into Ruth's bedroom, closed the door. Ruth could be certain her ear would be pressed against it, but she was growing tired of secrets.

"Where were you?" Gerry asked.

"At Bop City."

Gerry just nodded like he was bracing himself. He paused for a long time before he asked the next question.

"You got another man you meet there?"

"No, no." She approached him, sat beside him, and took his hand. "Of course not."

He shook his arm free.

"I'm not stupid," he said. "How long you been seeing him?"

"There is no him," she said back. Her voice had risen; she heard the baby startle and she lowered it.

"There is no other man," she repeated. "Just the music. I've been so miserable, so worn out, so dead inside, it's all I have to keep me afloat." For a minute she was embarrassed that there wasn't an actual other body to pin this on.

"You could have told me," Gerry said.

"I didn't want to worry you. You got enough going on in your own life."

"You are my life," he said.

The baby was full-on crying now, and Mary walked back in.

"I better be on. She needs you now." She handed her back to Ruth.

At the door, she looked back.

"Every couple got problems," she said. "You're better than I was. You'll find your way." She opened the door, then turned again. "You're going to have to," she added. "He won't always be able to call me. The white men came back. This time, they told me I don't have a choice. I haven't had the heart to tell your mama. I'm not going to fight it, I done got too old for that now. I'll be out of here on the first of the month, going to stay with my sister in Oakland. She got a room for me for as I long as I need it. You're the woman of the house now. You got to act like it."

The baby had been quiet with Ruth but woke again at the door's sharp click. Ruth stood and bounced her around.

"I can take her, baby, if you're tired," Gerry said. He whispered it, though, like he didn't know if this angle he was trying was the right one. "You just have to tell me," he went on.

He didn't seem bowled over by Mary's news, the way Ruth felt; it was almost like he hadn't heard it at all. He must have known, just like that bartender had known about Chloe. Suddenly she didn't feel like she'd been living in the same world as everyone else. So much had changed since she'd walked through that door, and so much had stayed the same. She leaned into what couldn't bend: the smell of the top of the baby's head, Gerry doing anything he could to keep her.

"I'm okay, baby," she said after some time. "At least I think I am." She took a breath, let it go. The baby seemed to sigh with her.

"I know I will be."

ESTHER

Horace was losing faith. They hadn't protested in two weeks. The last time, there had been a hundred people beside them at the Champagne Supper Club, holding signs that read KEEP THE FILLMORE SOULFUL, KEEP THE FILLMORE BLACK. But once the bulldozers started revving, Esther had pulled Horace to her, and convinced him the only responsible thing to do would be to send his followers home. They hadn't gone back.

Since then, Horace had still been in talks with Mr. Belmont, demanding with signed petitions that the City designate a certain number of new building units for Negro housing and businesses. Belmont wasn't even pretending to agree anymore. The City had eminent domain. They didn't have to do anything with the property they didn't want to do. The displaced owners would get compensated for the property outright; the renters would get fifty dollars. They'd all have thirty days to pack their things and leave.

Horace had begun taking his meals in the back room. They still hung out at the beach, but they were silent mostly, fingering pebbles, then tossing them into the ocean. Every toss felt final in a way Esther hadn't considered before. There was a pang in knowing she'd never see that particular stone again, that it would be lost in the tide sweeping it up, like it hadn't existed to her in the first place. Finally, she couldn't take it anymore and she turned to him.

"What's going on?"

"Oh, not too much."

"Don't lie to me. Used to be I couldn't edge a word in, what with all your talk about a revolution coming."

"Yeah, and that's all it turned out to be," Horace said. He was getting ready to spring something into the sea. "Just talk."

"Oh, now look, don't say that, you put more effort in than I've ever seen somebody put in a thing."

"Wouldn't know it by the end result."

"Well, it's not that kind of a thing, though, where you'd see an outcome so fast," she said. "Rome wasn't built in a day."

"Yeah, but it was white people building Rome. I must have gone and forgotten who I was."

The baby stirred then from his blanket on the sand, not crying, just announcing himself, and Horace lifted him. He fed him his bottle and Esther counted out some stones again, finding solace in their roundness. She threw one out farther than she had imagined she could. The truth was she'd become sullen too. She'd written more songs in the past weeks than she had in her life, and at every protest, someone asked her to open up with one like she were a preacher blessing the event. When she finished, she could feel the people's new contentment. But then their efforts had stalled. Horace's momentum had too. There was no more rehearsal, not for her anyway, and she'd been overjoyed at that at first, at finding a talent she was graced with, not one she had to hunt down. But without anything else on the horizon, the gaps in the day wanted to swallow her whole. She remembered Mr. Franklin's words. "Unfortunate," he'd said, and it was difficult not to wrap that description around herself, nudge into its sad contours.

"I talked to my cousin in Baton Rouge the other day," Horace went on. "They just reached a compromise with the City. Whites still get the two front sideways seats, but if it's just Negroes on there, they can sit. People are pissed that he settled, but he said something shifted for him after that, that it shifted for a whole lot of people. He said the South is on the verge of a change that will uproot the rest of the country." He paused. "I want to be a part of something like that."

"I want to be too," she said, but then she didn't say anything more. He didn't either. What was there to say? The sea washed up, then receded once more.

THE NEXT DAY AT WORK, HORACE WASN'T MUCH BETTER. HE SULKED IN the back room while Esther counted out the register. She was getting tired of his shit. Her dream had died too, but you didn't see her pouting over it. You didn't see her dragging out her own pity. They didn't have the luxury of bottoming out. There were other people depending on them now. She was depending on them herself.

"It's not just you, you know," she called out. She'd had to scream so he could hear her, and he stood from the couch where he'd sat all morning and hurried into the main room.

"What you talking about?"

"You're not the only one who's disappointed. I've been onstage my whole life, until now, and I would be still if I hadn't overheard that terrible conversation."

"It wasn't true, what he said."

"Yeah, well, it's hard to remember that sometimes. You're not the only one at war with your own mind."

Horace nodded. He walked closer to the register.

"I didn't know it was still bothering you," he said. "You could have told me."

"No, of course you didn't know because I wasn't hitting you over the head with it. I sucked it up, and I found something else that could hold my attention. I didn't give up on life."

He walked behind the counter and tried to embrace her, but she resisted.

"Maybe you're stronger than I am," he said.

"I don't want to have to be, though." She could feel tears forming and she willed them away, but they didn't heed. She wasn't supposed to be doing this now. She was supposed to be accounting for every dollar they'd made. She'd never been off by even a dime, and today was no different. They didn't earn much, but they could manage their expectations. They could predict a lull when layoffs hit at the Ford plant. They could predict a resurgence in December when the holidays rolled around. There was a simplicity to life when you didn't want for more than you could hope to achieve.

He reached for her again and she let him this time.

"It hurts," she said.

"I know."

She pounded his chest with her fists and he gripped them and moved them behind his back.

"I had wanted it so bad and I just feel like a failure," she said.

"Don't," he said. "I talked to my connect at the agency again. It was never going to work. All this time, the City was going to declare us blighted so they could get federal funding to redevelop the neighborhood. We never stood a chance." He paused. "At least if I move on, I could put what we learned to use. They're on the verge of something down South—"

She cut him off. "I'm sure they are, but I don't want the City to run you out."

"They're running us all out," he said, looking up at her and holding her gaze. "The bookstore will be next. We have to face that now. Any minute, there will be a notice on this door. At least I can see to it that the same thing doesn't happen elsewhere."

WHEN ESTHER GOT HOME, SHE HEARD CHLOE UPSTAIRS RUNNING CHORDS. She joined her in her room, sat on the edge of her bed.

"The audition's coming up," she said when the girl finished.

"And it's just you, right?" Esther asked. "No Lucinda and Joyce?"

Chloe nodded.

"I'm happy for you," she said.

"Thanks." Chloe smiled like she was trying to hide it.

"Really, I am."

"How's Horace?" the girl asked. "You write any more songs about him?"

"Girl, those songs aren't about him." Esther threw a pillow at her face.

"Well, did you write any more?"

"Just one you haven't heard." She pulled her notepad out of her satchel and sang the first verse the way she'd intended for it to sound.

You put words to the music inside my heart
You showed me the world could be its own art
I'd never felt myself so whole before
I'd never known how much I could reach for

"Wow, Esther, that's beautiful," Chloe said.

"Thank you."

Chloe let her smile bloom now. "But I have to say, there's no way this ain't about Horace."

And Esther threw the pillow at her again; Chloe knocked her with another one, and they rolled around on the bed swatting each other and laughing until they had to stop to catch their breath.

When it was time for dinner, Esther stood to freshen up. Her sister called her name as she stepped into the hallway.

"Esther?"

She turned back.

"I was serious about what I said. Someone should be singing those songs. They're amazing."

Esther had been about to go to dinner, but hearing that, she stopped in her room and lay down. She had been honest: the song wasn't about Horace; it was about herself. It was about her own uprising, albeit quieter than the one they'd envisioned. Before she'd left work, she'd told Horace she understood why he might leave, though she'd miss him desperately. He'd asked her to go with him, and she hadn't said yes. She hadn't said no either. She didn't hold the thought at all; rather, she let it pass. If there was enough gas behind it, it would summon her. Now, lying down, she imagined herself on the other side of the country. There was momentum there, he'd said. A couple of weeks ago, when they'd stood in front of that bulldozer, there had been a hundred attendees; maybe in the South there would be a thousand. They'd have enough people to cover shifts; they'd rotate every few hours, but at least fifty would always be there, standing arm in arm, Esther's songs like a blanket covering them. From her vantage point on the bed, staring up at the ceiling, she could hear a chorus.

VIVIAN

Ruth attended Wednesday night service for the first time in a long time. After Preacher's sermon, Vivian hurried over to her for the distraction of the baby more than anything. She had just cornered Lucinda and Joyce, told them straight up they'd beat out seventy other girls for a spot in the group. Of course it was a lie, and their squeals of excitement had made Vivian sick to her stomach. It was only Denise fussing in her arms that took her mind off it. She was getting too old for this.

Ruth hadn't been to Shiloh in so long, there were several friends to greet, to tell about the sleepless nights, the fulfillment. Vivian could see in her daughter's eyes there was more of the former than the latter, but that was how it was. By the time the crowd surrounding her died down, the baby had fallen asleep in Vivian's arms. It didn't make sense to wake her, so they sat.

"There's something I've been meaning to talk to you about anyway," Ruth said.

"Oh yeah?" Vivian snuck a glance down at her daughter's stomach. It was flatter than it had been, it seemed. With a second baby, by the time she would have gotten around to telling her mother, she would have popped.

"It's not that, Mama."

"Well, what is it then?" Vivian asked. "I can tell from your eyes it's not good news."

Ruth shook her head. "No."

At this point Vivian was too tired for concern. Not everything needed to be known. If the baby woke up, she might dash off, say whatever it was could wait until next week. But the baby stayed silent. Vivian was filled with a sudden, new worry.

"Is everything okay with her?" Vivian asked.

"Oh yeah, Mama, of course. In that way, everything's fine then."

Vivian nodded. "Exactly, she's all that matters now."

And saying that seemed to confirm something for Vivian. The baby hadn't stirred, but it was no matter. She stood, handed Denise to her mother, and walked past Ruth. She turned back, and she kissed the baby. She was still asleep. That was for the best.

"Get her out of this cold, Ruth," she said. "A baby ought to be home at this hour."

She had planned to wait for Preacher, but she wasn't in the mood any longer. Outside the air hit her like a punch to the gut. She was halfway home when she heard Freddy's familiar whistle. She turned back. If she hadn't heard the whistle, she didn't know if she would have placed him. He had shaved, changed into a pullover sweater. He didn't smell like vodka either, nor was he carrying it with him. She didn't know if she'd been as happy to see someone in all her life.

"Look at you," she said. "If I hadn't heard you, I would have walked right past you on this street, boy."

"Yeah, I been busy. Staying with a cousin. Looking for work, if you know of anything."

"I see that. Yes, Lord, that much is clear. I'm proud of you, Freddy."

"Well . . ." He hung his head for a short time, then lifted it. "I been looking for you actually," he said.

"Is that right? Walk with me, boy, I had a long day. I need to get off these feet."

He walked with her, slowly, though, and she had to reduce her own pace. Still, he kept on talking like there had been no break in the discussion.

"I had an epiphany one night. I moved here how many years ago?"

"Boy, you know we too old for equations now. And it's too late besides."

"A long time ago, right?"

"Yes, we can agree on that."

"But then one night, I couldn't sleep. It's quieting down some now, you noticed that? Not as much festivity as it used to be."

"People losing work."

"Yes. And I find it's harder to rest in the silence."

They were almost in front of Vivian's house now and she had just heard a sermon from Preacher. She wasn't in the mood for another.

"It hit me that I've been so afraid of the change happening here. I thought I could control things better if I didn't see it at all. I was so rigid."

"Don't be so hard on yourself, Freddy. You're doing great now."

"Now I see we can't escape forward movement. It's coming. Even if we don't bend to it, it's here."

"Yes, Lord, well, you always were the philosopher. It's good to see you on your feet, Freddy. It really is. It gives me hope. I'll see you tomorrow."

"That's not it," he said. "I told you I need to talk to you about something." He paused. "It's about your daughter, that third one."

"What about her?" Vivian turned to him fast.

It was clear he hadn't been drinking in some time, but the booze had surely dulled his brain and he had to search himself for the answer to her question, though it seemed it had just been on the edge of his tongue.

"She's been hanging out with the wrong crowd," he started.

"Oh." Vivian felt her own relief settle. He was talking about Tony. She had heard that since the girl was nine and she and Tony had both worn black pantyhose to the Christmas pageant. She flung her wrist at Freddy now.

"Now you know it takes all kinds, Freddy. What does the Good Book say about judging? You remember, don't you?" She was at her house now.

"I'm not talking about that," he said.

"What are you talking about then?" She felt restless in her spirit. She touched the bottom step of her staircase with her toe. She could feel the shoes sliding off; then it would be her bra. She didn't know if she would even eat. She might just carry herself upstairs and collapse.

"That white boy I keep seeing her with. I thought maybe it was somebody in the industry at first. He's always hanging outside the clubs at night. But then I saw him with those other men. The ones going knocking on everybody's door offering them money."

"Excuse me?" Vivian said.

"The displacements," he repeated.

"I'm not talking about that. I'm talking about Chloe. You're confused about her. You know better than anybody, that child's got a familiar face. Everybody's always saying that, always did, asking her if they know her from somewhere, but it's never her. Hardly ever. Excuse me, Freddy." She conquered one step.

"It was her, Vivian," he said back. "I'm certain of that. Kissing him one night. Then another. Wasn't going to say anything, but my spirit wasn't right holding it in. I'm just telling you what I saw."

"Kissing him? A white man?" She swung back around. "Did he force himself on her?"

He paused then before he answered. "No, Viv, she had her hands wrapped around his neck."

"Freddy, I don't know what you done replaced that drink with." She was screaming now. She couldn't control it. "But whatever it is, it'd be better to stick to the vodka. At least it didn't have you seeing things that weren't there, coming to absurd conclusions."

"Alright, Vivian, don't fight the messenger, I just had to tell you." He turned, but Vivian didn't hear or see him. She was too busy opening her front door. The whole rest of the while she called out to him, she kept her face fixed ahead.

"Ain't no way, is the thing. If you think I'd believe that, you must not believe I know my own daughter. And I know her. Know her better than any of the others, matter of fact. See, she's my miracle baby, the one Ellis sent me, and I believe our minds are merged." She was inside now, but she kept talking, all the while she slid out of her shoes. She had decided without giving the matter another thought that she wouldn't eat, but she'd make sure to take a bath. She needed to relax. Wash those words out of her consciousness, frankly. The silliness, the blatant untruth.

In the tub, she found her distress renewed and she burst out to no one at all:

"Not that I think you're lying, Freddy, just that you confused. Could be withdrawal. That happens sometimes. The body becomes so dependent on the substance and then, when it's taken out, especially so suddenly like that. Did you wean, Freddy? Let me ask you again, did you wean?"

She stayed in the tub for some time tossing out rebuttals to what she'd just heard, and they'd stick for a minute, then fall away. By the time she was dry, though, she bypassed her pajamas, settling instead on a plaid housedress. She walked downstairs, then outside, and closed the door behind her. She knew exactly where she was going and why. On the way, a note of rebuke toward Freddy would ring through her mind, but she didn't shout it out anymore. Preacher had given her a key and she found him in his sitting room. Vivian sidled up beside him and rested her head on his shoulder.

"I didn't think you were going to make it tonight," he said.

She wanted to tell him what had changed, but it wouldn't come out.

"How did it go with the new girls?" he asked.

And she shook her head.

"What's wrong, baby?" He sat up and looked at her, really looked at her.

"Everything, Preacher," she said. She wanted to cry, she could feel the great weight atop her chest that would be transferred if she could, but it wouldn't come out; it couldn't.

She parsed her words out, thick and measured.

"Chloe, she's out. I'm not going to get into why just yet. But I can't count on her anymore, not for this and not for anything."

"That's your baby."

"Yeah, she'll always be my child, and if she needs anything, I'm there, but everything I've given them they've kept for themselves and come back for more. It's not an even trade. They dig me out. I'll never be as whole as I was when I was nursing their dreams. I'm old now. I'm tired. I have to think about me.

"If you want more of me now, you can have me, Preacher," she said finally. "I don't belong to anybody else any longer."

"That's not how I wanted you to come."

"Me neither, but that's how I got here. That's how I'm here for you now." She paused. It was her turn to ask. "Will you take me?"

And he stood over her, lifted her like she was someone's child, carried her upstairs, and laid her down. When he was done, the tears still hadn't come. For a minute, when she was arriving, she had forgotten Freddy's words, but they were back, of course they were, skating across her mind in bold and large print. Every now and then, she'd remember a new point to scare them off, but finally even those points lapsed, and it was only Preacher snoring beside her to keep her from the brink.

She thought back to his sermon the other night, the one about God's voice, how to capture its essence. If He was speaking to her, she couldn't hear it.

CHLOE

Ruth's baby took an extra-long afternoon nap. Instead of sleeping, Chloe lay down beside her, reminiscing on the night she'd spent with James. The whole while, she hummed Esther's music to herself:

I'd never felt myself so whole before
I'd never known how much I could reach for

RUTH KEPT LOOKING AT HER FUNNY ONCE SHE CAME HOME, AND OUT OF nervousness Chloe lingered and played Monopoly with her and Gerry. Then they all listened to Fats Domino's new song and Chloe and Ruth danced along. Denise squealed so loud it was hard to hear the music. She was starting to favor Chloe, if she said so herself. When Chloe stood to go home, Ruth tried to keep her longer. She had to talk to her about something, she said, gripping her wrist. But Chloe had to go. The audition was the next day, and she still had to rehearse one last time.

"I feel good about it," she said as she slid into her coat. And it was true; there was something about the way it hadn't been expected, how the manager had explicitly asked for her alone. Vivian had started to express doubt about that aspect last week, volunteered Lucinda and Joyce for backup, but Chloe had said no in a voice that surprised even herself.

THE DAY OF THE AUDITION, CHLOE AND VIVIAN HAD AGREED TO MEET AT home at six. Chloe had been glad for the quiet house when she first arrived mid-afternoon, but now, as the hour approached without Mama, she had started to worry about being late, or worse. She sat in the kitchen drumming her fingernails against the table. She knew the song; she knew the routine. The manager had ridden the train to the San Francisco location just to hear her, and she could find the place the same way she and her mother would. Mama normally took care of business matters so Chloe could focus on singing, but she could introduce herself. She had never met a stranger—everyone said it. She would make her way.

She was about to stand to call Vivian once more when she heard her mother open, then close the front door. The silence was what gave her away. Something was wrong.

When Vivian reached the parlor, Chloe stood but didn't move toward her. She wanted to be equal to her for this, whatever it was. She and her mother had never argued about her grades, which hadn't been high like Esther's or even Ruth's. They'd never had a sour word between them over Tony even, though there were whispers up and down the block, and her mother was a deaconess. This woman towering over her now with a hard, dry expression on her face was someone she'd seen mostly with Esther. They'd scream at each other so hard and so long you could hear it in Esther's voice the next morning, which Chloe believed was the only reason her mother practiced restraint. But Vivian was walking toward her now with so much malice, and all of it was aimed at her.

"What's the matter, Mama?" she asked, still clinging to a childlike hope that she had invented the tension between them, that drawing attention to it might wipe it clean.

Vivian shook her head. When she finally did speak, her words came out so low Chloe had to strain to understand. "I wasn't going to say anything. I told myself to leave it alone. You drift off that far there's no turning back anyhow, not behind anything I might say."

"Okay," Chloe said. She didn't know what else could come out next.

"But looking at you here, after everything I taught you, after all you've seen me go through, after everything you knew I left behind, you trying to chase the trouble back. I don't understand." Whatever resignation Vivian claimed she had assumed was fading.

"What are you talking about, Mama?"

"Oh, you know what I'm talking about." The look in her eyes held so much disdain there could only be one thing she was referencing.

"Oh," Chloe said.

"'Oh'? 'Oh'? That's what you're going to say after you do such a thing? Not 'I'm sorry.' Not 'What was I thinking, Mama?' Not 'I'll leave it alone.' None of that. You've seen how I've suffered, and you're throwing it away to the one who started it all. These people aren't like us, why I ran so fast to get away from them. And they're like fleas or, worse, rats, there's always more, and now you're trying to invite them back in, you're trying to tether yourself to the worst of them, I won't do it, I can't do it. Not this time. Not now, not ever."

"Well, I'm not asking you to do anything, Mama," Chloe said. Her hands were shaking, but you wouldn't know it by listening to her.

Her mother looked at her like horrifying questions had splayed themselves out across her mind's eye, questions that would haunt her, forever unfastened to the resolutions she had assumed for them. Her head slanted, her eyes red, she asked, "Who are you, child?"

And Chloe couldn't look at her, only around the room. The sudden tenderness of her mother's eyes had caught her off guard, and she didn't know what to say. She understood now why Ruth got pregnant, why Esther got militant. It was easier that way, easier than standing here and telling her she wanted something more than what the woman had picked out for her.

"I'm the same, Mama, just in love," she said, and that seemed to set the woman off again. Chloe was relieved for the decline.

"After everything I did, after everything we been through, it was all for you, can't you see that? You were always my priority, and this is how you repay me."

Something about those words released a rage in Chloe she didn't know had taken on a form. "Why do you care, Mama? You ain't never here. It's you and Preacher all day and all night long, and you expect me to just be here by my lonesome. On the rooftop every day of my life while everybody's left me, listening to the sound of my heart breaking? I can't anymore. I can't."

And Vivian was quiet. She sat. Chloe collected herself in the silence. She looked ahead at the clock.

"Can't we talk about this later, Mama? We got the gig in a few."

"I'm not going to that gig." Vivian had calmed. Her voice was even lower than when she'd walked in. "You don't get it, girl. I'm done. This isn't having a baby with the neighborhood butcher. I managed, and I love that child. This ain't even Esther throwing herself into a cause that won't love her back, this ain't it." She began to whisper: "Drunk Freddy told me that you were kissing a white man outside. And you were hiding it 'cause you knew, I believe, deep down you knew it was too vile to speak of, but it's not just too vile to speak of, it's too vile to do." She had been clutching her pocketbook to her waist, but she let it fall to the floor now. "Say something," Vivian said. "Say something to redeem yourself."

But Chloe wouldn't. The only words that would come to her were apologies, and then she'd remember how she felt walking home that last morning with James, like she was dancing across clouds. As much as she wanted to bring her mama back, as much as she wanted to go back to being the child the woman had cherished, the miracle baby, they had moved so apart from each other since Preacher had come in, since James had too. She was glad in a way because it hardened her. She wasn't going to say, no matter who needed to hear it, that she was sorry for a feeling that had become her balm.

AS SHE'D IMAGINED WHEN SHE'D BEEN SITTING AT THAT TABLE THIRTY minutes earlier, she walked to the venue alone. She met the manager, a tall skittish man who barely looked at her and nodded at the dressing room in the back. She had already applied her makeup; she just had to cinch up her girdle, then her pantyhose, slide into her gown. When it was time, she stepped right onstage from the back without even glancing in the mirror this time. Mama had suggested "Angel Eyes," but everything was different now. She hadn't been able to get Esther's song out of her head. She had spent all week absorbing the lyrics, pouring her heart's contents into each word, and she would do the same, she knew, when she delivered here now. The manager hadn't seen her when she walked in, not really, but he would. She closed her eyes before she started. She had never sung the verses aloud, not like this, but the lack of practice seemed to soothe her, like she was inviting in a force beyond her and everyone in this room. They were all bound by this force too, and this song would be their communal invocation now. She wouldn't dance to this; she'd only sway. It was her pain they'd pay attention to tonight, how it leapt, then hunched back; then she would show them her joy, how she was learning to let it reign.

I didn't know that I could feel this way

The manager was with her here. She couldn't see him, but she could feel the heaviness in the quiet. Esther's words called a part of her forth that hadn't been released before, not with her sisters or Tony, not onstage, not with James, not ever. This part of her seemed to leave her person and ascend and sweep across the room, and it was directing

Chloe's body now; it was extending her lung capacity; it was inducing the trance that anybody watching was forced to enter.

I can't believe I know this depth of love
I thought it had to come from up above

She was almost finished, and when she was done, it would just be her again, her and this love that was mounting inside her. She had found a way to reveal it to the world in a way they could wrap around themselves. It was almost enough, even if it didn't pan out, even if she never saw James again. She had made it concrete, and maybe she could touch it later. For now, at least, it was in her grip:

I'd never felt myself so whole before
I'd never known how much I could reach for

She let it go and watched it fall away, and the manager roared, but she barely heard him. It had never been about that for her.

Typically, her mother was the one she rehashed the performances with, the triumphs, for the most part, but sometimes the hiccups, and Vivian was loving about guiding her toward her best. If Vivian had come home that night, Chloe would have told her she had finally reached it.

THE NEXT MORNING, SHE WALKED TO TONY'S. ED WAS OVER, OF COURSE. He had essentially moved in, and it didn't irk Chloe so much now that she had James. In fact, Ed was the one who listened to her recap today, while Tony got dressed upstairs. He didn't have the attention for the details the way her mother might, but Chloe told him that she'd put on a good show, and he patted her on the knee and said, "You always do."

She almost corrected him, emphasized she had reached a new level, but she savored the details for herself instead: the silence, the relief, the pain circling home, the love. She practiced the way she might relay them to James when the time came.

There was a knock on the door. Tony hustled down the steps. "Oh, I didn't know you was here, superstar!" he called to Chloe. "How did last night go?"

He opened the door before Chloe could respond. From her seat, she could only hear his side of the conversation. He was curt off the bat, but she didn't make anything of it. Tony ran cold. Then his voice rose.

"What you mean, 'order'?"

Then, "How I don't have a choice about property with my name on it? . . ."

"Eminent what?"

That's when Ed and Chloe walked over, hand in hand now. Chloe wasn't surprised to see Mr. Belmont and his crew at the door. They carried their signature black leather briefcases and wore wide-brimmed hats. Mr. Belmont held a handkerchief and wiped his neck with it once, then twice, then once more, though there wouldn't have been enough time for more sweat to gather.

Tony was still carrying on, the paper they'd given him swinging in his hand.

"Let's just talk to someone about it." Chloe tried to pull him back into the house. "Horace knows an attorney who could help us."

"I'm going to say it right here and right now," Tony went on like she hadn't said a word. "Y'all ain't getting my aunt's house. It's mine, it's my blood's, the only thing I got left of it, and there ain't no way." He spread those last few words out, and the men didn't respond, only glanced at each other one by one and seemed to share an understanding.

"Look at 'em, all smug and such like they doing the Lord's work. No idea they goin to hell in a handbasket," Ed whispered.

"Come on, men," Mr. Belmont called out to his crew. "Let's go get some lunch, give them some time. I got to meet my son anyway"

When the door closed, Chloe expected relief, but instead she and Tony just stood in the hallway in silence. Finally, she said goodbye and walked home. The same horrible men stood on the corner of her own street now, sneaking sandwiches in front of a household they'd harass when they were done. She crossed the street so as not to have to view them up close. She had crossed again and was almost at her stoop when she heard someone call out, "Where are you going, James?"

Chloe turned back toward a voice, Mr. Belmont. He called out louder this time. "Son?" A man walked away from him in the other direction. Tall and lean but not too much so. Chloe hadn't noticed him earlier, and she could only see his back now, but that image was enough.

"James?" Chloe said. "James?" She still hadn't spoken loud enough for him to hear. He turned, though. He looked between Mr. Belmont and Chloe several times, and even though she'd known it was him since she heard his name, saw his back—there was no way she could have mistaken his gait—seeing his face was another experience altogether. If a higher part of herself had been revealed last night, the lowest one sprang forth at this moment, and she raced up the steps and through the door of her own house, up the steps again and into her bed to begin the awful weeping that wouldn't let up until morning. Through the window all the while, she could hear James yelling, "I'm sorry."

SHE SPENT THE REST OF THE WEEK AT TONY'S. HER MOTHER WASN'T HOME anyway. She thought at first it might be hard to see him and Ed loving on each other, knowing what she'd lost, but it soothed her in a way. So many times she had been the one to cook oyster soup for Tony, sprinkle day-old bread on top. To watch him now, his man's hand on the small of his back for no reason in particular, it didn't do anything for the pain, which was steady, but it made her feel like it was possible that she might be okay in spite of it.

Midway through the week, she went home for clothes. While she was on her way out, the phone rang, and for a minute, she wondered if she had the right to answer it. Still, her mother was at work—Chloe had timed the visit that way—so after two rings, she hurried for the receiver.

She recognized the man's voice off the bat.

"This is Warren Hayes," he said. "The manager of the Dunbar. We've been calling and calling. I didn't expect to get you this time. This is Chloe, right?"

"This is," she said back.

"Congratulations, young lady. You got the job. Starting next month, you'll be the opening act for every big-name show we run out of this hotel. Your name will be on the marquee every week, smaller than the star's, but that's just a start. You're still able to move out to Los Angeles, right?"

Chloe wanted to respond, but nothing would come out.

Then the manager paused and said, "There's something in you, girl, just waiting to be let out. Whatever it is, it's going to restore people. I want to be there to see it. Are you ready?"

Vivian had always told her to wait to respond to any news, good or otherwise, but Vivian wasn't here. He was asking her.

"I'll be there," she said in a voice that didn't sound like hers. "Thank you," she added, and the tenor was still off, but she could adjust to a new thing. She set the phone down. Vivian had been waiting on that call for over a decade. Getting it without her there halved the thrill of the news, but there was still enough left for Chloe.

SHE HAD BEEN AT TONY'S TWO WEEKS WHEN SHE SAW HIM, SPEAKING TO Tony in a hushed voice in the entrance parlor. Chloe had been walking downstairs. She would have turned right back around, but she didn't want him to see her affected by his presence.

"I see you let just anybody in your house, Tony," she said, loud enough for James to hear.

"And I'll let him out if you say so," Tony said back, his eyes still on the white man at the door.

She paused before she answered, though she already knew what she would say.

"You can allow it."

Tony opened the door wider, then closed it and headed for the kitchen.

She and James both walked through the hall and ducked into opposite entryways to meet in the living room. They sat on opposite ends of the sofa too; things were different now.

"What is it?" She wanted him to leave, but she wanted to keep him there too.

"I gave you some time, but I couldn't wait anymore. I came to see you, to apologize."

"To apologize for what?"

He was silent.

"To apologize for what, James?" She was talking softly, but her sentiments were so loud. "It's not like you were five minutes late for a date, it's not like you forgot to buy a bouquet of roses. Your father is destroying the only home I've ever known. It's unforgivable, and to think you knew all this while and didn't tell me." She didn't want to start crying. She didn't think it was about him wholly; she had just met him, but the idea of all the relief he'd granted her disappearing . . . "It's unforgivable," she repeated.

"I know." He grabbed her arm.

"Don't touch me," she said. "You don't get to touch me." Seeing him again, connecting with him again, only to be reminded of the futility of it all would be torture. He dropped his hand at his side.

"Chloe, please," he said, "please stop. Just listen to me. I'll say my piece, and if you want to keep going, you can. Okay?"

She paused. "Okay."

"I know we just met, but I've never felt more strongly about anyone in my life. I knew when I walked you home that this was the neighborhood my dad had pinpointed. I went home that night and told him how reprehensible it all was. He said it was all about money; he said he could breathe more life into this place, but I know how the story will go, and I know that it would go differently if you weren't Negro. That day you saw me, I was dropping off something to him for my mom. I was going to tell you what he was doing even if you hadn't seen me, I was only waiting for the right time.

"I don't want you to think I'm like him," he went on. "I put a deposit down on my own place last week. I don't want to be benefitting from what he's doing in any way. It's not just 'cause I know you either. It's 'cause it's not right. I always knew that from the moment we moved here, but until I met you, I didn't have the courage to say it. You gave me that."

"Well, I'm glad I taught you courage then," she said.

"Chloe, please. What do you want me to do? I gave it up. There's nothing between you and me now. That part is over."

She almost felt sorry for him. There was so much earnestness in his voice, so much conviction in his eyes. And she didn't know if it would pan out.

"It's far from over, that part," she said. Her voice came out the way her mother's would have, firm, but she was calm too, like herself. She had wanted him to come for her; she had wanted herself to accept him again. She had thought that there was a stability that knowing him had given her, but maybe it hadn't only come from him. There was the new depth she'd found onstage weeks earlier, the new bounty it had yielded. It had been a miracle, but that didn't mean it had come easily. Everything with James would be the same, a fight. She could only imagine what it would take from her; she didn't know if she needed what it would give back.

"It's not just this, it's the whole wide world out there. If it's not your father, it will be your next boss; if not that one, the one behind him. What we had was sweet, let's leave it there. Something we can always remember. Something we can tell our grandchildren about."

She wanted to stop there. If she could stop there, she knew she could move past him. It would take a few months, but she would. It hadn't been much time, a few conversations; she barely knew a thing about him. She would meet someone new. Of course she would. She didn't know why it felt like she wouldn't.

"Chloe." She heard him, his voice faded from the distance that had grown between them.

She stood then in front of Tony's aunt's window, the one with white lace curtains on its back. He walked toward her, but he didn't touch her this time.

She didn't say anything. She thought of Tony and Ed, and how they were making their way. Maybe she could follow in their footsteps, but—

"I'm sorry," she said. And he looked at her with a desperation she'd never seen in a living being. It unnerved her because she understood it. She had felt it too at one time but not about him.

They held each other close before she pulled away.

"You need to go," she said, and he obeyed, his head turning back more than once, but he walked through the front parlor, then the entrance, and out the door.

Several times after he had gone, she wondered if she should go back out for him. He might still be on the stoop. At the very least, he would be on the street. She would say they should talk more. She would say they would figure out the rest. Several times, she might have stood if she had felt any emptier inside than she did. But there was something growing.

VIVIAN

Vivian wasn't surprised when she got the notice her neighbors had been whispering about for months. She had been gutted by her children. This was only cleaning up the mess.

She spent the rest of the week packing. There was the punch bowl that Vivian had set out for after-parties every Friday night; the maternity clothes she'd sewn for each of her pregnancies; Ruth's white Buster Browns that Vivian had handed down to Chloe—she would have given them to Denise too, but Ruth had wanted to start over.

"There'll be more space at least," Preacher had said the day the notice arrived. He was sealing up his church too, under orders. He had a cousin pastor nearby, and he would share Sundays with him until he gathered his own new congregation. After the notice came, he had knelt with a ring and asked her to marry him. She finally and happily obliged. He had carried her this season, and the joy in that surrender had astounded her; she didn't think she'd be owed it in this latter stage of her life. Still, there was a melancholy in her response that had come to blanket her since Chloe left. Her miracle child, and Ellis's final gift to her. The others' absences she had managed because there was so much promise on the horizon. It had been a month since she and Chloe argued, and it still seemed unreal, too sudden, too unlikely, like the morning Vivian had woken up in Louisiana after her bedroom window had been shattered. There was glass just beside her pillow, and instead of cleaning it, she'd walked outside barefoot and hid in the swaying stalks of corn until nightfall.

Everyone except Chloe joined Vivian now while she packed. Vivian, Preacher and Ruth's family would buy a small home in Vallejo. Mary planned to join her sister in Oakland; Esther was talking about moving down South, and Vivian had felt the urge to protest; then she'd felt that same urge subside. Life had taught her that, oh, yes, change blew in like the wind, and she wasn't any the wiser on where it would sweep her, or how.

Now Mary didn't lift a finger, but she busied herself relaying old neighborhood gossip, who was leaving, who was staying, who she wished would leave the state itself, but the devil himself would have to capture his own.

"It will be good for me," she said, "a change of pace. It's time for us to slow down anyhow. We're getting too old for this city life."

"Speak for yourself. I'm younger than Ruth," Vivian said and they laughed. "I'll miss you, old lady," she added.

"Oh, I'll just be a few miles away. We'll see each other all the same."

"Yes, that's true," Vivian said, though she knew it wasn't, and her heart swelled up again but she wouldn't let it spill out.

Ruth and Esther argued over mementos.

"I want the Nat King Cole records," Ruth said, and Vivian expected an argument, but Esther just shrugged.

"Okay, you always preferred him anyway."

"I mean, you could have one of them if you want." Ruth seemed embarrassed now.

On the mattress—because the bed frame had been packed—Denise squealed, and Esther leaned down and kissed her on the cheek. The doorbell rang as Vivian finished with one box, and she set the wheel of tape down and hurried to answer. There was no one there, just a note. It was from Mr. Franklin. He wanted to meet her at Bop City. She didn't discuss it with Mary. It wasn't meaningful enough to repeat to a soul.

THAT NIGHT, ONCE EVERYONE HAD GONE OFF ELSEWHERE, VIVIAN dressed. She had wanted to decline the invitation, but Mr. Franklin hadn't been at the door, and she supposed she owed him the courtesy of explaining in person that they had no point of connection any longer.

When she arrived at the entrance, one of the workers escorted her to a table in the corner. She was halfway to it when she saw Mr. Franklin was already sitting there, waiting. Unlike him to arrive early, but she was relieved. She could feel her pillow like it was beneath her head as she spoke. But no, the stage lights shifted, and it wasn't Mr. Franklin at all. It was her baby, a stranger to her now.

"Hi, Mama," Chloe said when Vivian was close enough to touch her. She looked as surprised as Vivian felt. Vivian started to turn away. She hadn't meant for this.

"It's okay, Mama. You can sit. I didn't know you were going to be here. I got a note from Mr. Franklin and I didn't ask any questions, I just came."

"Same with me." Vivian sat down slowly, like before she completed the act, she might reverse course. "Ruth told me you're staying with Tony."

"For now. It's just a matter of time before they kick us out of there. But it's okay. I plan to get my own place. In Los Angeles, Mama. They want me at the Dunbar Hotel regular, you know. My audition—"

Vivian held her hand to her heart. "You got it?"

"Yes, Mama." She nodded. "I got it."

"My girl."

"It's what we always wanted, Mama."

"I'm so proud of you, baby," she said.

"Mama, it wasn't only me." She paused. "It was us."

Vivian wiped the corners of her eyes and looked up to where Ellis was surely smiling down on her. And there was Mr. Franklin in her periphery.

"Hello there, I'm sorry to keep you two lovely ladies waiting." Vivian stayed seated, and Chloe followed her lead, but Mr. Franklin stood at the edge of the table as if he were waiting for them to change their minds. Finally he sat between them. Chloe's feet jiggled across from her own. It had been a habit she picked up in grade school that never departed. Vivian wanted to set one of her feet over her child's, but she left her alone. She was grown now. With a detachment so thorough it was eerie, Vivian waited for Mr. Franklin to speak.

"I'll keep it short and sweet since it's so late," he said. "I got a call from my connect at the Dunbar. They told me Chloe got the gig. Remember I told you"—he turned to Vivian—"if the girls picked up something big, I could do something with them."

Mr. Franklin looked between the two, again like he was waiting for something, but he was met with silence.

"It's only me now," Chloe said. And Vivian could see in her eyes how sad it made her to have to say that.

"You're enough." Vivian didn't know if she'd said it aloud.

"Your mama's right," Mr. Franklin went on. "The tide is turning, girl." He gestured to the waitress for a drink for them all. Vivian shook her head. She wouldn't be staying much longer.

"Just the two of us then," he said, and he was addressing Chloe. "Talent is talent. Ambition is ambition, girl group or not. The man at Dunbar told me he'd never seen anybody with range like your daughter." He was talking to Vivian now. "I want to try this again, for real this time. I want to manage her."

Chloe gasped; then she turned to Vivian, speaking to her with her eyes again, this time pleading. Vivian had been too stunned to notice that she was waiting for her mother to direct her course.

"What do you think?" she asked.

And Vivian shook her head. "It's you," she said. "What do you think?"

And the girl hesitated before she nodded. Mr. Franklin glanced back at Vivian as if for confirmation, but Vivian stared at her daughter. "It's her decision," she said, and Mr. Franklin turned back to Chloe.

"Yes," she said.

"It's a deal," Mr. Franklin said, and he stood. He and Chloe clinked glasses. Like the last time, the tables beyond them joined in cheering. And just like the last time, Vivian was overjoyed, but this joy settled deeper. It was Chloe now who sprang upon her and gripped her so hard she thought she might fall back.

They came apart finally, their shoulders where their faces had rested wet.

"I love you, baby. I'm so proud of you, even without all this . . ." Vivian didn't know how to finish, but maybe that was enough. The girl turned toward the group that was already gathering in the center of the floor.

"You better go ahead then and celebrate, you hear? You earned this."

"It was us, Mama."

"No, child, it was you."

And the child smiled at that, her eyes sparkling, before Mr. Franklin swept her away.

Vivian watched her for as long as she could, but then she couldn't stand to not be in her house any longer. There were only a few more days before it would be gone. She picked up her pocketbook and walked the few blocks. She sat in the kitchen in the silence. She hadn't been to the roof on principle, but she'd known that she would have to visit it before they left for good.

The house was empty. Now seemed like as good a time as any.

Once she climbed the steps, she sat on the same seat she'd sat on for many years beholding the girls in some aspect of their routine. Imagining it all now made her want to be ill.

She stood and walked to the edge. She'd been listening to the same record every day that week, the first song the girls had learned, the only one they all still adored, “Underneath the Harlem Moon.” She started singing it in a whisper; then she let her voice rise. The song signaled such a fabric of emotion for her, she didn’t know which aspect would make it to the forefront. She was surprised to see it was peace.

She tapped her hand on her thigh without noticing. Her foot slammed against the ground.

The chorus just delivered itself from her lips. And she couldn’t stop there. At some level, she guessed, when she was training those girls, she was training herself. She was the heart of the matter; she was the source of the steps; she was the one who copied down movements in her mind, translated them; she was the one who noticed if they stepped an inch to the left closer to their sister than was balanced; she was the one who felt the music up her spine when they reached a high note, and she hadn’t sung in years, hadn’t wanted to, but something in her set loose at the break, and her voice carried out wider than she’d known was possible. The release inside her was more magnificent than crying those early years after Ellis. It was more consuming than sex too, that brief window after she’d arrived and she flitted above the outer edge of the world, never entering it. It was heavier than church because Preacher could get her here by the end of his sermon, but an hour after she’d left Shiloh, a harsh word, a pitying thought, might wrench her from the sky. If she had guessed this was out here for her, inside her rather, she would have tried it sooner. Nobody could hear her, but there could have been a mountain of applause zeroing in, a whole city of people reaching for her, for her song to descend. That’s how high up she was. That’s how close she had made it.

ACKNOWLEDGMENTS

I am immeasurably grateful for my team: Michael Carlisle, who's been guiding and protecting me since the beginning; Helen Atsma and Sara Birmingham, whose brilliant insights and devotion to Vivian and the Salvations have elevated and transformed this book; Sonya Cheuse, for your vision and your unwavering belief in me; Vivian Rowe, for your gorgeous, emblematic cover; TJ Calhoun for your patience; and everyone at Ecco who has shepherded *On the Rooftop* to its destiny.

Thank you to V. Shayne Frederick for your jazz and literary prowess; to Chuck Collins, your perspective and influence on the Fillmore are unparalleled. I am indebted to *Harlem of the West* by Elizabeth Pepin Silva and Lewis Watts. The following books were also indispensable: *I Know Why the Caged Bird Sings* by Maya Angelou; *Victorian Architectural Details* by A. J. Bicknell and Company; *Queen: The Life and Music of Dinah Washington* by Nadine Cohodas; *A Brighter Coming Day: A Frances Ellen Watkins Harper Reader*, edited by Frances Smith Foster; *Jazz Masters of the 50s* by Joe Goldberg; *Sweet Soul Music* by Peter Guralnick; *The School Choral Program* by Michele Holt and James Jordan; *I, Tina* by Tina Turner with Kurt Loder; *Ella*

Fitzgerald: The Complete Biography by Stuart Nicholson; *Respect: The Life of Aretha Franklin* by David Ritz; *Billie Holiday and Etta James: The Lives and Legacies of the Famous Jazz Singers* by Charles River editors; *So You Want to Sing Jazz: A Guide for Professionals* by Jan Shapiro, and *Sign My Name to Freedom* by Betty Reid Soskin.

This work is written in homage to my inspirations and prototypes, *Fiddler on the Roof* by Joseph Stein (with music by Jerry Bock, lyrics by Sheldon Harnick); and *Tevye and His Daughters* (or *Tevye the Dairyman*) by Sholem Aleichem.

My writing group makes me better. Thank you, Ingrid Rojas Contreras, Anisse Gross, Rachel Khong, R. O. Kwon, Caille Millner, Esmé Weijun Wang, Andi Winnette, and Colin Winnette.

Big love to my pandemic crew for keeping me sane enough to write this book: Lucy Alvarez; Katherine and Egan Brinkman; Vanessa and Lowell Coleman; and as always, Nubia Solomon: special and eternal thanks for the counseling, the hype-ups, the wisdom, and of course the humor.

On the Rooftop was my mother's idea, and I owe the book and everything to her. LJ, my first baby, thank you for always supporting and affirming me.

Nina, you are already the wisest, kindest, bravest, and coolest girl I know. I'm so blessed that you're mine.

Carter, my mini genius, my prolific comedian: I'm in awe of your wit, your compassion, and your curiosity. May those gifts and your beautiful heart forever keep you.

Miles, my charming, break-dancing, Encanto-singing star: your confidence, humor, and spunk light up our lives.

Thomas, I'll never be able to thank you enough, or thank God enough for sending you.

To displaced people all over the world—especially the thousands of Black people forced to leave the Fillmore in the 1950s, 1960s, and beyond—may you find home.